C.M. O'NEILL

Good Hope

Based on a true story

Copyright © 2022 by C.M. O'Neill

All rights reserved. No part of this publication may be reproduced, stored or transmitted in any form or by any means, electronic, mechanical, photocopying, recording, scanning, or otherwise without written permission from the publisher. It is illegal to copy this book, post it to a website, or distribute it by any other means without permission.

C.M. O'Neill asserts the moral right to be identified as the author of this work.

Good Hope ® is a registered trademark of Cynthia Rutledge

First edition

Cover art by Alejandro Colucci

This book was professionally typeset on Reedsy. Find out more at reedsy.com

To my husband,

I love you with all my heart, but I must inform you that you are a deeply flawed man.
You are completely blind in your faith in me.
You are a mulishly stubborn supporter of all my endeavors.
And when loving me, you do not know when to stop.

Thank you

Contents

Prologue	iii
Chapter 1	1
Chapter 2	18
Chapter 3	23
Chapter 4	37
Chapter 5	50
Chapter 6	69
Chapter 7	83
Chapter 8	98
Chapter 9	115
Chapter 10	136
Chapter 11	153
Chapter 12	160
Chapter 13	179
Chapter 14	192
Chapter 15	199
Chapter 16	207
Chapter 17	226
Chapter 18	233
Chapter 19	246
Chapter 20	266
Chapter 21	283
Chapter 22	293
Chapter 23	302
Want more?	316
Aknowledgements	317

Interview with the Author 318
Other works 322

Prologue

PRECIS OF THE ARCHIVES

OF THE

CAPE OF GOOD HOPE

LETTERS AND DOCUMENTS RECEIVED

No1. – A Short Exposition to the Advantages to be Derived by the Company from a Fort and Garden at the Cape of Good Hope.

Though some who have visited the Cape, but without paying attention to its resources, will say that the place is altogether unfit and will not repay the expenses incurred, as nothing is to be had save water and wild sorrel; and others, that the Company have forts and stations in sufficient number to take care of, and therefore ought to make no more; we will endeavour to show according to our understanding, and with brevity and humility, how serviceable and necessary such a fort and garden will be for the convenience and preservation of the Company's ships and men; and also that they can be established with profit and no cost...

... The soil is very good in the valley ... Everything will grow there, especially pumpkin, watermelon, cabbage, carrot, radish, turnip, onion, garlic and all kinds of

vegetables, as those who were wrecked in the Haerlem can testify.

It is also beyond doubt that all kinds of fruit trees will thrive there, as orange, lime, apple, citron, shaddock, pear, plum, cherry, gooseberry and current, which can be kept on board for a long time...

... Please therefore to consider when all the fruit mentioned can be procured there in abundance, how many sick will be restored to health by God's goodness; especially when a large number of cattle and sheep have been bartered from the natives for supplies, and which could be procured for a small amount.

... it is plain how necessary the said fort or garden has become, as it is well known how difficult it will be for the sailors to reach home without intermediate refreshment; and the company's ships would be liable to great peril from severe sickness coming from India, especially if the officers were ordered whenever practicable, not to pass but to touch at the Cape for refreshments.

The officers of the outgoing ships, generally well provided in the cabin with everything, and more anxious to secure the premium (the good ones expected) than to benefit the service, when not able to reach the Cape with ease, immediately resolve to push on straight for Batavia, and the crew in consequence of an inadequate supply of water, receiving no more than four or five glasses per diem, whilst the cook can provide nothing save salt meat and pork, must become sick, so that the hospital at Batavia is filled with patients, causing great expense and loss to the Company; said patients remaining there often for months without doing any work, and nevertheless drawing pay.

All this can be prevented by having a fort and garden at the Cape. For the crews would be well refreshed there and provided with cattle, sheep and greens, and abundance of water...

(Signed) Leendert Janz,
N. Poort

Amsterdam, 26th July, 1649

Chapter 1

In the Wadden Sea off the coast of Holland lies the Isle of Texel. It is a spit of land that can be crossed from north to south on a robust horse in one day. Where rolling grass-covered dunes swathed ivory-white beaches, the smooth coastline opened into what would soon become the sought-after Texel harbor.

The small, narrow village of Oudeschild guarded the harbor as it gave shelter to ships from the rough sea. Up to a hundred and fifty yachts could drop anchor in the port as they awaited favorable sailing conditions.

In 1602 a commercial giant created far to the south, in Amsterdam, would change the face of the town forever. When the government forced several rival Dutch trading companies to merge, they formed the world's largest shipping corporation, the VOC, short for *Vereenigde Oost Indische Compagnie* – the Dutch East India Company.

The Texel harbor became the last port of call for VOC ships leaving the Netherlands, bound for the Orient, and the first safe port upon their return, brimming with spices and silks. Seeing the potential of the harbor, the Dutch government used its deep pockets and full coffers to build a seaport that would rival most. The rest of the town was left to develop at will.

Fifty years later and very little remained of the sleepy grey village. Cobblestones had replaced the rough dirt roads, with merchant shops and street vendors lining both sides. The streets were decorated with all manner of urchin, stray, and whatever was left behind from a long night at the dimly lit tavern. It had become a place where the wealthy clutched their coin purses, the poor kept their eyes peeled, and everybody sidestepped the dark corners.

Like the village itself, the inhabitants became open-minded with an elevated sense of awareness. Whereas the rest of Europe was distinctly fair-skinned and blue-eyed, the island population started to morph into something altogether different. Ships returned laden not only with spices and cloth but with refugees and stowaways fleeing from various kinds of persecution. Some were trustworthy and honest, others shady and nefarious, but all eventually found a home on the island.

Unlike the rest of Holland, life on Texel was unpredictable and curious – the extremes seemed to have converged there. In the village, no two shops were the same. The silk merchant's emporium was small and overstocked, with rolls of exquisite fabrics reaching the ceiling. The owner was loud and loved to haggle, overcharging any unsuspecting buyer. Of course, he had his favorite customers for whom his prices were quite reasonable. However, not a single beggar nor street rat dared venture near his bright red shop door. Next to the silk merchant was the candle maker. Large windows adorned with small copper bells displayed beautiful candles of all sizes, shapes, and scents. The proprietress was a plump, middle-aged Dutch widow with an infectious laugh and three beautiful daughters.

Music from street musicians and exotic smells of foreign food created an intoxicating blend of sensations lending a unique brand to the city and its people.

A small cart sold strange curries in wooden bowls to famished sailors and peckish businessmen alike. The food vendor was a tall, thin man with cinnamon-colored skin. He didn't speak much, for the local language was foreign to his tongue. Still, his business operated effectively, with customers handing over the number of coins equal to the number of fingers held aloft. After his paying customers were satisfied, he let loose an ear-splitting whistle, and every orphan and street urchin would flock to his cart, each receiving a bowl of the day's leftovers. He made them sit in a neat row and watched with pure joy on his face as they ate their meals. Then he would collect the empty bowls, pick up his cart, and wheel it home.

The Italian butcher and the French wine merchant were neighbors and enemies for no apparent reason other than their heritage. Fortunately, their

CHAPTER 1

quarrels remained verbal and never severe enough to require settlement of a physical nature. Interestingly, both merchants sold the same cheese to complement their signature products, acquired from an alluring, shy Prussian woman who kept both the secrets of her trade and her past close to her chest.

On a busy corner one street from the docks, were the bakery and tavern. The two were neighbors at one point until the owner of the latter married the owner of the former, knocked down the dividing wall, and combined the two businesses to form a warm and cozy spot by day and a discreetly lit haven by night.

The dockside was a hive of organized chaos, no different from the rest of the town. Heavy ships were in the process of being unloaded while impatient crewmen shouted at dockworkers loading the yachts soon to set sail.

December 23, 1651.

A deep frown marred the smooth skin of her forehead as she concentrated on pouring medicine from a large jar into a row of small bottles. Her father paused for a moment in his task and stared at her. At nineteen, she looked so much like her mother. Only, her mother's hair was blond, like wheat ready for the harvest, and his daughter's was like his – dark, almost black – but the face, oh the face was the same. He felt his heart tighten at the thought that one day she would leave his side and start a life of her own.

"Mrs. Colijn's baby will be born soon," he said around the knot in his throat, not taking his eyes from her.

"Hmm," she made the sound without looking up from her work, and a wistful smile curved her mouth – there and then gone.

"The boy from the bakery came by today when you were out," he ventured, wondering if the quiet, lanky young man had managed to make an impression on his daughter.

"Father..." she spoke gently, but the warning was clear. *"This* is my life. I am happy like this. You know I don't like distractions." She looked up from her work, and for a second, their eyes met. Her gaze was serious and determined; his remained soft.

"Life evolves, my darling. Nothing stays the same," he said as he turned back to his workbench and the bundles of clean bandages that needed rolling.

"Not this," her voice was edged with a finality that made his heart glow. She was still his – for now.

Their easy banter was disrupted when the high-pitched howl from a mongrel dog preceded the loud voice of the driver of a horse-drawn cart, floating in on the evening breeze as the door to the surgery was pushed open. A pair of expensive, soft leather boots of foreign make strutted across the threshold and entered the warmly lit space.

Aard Van Meerhof's surgery was part of a series of dockside warehouses, with a faded green door adorned with a tarnished brass knocker and a plaque that read *'Arts en Apotheek,'* Physician and Apothecary.

As he entered, the man took note of the generous open space of the surgery. Floor-to-ceiling shelves stacked with cloth-bound books, herbs, bottles, and jars of various sizes filled with oils, tinctures, and ointments covered most of the back wall. In front of the shelves was a long and wide counter containing mortars and pestles, bowls of dried herbs, plant debris, and whatever could not fit on the shelves. A comforting smell of camphor and wood smoke hung in the air.

A young assistant tried to bring some form of order to the remnants of what looked like a hectic day. The man tilted his head a fraction of an inch; something about the assistant gnawed at his gut and demanded more than just a sweeping glance – faded green vest over a many-times-laundered shirt, all plain and work-worn but clean. A generous leather cap was drawn low over the brow as if to hide something. His eyes squinted, and then it dawned on him – the feminine nose, high cheekbones, delicate face, full lips, and slender throat. The assistant was a young woman dressed as a boy – clever. Storing the information for later use, he continued his perusal.

Deeper into the room, against the far-left wall, was a curtained single bed and a chair in the corner. Both were empty – no patients tonight.

His eyes continued the anti-clockwise sweep, then stopped at the physician standing at a workbench by the window, rolling clean bandages of various lengths into neat rolls: delicate work done by patient and dexterous hands. His clothing was confidently understated, wide pants gathered at the top

CHAPTER 1

of calfskin leather boots, a loose-fitting white shirt with rolled-up sleeves, turned slightly grey from many washes, and a comfortable yet unadorned leather vest.

"Van Meerhof," the man's voice possessed an easy eloquence. The physician looked up from his work, half turning to greet the newcomer. The assistant's eyes flicked under perched brows, head downcast and cautious.

"Yes?" the physician confirmed, his voice soft and pacifying by nature. "Can I help you?"

Van Meerhof noticed the man's dark woolen overcoat, topped with a wide, crisp, white collar and silk vest. His clothing was fashionable, made from expensive imported fabrics with subtle dramatic flair. He was in his forties, ruggedly handsome, with dark hair and an unmistakable swagger.

The faint white scar running from the bridge of his nose to the corner of his mouth immediately identified him as Captain Alain Du Bois. Rumor had it that he was of French nobility, which would account for his severe lack of scruples and abundance of arrogance. He was the type of man women swooned over and men avoided or aimed to please. Van Meerhof never had the misfortune of meeting the man until now.

Two sizeable specimens of men followed the captain, filing in sideways through the open door, one after the other, the second closing it behind him with a sweep of his foot. They stood slightly hunched over like they were still on the ship and the cabin ceiling was too low. Their knuckles were dark, their hands scarred, and their bare arms bulky and corded with muscles and veins. One had a scar along the side of his face, which interrupted a dense stubble beard, and the other a dullness behind his eyes that told of a sincere lack of wits. Du Bois's lip curled up in a smirk beneath his dark mustache.

"Yes," the captain spoke in accented Dutch. "You can help me." He confidently strode to Van Meerhof's desk and sat down in the physician's chair, leaning back comfortably. He snapped his fingers at a stool, and the bearded sailor placed it at the opposite end of the desk, between himself and his fellow giant. Du Bois rubbed the hairs on his chin while his eyes traced the movements of the assistant, who continued gathering up pamphlets and books and dutifully filing them away.

"Have a seat," Du Bois commanded his host with a bored flop of his hand.

Van Meerhof examined the burly sailors he was to be perched between, forcing his features to remain still. The odors from their unwashed bodies left a bitter taste on the back of his tongue. He threw a moment's glance at his daughter and gingerly took his appointed seat, back stiff and straight, hands folded in his lap.

A fragile silence filled the room. The captain's nimble fingers played with the quill standing on the desk; the light *'plink, plink'* of the feather falling against the inkpot being hardly enough to disguise the surgeon's heart beating visibly against his rough linen shirt.

"You combine your physician's surgery with a pagan apothecary?" Du Bois's tone was neutral and devoid of judgment.

"Yes." In other parts of the world, this might seem odd, even blasphemous, but here in Oudeschild, it was just another oddity that became the norm.

"Why?" Again, no judgment.

"I blend the classical teaching on healing with the more unorthodox methods of apothecaries. Healing is not about ego but outcome. I will use whatever cures the sick or brings relief." The physician kept his eyes on the captain, though he could sense the menacing energy radiating from the men on either side of him.

"I smell camphor in the air."

Van Meerhof was uncertain if he should respond; it was not a direct question, merely a statement. He decided to err on the side of caution and kept his mouth shut.

"Do you make the camphor oil yourself?" Du Bois asked, pointing to the apothecary table.

There was a definite direction to the conversation now, but the destination was unknown. Van Meerhof was sure the captain had not dragged his two disciples to the surgery for a lesson in the production of camphor oil.

"I import it from Japan and lately from China. The quality of the white camphor oil is much higher than anything I can source locally." His tone was steady, but he could not shake the uneasy feeling that crept higher up his spine with each question.

CHAPTER 1

"You also use laudanum on your patients, correct?"

Van Meerhof remained still for a moment.

"Yes, not many surgeons do, but I insist on it. I believe patients heal faster when sedated during painful procedures; it is less traumatic. Mental pain often lasts longer than the physical and is harder to cure." Seeing Du Bois's eyes glaze over, he ended his explanation with a shy smile.

"Remarkable," there was an eloquent lilt to Du Bois's voice. "Very commendable… and I assume you require opium to concoct this anesthetic of yours?"

"Well, yes. But I don't see why that is a concern. The amount I use is hardly enough to –"

"There is no concern," Du Bois interrupted impatiently as if he just remembered that he needed to be someplace else and wished for this conversation to end.

"Van Meerhof, let's get to the point. I have a proposition for you," he continued in a low voice, leaning forward to rest his arms on the desk. "One that will benefit both of us." He paused, and the physician could finally see where the conversation was heading. Du Bois was looking for a new ship's surgeon, and this was nothing but an interview. His posture relaxed slightly. It was not the first time such an offer had been made to him and almost certainly would not be the last. He would have to disappoint the captain diplomatically; if the gossip were true, Du Bois was not a man who responded well to not getting his way.

"As you know, the VOC imports spices from the East Indies, cotton and silk from India, gold, silver, and copper from Japan, porcelain and opium from China, and all of it is carried every year to our shores by ships under the command of men like me." This was hardly news to the physician; the VOC owned hundreds of ships and employed thousands of crewmen, including the vaunted captain Du Bois. It was also no secret that most of these ships' captains ran very lucrative smuggling businesses on the side.

"However, the demand for opium has surpassed the very regulated supply. As an avid businessman, I have taken it upon myself to ease the growing need to some degree. Since you also require opium regularly, you would be the ideal business partner for this new venture." The way the words flowed from Du Bois's mouth gave Van Meerhof the impression that his acceptance or denial was not required, that he was merely receiving his orders.

"You will order four crates of opium every week –"

"Four crates!" Van Meerhof blurted out in surprise. "I do not need that much. I hardly use more than a thimble full per week, and besides, how on earth would I be able to afford four crates of opium?"

A deep crease formed between Du Bois's brows at the physician's outburst; his black eyes grew cold and hard as obsidian when he repeated his statement in an ominously calm voice.

"You will order four crates of opium every week. You will fill in the order form along with the amount of camphor and whatever else you may require. And you will sign the bottom of the document." He waited for another objection from the physician, and when none came, he continued.

"The four crates will be taken off the ship and be stored here, at your surgery, for one night only, and by morning when you step in to rid your first sailor of some form of pox or parasite, it will be gone."

"I don't understand why –" Van Meerhof began, but the captain continued as if he had not spoken at all.

"You will, of course, not pay for the four crates. I merely need the legal documentation with your willing signature at the bottom. When that old fart of a harbormaster sees your signature on the order document, he will not come sniffing where he is not needed. In return, you can help yourself to as much opium as you need, free of charge." He fanned his fingers out, palm up as if to suggest that those were all the cards he held.

Van Meerhof sat motionless, feeling the burn of his daughter's eyes on his back.

The captain sat back again, letting his left ankle dangle over his right knee, and with long, well-manicured fingers, he plucked pensively at a little pink bow sewn onto the rich, black fabric of his tunic.

Van Meerhof leaned forward, resting his elbows on his knees, and hung his head while shaking it slightly from side to side. He mistook the aim of the meeting. It was not an interview but rather an ultimatum.

CHAPTER 1

"No," his voice was quiet and low.

The captain's hand stilled.

"Perhaps you want to reconsider your response," he warned.

"I cannot be a part of this." The physician's lowered eyes darted back and forth as the thoughts raced through his mind. He could not bear to look at the man in his chair. "You're planning to distribute opium among people who are completely ignorant as to its effects. It will ruin their lives and their families. An opium addiction is an inhumane condition. If one is not mindful of the quantity taken, it can even lead to death. In its raw form, it is an abomination. *Four crates* every week, my God!"

"I am not holding a knife to my customers' throats," the captain interrupted with the bored eyes of a dead man. "The demand is much higher than the supply. If I'm not careful, they'll grab it straight off the damned ship," he paused. "And besides, it won't affect anyone you know or see regularly."

Van Meerhof lifted his head. "How do you mean?"

"Come now, you're a smart man," Du Bois delivered the false compliment without a twitch in his brow. "Surely you can piece it together. Your patients can hardly afford *your* services, let alone mine. This indulgence is not for the riffraff, but for the rich, the bored and frivolous who have nothing better to do than eat, fornicate and dish out taxes to the downtrodden poor." He looked at the physician with raised eyebrows. Conveniently not including himself in the aforementioned group.

The physician refrained from commenting on the captain's litany. Du Bois mistook Van Meerhof's silence and continued.

"I know you don't charge your clients. They pay or barter as they can for your care, and you are right, opium is expensive." He moved to lean forward again; a slow smile softened the curve of his mouth. "I am offering you a lifetime's supply, free of charge. Take it and fulfill that naïve little fantasy you have of numbing all the world's hurt. You don't want your patients to feel pain, and I don't want anyone sniffing around my ship." He nodded his head, willing the physician to see the sense of his offer. "Place the order, sign the piece of parchment. You and I can have our happy ever after, and so can everybody else, for that matter."

"The harbormaster is an old and trusted friend. I am not in the habit of deceiving my friends," Van Meerhof whispered, looking into Du Bois's expressionless face, knowing it was a sentiment the man did not understand.

"I'm counting on that friendship," Du Bois returned. "You do understand that this is not a proposal I am going to canvas the neighborhood with. It is an opportunity for you and you alone."

For all of life's intricacies, conflicts, and joys, Van Meerhof viewed it through a lens of simplicity. He was incorruptible; he did not judge others for their choices, nor was he impressed by wealth or power. He lived by a simple code: *Do no harm to others*. In a world devoid of compassion and consideration, this man in front of him was thriving like a weed; Van Meerhof was not about to feed and water it.

"No," Van Meerhof said for the second time. He shook his head and spoke with a clear and decisive voice, and with that one simple word, her entire world changed.

The assistant watched the events of the next few seconds unfold as if performed underwater with slow and fluid motions. Du Bois's eyes hardened; he put both his hands on the surface of her father's desk and pushed himself upright. A look passed between him and his sailors; his lips relaxed, and his nostrils flared.

The sailors reached down, took hold of her father's arms, and lifted him. He hung helplessly like a child between them. Her father turned his head, found her eyes, and mouthed, 'GO.'

Go where? She could not move; her feet felt riveted to the floor, her breath left her nose, and her ears popped with the force of her heartbeat. But there was no more time, for his head turned back to Du Bois, who was moving around the desk in a smooth motion; he came to stand in front of her father, black snake eyes riveted on the older man's face. Reaching across, he pulled a dagger from his sleeve. The blade moved forward and upward in one, well-practiced thrust, passing neatly between two ribs and piercing the surgeon's heart from the bottom. At first, she thought Du Bois meant only to threaten her father with the blade, but the finality of the act left her aghast, the scene impossible to comprehend.

CHAPTER 1

She saw her father's body go rigid as Du Bois pushed the dagger to the hilt, then the physician's chin dropped to his chest, the tension left his legs, his feet twisted inward, and his shoulders relaxed.

Everything her father had ever told her about making herself disappear into the background, not draw attention to herself, be as inconspicuous as possible left her as a scream, feral and raw, tore from her throat.

In the moment of indecisiveness, when the two goons did not know what to do with the body hanging between them, Du Bois looked up with a quick jerk of his head, his ugly eyes cataloging her face.

The urge to rush to her father was overwhelming. She needed to hold him and ensure he was still alive, but above all, she needed the safety of his arms around her. The shock of seeing violence done was different from dealing with the aftermath of stitching wounds and setting bones. Seeing violence done to somebody she loved, her only person in this world, was enough to rip her soul from her body.

Just moments before, they had discussed Mrs. Colijn and how her baby was due any day now. Blinking the thought away, she stared at her father's back. If only she could reach him and staunch the bleeding, but the three men were crowding him. If she ran, they would follow. She could lead them away from her father and come back. Or she could find a dark corner and crawl into it, close her eyes and ears, and hope against all odds that this was nothing but a bad dream. Then she remembered her father's plea.

Numb with shock, her feet took charge, moving her torpid body to the back door of the surgery with the agility of a street cat.

This evening, there was a bite in the air, but she hardly took note. There was no right or wrong direction to take. Now that she was moving, she knew the only mistake would be to hesitate. To her left, many more warehouses disappeared into the darkness. Driven by sheer instinct, she headed in the opposite direction.

Running away from the surgery and leaving her father behind felt like a betrayal. The knowledge that she would never see him again choked a strangled sound from her throat. The last moment between them would forever be seared into her soul. His eyes were filled with resolve as he urged her to flee. Even in those dire few seconds, he was thinking of her safety. He had died as he had lived, a good, honest man, protecting his daughter.

She felt like a snail whose shell had been ripped away, exposed, and vulnerable. Her father was her shell, her safe place, guarding over her, her entire life. The loss of his protection threatened to suck the strength from her pumping legs.

Not for the first time did she thank him for dressing her as a boy when she was little. Over the years, the garments became her preference, for they allowed freedom of movement. She could go about town more freely and without the usual gawking and whistling that followed most females. Once her breasts were bound and flattened with a long cotton strip and her ample ebony curls were tightly pinned and tucked under her generous leather cap, not many gave her a second glance. Her father had foreseen the dangers of a young woman growing up in a harbor town crowded with rough and often dangerous men who had stopped at Texel after months at sea. He had devised the ruse allowing him to keep her close at all times, never letting her go anywhere alone. When he was busy with patients, operating, consulting, or examining, she was given small tasks to keep her occupied and under his ever-watchful eye.

She needed to find help. Her mind raced as she tried to think of where to go. Over the years, she had refused to forge lasting relationships with anybody save her father. Her mother had died giving birth to her; her beloved grandmother passed away nine years later. The two powerful events instilled in her the belief that whomever she loved would leave her, that she was meant to go through life alone. The only exception fate had allowed was her father's love, but even that now proved to be an illusion.

She would go to her father's friends for help. He had a standing card game on Saturday nights at the barracks with the harbormaster and the barracks commander. They would be waiting for him.

Over the years, her love for crafting medicines and potions had granted her the title of 'witch' – mainly whispered behind cupped hands and open fans for fear of insulting her father. As a result, most interactions with others made her crave the safety of her father's company and apothecary, thereby lending

CHAPTER 1

to her reputation of being strange and distant, even in a place as contrary as Oudeschild.

One day she would live as she pleases with nobody to judge her. She would not need the protective shadow of another and would live by her own rule and decree if she could make it to tomorrow.

Running through the back alleys of a harbor town after dark was an ill-conceived notion, but hazards fade when one is driven by raw fear and the need to survive. The small knife she used to cut twine was still in her hand. Tucking it away, she sprinted down the alley, heading north toward the barracks.

The alley was pitch dark, lined on both sides with the back doors of soot-colored warehouses. She knew the terrain like the back of her hand but had never ventured out here in the dark before. Everything seemed different and threatening now. She stayed close to the walls, trying to minimize her silhouette. Somewhere behind her, the surgery's back door slammed open and bounced off the wall. Stealing a glance over her shoulder, she saw one of Du Bois's men exit the surgery and turn left toward the row of dark warehouses, his heavy footsteps drawing away from her.

She practically flew down the alley, dodging a cat and sidestepping a group of stacked barrels. For a surreal moment, she wondered if her feet were touching the street's surface as her legs carried her swiftly into the darkness.

She was increasing the distance between her and the sailor with every stride. With eyes not fully adjusted to the dark, she blinked hard several times, forcing her night vision. Her pace was grueling and could not be maintained for much longer; she needed a place to rest. The alley did not offer much in the way of hiding places. Scanning her surroundings, she searched for a shadow deep enough to disappear into when her foot hooked on something, and she crashed onto the cobblestone street, scraping her hands and knees.

Instinctively she tried to crawl forward, away from the obstacle that had tripped her, but a firm, rough fist closed around her booted ankle and yanked her backward. She turned onto her bottom, trying to find purchase with her fingers dragging over the uneven surface behind her. The man was surprisingly strong and determined as he hauled her toward him. He was drunk, sitting with his back against a wall, his legs stretched out in abandon. As he pulled her closer, she could smell vomit and piss everywhere, and for a horrifying moment, she feared that he was dragging her through his filth.

The breath that reached her was sour with the contents of his stomach and freshly consumed alcohol. There was a sluggish eagerness in his grasp. He gave a vulgar open-mouth laugh displaying black and rotten teeth with a wide gap where the central top incisors were supposed to be.

The tosspot had dragged her close enough to grab hold of her left calf; his mouth was moving, spittle flying as he slurred, but she could hear nothing above the rush of the blood in her ears. Looking up, she saw the faint outline of her pursuer. He must have turned around and was now heading in her direction. She was out of time. If necessity was the mother of invention, then desperation was the father of brute force. She pulled her right knee close to her chest and extended a vicious forward kick. Had he been sober, he would have recognized the movement, but he was too inebriated and too focused on moving his hand higher up her leg to pay the necessary attention. The heel of her boot connected with his face between the nose and the upper lip; his eyes lost focus as his head snapped back and hit the wall with a wet slap. His hand released the grip on her leg, and she turned on her hands and knees and crawled a few paces before she gained her feet again.

Glancing over her shoulder, she saw Du Bois's man coming down the alley; his pace was slower than hers for now. Her running was becoming labored; there was a piercing pain in her side, and her heart was beating frantically. The struggle with the drunkard had drained the life from her muscles. A few strides more, and she knew the sailor was gaining on her. His footsteps were falling hard on the cobblestones, uneven but determined, and his breaths came in short bursts. When she saw him in the surgery, she noted his thick, short neck, broad shoulders, and large thighs. He was built for brawling, not sprinting. *May the good Lord grant him apoplexy this very moment.* Her prayer was in vain, for the man kept his pace and advanced relentlessly. Momentarily distracted by the advancing man, her step faltered, and her leg buckled as her foot stepped deep into a depression in the cobblestones. She snapped her hands out to break the imminent fall when she heard his voice from behind.

CHAPTER 1

"Avast!"

He was closer than she thought, and with the last of her strength, she righted herself and commanded her burning legs to keep moving.

The row of buildings ended with the tavern on the corner. It was not an ideal hiding place, but she headed for it regardless. Approaching the tavern, she flattened herself against the wall. Her hand curved around a pillar. Advancing carefully, she felt the rise of a step. At the top of the step was a tall narrow door. It was once the front door of the bakehouse. She had often sat on this step, basking in the morning sun when her father went next door to get something for them to eat. Every brick and stone of the small porch was known to her, but now it seemed cold and foreign. The familiarity of her surroundings brought with it the need for more. She wanted to go home, crawl into bed, and wake up with her father preparing their breakfast. Right now, it felt like she existed in somebody else's world. Her father was dead – murdered, torn from her life in the blink of an eye. Between one breath and the next, all had irrevocably changed. She was no longer the girl from an hour ago and never would be again.

The pillar cast a dark shadow over the door, and she wedged herself into the tight corner. She could hear the goon's footsteps; he was close. The large sailor came to a stop less than twenty feet from her. He scanned the street. He had stayed close to the middle of the narrow alley, sacrificing stealth for the benefit of sight. His breathing was ragged; he coughed, then spat, and she heard the gob splatter on the cobblestones.

Standing motionless, she feared he might hear her heart's hammering. Her breath formed small, white ghost clouds in front of her face. If he looked just a little more to his left, back over his shoulder, he would see it. If he got his hands on her, her life would be over one way or another. Would he murder her here on the small porch, cut her throat, and walk away? Would he rape her first? He was a big man; she would not be able to fight him off. Or would he take her to Du Bois? All three options made her knees weak and her chest tight with dread. There was only a thin layer of darkness shielding her from her pursuer. Taking a slow deep breath through her nose, she held it; her heart slammed against her breastbone in protest.

The sailor was unsure which direction to take. The bitch could not have gone far; she was in front of him just a moment before, but he had wiped his face, and when he looked again, she was gone. He looked toward the corner tavern. The alleyway opened into a wider perpendicular street. To the right was the wharf, to the left, the tavern, and further up the street was a brothel. All offered excellent concealment. He made up his mind and started toward the tavern when his companion came around the corner from the harborside. The man was similarly out of breath. He must have left the surgery through the front door and searched up and down the dockside in the event she made her way back.

Her original pursuer moved toward the newcomer, further away from her hiding place. As dark spots began to dot her vision, she slowly released the breath from her burning lungs through her nose. A few quick blinks and short breaths seemed to ease the discomfort. The two men were moving again, one toward the tavern, the other toward the brothel.

Instinct warned her that fleeing back up the alley was a death trap. She could not stay put either; she needed to move to stay alive. There was one option left: to run in the direction of the docks. The downside was that it would lead her away from the barracks and toward the unknown position of Du Bois. 'Go!' her father's echo urged her on. She left the safety of the little step-porch and darted across the alley, fearing the first goon would emerge from the tavern at any moment.

Sticking to the shadows, she reached the docks and detected the tang of smoke in the air. Even after dark, the dockside was still busy. People were milling about, some with more urgency than others. A lusty giggle bubbled from nearby shadows, and further away, four young sailors were serenading the night as they drunkenly stumbled away, clinging to one another. Rather than darting from shadow to shadow, she slowed to a walk and kept her head down. She needed to consider her options.

Continuing down the wharf, in the direction of the warehouses, would eventually lead her to the surgery's front door. The prospect of running into Du Bois made that a less-than-favorable destination. If she headed in the opposite direction, the docks would eventually end at a small white sandy

CHAPTER 1

beach with tall grasses. It would be a good hiding place, but the sand would hinder her if she were forced to run again. She could make her way to the back of the barracks past the beach; it would take longer, but it was doable.

A booming voice from the deck of one of the large yachts drew her attention, and she looked up. A freshly painted yacht lay close by. Its gangway was lowered and creaking with the gentle movement of the water. The ship towered over her, its white sails neatly tied to the yardarms and lanterns sparkling at uneven intervals across the deck. A large man was leaning against the side, his long dark hair stirring in the breeze.

"You, boy! Yes, you, you scrawny piece of rat shit," he called as she looked at him, "make yourself useful and bring up those crates! We're short on hands tonight."

Chapter 2

The meeting was a colossal disappointment. The physician was painfully naïve, blinded by his principles and good intentions. His foolishness had cost him his life. Du Bois flicked the collar of his cloak up against his neck and lengthened his stride. He was heading toward his yacht, the *Goue Duif* – Golden Dove, which lay anchored at the far side of the harbor, still heavy with cargo.

The sun had long since set, and the dockside's pulse beat was dark and depraved, the type that resonated with his own. Another explosion sent a rush of warm air crashing into his back. He had doused the physician's body, the rug in front of the hearth, and most of the work surfaces with alcohol before setting it ablaze. The fire was hot and fierce and would erase all evidence of foul play. With so much alcohol stored at the surgery, it was a miracle it had not self-combusted hitherto.

The physician's death was regrettable but necessary. Men like Du Bois were the very essence of trade and commerce. Men who dared to skirt the law and walked that infinitesimally thin line between freedom and enslavement. They kept trade alive and flourishing, and if an obstacle presented itself, they either used it or removed it, and the physician was an obstacle that could not be used. He might have been a saint amongst the needy and ahead of his time with his healing methods, but he lacked business acumen and foresight, curse his worthless hide.

Not much he could do about it now, but he would be damned if he let a lowly assistant ruin his carefully laid plans. One word to the harbormaster and the Texel harbor would be closed to him, that is, if he didn't find himself

CHAPTER 2

swinging from a noose in the village square. Hung by his aristocratic neck until dead, and he doubted God would have mercy on his illustrious soul.

He had given his men strict instructions to find the assistant and bring her to him unharmed, knowing they would not return to the *Goue Duif* without her. If there were so much as a scrape on her body, he would split them open like cheap dockside herring.

Du Bois's fury grew with each step and, with it, his craving for violence. He wished he could reach into the physician's chest and squeeze the life from his bleeding heart all over again. He would have to settle for the assistant. Once his men found her and brought her to his ship, he would sate his anger. His spine tingled with anticipation; it had been a while since a woman had died by his hand.

His booted footsteps fell with a sure and rhythmic pounding on the cobblestones. The smell of smoke was thick, almost strong enough to choke the stench of the open sewer, rotten fish, and unwashed bodies. Scanning his surroundings, his eyes judged angles and distances, watching hands, especially those in pockets, while keeping his loose and relaxed, swinging at his sides. Footsteps were coming fast from behind; shifting his gaze, he scanned the faces around him. No eyes were on him for longer than needed, and there were no quick and belatedly averted stares; all the faces he met were fleeting and uninterested. He silently slipped the dagger on his wrist into his palm. The footsteps were close now, and then a barefoot sailor passed him, rushing toward a group of men, calling and swinging his arms while pointing in the direction of the burning surgery. Du Bois pushed the dagger back into place with the tip of his middle finger and continued down the pier. More feet rushed toward the fire, and buckets dropped into the water.

Fire was a sailor's worst enemy. On the wharf, it could swiftly spread from one building to the next before the wind whipped it onto the yachts, and then the disaster would become vigorously impressive. Men swarmed from the ships like ants from their nests toward the burning building, shouting instructions and calling on others. Two dirty boys pushed and shoved at each other, trying to reach the tragedy first. A forgotten whore clutched an ill-fitting shawl to her ample bosom, looked toward the source of the smoke, and turned in the opposite direction. Du Bois kept his head down and his pace steady as the dregs of society flowed around him like water around a steady rock in the middle of a stream.

For once, could his plans not just work as they were intended to? Every year the Dutch East India Company's rules became more draconian. More and more officials littered the ports where the VOC ships docked. With inkpot and parchment, these vermin oozed their way onto the yachts. Crawling through every inch of the vessels, tallying, measuring, and weighing. Their beady little eyes that peered down sharp noses missed nothing. The officials created painstakingly accurate records; these were then compared to the port records where the ships were discharged. There were no rules on what could and could not be carted to the Netherlands. Anything went, just so long as the profits went into the coffers of the VOC. He shook his head in quiet disgust.

Du Bois felt like nothing better than a faithful servant dangling from strings pulled by his VOC puppet masters. The thought rankled; if there were any strings to be pulled, he would prefer to be the one pulling them.

He had found a way around these snares and hindrances. Over the years, he had amassed a fleet of small vessels on all the regular trade routes that met his *Goue Duif* off the coasts of Batavia, Africa, and the Mogul empire, with an exotic variety of treasures. He procured precious gems, porcelain, gold, silver, rare spices, and opium – anything that could be stored underneath the VOC cargo in the false bottom of the *Goue Duif's* cargo hold.

Du Bois sported a dark reputation, and proudly so. Men, and especially women, seemed to be drawn to it, which opened endless doors previously closed. But there was a very definite line between a reputation built on rumor and one built on evidence, and that line was about as thick as the rope around a man's neck. He was nothing if not the seeker of opportunity and the hunter of fortune, the perfect blend of his title-rich but cash-poor father and his cash-rich but title-poor mother. Only, he was the second son and therefore had to work for a living, for his brother, the tight-fisted sack of shit, had quite literally chewed his inheritance away on opium. But Alain Du Bois had landed on his feet and secured himself a lucrative opportunity with the VOC as captain of the *Goue Duif*.

CHAPTER 2

Turning to the Dutch East India Company was not his first choice. Still, his options were limited, for he was no longer welcome to dock at any French port due to an unfortunate incident concerning the death of Cardinal Mazarin. The man was Italian, for the love of all that is holy.

He was rudely pulled from his musings by a loud voice yelling down at somebody on the docks.

Du Bois's head snapped up, and he slowed his pace, for dead ahead stood the assistant from the apothecary. She was standing next to a pile of small crates, looking up at the man on the ship. He watched as she bent to pick one up and headed up the gangway. Stepping deeper into the shadows, he waited, but she did not return.

He suppressed a roar of frustration as he noted the name on the side of the ship – *Drommedaris*. If it were any other vessel, he would step aboard and demand the assistant be turned over to him immediately, and his request would have been granted without delay or inquiry. But not here, not now, for the man behind the voice, Arent Van Jeveren, had vowed if he ever laid eyes on Du Bois again, he would tear him limb from limb. Du Bois was not fool enough to take the statement as a figure of speech. It was a promise the blackguard of a boatswain would keep, for he had the full support of his captain, Davit De Coninck. All this unpleasantness over the inconsequential death of a Mussulman slave woman and the orphaning of a small child to which Van Jeveren had seemed to form an attachment of sorts.

No, this situation with the assistant required discretion. Du Bois was not afraid of the *Drommedaris* crew, but a ruckus could loosen the assistant's tongue, and he would rather it stayed silent.

How hard could it be to capture this chit? Cursing under his breath, he knew he needed to get those two mongrels off the streets. They had failed him, and he would take it from their flesh. For now, the only solution was to post a man to watch the *Drommedaris* until she set sail or the assistant emerged.

When the sailors raised the gangway, he headed into town, confident that she would remain aboard until morning.

The tired and misbegotten shack near the edge of town was easy to find.

GOOD HOPE

Du Bois hammered on the door until the frame shook. A man opened, his left arm shielded by the door, no doubt clutching a dagger. Squinting into the dark, his eyes widened with recognition.

"Captain Du…"

"Shut up, you imbecile," Du Bois growled in an ominous whisper.

He motioned the man outside and away from the hovel with a single sideways nod. The man closed the door behind him and followed, subdued, with hesitant footsteps.

"I have a task for you." Du Bois did not wait for the man's response. "You will board the *Drommedaris* tomorrow morning. Report to Captain De Coninck, convince him of your worth, and get him to allow you to join the expedition." That seemed to stir a reaction from the man, but it never made it past his lips. Du Bois speared him with a cold glimmering stare, and the man swallowed his words, the stench of his fear filling the night air between them.

"There is a young woman aboard, the physician's assistant; she's dressed as a man. Find her and end her." If the *Drommedaris* set sail with her still aboard, having her killed was the only option left to him.

"Is there not somebody else more suited to the task?" The man's voice shook as he forced the question between his terrified lips.

Du Bois was in the process of replacing dock officials with his own men. He found the process tedious and expensive. But with the new settlement to be established at the Cape of Good Hope, Du Bois had an opportunity to do it right from the beginning. His man was already aboard one of the expedition ships and highly placed. No doubt the halfwit in front of him was aware of that, but he did not need to know who it was.

Du Bois's hand snapped out like a snake striking its prey and closed around the man's throat. He squeezed until he could see the white of the man's eyeballs in the darkness. The man made no effort to resist.

When the captain spoke again, his voice was cold and sharp.

"If you fail me, I will slaughter everybody dear to you and make you watch. Do you understand me? Nod."

Chapter 3

The three-master was lying just outside the Texel harbor. She was one of three ships carrying tradesmen, building supplies, soldiers, and merchants to the southern tip of Africa. Being the expedition's flagship, the governor, Johan Antonizoon Van Riebeeck, his family, and his most trusted merchants and advisors were aboard. The mission was to establish a trading station for VOC ships to replenish their fresh food and water supplies before continuing their arduous journey to India and the Far East.

The ship was a Dutch East India Company trading yacht, the *Drommedaris*, named after a camel used by traders to transport goods across the desert in Arabia. Built from the finest Belgian oak, the *Drommedaris* was sleek and elegant with square rigging, her three masts stained the same color as her hull. The aft mast supported a large triangle lateen sail, making her fast and easy to steer, needing no more than thirty-five men to handle her.

Her eighty-two-foot deck was painted in the same crisp white as her hull, and like any good woman, she was slender up top and wide in the hips. Above the waterline, the deck was only twenty feet wide, but below, the hull bulged outward, giving the yacht a distinct pear shape. The VOC ships were the only ones in the world built this way. The design came to life after Belgium started taxing ships according to the size of their upper decks. Therefore, the VOC designed their yachts with narrow decks and wide hulls, allowing them to pay the minimum amount of tax while carrying the maximum amount of cargo.

They left Amsterdam ten days earlier and had spent the last three loading more provisions and passengers from the port of Texel.

This afternoon, the port was abnormally busy, with more than a hundred merchant ships departing simultaneously, leaving the *Drommedaris* crew to row themselves out instead of being assisted by harbor rowers. They still had much to do, and the captain wanted to be well clear of the harbor traffic come nightfall. Even though it was still early afternoon, dark came quickly this time of year.

After days of inactivity, the crew was eager to set sail, and not a soul among them could bear the thought of his hands idly stuck in his pockets. The deck was bustling. Sure hands coiled neat piles of thick ropes at the bottom of the shrouds. Here the ropes lay like cobras, biding their time, waiting to snap out as soon as the sails were released to the wind. With a rushed hiss, they would uncoil to feed the sails, and at the very last moment before the end slithered through the deadeye, a well-timed sailor's hand would stay its bid for freedom, give it a firm yank and deftly tighten it with a knot around the wooden hook on the inside of the bulwark.

Between the shrouds, at the port side, a group of sailors was hauling two sloops back on deck, one after the other. The rowboats would later be taken apart and stored below decks.

Far above the water, Sebastiaan De Vries was standing barefoot on the footrope of the main mast's top spar. The wind tugged at the loose trunks of his sailor slops while his golden blond curls danced freely and uninhibited in the breeze. His movements were relaxed but efficient as he checked the last of the fastenings around the clewed sails.

It was late afternoon, and the sun painted the young sailor in a shy orange light. The little heat hidden in the last rays of the day was quickly whipped away by the breeze.

A content smile spread across his face as his feet danced along the footrope. These were sacred moments, being alone and high above the water with the wind in his hair and the salty ocean air filling his lungs.

When Sebastiaan heard the boatswain's voice, he looked down, scanning the activity below. He had known Arent since they were boys of twelve and fourteen. Arent was the night to Sebastiaan's day, for he was dark-skinned,

CHAPTER 3

with long black hair that fell straight between his shoulder blades, a gift from his Javanese mother, and a height that reached well beyond six feet, a legacy inherited from his Dutch father, whereas Sebastiaan was light of skin, with shaggy golden curls and a frame just touching the notch past six feet.

"Up, pull her up, lads!" Arent Van Jeveren was pacing up and down the upper deck of the *Drommedaris*. His voice carried like a seasoned politician's on the breeze. Yelling, backslapping, and smiling every time the sailors pulled. They adjusted their hands and pulled again with a collective *'Heave.'* Smoothly and slowly, a large sloop was hauled back on deck.

The ship's head carpenter was making his way to where Arent was guiding the men, grumbling and shuffling in the manner old men do. Sebastiaan wondered how old the carpenter was. When he had joined the crew, Mattheys was already gnarly and grey, and that was more than ten years ago. He must be close to his sixties, if not more.

"They're scratching my paint," the old carpenter sourly grumbled as he came to stand next to Arent, his small sinewy body made to look even more scraggly by the bulk of the boatswain. In one hand, he was clutching a bucket of paint. His bristle brush was in the other, ready to repair any damage to the hull.

"You can patch her up in a moment, Mattheys. Keep your slops dry, hey?"

"That's all I've been doing for the past three days, patching and painting, and patching and painting, while everybody else was getting drunk and chasing *chat.*"

"You wanted to do some chasing, Mattheys?" the boatswain asked with a skeptical raise of his eyebrows, appraising the old sailor's weathered body, which bore the distinct look of being prematurely mummified.

"Well, at least your French is improving," the boatswain said as a chuckle rumbled up his chest.

The old carpenter gave him a dirty look and disappeared over the bulwark just as the sloop cleared and the last rowers clambered aboard.

Sebastiaan smiled at the scene and shifted his attention to the quarterdeck where *'Lord'* Niklas was fiddling with his ever-present astrolabe, plotting their best course. The man's mind worked in mysterious ways. The navigator looked up and frowned at the descending sun, then turned his attention back to his calculations. The signet ring on his little finger was tapping impatiently on the wood of the whip staff. Sebastiaan could see the small annoying movement even from a distance. Niklas was the best navigator in the business, and other captains constantly hounded him to sail under their command. But he was loyal to the *Drommedaris* and her captain, and no amount of money or promises of power had been able to lure him away.

A small boy rushed across the upper deck, dodging lines and sidestepping sailors with pickpocket sprightliness. The boy ran past Arent on a single-minded mission with bare feet hitting the deck, skinny arms propelling him onward, and shaking his head as he went, dislodging a black lock of hair from his eyes. Arent's arm snapped out and grabbed him by the scruff of his shirt, lifting him clean off his feet. "Where are you going?" he barked as he turned the dangling child to face him.

"I wanna see the coils snap out." His impish face scrunched in a scowl.

"Not this time. Go see if the cook needs a hand. It's almost time for supper. And don't you be coming back until we are moving. I don't want one of your feet getting in the way of the sheets, like last time." The boatswain set the boy down and watched him dart in the opposite direction toward the galley.

From the set of his shoulders and the swiveling of his head, Sebastiaan knew Arent was looking for somebody. The boatswain scanned the sails and the rigging.

'Of course.'

The instant he heard the raucous bid from below, he knew his peace and quiet were done for. Looking down, he saw the impatient flick of Arent's hand as he beckoned him down.

Clewing the last sail, Sebastiaan started his descent; his hands and feet moved down the shrouds with the agility of a monkey with a stolen treat.

"You bellowed?" he sardonically said as he landed at Arent's feet, who draped a heavy arm around his shoulders and led him toward the forecastle.

"Since you are the captain's beloved nephew and not officially part of this scruffy crew, and neither are you one of the dandy passengers, one can safely assume you are something in-between," Arent spoke in a sinisterly soft and

CHAPTER 3

reasonable voice – the kind he reserved for cheating and gambling.

"I'm getting the distinct feeling you are putting your hand on my shoulder so you can better piss on my feet. What do you want?" Sebastiaan demanded.

Arent looked at him with feigned offense, then continued, "I need you to settle the passengers in their cabins."

"No," Sebastiaan refused and stopped dead in his tracks. Arent released a short burst of laughter, then slapped Sebastiaan on the back and left him as he made his way to the navigator on the quarterdeck, obviously not sated in his desire to spoil somebody else's afternoon. Sebastiaan felt his face contorted as if he had just bitten into a rotten apple. With a visible effort, he relaxed his shoulders, rolled his head to the heavens, swallowed a violent curse, and set out to follow the boatswain's orders.

The passengers were like a group of toddlers; not a minute passed without one developing a pressing need of some sort. The sailors avoided them like watered-down rum. The crew had done everything they could to make the subsequent four-month journey as comfortable as possible, considering that the *Drommedaris* was a merchant trading vessel with the most basic amenities. Additional cabins were constructed for privacy and comfort. They'd even turned the dayroom into something resembling a boardroom where the governor and his advisors could have their daily meetings.

The passengers, unaccustomed to the rigors and hardships of a lengthy sea voyage, were entitled and demanding. Sebastiaan's even temper and boyish good looks made him an excellent choice for smoothing over difficult situations. He accomplished much with a grin, a wink, and a soft word.

Squinting his eyes against the sudden darkness, he entered the cluttered area of the forecastle where the sailors and some of the passengers slept. A long table with benches on either side stood in the middle of the space. Trunks containing personal belongings, with neatly rolled bedding on top, lined the sides. Most passengers were already settled, except for one family huddling together by the dining table. Seeing Sebastiaan enter, the man got up and smeared a cap from his head. He was sun-browned and had laugh lines around his eyes. His wife was calm, but clearly annoyed, and the two teenage daughters looked at the broad-shouldered young man with the eyes of a drowning sailor spotting a life raft with a barrel of ale strapped to it.

"Hendrik Boom, at your service," the man introduced himself. "I am a gardener, bound for the Cape, but I am afraid, with all the confusion on the docks, we boarded the wrong yacht." He looked apologetically at his wife.

"At least you are heading in the right direction," Sebastiaan said with a smile, nodding his greeting to the rest of the family whom the gardener forgot to introduce.

"Sebastiaan De Vries." He stuck out his hand and gave the gardener's a firm shake.

Sebastiaan settled them in the dayroom while he arranged their private sleeping quarters. Then he headed to the stateroom to inform the captain of the four extra souls on board.

Tomorrow an extra cabin would have to be constructed, somewhere. Space was a problem. Perhaps they could steal a little from the neighboring cabins. Either way, he would talk to Mattheys and Arent to see what could be done. He was deep in thought when his uncle's steady voice allowed him entry to the stateroom.

Captain Davit De Coninck looked thoroughly at home in this fragile wooden world. He was utterly relaxed as he stared out the bank of windows lining the back wall of his cabin. They shared so many features; Sebastiaan knew he looked more like his son than his nephew. Both were broad-shouldered and narrow-hipped, with the same blond hair and sharp facial features. Even though his uncle was in his early forties, there was not a trace of silver in his hair or extra weight around his waist. The man was as lean and fit as a lion in his prime.

His uncle turned to him. As usual, he surveyed Sebastiaan with a quick glance, but instead of his usual strict frown, this time, a slow smile spread across his face. His uncle stepped closer and handed him a heavy crystal glass of brandy, then turned to pour himself another. Sebastiaan looked down at the golden-brown liquid, raised it to his nose, and inhaled deeply.

He was twelve years old the night his father left him in his uncle's care, and as the sun's rays lengthened the next day, so did his list of chores. He had started in the galley, carrying food to the sailors and cleaning dishes

CHAPTER 3

afterward. His quick wit and sweet nature had soon made him a favorite among the seamen, and ere long, everybody needed him as their assistant. He learned to boil pitch and make barrels, mend sails and tar rigging, and the first time he and Arent raced up the shrouds to clew the topsail, he learned what heaven felt like. With the salty wind in his face and his feet dancing along the footropes, he was sure he had left earth and was touching God's feet. Soaring eighty feet above the waves with his arms hanging over the boom, his tiny hands open and mimicking the roll of the water far below – he was flying. Being two years older and therefore stronger and wiser, Arent had done all the clewing. When all was done, they had raced down the shrouds to see who could reach the deck first, but the moment their feet hit the white wooden planks, they were met with the captain's stern mien and immediately sentenced to four days of deck scrubbing and head cleaning. Though his uncle's voice was angry, his eyes shone with pride. Now, a decade later, his adventure was coming to an end.

"To your last voyage," Davit De Coninck said with warm eyes and a nostalgic smile, raising his glass to Sebastiaan.

* * *

A deep frown etched between the assistant's eyes as she surveyed her surroundings. Her body was stiff from sleeping in an awkward position. For a moment, confusion clouded her mind, and then the events of the previous evening came crushing over her.

She remembered standing on the wharf, hearing a man calling to her. She had looked up and then down, following his outstretched finger to a pile of small crates at her feet. Bending down, she had picked the closest crate and made her way up the gangway. There was an odd sensation as the wooden walkway pushed against her stride with the movement of the water. Reaching the sparsely lit deck, she had not dared to glance back from where she came, fearing somebody might recognize her. Her fears were quickly pushed aside as more rough hands and gruff voices guided her toward what she could only assume was the galley. There, the cook, without looking from his task of beheading a fish, then deftly launching the head into a large pot, had ordered her down a steep ladder and into the hull, with pointed instructions on where to store the crate.

After stowing the crate, she gripped the ladder's sides to start climbing, but the sudden rush of voices from the galley above had stayed her movements. Retracting her foot from the rung, she moved away from the ladder and quietly took a sidestep into the deep shadows of the hull. The men talked about a fire at the physician's surgery. Many sailors helped to put it out, and somebody had dragged a dead body from the building; the harbormaster was summoned and had confirmed the body was that of the physician and declared it a terrible accident.

She had listened to the excited voices and the detailed recounts, and only then had reality slammed into her like a fist to her stomach. They were talking about her father and the surgery, confirming her worse fears. Her father was dead, and she was alone, her life utterly destroyed.

She had seen people in the grips of panic before. It forced them to run blindly, often even toward the danger. Sometimes they screamed, sounding raw and looking detached from the awful sound. Once, she witnessed a woman in a catatonic state, staring blankly, seeing nothing, only blinking occasionally.

Standing in the dark hull, she listened to the sailors above her discussing her father's death and the destruction of their apothecary. A need to move washed over her. She suddenly understood the desire to run – anything to escape the sound of their voices – but her feet stubbornly remained, and her ears continued to hear.

For the first time in her life, she panicked. Her stomach had given a violent churn, making her chest and throat burn as the bile rushed upwards. Somewhere a speck of reason made its way to the front, and she knew that if she allowed the nausea to continue, the sound of her retching would announce her presence to the men above.

The dread inside her was boiling like lava, looking for a weakness in her crust from which to erupt. She felt short of breath. Her chest was so tight, the air wheezed in and out of her lungs. Tamping down on the noise was futile.

CHAPTER 3

Her mind had lost its hold on her body and instead acted like a spectator.

What an odd sensation: to feel like she was a dispassionate outsider observing herself. Was she dying? How was it possible to see oneself through what must be somebody else's eyes?

She was cold, typical for December for sure, but this was a different cold; it came from her bones and not from the wind or the water outside. It was a cold that burned like frostbite, creating a thin layer of sweat on her upper lip. Her vision started to blur at the edges, and for a terrifying moment, she thought she was gradually going blind. The room had spun and flipped, and then all went black.

Still hearing the infernal wheezing of her breath, she had come to herself in increments. Her brain recalled its duty and connected with the rest of her body. Opening her eyes, she discovered that she was sitting on the floor. She must have stumbled until her back met with an obstacle. Looking over her shoulder, she saw a neat stack of sails pressing against her back. Her knees were tightly drawn to her chest, one hand splayed out on the floor, the other clutching her stomach.

With every passing second, the connection between her mind and body became stronger. She licked her lips and tasted salt, then lifted her hand and felt the wetness on her cheeks. Closing her eyes, she tried to listen to her heartbeat, finding it fast but strong. It sounded familiar. The sound was an anchor that grounded her, and she took comfort in the steady rhythm.

The ship was an excellent temporary hiding place from the men chasing her. She only needed to stay out of sight for a bit longer. Crawling deeper into the dark, she had found a tight corner created by the hull and the neatly folded sails. The tightness of the gap was oddly comforting, and she had nestled deeper into it until her back had once more pressed against the wall of folded sails.

Captains usually do not like to leave the Texel harbor after dark, for the entry was narrow and guarded by jagged cliffs. She reckoned there was enough time to wait and make her way back to the docks once the sailors had settled down for the night. It was a sound plan had she not made the terrible mistake of resting her head against the pile of sails and closing her eyes for a moment.

She must have slept through the night. Daylight was coming in grey shafts through the latticed hatch above the goat pen. Four goats were happily huddled together, seemingly unperturbed by the movement of the floor beneath their hooves. She realized with a start that the ship was no longer in the harbor. The hull made unfamiliar creaks and sounds as it moved in leisurely rolls. Too frightened to move, she let her senses hoard as much information as possible. Scanning the space, she noted that the hull was divided into three parts. Her part was orderly, arranged with sails and wooden barrels, rolls of cheese, and crates with herbs and vegetables. The part in the middle housed various animals, such as chickens and goats, suggesting a long journey ahead. She was in the section directly beneath the galley at the ship's stern. On the other side of the goat pen, large crates, bundles of tools and construction equipment, wood, luggage, and furniture were tightly packed – it looked like they were on their way to building a house on a remote island.

Pressing her hand against the wooden surface, she battled another surge of panic that threatened to overwhelm her once more. She was trapped in a nightmare from which she seemed unable to wake. The ship was no longer at anchor, and judging by its even roll, it had also exited the harbor and was now most likely on the open ocean, heading toward its mysterious destination.

She was not in Oudeschild anymore, not on the island on which she had grown up and spent her whole life. She was being whipped away from the only life she knew, and nobody was there to rescue her. There was no large familiar hand to take hers and say, *'this way.'* How was she to make her way back? Her father would be buried on the hill outside the village without her. She would not be there to say goodbye or to put flowers on his grave. What would become of their home? Would somebody look for her? How had it come to this? The need to escape was strong. She closed her eyes for a brief few seconds, wanting sleep to claim her.

She was not particularly religious by nature, understanding that there was never a need for her to be – until now. Instead of falling asleep, she prayed for the first time in her life. Not the prayer of a small child thanking an invisible, benevolent God for her papa and her food and her bed and her doll, but the desperate prayer of a woman alone and adrift, everything lost and heartbreakingly vulnerable.

Slowly, small pockets of information invaded her senses. The air had a hint of juniper and pine tar, suggesting the hull was recently subjected to a thorough clean. Cooking smells were coming from the galley above, and she imagined her father cooking dinner for them. The thought made her snap her eyes wide open, for she could not afford to fall apart again. Now was the time to think, to plan, to stay alive, and above all, it was imperative she stay sane. Searching for more distractions, she focused on the sounds drifting from above: shouts, scrapes, and laughter.

Looking down at her clothes, she felt a small measure of comfort. They were the same clothes she'd worn the day before, donned in her small attic bedroom, worn sitting down to breakfast with her father, worn mixing the herbs while the morning sun shone through the surgery windows. This clothing was the only familiarity in her entire existence, a lifeline tying her to the safety of everything that came before.

Yesterday seemed a lifetime ago. The clean smell of her father's skin as she kissed his cheek, their home with its soft, worn furniture, her bed with the green counterpane, the surgery – it all felt like it belonged in a book she once read. Her throat was thick with feelings of loss and being lost. Emptiness wrapped around her and forced her deeper into the stack of folded sails as her need for shelter amplified.

A painful lump started to swell in her throat, and she focused on it, feeling it move up until it touched the back of her tongue, but then it faded.

Turning her focus away from her emotions and onto her immediate needs, it became blindingly apparent that she needed to relieve herself, and soon, but where? Her bladder was quite literally pulling her mind from the depths of despair.

Searching the space, she tried to find a spot unlikely to be frequented by anybody else. Her eyes followed the wooden ribcage of the ship; it dipped below the floor into the bilge. Water and waste eventually made their way down there, and the bilge pump would pump it overboard. She noticed the slats on the floor of the goat pen were slightly further apart than other parts of the hull, allowing for urine and pelletized droppings to fall through. So far, nobody had come down to check on the goats. Assuming they would need daily tending, she decided to wait a while longer; her bladder protested the decision, but fear was a ruthless master.

She did not have to wait long. The hatch above opened. A potbellied man and a small boy descended into the hull, each carrying a wooden pail. The man climbed into the goat pen and settled next to a goat. The little boy disappeared from her view but returned and dropped two large squares of dried alfalfa hay into the goat pen, then filled the water trough from a nearby barrel. Having finished his chore, he kneeled next to the man milking one of the nanny goats. The man spoke softly to the animal, stroking the white hair on her back and playfully ruffling her ears.

She could see the expectation on the boy's face as he watched the older man's fingers squeeze and pull each teat, aiming the thin stream of milk neatly into the pail.

"Did you check for eggs this morning?"

The boy looked up at him and shook his head.

"Well, off you go then, see if you can find some before they settle for the night. No need to disturb them once they're comfortable; they need their rest."

The boy crawled into the cage housing ten fat chickens and scratched through the hay-covered floor, placing a few eggs carefully into the pail by his side.

"You know they don't work all that hard. All they must do is lay an egg every day," the boy said.

"And how would you like that job, you little shitweasel?" The cook laughed at the disgusted expression on the child's face. She was not sure if the child took offense to the moniker or the unpleasant task of laying an egg.

The pair moved from her view, and moments later, the hatch slammed shut. The girl moved slowly from her hiding place and headed for the goat pen. Hoisting herself over the slatted railing, she crawled to the center. Not wanting to cause a disturbance among the goats, she stilled, but the animals were absorbed in their dinner and paid her no attention. Loosening the cords of her pants, she pushed them down. The forgotten knife in her waistband clattered to the floor. Her heart missed a beat as she grabbed it before it could slip through the slats. Keeping her eyes on the hatch, she fully expected the cook's face to appear at any moment. She waited, but nobody came. Slowly and carefully, not looking away from the hatch, she squatted among the goats, their warm bodies rubbing against her face. Staying on her haunches for a while longer, she listened for more sounds from above, holding the knife in a grip that turned her knuckles white. With her most pressing need taken care of, she crawled to the water barrel, quietly lifting the lid and using the jug the boy had left by its side to slake her thirst.

Leaving her hiding spot among the sails had set her nerves on edge. Exhausted from her outing, she crept back into her corner. Tomorrow she would focus on finding food. Relieved to have a plan, she stretched her legs out and allowed sleep to claim her once more.

Her sleep did not last until morning. Somewhere in the small hours of the night, she became aware of a weight on her lap. When her hand hesitantly moved to investigate the object, her fingers were met with soft vibrating fur. Her first instinct insisted that it was a rodent of sorts. With a herculean effort, she swallowed the scream that most certainly would have alerted past and future generations to her presence. Taking a few calming breaths, she cleared her mind, and it became apparent that the object was too large to be a rat. She chastised herself for her foolishness, and besides, rats do not purr.

The cat felt her body tense and dug its claws into her thighs. It looked at her with deep suspicion, its purring suspended. Exhaling slowly, she felt her way over the animal's body. The fur was warm, thick, and soft, and she sunk her fingers deep into it. A raspy tongue appreciatively licked the side of her hand. Her shoulders dropped, and her body relaxed, grateful to be able to hold another living creature close.

All was quiet. Only the ring of a bell far above signaled the end of one shift and the start of another. Above, the galley remained encased in darkness. The loud growl of her stomach elicited a companionable moan from the cat as it got up, turned several times on the same spot, and lay down in precisely the same position as before.

"Aren't you supposed to hunt at night? No?" she whispered while clutching the snug body. "Well, then, I suppose the task will fall to me. What would you prefer, salted meat or cheese? I must confess I've never milked a goat before, but I suppose one could try. If I succeed, we can wash it all down with goat's milk."

From the moment she pried open the barrel of salted meat with her knife, the cat had turned into a screeching and howling hellion. Her blood froze with the surety that somebody would come to investigate the source of the distress. Trying to hush it only served to increase the pitch of the racket. The only solution to the predicament was to offer it something to eat immediately. After the feline had consumed several bribes, cut from the piece of meat she had scraped clear of the salt, it quietly followed her back to their corner.

Another ding from the bell on the upper deck pierced the dark hours of the night. Every half hour, the hourglass turned, eight turns marked a shift, and two shifts marked the morning – for now, she could do nothing but wait.

Chapter 4

They had left Texel six days ago. Captain De Coninck was standing on the quarterdeck with his navigator, Niklas Jansen, and his boatswain, Arent Van Jeveren, locked in deep discussion. Every man on deck was keenly aware of the captain's presence, although the sailors did not stop in their industry to look at him; rather, they *felt* him. He brought with him a pride and purpose that strengthened their grip and sharpened their wits.

The *Drommedaris* was the love of his life and had been for the last eight years. She was a dream to sail, plain to the eye with not many frills and fancies, but she was fast and elegant, and he knew every inch of her from the depths of the bilge to the top of the main mast. He knew how to shorten or increase her sails to push her to the limit, and when his demands were harsh, she complied without complaint or restraint.

He was a purist, if such a thing was possible among mariners, with a deep love and respect for the ocean, and unlike so many other men who captained the VOC ships, he was incorruptible. He had no interest in running smuggling businesses on the side, for he was a rich man by birth. He took to the seas because it was his passion and what he had wanted to do since he was a boy. Inhaling deeply, he let the salty air coat his tongue.

"Look, lads, I love a rough ride as much as the next man, but this is fast becoming tiresome. We're getting punched in the ribs with every gust coming our way," De Coninck said, switching his eyes between his two officers before finally settling on the horizon.

The ship was not heavy enough. The stowers should have loaded them with more ballast stones back in Amsterdam. De Coninck also knew that the men on the docks acted on the orders of the higher-ups in the VOC, men who spent their days in offices and their nights in warm beds, to whom life on a ship meant adding profits and subtracting losses.

"We're working on it," came Niklas's short reply, followed by a click of his tongue in annoyance, his sharp eyes moved in a constant sweep from the man in the lookout basket over the vast expanse of water to the sailor on the weather deck above and behind them. The captain, used to the man's social awkwardness, had learned to trust his ability to navigate rather than communicate.

"In *short*," Arent said with a slight shake of his head, "we've been tacking towards the English coast since yesterday. It's not helping much with the wind, but at least we wouldn't have to worry about Portuguese pirates biting us in the arse. It's a pity we can't use this wind to our advantage."

The ship had been in trouble since leaving Amsterdam, but they managed because the wind was gentle and not too demanding. Even so, they were bobbing like an empty barrel. When they reached Texel, Arent had ordered the storm sails brought up from the hull, just in case.

"She's too light for heavy canvases, so we've been on shortened sails since yesterday. It gives us more control, but it makes us slow – pirate bait," Arent continued.

"Has anybody seen the cat today?" De Coninck asked. The quick change in topic caused a hitch in the conversation.

"He came up this morning. We tried feeding him, but he didn't want to eat. Jumpy as all hell, though. Why, Cap, you feel something?" Arent asked with a lift of his chin.

Pinching his lips, De Coninck nodded slowly, an uneasiness filling his gut. The air felt heavy and thick, and there was a heat to the wind he did not like.

"Arent, keep those storm sails and hatch covers close by. Close the gunports and tie up the cannons – the wind feels angry." Not sensing any change in the wind but trusting the captain's instincts, Arent turned on his heels and left to see the orders carried out.

The small dark-haired boy scampered on deck with refreshments for the captain, compliments of the cook. De Coninck reached for the proffered cup

CHAPTER 4

of tea. "Thank you, Master Orion," he smiled as he poured the spilled tea from the saucer back into the cup. The child executed a bow that needed practice and flitted down the companionway, forgetting to wait for the empty teacup.

"Put us in an English port, Nik, and we'll weigh her down with more cannons. Signal the *Reijger* and the *Goede Hoop*." He referred to their two sister ships without taking his eyes off the horizon. Niklas gave a short nod, and the captain left the deck, his booted footsteps sounding in measured strides.

31 December 1651 – The day broke with a red sunrise over uneasy seas.

Governor Van Riebeeck and Captain De Coninck stood on the quarterdeck. Having spent much of the early years of his career as a ship's surgeon, Van Riebeeck understood the significance of all the goings-on aboard. This morning he noted the crispness in the sailors' movements, how the deck seemed more tidy than usual, and the way Arent came around the foremast like a bull rounding a narrow street corner in Pamplona.

"Are we preparing for a bit of rough weather?" He didn't look at the captain but tilted his head backward to enjoy the sunlight.

In his early thirties, the governor had an intelligent face and dark hair. His clothing was simple but elegant, and he wore his responsibilities with the confidence of someone twice his age.

The captain had known the young governor for only two weeks, but what he saw, he liked, for the man was understated and efficient.

"*Amat Victoria Curam.*"

Touching his earlobe, Van Riebeeck looked at the captain with a question on his face.

"Victory likes careful preparation," De Coninck translated.

"I always thought victory favors the bold, but I suppose if the bold is unprepared, it becomes a question of fatuity."

De Coninck smiled at the governor's wry wit, but his eyes stayed fixed on the horizon where a large bank of heavy, dark grey clouds was forming. A well-rested and fresh-faced Niklas joined them, greeting both men with his signature short nod. De Coninck stepped away from the whip staff, allowing Niklas to resume the navigation. He hinted to the governor, and they walked a few paces.

De Coninck lowered his voice when he next spoke. "If we do get caught in a storm, I will need a strong hand to guide the passengers."

Van Riebeeck immediately understood the unspoken question. "Done," he replied with a relaxed smile, but when he descended the companionway leading to the cabins below, there was an urgency to his stride.

The smell of beef stew wafted from the galley. Barent, the cook, received his orders from the captain early this morning. He was to serve a simple breakfast of porridge and dried biscuits, then start on the stew and douse the galley fire as soon as possible. There would be no cooking for the rest of the day as a precaution in case the weather should turn quickly.

Half an hour later, the sea was rough. Van Riebeeck knocked on the door of each cabin, breaking the news of the possibility of bad weather and ordering all portholes shut, all lanterns lit, and everything to be stowed away or tied down. He ensured each cabin was equipped with empty buckets and extra blankets. The water was choppy, causing an uncomfortable roll to the ship, and he steadied himself against the door jamb while he spoke words of encouragement to the taut faces in front of him. All were to remain in their cabins and not venture out on the decks until he gave the all-clear.

Finally, he reached his own cabin. His wife, Maria, was cradling their eighteen-month-old boy, Antoonie, on her lap, whispering soft words against his temple. The boy looked so much like his mother, with the same pale blue eyes and flaxen hair. Unlike most children his age, he was quiet, with a serious demeanor and a delicate constitution. Van Riebeeck kneeled next to the bed, resting one hand on his wife's knee and touching the child's warm cheek with his other. He held her gaze for a moment, noticing the worry lines between her eyes and around her soft mouth. She looked at him and bent forward to lean her forehead against his.

"Is there a storm coming?" she whispered.

"We'll be fine," he said without withdrawing.

"I know," her voice faltered only slightly.

* * *

CHAPTER 4

The sea was getting angrier by the minute, but the storm was not upon them yet. It still churned and threatened some way off in the distance. A warning call roared from the lookout, piercing the whining of the growing wind. "FREAK WAVE!"

De Coninck reacted without a moment's hesitation, ordering the sailor down from the lookout in a voice that brooked no arguments, not that he had expected any. The sailor was already making his way down to the safety of the deck.

"Safety ropes! Hunker down!" The captain's voice thundered over the upper deck, reverberating down the spine of each sailor. All the men aboard scampered to take shelter against the bulwark, hooking their arms around the safety rope installed on its inside, bracing themselves for the event most of them had never experienced but feared the most. Freak waves did not occur frequently, and only a precious handful of ships survived an encounter with one. Stories of these incidents were embellished and shared liberally among sailors to the point where it was impossible to distinguish fact from fiction.

Sebastiaan stood next to Arent, their arms laced through the shroud supporting the mainmast. He looked up to the quarterdeck and locked eyes with his uncle, who stood with his arms braced on the railing and his blond hair flying in the wind. The man reminded him of an African lion he once saw – alert, strong, and fearless.

De Coninck scanned the deck, taking note of each sailor and his position before pausing at the sight of his nephew standing among the crew with a cocky smile on his face. The lad had turned out all right. The thought struck him hard as he turned back towards the whip staff.

The rolling hill of water was approaching them head-on. "A fifty-footer! Don't back down!" De Coninck yelled to Niklas over the noise of the wind.

"Better not be an inch more! We're good; it hasn't curled yet!" Niklas yelled back. De Coninck was stunned. It was the longest uninterrupted sentence he had ever heard from the man's mouth. The intensity of the moment seemed to have loosened his tongue. The wave was heading towards them, feeding on the ocean in front of it, growing higher. Their best chance of survival was to face it head-on. Both men took a firm hold of the whip staff. The rudder needed to be kept steady against the force of the water and not be allowed to turn the ship sideways. For if that were to happen, they would capsize and sink. With luck, the wind would push them up and over; if not, they would slide back down the wall of water, and the wave would crash over them, sending them to the bottom of the ocean. There was only one option left, and De Coninck liked that, for, in a crisis, simplicity was key. Keep the rudder steady. He had ordered the sails to be wetted earlier, and he was certain they would hold – the moisture in the canvas would keep them from tearing. All that was left was for the wind to fill them hard.

The towering wave reached them with an uncompromising force. The deck rose under their feet as the *Drommedaris* started her uphill journey. She moved stoically up the wave, like Joan of Arc walking towards her pyre, shoulders back, chin up, defiant to the bitter end. The climb continued, and their progress slowed until she tilted into a near-vertical position, her three masts almost parallel to the ocean below. On the upper deck, sailors were suspended in mid-air, hanging from the safety ropes like laundry on a line. The wind kept steady pressure on the sails, pushing against the wall of water and causing spindrift to fly from the top.

Muffled screams from the passengers below deck drifted through the floorboards, mingling with the creaking of the hull. Niklas caught the hourglass as it swung loose from its hook and tucked it beneath his crouching body while looking up at the ship's bow, stunned by the unusual perspective.

When De Coninck was a fifteen-year-old navigator's assistant, he had encountered his first and only freak wave. What stayed with him through the years was the captain's composure. He had taught him that fear and panic killed sailors and sank ships, not the water and the wind. The memory of the captain's words brought a sardonic smile. He loved the ocean and every minute on it, but he had never felt more alive than he did at this moment.

Gradually the ship tilted forward. The *Drommedaris* sat motionless on top of the wave for a few moments, surrounded only by sky, the rest of the water far below. It was not hard to imagine that they had gone to heaven. In the next moment, the illusion came to a crashing end. The ship plummeted into the depths of the trough behind the comber. The deck that had, moments before, pushed against their legs now fell away like the platform under a condemned man tied to the hangman's noose. As terrifying as the wave was in its approach, so was it anti-climactic in its departure. The wave discarded the ship like an unwanted toy, leaving it to bob in its wake as it continued to roll away. Men rose from their crouched positions, looking on as the wave crested and crashed into the ocean.

A stunned silence fell on the deck. They looked at each other with blank expressions as they came to terms with just how close to their deaths they had come. Arent lifted his chin and rubbed his neck as if his shirt collar was suddenly too tight.

"What are you doing?" Sebastiaan asked, his voice a notch higher than usual.

"Just making sure I'm not wearing my arse around my throat."

Sebastiaan was still barking with laughter when the captain came flying down the quarterdeck companionway. He patted each sailor on the shoulder with a wide grin, shouting bawdy encouragements.

Their reprieve was short-lived, for the bank of storm clouds was advancing on them with inexorable determination. The horizon was a golden line against the black mass of the storm. Furious veins of white lightning licked across and down to the water. It could have been a painting on a gallery wall for all its terrifying beauty.

Arent ordered the storm sails hoisted and the hatches to the lower deck covered. Four men carried the lowered sails into the forecastle, where the sailmaker and his assistant went over every inch, searching for tears or worn patches. The men moved across the deck, checking safety ropes and tying loose lines. They were about to be locked in a duel, armed with a slingshot against an advancing army.

* * *

The moment the ship started to rise in the unnatural upright position, Maria locked her arms around her child and clutched him to her body. They were thrown from the bed, skidding across the cabin floor, passing underneath her husband's desk, and, together with the chair, colliding with the back wall. Books and letters bundled up next to her on the floor. The desk's drawers slid free; one crashed, edge first, onto her shin, causing an ugly green and purple swelling with a deep cut in the center.

The child was viciously clinging to her, his small nails scratching her neck. She grabbed the flat cushion from the overturned chair and draped it over the boy's head. It sounded like the ship was being torn apart plank by precious plank, as it elicited gut-wrenching creaks and moans like a woman caught in the grips of labor pains. Water was seeping through the walls, although there were no apparent leaks. Where Maria's back pressed against the wall, she could feel the dampness on her skin. She looked into her child's angelic face, pressed her lips to his forehead, and held them there for a while.

"Angel, will you pray with Mommy?" she asked and smiled at his eager nod. She started with a simple prayer, pausing after each sentence and allowing him to babble his baby words before continuing.

"Our Father in Heaven." Pause

"Do not forsake us." Pause

"Please keep –," the pressure at her back eased, and she slowly opened her eyes, understanding that the ship was level again. The child gave a shrill shriek when he and his mother were suddenly left suspended in mid-air as the ship fell away with a deep moan.

"Oh God, help us!"

* * *

Her husband came crashing through the cabin door, disheveled and shaken. Scanning the cabin, he searched for his family. He fought a wave of panic, not seeing them at first. Then he found them on the floor behind the desk. Reaching them with stunning speed, he fell to his knees and hugged them to his chest. Pushing her face into the crook of his neck, Maria slipped her arm around him. They stayed interlocked until they felt the baby squirm between them. Releasing her, he assessed them both for injuries.

CHAPTER 4

"What happened?" he asked when he discovered the gash on her lower leg. While listening to her explanation, he ripped a strip of cotton from the bedsheet and gently wrapped her injury. When he was done, he reached over to take their son from her arms and placed him on the floor between them.

"Is this what usually happens during a storm on the ocean?" Maria asked as she started to gather the contents of his desk.

"No, I think a freak wave hit us. It's quite rare. It won't happen again."

From the look on her face, he could see that she was not so easily appeased. He continued his explanation. "Sometimes a storm pushes strong winds in front of it, which then create a wave many times the size of the other waves, but once it passes and the storm is upon us, everything becomes normal again."

Her hands froze as she slowly turned her head to face him.

"Normal?" she asked, listening to the storm outside. Waves were slamming into the sides of the ship, rocking it violently. The wind was making unworldly sounds as it howled. Thunder was clapping and cracking above. They were sailing amidst all of it in a wooden box that leaked, on an ocean hell-bent on breaking them apart, and her husband was using the word *normal*? Van Riebeeck watched the emotions play across her face and knew the exact moment she reached the end of her tether.

"What is it?" he asked, handing the baby a dried biscuit fished from his pocket.

She had a stubborn glint in her eyes when she replied. "I will not sit in this cabin waiting to drown."

"Sweetheart, we are not going to drown –" he started, but she interrupted him.

"You don't know that." She looked up at the ceiling as the bell above announced the shift change. "Husband, who cares for those sailors as they finish their shift?"

Not waiting for his reply, she bent down, scooped up their son, and headed for the door. Not sure what she meant to do, he tracked along behind her, smiling at how the child's chubby little legs bobbed rhythmically with the assertive bounce of Maria's strides. She went straight to the gardener's cabin and briefly rapped on the door. A plump middle-aged woman answered. Recognizing the determination on the younger woman's face, she asked before Maria had a chance to speak, "You need all three of us?" Van Riebeeck took this as his cue to leave and assess the situation among the rest of the passengers.

"I do indeed," Maria replied, smiling as Mrs. Boom snapped her fingers at the two teenage girls who swiftly came to their feet like well-trained soldiers.

* * *

With the start of the afternoon watch, the captain once again assigned specific jobs to each crew member. The first man on deck was sent to the suction pump on the forecastle and four men to each line securing the sails. Waves crashed over the bulwark, submerging the deck in knee-high white foamy water.

"Stay on your feet, lads!" De Coninck commanded in a voice made for rough weather. "You fall, you drown!"

He backslapped each man leaving the deck as the new crew came on for the start of the next shift. Spotting Arent, he waved him over. "Boatswain, get your arse to the dayroom. Your shift is over!"

Arent waded his way through the water to the captain. "No disrespect, Cap, but I'll go when you go." They stood a foot apart but had to yell to hear each other over the wind.

"I'll flog you myself for your disobedience, boy!" De Coninck threatened with a hard look.

"Five minutes, Cap. Let me hand over to the lad," referring to Sebastiaan. De Coninck nodded, turned around, and ascended the steps back to the quarterdeck where a drenched but stubborn and straight-backed Niklas was guiding the ship like a lighthouse. His wet linen shirt and black breeches clung to his body like a second skin, and for the first time, De Coninck noticed how slender of frame the man was. What Niklas lacked in physical prowess, he made up for in intellect and, judging by the determined set of his jaw, also in stubbornness.

CHAPTER 4

Even though it was just past midday, the sky had turned an unusual shade of pink, with silver-white lightning running in horizontal and vertical cracks, ripping and scratching at the clouds. As the storm gained strength, the water turned into a rough confusion of ink-black waves with white foam clinging to them like fur on a stray dog, uneven and ratty. There was no order or pattern to the waves; no two were coming from the same direction. The only noticeable commonality was the single-minded objective to obliterate the small wooden ship. But in their confusing fury, the waves worked against each other. Directing all their force from different angles, they inadvertently kept the ship upright.

Sebastiaan spotted Arent as he made his way to the middle of the deck, yelling something at him. He shook his head and pointed to his ear, signaling that he could not hear above the wind, when he spotted a movement just off Arent's right shoulder. Identifying the flying object, he rushed forward to push his friend out of the way, but the water surrounding his legs hindered his agility. He knew the moment when Arent realized the danger, for he searched Sebastiaan's face, and the words he was about to utter died on his lips.

One of the smaller deadeyes had broken loose and was flying like a wrecking ball on a chain, clearing everything in its path before connecting with a dull thump with the back of Arent's head. The large man tilted like a felled oak. Sebastiaan reached him before his knees could touch the deck, grabbed his arm, and swung it over his shoulder. Blood was running in rivulets over Arent's shoulders and down his back, mixing with his long black hair, giving him a savage look he would have been proud of. The sailmaker was the closest man to them. Lukas wedged his shoulder under Arent's left arm, and together they hauled the boatswain across the deck toward the shelter of the dayroom.

Ordinarily, the dayroom was where the governor and his advisors held their daily meetings concerning the start of the new trading station at the tip of the African continent. It was in the stern, directly beneath the captain's cabin and beside the galley. The room was not large, but comfortably accommodated a table and twelve chairs. Today, the solid walnut table was pushed against the back wall. Circumstances had reduced the stately piece from witnessing historical declarations and decisions to shelter, sickbed, and general kitchen table surrounded by women with blankets and food and the smell of many wet bodies in close proximity. Sebastiaan and Lukas lowered Arent onto the table and were immediately pushed aside by the surgeon.

Heading for the door, Sebastiaan turned as he felt a hand on his shoulder. He found himself face to face with the calm façade of the governor.

"That's the boatswain?" Van Riebeeck asked, looking over Sebastiaan's shoulder to Arent's large limp body.

"Yes, sir."

"Who will take his place?"

"That would be me, sir."

Sebastiaan didn't know much about the governor other than that his uncle liked and respected him, but that was of little significance at this moment. He had no interest in entering a pissing contest with the man. He had practically grown up on this ship. He was never sheltered from the life of a sailor, and he had worked every job from cabin boy to filling in for his uncle when he had a fever. His uncle had told him long ago that if he hungered for a position of power, he would have to get it elsewhere, for loyalty and respect were earned, and earning them meant being the best at every task put before him. He accepted and enjoyed the challenge and rose above it. He knew the men needed leadership now. With Arent injured, they would naturally look to him. That was how it had always been, but there was no way this dandy toff with his soft hands would understand that, and he did not have the rank, time, or inclination to explain it.

Van Riebeeck surprised him by asking, "What can I do?"

"Sir –?" Sebastiaan was momentarily at a loss for words. This man was the governor, for God's sake, but Van Riebeeck looked to him with eager anticipation, his gaze level and sturdy.

"Governor, it is a mess out there. The rain is coming down so hard it feels like pebbles hitting us, and we can't even see the deck beneath all the froth and water." Pausing, he saw that the man was not intimidated. Sebastiaan grinned.

"Sir, we need help on the suction pump. A four-hour shift is too long for

CHAPTER 4

a single man to operate it," he said, gesturing to a sailor with shoulders so cramped he could hardly sit upright. "If we are to stay afloat, that pump needs to work without pause. It's backbreaking work, but it doesn't require skill."

Van Riebeeck looked at the drenched, barefoot young man in front of him. He was tired but far from exhausted. The lad was a fighter with a stubborn set to his shoulders and defiance in his eyes; he could respect that.

"There are twenty-four of us." Meaning himself and the rest of the male passengers, for De Coninck had already commandeered the soldiers aboard to assist the sailors. "We'll work in half-hour shifts under your command," the governor said, barely containing the excitement in his voice.

Sebastiaan nodded and resisted the impulse to slap the governor on the shoulder.

"That can work."

Chapter 5

He was trying to get out of this killing business. Not for moral reasons, of course, for life had stripped him of that illusion a long time ago. He was the product of a mother with stars in her eyes, making him believe he could be a king, and a father with mean fists showing him that he was nothing but vermin.

The two ideas had never really left him, and as he grew older, they took a form of their own, guiding him, pulling at him, forcing him to choose.

No, the problem with killing was that he liked it too much, but it messed with his head, especially the part where he studied his victims. That was when the vermin side of him grew strong, for he liked to sneak into their lives, learn from them, feed off them, take their sins and make them part of him. He learned the games they played and joined in without them even knowing; it filled him with anticipation and heightened his pleasure. Though he could never understand how his prey could not find delight in it as well; it was positively exhilarating.

Then when it was time to strike, the king came to life, and he was strong and ruthless. He served justice upon those condemned creatures, a death befitting their sins.

It was dark as sin in the cabin. He dipped to his knees to search under the bed. His hand connected with a trunk, a chamber pot, and a pair of shoes, but nothing else. Rising, he scanned the room; another trunk stood to the back. Three clicks of his boots' wooden heels and the screech from the hinges filled the silence of the deserted cabin. The trunk was large and filled with garments; he patted them down, felt resistance, and searched deeper,

CHAPTER 5

discovering books, more shoes, and a wooden box. He slammed the lid shut.

The storm offered him a small window of opportunity to search the cabins. It was a chance he would most likely not have again. On to the next one, different objects, same results. More cabins, more trunks, beds, empty spaces. Too dark to see, he relied on the information his hands and nose gave him. He touched everything. His boot clanked against an overturned chamber pot; the stench of the spilled contents made his lip curl, and he kicked it to the side. Deeper into the cabin, he slipped in a pool of vomit but steadied himself with one hand against a bed frame.

He was once more in the passageway, stumbling his way to the dayroom. Scanning the room, he searched every face. Then his eye caught the slender shape of a young sailor tucked in the corner. He paused in his stride. His increased heartbeat made the air whistle through his nose like a breeze through a forest. It tickled the hairs close to the entrance, and he flared his nostrils to rid himself of the annoyance. It was her; he was sure. He had found her. The young sailor's slender shoulders stood out under the damp shirt. A large leather cap was pulled low, obscuring the face and casting deep shadows over the pronounced cheekbones. The fingers clutching the bowl were long, elegant, and feminine. He clamped his jaw tight to stifle the sound his victory was forcing to his lips. He must remain calm and not rush – deep breaths, more wheezing.

He scanned the body for more evidence. His eyes dipped to the sailor's chest, but the shirt was baggy, and the sailor was hunched forward, offering nothing conclusive. He approached slowly, concentrating on reducing the length of his strides – *don't rush, don't rush*. He forced his heart to follow the rhythm of the silent words. Pungent sweat dripped from his armpits down his sides. He came to a stop mere inches from his quarry. It was her; he was so sure he could taste it. Resisting the need to lick his lips, he marveled at his self-control. Oh, how he would relish the feel of her skin, warm under his constantly cold hands, the scent of her fear when she realized that her game was done.

He knelt in front of the young sailor. There was no reaction to his presence. Did she not sense him? Her daring only managed to increase his excitement.

Then there was movement. A fine-boned hand stretched out, handing over the empty food bowl without looking up. She thought he was here to aid her: how innocent. The man could not resist the need to touch her. He overextended his reach for the bowl, allowing his fingers to slide over the sailor's. When they touched, he knew she would feel the connection between them and look up; when she did, they would be face to face. He wanted to see her eyes, learn all her secrets. The instant their fingers touched, he felt a sharp jolt of excitement pulsing through his hand, but the sensation faded quickly, replaced by a serpentine calmness. His heart slowed down, his breathing evened out, and the clamminess of his skin seemed to dry in that split second. Now that he had touched her, he knew he would not deliver her end too soon. He would keep watching her for a while longer. Let her play their game until he decided that it was time.

The sailor's reaction to their touch pulled him from his fantasy. The young hand snapped back, dropping the bowl to the floor, and the sailor's eyes jerked up, scowling at the man with a deep frown instantly carved between tired but wary eyes. The light from the lantern on the wall washed over the previously hidden face and glittered off the fine stubble coating the sailor's cheeks. It was not her.

He gained his feet and stepped back with a growl, almost losing his footing. Leaving the bowl on the floor, he turned and forged on deeper into the dayroom. He was so sure it was her – he felt it. How could his instincts have failed him so badly? After a few strides, listening to the clicking of his heels competing with all the other sounds, a slow, cold smile creased his face as sudden understanding dawned. She knew; she knew he was looking for her. Perhaps she was watching him, avoiding him. She wanted to play their game, craving the thrill of being hunted – how intoxicating.

* * *

"Madam, no disrespect, but water is for washing," one sailor grumbled while squinting into his mug of water, his lip curling as though he detected something floating in it.

CHAPTER 5

"You can hand that warm blanket and stew back, along with the water, if it's not to your liking," Mrs. Boom challenged with elevated eyebrows and fists on her hips. She pinned the man to his sleeping pallet with her stare until she was satisfied that he was eating and drinking sufficiently before collapsing.

Maria watched the interaction, admiring the older woman for the easy charm and unaffected care she showed. Being here aiding others kept Maria's fears at bay, and for the first time since the expedition started, she did not feel like an outsider.

Time had lost its meaning with the sky so dark, and their small existence held tightly in the grip of the raging sea. Ship and crew were mercilessly set upon by the sudden and fierce storm that had left them little time to recover from the shock of surviving the freak wave that hit sometime before midday. With so many demands around her, there was little time to worry about capsizing, sinking, or drowning; being useful far outweighed being afraid.

She took pity on the row of bedraggled men as they sat against the wall of the dayroom, stopping by each one to collect the dirty dishes from their hesitant hands. They were uncomfortable having the governor's wife serve them and hid their unease behind grumbling and minor complaints. She assured them that she would personally listen to each of their grievances once they were warm, fed, and rested. One poor man's shoulders were cramping so badly that he could hardly hold his bowl of stew, but after Maria offered to feed him, he recovered sufficiently enough to manage. Since their sleeping quarters were flooded and their bedding soaked, they had no alternative but to lie down on the floor as they were.

"Show them no mercy, Mistress, or the lot of them will turn into a bunch of whining babes," Mrs. Boom said with a wicked glint in her eye. Maria instantly took comfort in the older woman's raucous nature. She had not had an opportunity to spend time with the Boom family since she mainly kept to her cabin, with Antoonie being so small and her fear of being underfoot. Being the only child of a protestant pastor and almost ten years younger than her husband, her marriage to the governor had catapulted Maria into a life she was unprepared for. Therefore, she was grateful for the four-month sea voyage ahead of them, as it would allow her time to find her feet. Mrs. Boom, having misinterpreted the younger woman's uncertainty and consideration as aloofness, had kept to herself as well.

The storm and their current circumstances had forced a camaraderie between them. Mrs. Boom had the innate ability to transform a threadbare room filled with sodden sailors into a home. She seemed in perpetual motion, always busy, with little escaping her notice, yet she brought order wherever she went. Her body was lush and comforting, and her garments made swishing sounds when she moved, but her most endearing feature was being one of those refreshing, unfortunate souls bestowed with a glass face. Every thought that popped into her mind immediately revealed itself in her features before manifesting in unguarded words that tumbled from her mouth; there was simply no time for censure or deceit.

"Mrs. Boom – " Maria was about to offer her some stew and a dry biscuit when a quick reply brought her up short.

"Mistress, just now when you said, 'Mrs. Boom,' I had a chill run down my spine, thinking my mother-in-law had somehow found her way here. Please call me Anke if it's all the same to you." Maria gave a short burst of laughter at the woman's earnest and slightly panicked expression.

"Very well then, Anke. I need you to sit down and eat something, please. If you continue in this manner, you will drop from exhaustion, and I can't do this without you."

"Mistress, exhaustion is the furthest thing from my mind. Right now, I'm more concerned about getting those wet shirts off the men's backs. They will all turn sick if they sleep in them." Her brow knotted with concern, and her head tipped in the direction of the men.

It was a valid concern. As a solution, Anke would beg dry shirts from the passengers. Maria had an inkling that there would be little begging and a lot of bullying, judging by the purposeful tilt to Anke's chin as she marched out of the dayroom and down the corridor. 'No' did not seem like a word she would suffer lightly.

A large, unconscious man was lying on the walnut table. Maria's eyes traced a path from his long, broad bare feet to his calves which were easily the size of her thighs. She had never seen the like before. Even relaxed, the muscles

CHAPTER 5

on his legs bulged. His linen slops were blood-splattered, as was most of his shirt. His shoulders were impossibly broad, and she wondered what force of nature had incapacitated him.

Maria watched as the surgeon grabbed his shoulder and pulled him onto his stomach with a sudden harsh movement, exposing the wound on the back of the patient's head. A soft moan escaped the sailor's lips. The surgeon's face scrunched as he looked down at the injury in a manner advertising disgust or, God forbid, short-sightedness. Maria was unsure what to make of the surgeon. He had offered very little assistance to anybody since the storm started. She had also learned that his family was aboard and his child was ill. Perhaps it was the reason for his standoffish behavior. Looking up, he found Maria's eyes on him. With a frown, he barked, "Water."

After sluicing the wound, he opened his black leather satchel. A musty, sour smell wafted from it. He extracted two pieces of stained cotton strips, and Maria winced at the sight of the dirty rags. Dousing one liberally with vinegar, he folded it in a square and plastered it to the wound. Then he wrapped the second rag around the man's head twice before securing the ends. Looking to the poor man on the table, she wondered which would be worse for him, the surgeon's ministrations or a ride down a rutted road in an open oxcart. With his patient successfully treated, the surgeon dropped the man's head carelessly back onto the table and left.

Anke and Maria exchanged a look that communicated such profanity neither woman felt equipped to utter. Anke opened her mouth twice, attempting to call the disagreeable man back, but no sound came forth.

"Satan's bollocks," the cook mumbled as he came to stand next to the two women. "He should not be lying down. Not with a head wound." Arent was still on the table, the bandage around his head soaking up the bloody puddle it was lying in.

"Let's lift him off the table and onto a pallet," Anke suggested. It took the combined efforts of all three to lower him into a sitting position against the wall and dispossess him of his wet shirt.

Maria placed a warm blanket around his shoulders and knelt next to him. She was worried about his condition and unwilling to leave his side. Instead, she leaned forward and unwrapped the dirty rags. Tipping his head forward and letting it rest against her shoulder, she gently applied a thick layer of honey to the open wound, then she covered it with clean linen strips cut from her bedsheet.

Arent was slow to regain consciousness. When he finally opened his eyes, they were glassy and unfocused. Maria continued to talk to him in a soft voice, asking questions and voicing concerns.

"Mistress, I am fine enough, just a bit of a headache," he reassured her in a raspy whisper. She reached for a mug and brought it to his lips.

"Willow bark tea," she explained, "for the pain." He sipped the tea gingerly but felt instantly nauseous when she offered him a bowl of beef broth. The bowl was immediately retracted and put to the side.

"You took a blow to the head. We've cleaned and bandaged the wound, but it is important to stay awake a bit longer." He acknowledged with a barely perceptible nod.

She dispatched Antoonie to sit with him and keep him awake for a while when there was nothing more she could do for him. The giant of a man was infinitely patient with the toddler as Antoonie climbed over him, touching an old scar on his cheek, and exploring his long, matted hair. The child played a game with his fingers, running them over and around Arent's face and shoulders, tracing over the bridge of his nose, across his mouth, down his neck, and up again, making spluttering sounds of baby chatter.

Maria hadn't seen her husband in a while; she assumed he was in their cabin journaling the events of the day, but when she looked up from the pile of dirty bowls, her breath caught in her throat. He was standing in the doorway dressed in a rough, white linen shirt that clung to his body and dark pants gathered below the knee, barefoot and drenched from head to toe. He held her gaze, and a slow, tired smile spread across his handsome face as he approached her. Guiding him to a chair and handing him a bowl of stew, she noticed the state of his hands. Placing the bowl down slowly, she took his hands in hers and turned them over to reveal their blistered and bloody palms.

"What have you been doing?" she asked, her face contorted with concern.

CHAPTER 5

When he answered, his breath stirred the hair at the top of her head, "I took the first shift working the suction pump." She was on the brink of tears after seeing his battered state, but the boyish bravado in his voice filled her with pride.

News must have spread, for the surgeon came hurrying back into the room, eager to be of service to the governor, but Van Riebeeck kindly declined his services and returned his attention to his wife.

Maria draped her husband in a blanket. Sitting beside him, she took his hands in her lap and cleaned his wounds. After lathering his palms with an ointment of beeswax and sweet almond oil, she tightly bandaged his hands. Only then was he offered his food and mug of water. He wolfed the stew down, and when she asked him if he would like a little more, he declined on account of being too tired to chew.

Van Riebeeck scanned the room. It was such a contrast to the chaos on deck. The dimly lit space was warm and dry. Arent was sitting upright, his head resting against the table leg, Antoonie on his lap, the child's small golden head resting against the boatswain's heavy chest, both fast asleep. Somebody had placed a blanket over them.

A sound was coming from underneath the table, and he bent down to investigate. He found a cozy nest of blankets containing the little cabin boy and a large grey cat. The boy looked up and gave him a grin, displaying the gap in his front teeth.

"I lost my tooth today. It didn't even bleed," the little imp explained, holding out a tiny hand revealing a shiny white tooth.

"Congratulations," Van Riebeeck replied. "Did you make a wish?"

"Nah, I'll throw it in the ocean tomorrow, and then I'll make a wish when the mermaid catches it." Van Riebeeck nodded and smiled at the child's blind faith that there would be a tomorrow.

* * *

By late afternoon they had entered their third shift since the storm started. Mrs. Boom had managed to raid every cabin and clothing trunk for dry blankets and shirts. As the men filed into the dayroom, they pulled their wet shirts over their heads and traded them for dry ones, which they dutifully changed back once their shift started again.

The storm was starting to take its toll. The men were exhausted, and their hands were raw. They seemed oblivious to the roll of the floor and only noticed it when they saw how the women struggled to keep the food from spilling.

A man entered with a near-unconscious shipmate draped like wet laundry over his shoulder. "Old mate's just a bit unsure as to where to put his feet," he announced with slurred words as his whole body shook violently under the other man's weight. Anke and her eldest, Elsje, rushed to take the young sailor in their arms and guided the men to makeshift beds.

The twins ran back and forth from the galley to the dayroom, passing food and drink into rough, grateful hands.

Maria smiled softly, seeing Leesa, the younger of the twins, hesitate before each man, trying to grab their attention with a quiet, *'Excuse me,'* and shy away at their grateful smiles. The girl had been in the company of the sailors for hours, and still, she was desperately shy. The twins could not be more different. Elsje was blue-eyed and blond with a vivacious personality that brought sunlight wherever she went. Leesa was dark-haired like her father, with a quiet and observant demeanor, patiently waiting for her life to start.

* * *

The *Drommedaris* was fighting for her life. They were running heavy seas. Sailing at roughly two knots and at a sharp angle to the wind, trying to match the speed of the waves. A long line floated in the water, trailing behind her like a tail, providing a measure of stability.

"I can't see past my own eyelashes!" Sebastiaan said in frustration. He and Lukas, the sailmaker, were standing near the mainmast, legs wide apart, bracing themselves against the violent rocking of the deck, the rain slamming down on their upturned faces. They blinked and wiped the water from their eyes as they tried to see where the rogue deadeye was stuck. A network of shrouds supported the mainmast on either side, along with four individual stays tied to the bulwark. One of the stays had snapped neatly between its two anchoring deadeyes, swinging one around in the wind and causing havoc on deck before winding itself up somewhere amidst the intricate rigging.

"We have to find it and tie it back down, or the others will soon start to pop as well," Lukas said while securing his work basket around his waist. He waded through the water on the deck to the ship's side.

"Here's where it broke loose," he shouted to Sebastiaan over the howl of the wind, pointing to a lone deadeye missing its twin. Sebastiaan examined the break in the rope.

"Start fraying this end. I'll find the other end and bring it down," Sebastiaan ordered, spraying droplets in all directions as he shook the water from his face.

He grabbed hold of a stay and climbed onto the bulwark, stopping for a moment to find his balance before he latched onto the rope next to him. A wave sprayed up and over the side of the ship when Lukas yelled at him to get down, his voice grating and hoarse. In response, Sebastiaan flashed him a smile as he swung his leg around the bulwark's outside in one swift, cocky motion. With his body tightly pressed against the latticed ropes, the storm flung another wave against his back. The water felt hard and solid as it hit his shoulders. Shaking it from his face once more, he began to climb.

The shroud's angle lent him stability as his hands and feet moved upward. He pushed with his legs and pulled with his arms, finding comfort in the familiar rhythm of his limbs and the coarseness of the cross ropes beneath him. The key was to climb in a straight line and not look up. The shroud would lead him onto the first lookout platform.

Climbing the shrouds on a fine day was a beautiful experience, providing unhindered views in all directions. Doing so amidst a storm was slightly less thrilling; it meant fighting the ship for every inch gained. The shroud moved violently beneath him, trying to shake him loose. He was about to latch onto a higher rung, with one hand holding on and the other reaching, when a sideways wave rocked the ship sharply to its port side. The force of the movement made his arm swing wide, and both feet lost their hold. Hanging on by one hand, he felt a thousand sharp needles stab his fingers and toes from the inside as his body reacted to the sudden shock. He inhaled deeply to calm himself and then used the ship's momentum to reach over and latch on with both hands again. His heart was thumping against his wet shirt, and his breath was roaring in his ears. Blessed with good coordination, strong legs and shoulders, and no fear of heights made him one of the best riggers on the crew. He climbed the shrouds daily, clewing sails, tarring ropes, and fixing lookout boards, but never had the ship fought him like this.

He knew this was the moment when most men lost their heads. Their hands would lock around the ropes and freeze. He had seen it happen to others a few times. The biggest mistake they could make was to look down. The height that seemed normal on a calm, sunlit day became an instant horror during the dark of a storm with lightning cracking above and the wind pushing and pulling at their backs. When the primal need for safety was all-consuming, the body turned vulnerable as its senses became acutely aware of everything around it. Some were never the same after such an incident.

Steadying his breathing, he forced his feet back to the ropes, focused on finding a firm hold for each foot. In recognition of the moment, he lifted his face to the rain, then smiled and started climbing again. Passing the first yard, he knew the first platform was not far. With a few more reaches and pushes, his hands touched the slippery wooden edge of the platform. He let go of the shroud and splayed one hand wide on the flat surface. With the other, he clawed himself forward. Hoisting himself onto the platform, he grabbed hold of the safety rope. Up close, visibility was not so bad, and he started his hunt for the missing deadeye.

The deadeye being stuck this close to the mast would have been accommodating, but alas, it was not. From Sebastiaan's vantage point on the platform, he surveyed the yard below, not seeing anything foreign or out of place. The first yard was the widest of the three, stretching out far over the water. His eyes followed the length of it from left to right and back again. This high up, the violent rocking of the ship seemed amplified. Pushing his back against the mast for support, he shuffled around to get a better look. Scanning the yard from left to right again, he was about to start his climb to the next platform when a cluster of ropes caught his eye. He squinted into the rain and saw a tangled mess around the yardarm. The missing deadeye had wrapped itself around and between the yard and the Flemish Horse.

Cursing roundly, he climbed down a few rungs until his feet reached the footrope. He reached the yard, thick enough that a grown man could easily rest his belly on it, grabbed hold of the ropes on top, securing the sails, while his feet moved sideways along the slack line of the footrope underneath. With single-minded determination and a healthy dose of annoyance, he ignored the cacophony the storm was creating and focused on his destination.

The ship was pitching wildly, causing his position to become exceedingly capricious. With hand-over-hand movements and feet swinging back and forth on the unstable footrope, he inched closer to the end of the spar. There was no pattern or rhythm to the ship's movements; every lunge was random, either back or forth, left or right. He banned all unnecessary information from his mind. Instead, he focused on his hands and feet and breathed through his nose, in and out. Reaching the end of the wooden spar with the deck far below and to his left, he assessed the situation. The rope had broken just below the deadeye. It was a tangled mess, and he would have to free the deadeye and push the entire cluster off the end to untangle it.

Moving as close as he could to the end of the yard, he placed one foot on the Flemish Horse and forced the angle between the rope and spar to open slightly. With one hand holding onto the line running on top of the yard, he used his other to grab hold of the severed rope, just above the wooden disk, and started to pull it towards him. It slid free after a few powerful tugs and dropped a short distance.

"Oh, no, you don't," he muttered through tight lips, pulling the deadeye back up. God knows what mischief it would get up to if left to dangle freely again.

Sebastiaan set about his task, his movements awkward due to the beam's circumference and the rope's thickness. He planned to untangle the rest of the rope from the spar, tie the loose end of the rope with the deadeye around his waist, and then make his way back to the deck. Once uncoiled, the line would be long enough to travel the distance.

One after the other, he pushed the coils over the end of the beam. With all the coils freed, the line hung in a heavy, lazy loop, thick with water. He felt the rope's weight swaying back and forth with the ship's movement, each sway tugging on his body. With everything unwound and secured, it was time to head back.

Recalling the incident later, he could not be sure if he had lost his concentration in a moment of relief or if it was the unexpected movement of the ship, but in the next moment, the ship tilted dangerously, and green water rushed over her starboard side. The force yanked him off the footrope and away from the spar. With his left hand still holding the rope he'd freed moments before, he was flung out over the ocean, limbs dangling wildly in the wind. His right arm reached over, finding the rope above his head. It cut into his hands as he was tossed viciously from side to side. He tried to still his body and forced his legs closer to the line, but his legs never made it that far. Another savage gust rocked the ship again, and his hands lost their grip. He dropped into a free fall.

His mind was slow to grasp the suddenness of the events, and he experienced a moment of utter peace, with no fear or concern, his body consumed with the sensation of falling. He knew the moment the rope extended to its maximum, the loop around his midriff tightened unexpectedly, and then he was forcefully yanked back up. The rebound of the rope was so violent it threatened to cut him in half. The line thrust into his body underneath his ribcage, and air rushed from his lungs as he fell back down. Dangling at the end of the line like a ragdoll in a careless child's grasp, he struggled for breath. The ship was not done with him yet. The line began to swing sideways, gaining momentum. Helplessly, Sebastiaan swung across the black water with impressive speed and straight towards the fast-approaching hull.

In a last effort to save himself, he reached again for the rope with both hands but again failed to grasp it. There was nothing left to do except prepare for the impact. He clamped his eyes shut, clenched his jaw, and brought his arms up to protect his head, leaving his ribs exposed to bear the brunt of the collision with the ship.

The impact never came. As Sebastiaan raced towards the side of the ship, a

CHAPTER 5

gust of wind struck and heeled them over far enough for him to pass over the rail.

Many eager hands reached for him, but he was brought to a halt by a strong pair of arms catching him in a bear hug. When he found his balance, the arms around him relaxed, and he was slowly released.

"Easy, easy now," a rough voice spoke close to his ear. When he opened his eyes, he stared straight into his uncle's face. The captain's countenance was a mixture of urgency, concern, and pride. Sebastiaan had induced that expression many times growing up. It gave him a profound sense of safety, and he felt a sting in his eyes and throat.

The embarrassment at his rush of emotion was short-lived as a sudden hush fell over the sailors. His uncle looked up to the spars and rigging, and Sebastiaan followed his gaze. Purple-blue flames orbed around the end of each yardarm and the tops of all three masts. The ship looked like a Christmas tree in a town square, with candles hanging from the tips of its branches.

"What …?" he breathed.

"St. Elmo's fire," his uncle announced. "A good omen. The storm will soon be over, lads!" The statement was followed by cheering and backslapping from the men. What seemed like a fight to the death, moments before, had turned into a mere demanding chore.

* * *

Niklas had lashed himself to the whip staff, and after ten hours of steering the ship through the roughest of the storm, De Coninck ordered him off the deck.

"You are no good to me dead, or worse, dim-witted. Get some rest, Niklas," he said when he saw the man start to shake his head. The water was still rough and choppy, but the rain was beginning to ease, coming in spurts only.

By eight o'clock that evening, the rain had ceased, but the wind was still boisterous. Despite the change for the better, the suction pump would continue to pump for another twenty-four hours, if not more, draining the six feet of water from the ship's bilge.

De Coninck stayed at the helm; with Arent injured and Niklas exhausted, nobody else could navigate the ship in these conditions. The men were tired, but they still functioned well, and with Sebastiaan in charge of the upper deck, the captain relaxed for a moment.

A short three hours after he had sent Niklas to find his bed, his navigator was back on deck with Arent at his heels.

"What are you doing here?" De Coninck roared when he saw Arent. Neither man was sure who the captain spoke to, so as per usual, Niklas said not a single word and left the explaining to Arent.

"Cap, you and the lad need rest. You're pushing fourteen hours."

Checking his annoyance at the boatswain's newfound maternal instincts, De Coninck nodded. Walking to the railing, he placed two fingers on his lips and produced a shrill sound. Whistling aboard a ship was forbidden. Sailors believed it to be a direct challenge to the wind; however, that was not a whistle but a siren call directed at a specific person. Sebastiaan reacted immediately. Instinctively, his ears perked, and he looked over his shoulder, wide-eyed and tense. That whistle had been the definitive sound heralding every *'oh shit'* moment of his boyhood. He froze for a minute, blinking multiple times, trying desperately to remember what he could possibly have done this time. He looked up to the quarterdeck.

When his nephew finally looked up at him, De Coninck jutted his thumb over his shoulder and waited for the lad to obey the order. Sebastiaan was bone-tired. His limbs felt jointless and heavy. Giving his uncle a thumbs up, he turned towards the dayroom.

Passing Arent, he jabbed, "Nice turban, might wanna add a feather or something," pointing to the white bandage around his friend's head. Arent responded with a bored look and an obscene hand gesture.

Maria saw the young man enter the dayroom, bearing such close resemblance to the captain, she knew it must be his nephew. He was exhausted, dangerously pale, and his legs were unsteady. She moved to his side, putting her arm around his back, and leaned her body against his for support. Instinctively he placed his hand on her shoulder. She guided him to a chair and ordered the twins to prepare a bowl of stew and a mug of beer. A generous

CHAPTER 5

serving appeared; the twins were positively glowing at the chance of being near him.

"Thank you, ma'am," he said in a coarse voice as he looked at each of them in turn, unaware of the giggles his words unleashed. Stew had never smelled nor looked this good. He tried to lift the first spoonful to his mouth and couldn't remember eating being such a chore. If it weren't for the governor's wife sitting next to him, observing him with her calm blue eyes, he would've tipped the contents of the bowl into his mouth and be done with it. His hands were shaking something fierce, and he was worried he might spill on his shirt. After consuming the first few bites, he realized just how hungry he was. The task became more manageable as his muscles adjusted to the smaller movements.

Maria watched as he gulped the food down. She reached over and took the empty bowl when he picked up the last bit of meat with his fingers.

Turning his head sideways to face her, he saw how tired she was. Her pale blond hair hung in haphazard strings down the sides of her face. She was no older than he, but it looked like she bore the weight of the world on her slight shoulders. There were dark shadows underneath her eyes, and her complexion looked pasty. "The storm is almost over. You should get some rest; there is nothing more to be done here ... Ma'am," he added as an afterthought.

She smiled at the honorific and watched as his head dropped to his chest.

Clutching a dry shirt, Anke approached the young man sitting with Maria. "Turn this way, lad, and put your arms up." His response was a bit too slow, so a crisp rap on the table followed the voice. He turned and found himself looking into the round, pleasant face of the gardener's wife. Her mouth was set in a stern line, but her eyes were soft. Instantly he missed his mother. The sudden thought brought a wry smile to his face.

"Oh, but you are a charming one," she said in a teasing voice.

Without much ado, Anke bent down, grabbed hold of the hem of his shirt, and without a second thought, hauled it over his head and up until his arms were free. Maria heard a small sigh coming from the direction of the girls, no doubt in appreciation of the lad's bare, well-made upper body. Having heard the sigh as well, Anke barked over her shoulder, "Time for you two to retire. Go and take a nap. I'll be there shortly." Maria curled her lips in, hiding her smile as the crestfallen twins left the dayroom, looking over their shoulders and bumping into each other.

Turning her attention back to the young man, Anke stared at the ring of dark bruises around his middle. With a motherly furrowing, she leaned down to get a closer look at the rich purple blotches and patches on the raw skin.

"How did this happen?"

"A rope."

She reckoned a blind person could deduce as much but resisted the urge to slap him upside the head for the inadequate answer.

"Keep 'em up," she ordered when Sebastiaan's arms started to sag. A warm, dry shirt slid over him and was tucked deftly down the sides of his body. From there, the woman pointed him to a sleeping pallet near the wall.

Sometime in the early morning, Sebastiaan woke from a kick to his side. Arent stood over him; the man was not well. His skin had a green tinge, and he was swaying on his feet.

"Are you dying, or do you wish to?" Sebastiaan asked as he got up, knowing Arent would not wake him unless it were absolutely necessary. Arent shook his head in reply and promptly fainted. Sebastiaan gained his feet in time to catch him before he hit the floor and eased his heavy body onto the damp pallet he had been sleeping on moments before.

***

It was the dawn of a new day, with the sun not yet risen. The storm had subsided, and all that was left was a stubborn wind biting at the sails like a dog who knew it had lost the fight but was too stupid to roll over. Sebastiaan stood on deck with his hands on his hips, his blond hair flying around his head. He closed his eyes for a moment in a silent prayer of gratitude.

"Happy new year," he said to himself. On a spar high above the deck, somebody yelled: "Three cheers for the new year!" and as one, the sailors roared in celebration.

CHAPTER 5

It was Van Riebeeck's turn at the suction pump. The man looked nothing like his usual well-kept self. Wet clothes were glued to his body and his always neatly tied hair hung bedraggled over his shoulders. After a long day and a rough night, fatigue showed plainly on his face. The white bandages on his hands were now grey and pink as blood had begun to seep through. The rhythm of his arms faltered every so often.

"Let us do this for a bit, Governor," Sebastiaan said as he rested his hand on the pump lever. "It's done," he continued in a gentle voice. "You and your team have kept us afloat; now it's just a matter of drying her out. We can do that."

"My shift is almost over, and then I will be glad to return to my correspondence and strategy meetings." Even though it was meant as a light-hearted remark, the governor could not muster a smile. Sebastiaan nodded and signaled a young sailor on the upper deck to take over from the governor once his shift ended. Squeezing the governor's shoulder firmly, he left.

Mattheys was easy to find; Sebastiaan simply followed the string of curses and endearments. The old man was hanging off the bow in a three-loop harness seat formed by a double bowline, repairing the China-red figurehead. Sebastiaan found the rappel rope the carpenter had secured to the inside of the railing. Balancing his feet on either side, he lifted the rope and started to pull without warning. The old bastard was heavier than he looked. A splattering of curses and red paint emerged from the other side of the bulwark. Grabbing hold of the carpenter's wrist, Sebastiaan pulled him back on deck.

Wrestling Mattheys out of his harness, Sebastiaan traded places with him, securing one of the loops around his waist and pushing his legs through the remaining two. Mattheys' wrinkly body was positively shaking with the indignation of being manhandled out of his task.

"You little shit! How dare you … you can't just … are you listening to me!?"

Sebastiaan slapped the bony back and took the brush and paint bucket from the old man's hands. He maneuvered himself over the edge and around to the front of the figurehead, making a mental inventory of the damage to the prow.

"You can keep me company while I patch this puppy up," he called back.

"You know, you shouldn't be dangling out here by yourself. What if you fall? You'll pierce a hole in the ocean with those bony elbows of yours." He laughed as he saw the carpenter's disgruntled face appear above him.

"Refer to that proud dragon as a puppy again, and I'll cut this rope, I swear it, and don't slap the paint on! Spread it evenly, like I've been showing you for twelve years."

Sebastiaan feigned temporary hearing loss as Mattheys alternated between a steady stream of insults and prayers for patience. He paused his litany long enough to pay attention to the cook calling from the bow.

"Mattheys, is the lad with you?"

"He's busy; go away," the old man yelled back with a wave of his skinny arm.

"I need to talk to him," the cook called back.

Sebastiaan was already hoisting himself up. The tension in the cook's voice foretold that something was wrong. Reaching the railing, he handed the paint and brush back to Mattheys, then swung effortlessly onto the bow.

"What about my dragon?" The old carpenter called after Sebastiaan.

"Add it to the list, Mattheys. I'll finish it later. Go patch something else up in the meantime. God knows we're leaking like a sieve this morning."

Falling in step at the cook's side, they walked a few paces, then the cook stopped and scanned to see if anybody could overhear them. Satisfied that they were out of earshot, he said in a low voice, "We have a problem in the hull."

Chapter 6

"I lit a few lanterns as I was about to start the clean-up." Barent waved his hand in an all-encompassing gesture. Sebastiaan's eyes quickly scanned the hull's interior, from the traumatized chickens, the overturned luggage, and rolls of cheese to the scattered animal feed and tools. It was, as expected, in a state of chaos considering what they had endured over the last twenty-four hours. He gave a crooked smile as he noted the beer and brandy barrels were still upright, safely secured with ropes to each other and around a supporting beam – encapsulating a sailor's life.

"How are the animals?" he asked as he noted all the goats were lying down in their pen with their legs tucked beneath their bodies.

"One dead chicken, but all the others are fine. I will take them up to the deck for a bit of sun; it will put them to rights again." Barent kept his eyes on Sebastiaan's face as the young man took further inventory of the hull.

Sebastiaan turned to him with a frown. "You said there was a sit – " but stopped abruptly, his mouth still forming the rest of the word; no sound followed as he looked to where the cook was pointing. On the floor, next to the mizzen mast, behind a few stacked grain sacks, showed the lower half of a body lying on its side. Tilting his head, Sebastiaan noticed the black knee-high leather boots and brown woolen pants: expensive boots, workman's pants.

"Who is it?"

Barent shook his head, "Don't know."

"Did you check?"

"Not yet," he said without looking away from the legs.

Sebastiaan pulled a knife from his waistband and slowly approached the still body. He had no desire to be lured into a trap, facing the pointy end of some fool's weapon. The unmoving body was lying with its back to him, facing the mast. The rest now visible: white linen shirt turned grey, faded green vest, long black hair, narrow shoulders – a boy's body. Tools littered the floor: shovels, pitchforks, an ax. He shoved some of it away with his foot, the noise eliciting no reaction from the form on the ground. Reaching the body, he lowered to his haunches, knife at the ready.

"If he's not dead, he's gonna wish he was," Barent mused. "The captain don't take kindly to stowaways."

Sebastiaan touched the small shoulder and turned the body over; long black curls covered most of the boy's face, but the unmistakable curve of a female chest caught both men's attention. "Not a boy ..." Sebastiaan groaned. He swept some of the hair aside to reveal a delicate face.

"Dear God!" Barent breathed and took a step back. "I was down here after midnight, didn't see anything."

Sebastiaan's body went completely still as his eyes traced the thick crust of blood from her neck, up the side of her face, to the deep cut on her forehead. The wound was still wet. He reached over to remove a few strands of hair sticking to it.

"Is she alive?" Barent whispered.

Moving his hand to the side of her neck, Sebastiaan noted the clammy and cool, not cold, feel of her skin. He found her heartbeat even and strong under his fingertips. "Alive," he replied. Tucking the knife back into his waistband, he pushed his arms gently beneath her knees and behind her shoulders, lifting her as he gained his feet. Pausing for a moment, he readjusted his grip and hoisted her over his shoulder. With her legs clutched to his chest and her upper body dangled over his back, he headed for the ladder. "Keep this quiet, Barent," he said over his shoulder and disappeared into the galley.

Turning right, he entered the empty dayroom. Then he ascended the narrow companionway to the captain's cabin directly above. It would be best to keep the girl out of sight for now.

The cabin was not unoccupied as he had hoped. The small boy, Orion,

CHAPTER 6

was sitting among a pile of books, shoving one after the other back onto the bottom shelf of a thin bookcase. Sebastiaan carefully lowered the girl's body onto the bed, sweeping the hair from her face again.

"What is that?" the boy asked, extending his neck around the corner of the desk before he curiously approached.

"It's a girl," Orion observed with reverence.

The fact that the child reached that conclusion quicker than he and Barent had was not lost on Sebastiaan.

"Is she a pirate?" he asked in a whisper laced with awe as he reached out his hand to touch her boot.

"Master Orion, go find the captain if you please," Sebastiaan said without taking his eyes off the figure on the bed. She was young, older than the twins, but still, he would guess, not much older than eighteen. She had fine and delicate features, even and pale skin, thick and shiny hair. Nothing about her advertised a rough life on the streets; she was healthy and well cared for. The question then arose: What was she doing on the ship, dressed as a boy, hiding in the hull?

* * *

"What the devil is this?" His uncle growled from the door leading to the quarterdeck, his eyes riveted to the woman on his bed. He was disheveled and tired. There were dark half-moons under his eyes, and the lines around his mouth and brow foretold a short temper.

"Found her in the hull, unconscious. Not one of ours," Sebastiaan stated.

"Bloody stowaways. Did we not get rid of one in Amsterdam?" the captain asked, frowning while taking in the woman's condition from head to toe, noticing the injury to her forehead. "There is a medicine box underneath the bed. Ask Mrs. Boom for help and call me when she wakes up." The captain left the cabin without a backward glance.

Looking down at the woman, Sebastiaan could not help but feel that there was more to this than her simply being a stowaway. Until he knew more, he wanted to keep a lid on the situation for as long as possible, and Mrs. Boom seemed about as discreet as cannon fire. He did need assistance; the woman will have to be examined for further injuries. The surgeon was out of the question. Sebastiaan did not know him, for he was new to the expedition, and for some reason, he did not want the man's rough hands touching her.

***

Maria answered the soft knock on their cabin door. The physical demands of the storm, and her husband's boyish enthusiasm to meet it, had worn him out, and even though it was midmorning, he and their son were fast asleep. Quietly stepping into the corridor, she found herself staring into the face of the captain's nephew. As soon as the door closed behind her, he whispered, "I need your help."

Maria followed him without question to the stateroom and came to a dead stop at the sight of the young woman lying on the captain's bed. Her eyes darted from the girl to Sebastiaan and back again.

Sebastiaan bent down to retrieve the medicine box while explaining the girl's presence and all the unknowns surrounding her. Maria nodded while her eyes collected as much information as possible.

"What do you need?" he asked, correctly assuming she would help him.

"I need two cans of water, both warm, and the bedsheet – the one I used last night for cutting bandages. It's on the table downstairs." Her voice was sure, her mind racing ahead, calculating what needed to be done.

The girl was lying motionless on the bed, her dark hair fanning over the pillow. Her clothes were peculiar, men's clothing of good quality made to fit her slender frame. A stale smell emanated from her body, resulting from days without the luxury of a wash.

Maria removed the girl's dirty waistcoat, shirt, and bindings, taking care not to jostle the body too much. The eighteen months of being a mother had prepared her to effectively undress and redress a sleeping child without causing him to wake. Although the girl's body was much larger, Maria's tender touch was the same.

Unlacing the sturdy but elegant leather boots, she pulled them free and placed them by the side of the bed, followed by the woolen pants, undergarments, and knitted socks. The young woman was beautifully made, and in the dim light of the cabin, her soft, ivory skin stood in stark contrast to her harsh surroundings.

Reaching for the blanket at the foot of the bed, Maria quickly covered the girl, preserving her modesty, baring only the parts she needed to examine for injuries. Maria's fingers traced the delicate bone structure and long, toned muscles, searching for dislocations and swellings. She reached for the girl's hand and studied it for cuts and callouses, finding none. Instead, the slender hand resting in hers was soft and without scars – not a maid then. "Who are you?" she whispered. "Who were you running from?"

A gentle knock on the door followed the creaking of the steps, and Sebastiaan entered the stateroom. Seeing the pile of clothes on the floor, he placed the water on the bedside cabinet and went to stand in front of the large windows lining the entire back wall of the cabin, his back turned to the bed. "How is she?" he asked, keeping his eyes on the water.

"She is still unconscious. I think she hit her head, hence the cut and swelling. There are many bruises on her back, but they all seemed fresh. Perhaps she received them after she fell unconscious. Other than that, she suffered no other injuries, as far as I can tell. I will need to tend to her wound and wash her body and hair, so if you have somewhere else to be …" She spoke in a soft, even tone as she wiped a moist rag over the girl's face.

Sebastiaan stared out over the ocean. It was a beautiful day; the sun was dancing on the water, sparkling so bright it made his eyes smart. The wind was just strong enough to bulge the sails and push them in a steady southerly direction. They had planned to make it to an English port to load more cannons, but the storm had interfered to such an extent that they were now headed toward the Cape Verde Islands instead. Being a Portuguese territory, and considering that Holland was at war with Portugal, they would stay well clear of the islands and probably drop anchor somewhere off the African coast.

There was a lot to be done on deck today; sails and rigging needed repairing, Mattheys would need help patching the hull, decks needed scrubbing, and the forecastle must be dried out along with all the bedding and clothing. Barent would also need somebody to help him put the hull back to order. But as much as he enjoyed getting his hands on all that needed to be done, he did not want to leave her. The reasons for that would remain as they were – unknown.

"You go ahead, Mistress," he said after a while. "I'll keep my back turned, but I'll be right here should you need me."

* * *

She found herself staring blindly across a room. Waking from a knock to the head should have been more eventful; there were no strange dreams or tingling sensations. Her eyes were open, and since she was looking but not seeing, she closed them again. She tried to piece together the events to a point that felt real. Her mind was foggy, and her thoughts were disconnected, floating like feathers in the wind. Images drifted in and out, all loose and abstract – her bed, the apothecary, her workbench, her father saying something she did not quite hear, and then she remembered *everything*. The weight of it crashed over her so heavily that it caused a piercing pain to shoot through her chest, so sharp it forced a lone tear to escape her closed eyelids and travel down her cheek. She wanted to wipe it away, but her arm was too heavy to lift. Instead, a rough finger swept across the side of her face, taking the moisture with it.

Du Bois! Had he found her? No, she knew that could not be. She remembered the ship and her hiding place between the sails in the hull. She remembered the goats and the sudden violent angle the ship tilted, hurling her through the air before her head connected with the wooden beam. She recoiled from the touch. The movement caused the pain in her head to send sparks of white fire to her nose and cheekbones. Sweat formed on her forehead and upper lip, and she felt cold with the shock of its intensity. Her whole body shivered.

A strong hand touched the back of her neck and lifted her head, and then the metal rim of a cup touched her lips. She tightened her mouth in resistance,

CHAPTER 6

which only intensified the pain.

"Drink," a man's voice said, and the cup pressed against her lips once more. Slowly, it tipped until a few drops of liquid ran down the side of her closed mouth and chin.

"It will ease the pain." The voice was strong but velvety, soothing like a balm over coarse skin. She softened her lips, and the bitter liquid filled her mouth. She swallowed; the cup remained. After three more gulps, the cup was taken away, her head was slowly lowered, and another blanket's weight settled over her. She waited for the voice to return, but there was only silence.

Slowly she opened her eyes, wincing at the effort of focusing. A stranger was sitting on the edge of the bed, looking at her, patiently waiting. She noticed the calmness in his eyes before registering the color – hazel green, just like her father's. Only these belonged to a different, much younger face, with sun-brown skin and golden hair that glimmered as the light streaked through it. His mouth looked like he was on the verge of a smile, but that couldn't be because his face held no expression at all; it was carefully blank.

"Go back to sleep. You're safe now."

Safe. After all, she was dreaming, for this vision sitting next to her, offering concern and safety, was nothing more than a mirage her confused mind had conjured up, trying to reconnect with reality. Not caring much for its efforts, she closed her eyes again and let her body relax back into darkness. The apparition was saying something, but its voice seemed far away, and then it faded.

Sebastiaan knew she was in too much pain to answer any questions. He had watched as she opened her eyes and stared sightlessly. It was the color of her eyes that drew his attention. They looked like the ocean on a warm day, a light blue and green mixture, rimmed by a dark line. When she closed them, he swallowed a grunt of disappointment. She might have fallen asleep, but he saw the lone tear rolling down her face, evidence of the story behind the mystery. When she opened her eyes again to look at him, he was better prepared, but her gaze was unfocused and detached, and it didn't take long for her to slip into a deep sleep again.

The longer she slept, the longer he could keep her safe, for when his uncle learned that she was awake, he would not go easy. He would wring every last truth from her, whether she was in pain or not. For now, Sebastiaan still had control over the situation, but that would soon change, and her fate would be in the hands of others. An uneasy knot started to form in the pit of his stomach.

* * *

"You are not painting the Sistine Chapel. Get a move on!" Arent was yelling up at him, his fresh new bandage stark white in the sun. Sebastiaan was moving down the backstay on a gantline, covering it in a thick layer of tar from a bucket hanging from his waist. Down on the deck, Arent was impatiently controlling the gantline while barking orders at him.

"Slow down, will you?" Sebastiaan called back. Arent fed the line too much, letting him drop too far to cover the rope adequately. The drop came while he was still applying tar to the line, and he found himself painting air.

"It's good, let's go!" Arent yelled back.

"How can you possibly see from down there with your *bandeau* hanging over your eye?"

"What the hell is a *bandeau?*" Arent spat the unfamiliar word at him.

"It's a pretty thing women wrap around their heads," Sebastiaan informed him, circling the brush as a visual aid.

Arent promptly ignored that useless bit of information and turned his attention to the cook walking towards him. Barent gave a brief report on the state of the hull and a list of the repairs needed. Their words blew away in the wind, and Sebastiaan's thoughts returned to the girl.

After midday, Mrs. Van Riebeeck had revisited the stateroom with more willow bark tea, beef broth, and a slice of cheese. She also left some clothes. Sebastiaan had stayed by the girl's side, considering all the possible scenarios explaining her being there. When his uncle returned later in the afternoon, he was dismissed. She was still asleep, and he was reluctant to leave her, but there was a hard light in his uncle's eyes, so he left without a word.

CHAPTER 6

* * *

Back in the captain's cabin, sounds of shouting, scrubbing, hammering, and creaking ropes penetrated the fog of her sleep. She was lying on a bed; the linens smelled fresh, and she felt a rush of panic when she discovered that she was naked under the coarse blanket that covered her from throat to toes. Taking further stock of her body, she found her arms by her sides, heavy but unrestrained. The pain in her head was throbbing but not as blinding as before. A rustling of papers signaled that there was somebody else in the room. Slowly she opened her eyes.

De Coninck knew by the change in her breathing that she was starting to wake up. He pushed the charts he was studying aside, stretched his legs in front of him, crossed his ankles, folded his arms over his broad chest, and waited.

She looked at him. Their gazes locked and held. Working as her father's assistant allowed her to know most of the ships and their captains who docked at the Texel harbor. This man was Captain Davit De Coninck; she had seen him often but always from a distance. Stories of his ruthlessness and bravery at sea depicted him as something resembling a virtuous pirate, and no sailor worth his salt would give up a chance to sail under his command. Looking at the man now, she believed his reputation.

The way he looked at her scared her. She was trapped and uncertain, like a deer that knew the predator was close and there was nowhere to run.

"There are garments at the foot of the bed. Get dressed," he said, pointing a finger without lifting the hand from his chest.

Following the direction of his finger, she saw a brown woolen dress and fresh undergarments at the foot of the bed. The command horrified her. Was she to dress in front of him? Certainly, she could not, but then he looked like the kind of man who would pull her from the bed and see to the task himself were she to hesitate.

Captain De Coninck casually tilted his head back against the chair and closed his eyes. Ignoring the pain in her head, she threw the blankets to the side, reached for the undergarment, and pulled the chemise over her head.

An involuntary yelp escaped her as she accidentally touched the wound on her forehead. Fearing he would open his eyes to investigate, she forged on, pulling the loose-fitting day gown on next. The dress reminded her of those the girls wore on the island when they worked in the fields. It was clean, comfortable, and warm. With no time to further appreciate the garment, she swung her legs back onto the bed and hastily rearranged the blankets over her again.

"Decent?" he asked.

Hearing the whispered acknowledgment, he opened his eyes. The girl was sitting on the bed, back against the headboard, the blankets pulled to her chin. Her face was composed, but her eyes were round and frightened – good, truth and fear marry well. Then the sound of her growling stomach reached him. He nodded towards the cabinet by the side of the bed.

"Finish all of it," he said in a softer voice, though his face remained hard and unyielding.

The captain looked like an older version of her apparition. Only the hawkish eyes, staring at her now, were cold and unforgiving. Clutching the edge of the blanket, she swallowed. A droplet of sweat ran down her side, underneath the borrowed white chemise.

On the side cabinet was a mug, and judging by the minty smell, it contained willow bark tea, a bowl with beef broth, a wedge of cheese, and – her breath caught as she saw the medicine box with the neatly folded paper sachets, bundles of herbs and a few bottles of grain alcohol.

Her father's idea was to give a medicine box to each ship's captain. He said he would sleep better knowing that at least the barest of essential medicines were aboard each ship leaving the harbor. Reaching over, she picked a bottle, closed her eyes, and marveled at the knowledge that she was touching something that last left his hands. She could see him so clearly. He was standing at his workbench by the window, overlooking the pier, the morning sun playfully painting rainbows on the smooth surface. His hands moved with practiced efficiency as he poured the tincture from the large green glass bottle into the smaller ones, not spilling a drop. Taking a deep breath, she could smell the small bundles of herbs mixed with the musty scent of

CHAPTER 6

books on the shelf behind her long apothecary table, and she remembered the easy conversations drifting back and forth between them. Nothing work-related was ever discussed during their morning routine. Her father would sometimes share a bit of gossip he picked up at the tavern or the views of his favorite philosopher – Plato of late. She mostly enjoyed listening to his voice, deep and comforting like the morning sun, laced with warmth.

Tears gathered in a knot hard enough to sting, but she refused to release them in front of the man staring at her so callously. Instead, she returned the bottle to its place, picked up the willow bark tea, and drained the cup with a few gulps. With her appetite gone, she passed on the food and sat back, staring at her hands in her lap.

"Eat," the man commanded from behind the desk, but she shook her head. She did not think it possible, but his voice turned even more frigid when he ordered her again. Each word was slowly and softly growled, "I. Said. Eat."

She could almost hear the curl in his lip as he spoke. With shaking hands, she gripped the bowl of broth and drank from the rim, not daring to look at him but feeling his eyes boring into her all the same. When no more than a spoonful was left, she lowered the bowl to her lap and reached for the cheese.

There was a scrape on the floor when he got up and moved the chair closer to the bed. When he sat down again, he was near enough for his outstretched legs to close the distance between the chair and the bed.

"What's your name?" he asked, his voice still soft but no less firm.

"Danielle Van –" she said but was harshly interrupted.

"Look at me!" he barked unexpectedly, and her eyes snapped to his face. That proved to be a mistake, for now, she could see his eyes. They were the color of a cold winter's day, and they sent shivers down her body.

"Danielle Van Aard," she tried again and infused her voice with a strength she did not feel. "My father is Aard Van Meerhof; *was* Aard Van Meerhof." Her voice shook, but she bit back the sob that rose, lifted her chin, and did not dare look down again.

"How old are you, child?"

"Nineteen, sir." Her voice was still shaking but clear.

De Coninck regarded her for a moment, deliberately keeping any emotion from his face. He knew Aard Van Meerhof; the man was a competent physician. The medicine box on the cabinet was a gift from him. Of course, De Coninck had insisted on paying for it. That would explain the emotion the girl tried to hide when she saw it.

Something was not making sense. The girl obviously boarded the ship in Texel and had spent the last seven days hiding in the hull – why? Why decide to become a stowaway on the very night her father died in a fire? There could be but one explanation: she had played a role in the unfortunate events that claimed the physician's life. She was a good little actress – the show of emotion, the fight for control, very talented indeed.

"Did you have a hand in your father's death? Is that why you chose to hide on *my* ship? To escape any uncomfortable questions?" He watched as the color left her face, her brows knitted together, her lips pinched tight, and the shaky breath left her nose.

"No!" she almost shouted in a voice he did not think she possessed. All he had heard from her so far were soft murmurs.

"No," she said again, a bit more controlled the second time. She wanted to cry, tears welled in her eyes, but she knew it would not aid her cause, so she bit them back.

"No?" he asked. "Then explain it to me."

He thought her responsible for her father's death. He all but accused her of it. She hesitated, having relived every moment over the last seven days, quietly crying until she was sure there were no more tears left, and yet every time, she was proven wrong.

"I heard the men say that my father's death was an accident." She did not know where to start, so she started with the most crucial part. De Coninck did not respond. "It was not an accident." The scene replayed itself in her mind, and she saw her father's strong body go rigid with Du Bois's knife twisting into his chest.

"He was murdered?" De Coninck asked with a frown.

She nodded but remained silent.

"By you?" he asked again. That drew a reaction from her, not as acute as before but powerful enough.

CHAPTER 6

"No."

She'd whispered the denial, but she might as well have screamed it for the shattered look on her face. Again, De Coninck remained silent, only folding his arms over his chest.

Danielle knew that trusting the captain with the truth was her only hope of finding justice for her father. This man staring at her might be as cold and unforgiving as a winter's night, but her father respected and trusted him. She started at the beginning, telling him about Du Bois's visit to the apothecary, the proposal he put to her father, her father's refusal that led to his death, the chase down the alley, and her ending up on the dockside. The words flowed from her without thought or pause.

"I was unsure what to do or where to go when a man called down from the ship and ordered me to load some crates."

De Coninck remembered her attire and understood how someone could mistake her for a dockworker.

"Boarding the ship was a good escape from the men chasing me, and I thought I would hide in the hull until nightfall and then make my way back. But I fell asleep, and when I woke, it was well past midday, and we had left the harbor. I didn't mean to be on the ship for so long." Her voice was steady throughout the telling, only faltering at the last statement.

De Coninck considered her story and asked, "If what you are saying is the truth, then why did you not make your presence known at the very first opportunity? Why remain hidden?" It was an impressive story, but he did not live this long by believing fantastic tales.

"I wasn't sure which ship I had boarded or who the captain was. Some are no better than pirates, and I was afraid of what might happen to me if I made my presence known."

She looked him straight in the eye as if assessing his character. The little chit had grit, he'd give her that. Her concern bore some validity, and he could well imagine her reasoning, realizing she was the only woman trapped on a ship full of sailors.

"Why were you dressed as a boy? It seems a touch convenient, doesn't it?" He watched as a soft, wistful smile pulled at the corners of her mouth.

"My father started dressing me as a boy when I was nine years old. It allowed him to take me to work with him. I have no mother, and he wanted me close to keep me safe." Her eyes were staring at his chest but lost their focus. "At first, I helped clean the surgery and occasionally sat with the sick. But as I grew older, he taught me about herbs and medicines and how to prepare ointments and poultices ..." she gave a little shrug and looked up to his face. "I liked it, and I discovered I had a knack for it."

The captain stood abruptly, swinging the chair back to its place behind the desk. He looked back at the girl. She was a problem, innocent or not. She was a stowaway and would have to be treated as such. There was much to consider.

Sebastiaan was sitting on the companionway to his uncle's cabin listening to the girl's story. The captain hardly said a word, letting her speak freely. Tomorrow, his uncle would make her repeat it, looking for inconsistencies and picking up forgotten details. He was no fool. He was firm but fair, and Sebastiaan had faith in that. Hearing the chair scraping the floor, he left the dayroom.

"You will go back to the hull for the night. Tomorrow I will determine what is to be done with you," De Coninck stated in a firm voice. "Take the two blankets," he said over his shoulder as he walked to the stairs leading down to the dayroom, turned sideways, and waited for her to rise and follow him.

Danielle scampered from the bed, but the pain in her head made her lose her balance, and she sank to her knees on the floor, clutching the frame.

Still not convinced of her innocence, De Coninck watched as she gained her feet again, bundled the two blankets roughly in her arms, and then made to follow him. He slowed his step, ready to catch her should she lose her footing again.

Her legs shook as she climbed back into the dark cavern, welcomed by the familiar smell of chickens and goats.

Above her, the hatch slammed down.

Chapter 7

What about the sweat of another makes it so off-putting? Sebastiaan mused as he bent over the barrel of seawater to wash the dead man's sweat from his arms. He had worked two straight shifts cluttered with a hotchpotch of tasks, from realigning the seat in the head to mending one of the footboards of the lookout platform.

Symon Jansz, an unassuming forty-odd-year-old carpenter from Amsterdam, was one of the passengers aboard. Jansz had volunteered his services early in the journey, and Arent had quickly put him to work with the team constructing the passengers' cabins. Sebastiaan was acquainted with him. He passed him regularly on deck and shared a nod in greeting as they went about their respective tasks.

Jansz had the habit of calling everybody 'sir.' "Good morning, *sir*. Thank you, *sir*. Aye, *sir*." The epithet hinted more at the man's inability to remember names than a show of respect since Sebastiaan had heard him addressing the young Orion in the same manner. Symon was good at what he did. His work held an artistic quality in its precision. He preferred to work alone, and although he shared his living quarters with the sailors, he kept mostly to himself.

When Sebastiaan finally sat down for dinner, he found himself opposite the carpenter. They shared their customary nod and then turned to their food. Sebastiaan was about to shove the first spoonful into his mouth when Symon released a cough that sent food spraying across the table. The cough had scarcely left him when he shot up from his seat with enough force to send many mugs of ale clattering to the floor. His face had turned a dark purple-red, and his eyes seemed to bulge from their sockets. Sebastiaan's first impression was that he was choking, and he moved to pound him between the shoulder blades. But Symon clutched his chest, and when Sebastiaan reached him, he had already collapsed with sweat running in thick beads down his face and neck. Sebastiaan had gone down on his knees and tried to lift the stricken man into a sitting position, but Symon was limp and heavy in his arms, so he lowered him back to the floor.

The surgeon had entered the forecastle in a flurry of importance, gave Symon a quick examination, and promptly declared him dead.

Cause of death: apoplexy.

Symon Jansz was buried at sea less than an hour ago.

Sebastiaan felt detached from the events as he sloshed cold water over his arms and face. He didn't particularly care to go back into the forecastle. It was not the first time he'd seen death claim a man, nor would it be the last. However, this time, the man had died in his arms. They had battled and survived the same storm together, forging a bond. Sebastiaan found peace in the knowledge that the man had not died alone. Not wanting to entertain the direction of his thoughts any longer, he considered what tasks still awaited him. Anything to keep his hands busy. As his mind had been occupied with thoughts of the girl all day, it seemed natural that they turned in that familiar direction again.

His reasons for wanting to visit her were purely altruistic. He had discovered her, and it was only natural that he would feel some concern for her welfare. Satisfied with that explanation and the soundness of his reasoning, he gathered what he needed and headed toward his newfound responsibility.

Reaching the galley, he lit a lantern and descended into the hull. It was pitch dark, with only the faint outline of the cargo visible. He scanned the cavernous space while holding the light at arm's length. The girl was nowhere in sight. He could well understand how she had stayed undetected for so long.

Searching from left to right, Sebastiaan strained to see beyond the lantern's glow. He was about to call her name when a rustling to his right caused him

CHAPTER 7

to swing the light in that direction. The girl was creeping from behind a stack of sails. Her feet were bare, small, and elegant as she placed them on the floor's rough surface. Her movements were sure and nimble, undoubtedly honed from many hours moving around in the dark hull.

For a moment, Sebastiaan simply stared at her. She seemed smaller than before, her black hair fading into the dark. She looked fragile, garbed in a shapeless dress and deprived of the armor her male attire had afforded her. Standing outside the reach of the light, she fingered the fabric of her dress, advertising the desire to bolt at the slightest provocation.

"I wondered if you might need anything?" he asked.

She shook her head slightly. "No, thank you." Her voice, following the gesture, was barely above a whisper.

"Cook put aside some of the evening meal," he said, squinting at her before placing the lantern on the floor. "But I might need some help bringing it down." He waved her over and headed towards the galley. She followed but stayed at the bottom of the ladder, looking up into the dimly lit room.

Danielle was relieved to have escaped the captain's scrutiny when returning to the hull earlier. But the dread of what he meant when he said her fate would be decided in the morning made her too anxious to sleep. Being branded a stowaway had plunged her future into a pitch-black pit. Not once, until now, was there any doubt in her mind as to what her future might hold. She had planned to work alongside her father for many years to come. He would never have forced her into marriage, even though she was of age, and she would never have left him to enter his dotage alone. She had planned to care for him as he had for her, but now ...

Her musings were interrupted by two mugs appearing in the opening above, followed by two plates loaded with fishcakes, sauerkraut, and thick wedges of cheese. Placing the food next to the ladder, she watched as her dinner companion appeared at the top rung, arrogantly jumped down, and landed with a thud next to her.

"Voila! I made dinner," he announced with a triumphant smile, looking down at the food on the floor.

She regarded his antics with a skeptical mien. As he entered the hull and stood in the clearing surrounded by the lantern's light, she knew that her apparition was real and not some figment of her confused mind.

"What is it you want?" Her question was loaded with suspicion. Folding her arms tightly over her chest, she looked at the young sailor who stood staring at her with an arrogant smile smeared across his face.

"There is nothing for you here," she said, her hand closed on an empty fist. She wished for her small knife, which they must have taken off her in her unconscious state. Remembering her state of undress when she had woken earlier in the captain's cabin, a flush of heat covered her face as her embarrassment gave way to anger. Was this dolt responsible for removing her clothes, and with them, her knife? Uncomfortable with his presence and familiarity, she took a step back into the safety of the darkness.

"I mean you no harm," Sebastiaan said as he reached his hand out to stay her retreat, but the gesture only managed to push her further away. Temporarily at a loss for what to say, he knew he must win her trust, but he had not thought his actions through in his rush to escape the evening's events. *What was he thinking coming here?*

"You are right not to trust anybody," he said while holding the light at arm's length. "But I thought you might be hungry." He tried to read her face, but it was impossible in the darkness.

"I'm not. Please leave." Her voice was shaking with tension.

Sebastiaan turned and spotted an empty vegetable crate. Turning it over, he arranged their food on the makeshift table. Then he folded his tall frame into a sitting position, crossed his legs, and stuffed a whole fishcake into his mouth. He closed his eyes, released an exaggerated sigh, and savored the tasteless morsel.

"Suit yourself," he said around the food in his mouth, then swallowed. "Between rescuing you and keeping us afloat, I haven't had a single bite all day."

Feigning a complete disregard for her concerns, he bit off a large chunk of cheese and set about to finish his meal with a single-minded determination.

Danielle watched him from the darkness. The resemblance between him and the captain was unmistakable. He dressed like any other sailor, but his

CHAPTER 7

speech was refined. His tone and pronunciation hinted at someone with a gentle upbringing and education. As the captain's son, he would have access to such privileges. He would also be able to answer many of her questions.

Since she did not have a knife, she could not cut dried meat or cheese as she used to do until now and was quite hungry. Her stomach gave a loud protesting growl when Sebastiaan finished his food and reached for hers. Lout! she thought as he raised a knowing eyebrow in her direction at the sound of her distress. However, he pushed her food into a neat pile and quietly gestured for her to sit down opposite him.

Had he any thoughts of attacking her, he could have done so on many occasions, so she took a hesitant step into the light.

Sebastiaan watched as she stepped closer and slowly moved toward the upturned crate. She reminded him of a cat he had tried to tame as a little boy.

Every day, the cat would creep through the garden and sit at the edge staring at him with wide, distrustful eyes. At first, he tried to reach for it, but the unexpected movement sent the creature into the shrubs for hours. Then he started to leave little scraps of meat in the garden and retreated to his spot on the doorstep, waiting and watching. Every day, he would place the food a little closer to where he sat. It took him all of three weeks to win the cat's trust.

She was sitting down on her knees, with her bottom resting on her heels, ready to jump to her feet should the need arise. Nervous energy came off her body in waves, but he could not be the first to break the silence. He watched as she chased her food with a gulp of ale. Tension filled the air between them, and still, he did not look away.

"Thank you," she managed at last. He only dipped his head to her in acknowledgment. It was the first time since her father's... since the incident, that somebody looked at her with kindness. Although she was wary of him, she craved the company.

"I'm Danielle."

"I know who you are, miss," he said and reached across the crate to offer her his hand, but she flinched, and he retracted it immediately – cursing himself for his lack of judgment. "Sebastiaan De Vries," he returned. His voice was rough and low, tainted by a hint of exhaustion.

A confused frown creased her brows and wrinkled her forehead. Confusion was infinitely better than fear and distrust, but the sentiment was so violent that its effect lightened the mood.

"What?" he laughed. "Did I give the wrong name?"

"No… I thought you were related to the captain, but your name suggests otherwise." She felt instantly embarrassed for making such a personal observation. "Forgive me."

"You're close. The captain is my uncle. On my mother's side." The few words they shared could barely be called a conversation, but he could already feel her tension fading, and the weight of the evening was beginning to lift from his mind.

"How is your injury?" he asked as she scraped the last food from her bowl.

"It's fine." She did not want his concern. A conversation was something she longed for, but with so many questions crowding her mind, she didn't want to talk about herself or her reasons for being on the ship. Twice, she inhaled to ask the questions that plagued her most, and twice, she released her breath, frustrated with her inability to formulate, or rather to prioritize, her concerns.

"Spit it out," he commanded with a lazy smile.

"Did your uncle send you here?" That was, by far, not the most important of her questions.

"No."

"Then I don't understand." Her frustration was mounting, and she gained her feet with the impulse to move.

"Sit back down, and I'll explain," he replied, keeping his tone even and relaxed. Sebastiaan knew she was struggling with the uncertainty of her circumstances – he would have been driven out of his mind had he been in her position.

"I can hear you fine while standing." Her fear of him was slowly fading with the rise of her ire.

He made no effort to reply. Pinching his lips, he looked at her with the innocence of a puppy who had just puddled on the hearthrug.

CHAPTER 7

Annoyed at his childish game, she dropped to the floor with a grunt.

Not wanting to push her further, Sebastiaan took the gesture as a small victory and decided to reward her with information.

Danielle started to feel a sense of calm as she listened to Mr. De Vries explaining how he and the cook had discovered her, injured and unconscious early this morning. She learned that other women were aboard, and one of them had tended to her in the captain's cabin. A wave of relief washed over her at the knowledge.

He went on to explain about the storm and the damage to the ship. Some pieces of information were helpful; others drifted past Danielle, filling gaps and painting a picture of her new reality.

The words flowed easily from him, and as he lay back on one elbow with outstretched legs, she allowed herself a moment of peace, much as she had with her father.

"Normally, the ship is a trading vessel, but not on this voyage." His voice drifted back to her.

He continued to explain how the *Drommedaris* was one of five ships heading for the Cape of Good Hope to establish a halfway station. Once on land, a fort would have to be built. It would provide protection from natives and enemy ships alike. Gardens would follow to replenish VOC ships' food and water supplies en route to India and the Far East.

"Weather permitting, we will reach the Cape by mid-April."

She was struggling to sort through this last bit of information. Africa was wild and untamed, with stories of treacherous seas and dark-skinned tribes who decorated their bodies with the teeth and bones of their enemies. Many Dutch sailors had died violent deaths at the hands of the local tribes. Was this to be her future? Living life in exile on a continent she knew nothing of, among strangers, and most likely destined to die a violent death? Would she never see Texel or any familiar place again?

Sebastiaan had no idea how long he had been talking, but he had watched her relax, and at times, her eyes had turned glassy as she lost herself in her thoughts or memories. Her face held persistent lines of sadness. He could well understand the source of her sorrow, but as he continued to talk about the expedition, distress and uncertainty replaced her sorrow.

He wished he could put her mind at ease, but the more she knew, the better it would be for her. Her situation was uncertain, and he had no idea what would become of her, but they had a four-month journey ahead of them, and much could happen in that time. At best, she could be put on the first ship back to Holland. Then again, she could be kept as an indentured worker at the Cape. He wanted to tell her that all would be well, that he would protect her, but it was too late and too soon for any of it. Besides, it would be unfair to make promises he most likely could not keep. He had no claim to her, nor the authority to influence a favorable outcome for her.

"The other ships will depart for Batavia as soon as they unload their cargo, but we will stay on at the Cape for as long as needed." His heart felt a stab as she looked at him with eyes swimming in raw fear. "Until it's safe," he added to ease her thoughts.

Seeing the emotions ripple across her face and how she bravely tried not to cry, he instantly regretted the turn of the conversation.

"I'm sorry for upsetting you." He had no idea how to comfort her. "Perhaps I should go. You need to rest."

She only stared at him with an empty look, and the frustration at his inability to console her multiplied tenfold. He wanted to stay, but instead, he gathered the dishes in one hand and said, "Keep the lantern on." She nodded. "Goodnight, Miss Van Aard."

* * *

Danielle woke early the following day to a slight touch to her foot. The cook was standing at the end of her makeshift bed. Her breath caught when she saw the man, and she scampered back.

"Easy, sweets." He placed her boots, a tortoiseshell hair comb, and a light blue ribbon on the floor. She stared at the feminine items, and the anonymous, thoughtful gesture brought sudden tears to her eyes.

"Put your boots on and come for breakfast. You can eat in the galley. The captain will want to speak to you soon," he said while he turned to rummage

CHAPTER 7

through the chicken coop, searching for a few eggs.

Scampering her way up the ladder, she sat on the top rung, chewing on a hard biscuit and washing it down with goat's milk. The cook cared for her much in the manner one would a stray cat. Now and then, he cast an assessing eye in her direction and went on with the task at hand, which happened to be preparing tea.

"Send her in, Barent," the captain called from the dayroom. The cook picked up the silver tray from a battered sideboard and motioned for Danielle to follow him.

The dayroom was restored to its function as a meeting room for the governor and his four advisors, otherwise known as the Broad Committee. Captain De Coninck stood off to the side, keeping an eye on the ocean through the bank of windows. The other men were spaced loosely around the table; maps, letters, and parchments with diagrams littered the surface. The cook placed the silver tray with six delicate teacups in the center. Danielle stepped over the doorsill and stood with her back firmly pressed to the mahogany-paneled wall, dressed in the borrowed brown peasant dress and her boots. Instead of her generous leather cap, her hair was combed and tied at her neck. Her head was throbbing, and her stomach curled tightly into a knot.

Staring at the men around the table, she felt odd and unwelcome. The time alone in the hull had almost broken her. Yet she wished for it now – to crawl back into that black hole and disappear into its solitude.

The captain's stern, authoritative voice pulled her from her maudlin thoughts. He introduced her to the governor and the committee members and then relayed the circumstances of her discovery. All eyes in the room turned to her. Gesturing to an empty chair, the captain signaled for her to sit.

Moving to the chair was no easy feat. Danielle's legs threatened to crumple under the weight of the intimidating moment. She stepped away from the wall and sat down. Her throat was dry, and sweat trickled down her back. Folding her trembling hands in her lap, she tried to control her breathing without meeting any of the curious glances.

"Miss Van Aard, would you care to enlighten the gentlemen of the committee on how you came to be aboard the *Drommedaris*? As you explained to me yesterday." The captain's calculating, cold blue eyes never left her face. He was leaning against the wall, arms and ankles crossed. His relaxed posture only served to heighten her nervousness.

A tense silence filled the room. Fixing her gaze to a point in the middle of the table, she harrumphed twice but struggled to find her voice. Somebody pushed a cup of tea in front of her.

"Drink this first." She looked to the man at the head of the table who had given her his cup. He was in his mid-thirties, with soft brown eyes and gentle features. His almost black hair contrasted with his crisp, white wide-collar shirt. A quiet air of authority surrounded him. He must be the new governor, looking at her with no small amount of sympathy.

"There is no rush. We have time," he said and smiled.

De Coninck had developed a deep groove between his hawkish eyes at the governor's approach. With his irritation on abundant display, he gave her a single brisk nod.

Du Bois had no power, interest, or influence here, and even though she was a stranger among them, the knowledge gave her a feeling of safety and the courage to speak. Relaying the unfortunate series of events that led to her current circumstance, she talked without pause, much as she had the day before, to De Coninck. Nobody interrupted her, and she finished with, "I did not make my presence known because I was afraid of what might become of me once I did. I never intended to be a stowaway nor wish to be treated as such."

All around the table was silent. Danielle could not help the feeling that somehow, she had passed a test, for the air in the room seemed lighter.

"You said Captain Du Bois murdered your father?" the governor asked.

"Yes, I was in the room when it happened." Her voice was laced with pain.

A long silence stretched between them. The governor looked at the young woman. She was pale, her hands were shaking, and her shoulders were drawn tight. She was nervous. But was she lying? He knew the captain had interviewed her earlier, and if she was not telling the truth now, or if there were inconsistencies in her telling, he would have pointed it out. The years Van Riebeeck had spent as a merchant in Japan had honed his intuition and

CHAPTER 7

sharpened his instincts. Living as a Dutchman in a culture where nobody ever says what they mean had challenged and changed him.

The young woman was strikingly attractive, but she seemed unaware of it. Her eyes were clear and guileless, and her face was open and honest – time would tell, but for now, he was willing to give her the benefit of the doubt.

Danielle watched the governor as she completed her recount of the events. He was quietly studying her, and she could not look away.

"I don't doubt your word." He continued, "As far as we are aware, the authorities have ruled the matter an accident. This error must be corrected at the earliest possible time. Therefore, I will require an affidavit from you in which you will state the events you witnessed." The statement caused a rustling among the committee members. Accusing a captain of the VOC of murder was not done lightly. "I will also write a letter of support to accompany your statement," Van Riebeeck continued.

"Governor Van Riebeeck, if you will allow me?" A dark-haired man with a narrow aristocratic face spoke. Van Riebeeck turned to the man. "Of course, Mr. Coopman."

"This is a dire situation indeed. We might consider bringing it to the attention of the authorities in Amsterdam and the Seventeen Lords of the VOC. If Captain Du Bois attempted to smuggle vast amounts of opium into Texel, one could only imagine that he would do the same in Amsterdam." The man's voice held the deep and soothing lilt of a lullaby.

The VOC was controlled by seventeen of the Netherlands' most powerful and influential businessmen, known as the *Council of Seventeen*. Fifty years earlier, prosperous and powerful Dutch trading companies were on the brink of a turf war when the government stepped in and forced a consolidation – creating the largest company ever to have existed in recorded history.

"As you know," Coopman continued, "I have strong family ties to one of the *Council of Seventeen* and, therefore, volunteer to see the affidavit and your letter delivered into the right and most efficient hands. I will furthermore act as a liaison on this matter and ensure justice is served swiftly and proportionately." Danielle felt a moment of relief for the man's unexpected support.

"Thank you, Mr. Coopman. I accept your assistance in this matter." The governor considered the matter settled and turned to the captain. "Should we consider sending her back to Texel when an opportunity presents itself?"

Putting her on the next ship bound for Texel was not inconceivable. Indeed, they were bound to encounter VOC ships returning from the East en route to Holland. However, De Coninck shook his head slowly, his eyes staring at a vague point on the floor.

"I think she should remain aboard the *Drommedaris* for two reasons. The first, if her claims about her father's murder are true," he raised a hand when Coopman moved to interrupt, "her life would be in danger, seeing that she is the only witness." Some of the men around the table nodded, naturally pleased with the captain's concern for the young woman's welfare. But in the next sentence, they realized that his concern was not for her welfare at all.

"Also," he continued, "she might be a spy for the Portuguese, the English, or the French. In which case, I would prefer she remain where I can see her."

A painful silence descended on the room. Nobody else had considered that possibility. Danielle's eyes were large and round as she scanned the faces around the table. How could anybody believe that she could be a spy? It was preposterous. However, a few of the men could not meet her eyes. She looked to Mr. Coopman; his brow was furrowed with concern, but he remained silent. When her gaze reached the governor, her lips were cold as ice, and her skin prickled all over. She took deep breaths through her nose, determined to hide her rising panic.

"Both are sound reasons, Captain. Might I suggest she be conscripted as a member of the crew until we reach the Cape?" Van Riebeeck asked.

The captain nodded in agreement, keeping his eyes firmly planted on Danielle. "You are dismissed. Barent will return you to the hull where you will await our decision."

At first, she was stunned by the captain's words, but her brain quickly caught up to her outrage. All that was left of Danielle's initial panic was a few wispy clouds burned to nothing by the heat of her anger.

Her entire world had been ripped apart by sudden and unexpected events that left her reeling. Witnessing her father's murder, being taken from her home and all she had ever known, spending the last seven days in hiding, and now being accused of spying had finally eroded the last of her self-control. She rose from her chair in a fluid motion. Her eyes, brimming with naked recklessness, bored into the captains.

"How dare you accuse me of being a spy," she hissed between her teeth. "It is an absurd accusation for which there is no evidence whatsoever."

Her face was hot, and she could feel her cheeks burn. Looking each man at the table in the eye, she asked, "How am I supposed to defend myself against such rot? If I say 'No,' everybody will say, 'that is to be expected,' and I would be a liar if I confirmed this disgusting statement. You all act like a bunch of priests on a witch trial. Shame on you!" She was sure the last statement came out as a shout, but the blood rushing in her ears made it hard to determine the volume of her voice.

There was a collective gasp of indignation by the committee members. De Coninck almost laughed at the shock on their faces, except for that of the governor; Van Riebeeck watched the girl with a placid, absorbed expression.

"My father was a respected physician and devoted his life to serving others, and what do you do?" she shouted. "You spit on his good name by slandering his child. All I am guilty of is surviving, and for that, I will not apologize."

She let her head drop to her chest. Her arms were shaking as they supported her body on the table. The stunned silence in the room stretched for several seconds. Someone took a breath as if to say something but then remained silent. Her eyes were pinched shut, and her head bent down. She did not notice the quiet shaking of Van Riebeeck's head as he discouraged anybody from speaking.

"Are you done?" De Coninck asked in a cool and dispassionate voice.

Although the question was rhetorical, it snapped the last of her hope. Her thoughts came hard and fast, tripping over each other in her mind. Nobody was going to listen to her. They heard the word 'spy,' and all reason fled their minds. No matter if she was innocent, no matter that she witnessed a brutal crime, and the criminal was still running free. Accusing her of spying presented an easy way out of a difficult situation, and they took it. They were nothing more than pack animals targeting easy prey.

Spying was a crime punishable by death. The realization chilled her to her marrow. She raised her head slowly and looked at the captain. He had the power of life and death over her, and she had made a mortal enemy of him. He was the man who would hang her from the yardarm for a crime she was not guilty of, simply because he could. In this small wooden world, he was God. She moved without thinking. Pushing herself away from the table, she rushed towards him. If she were going to die, she would not do so on her knees. There would be no begging for mercy or pleading anymore. She would claw his cold blue eyes from his face before letting him lay a hand on her.

De Coninck was taken aback by her defiance. Not for the first time was he pleased to see that the girl had grit, but then she pushed herself away from the table and charged him. Had he not been leisurely leaning against the wall, he would have been quicker to defuse the situation. He was still uncrossing his arms when she delivered a slap to his face that echoed through the room; the girl had a good arm. His face was on fire, and his eyes watered, but he was finally ready to catch her wrist before she could rake her fingernails across his face.

With her wrist firmly in his grasp, he spun her around and twisted her arm high into her back. Taking a brutal hold of her nape with his free hand, he pulled her close to his chest.

"Claws in, cat!" he hissed in her ear in a tone oozing with menace but so soft only she could hear it. Giving her a hard shake for good measure, he yanked her arm a little higher, rendering her helpless.

She made a small sound as pain lanced through her chest. Danielle was sure her shoulder would pop from its socket. With her free hand still burning from the slap she'd delivered, she reached back to try and dislodge his bruising fingers from the back of her neck, but his arm was hard and solid beneath her touch, and she could do nothing more than scratch his skin. He hauled her against the wall of his chest, and his voice burned the side of her face. She could kick and scream all she liked, but the fight was lost, and she was now closer to her death than before.

De Coninck felt the fight leave her body and eased the hand on her back

CHAPTER 7

just enough to relieve some of the pain, but not all. He let go of her neck and reached for her other hand. With both hands firmly secured behind her back, he marched her to the middle of the room.

"This stunning display of disrespect in the presence of the governor, the committee, and *me* will cost you dearly. Do you understand me?" His self-control was in tatters, and his voice thundered through the room. His cheek was still burning from where she had struck him, and he wanted to throttle the wench on the spot, but he had never raised a hand against a woman before, and by God, he was not about to start now.

"I will flay the skin from your back for this temper tantrum," he sounded hoarse.

He was furious. Danielle could feel the heat of his rage radiating from his body and the ice dripping from his voice. Gooseflesh rose on her skin.

"Barent," the captain barked. The cook appeared immediately. "Take her back down."

The cook approached her. His hand closed around her upper arm, pulling her from the captain's grip. As they reached the dayroom door, Captain De Coninck spoke again.

"Five lashes at dawn – tomorrow."

Chapter 8

The ocean was awash with shades of pink and purple. De Coninck stood alone at the stern railing, enjoying the last of the sun's rays before it dipped into the water. He listened to the sounds from the upper deck and let the gentle roll of the ship soothe him. Looking down at the amber liquid in his glass, he sipped the last of the delicate French brandy, closing his eyes as the smooth fire slid down his throat. A few drops remained in the glass. Tipping it, he let the drink soak into the wood of the railing.

"You've earned it, my lady," he said as he traced his fingers over the smooth, warm surface and turned toward the stateroom. It had been a long, taxing day, and he was looking forward to a quiet evening alone with his books and charts.

* * *

Shortly after the meeting with Danielle and the Broad Committee, Governor Van Riebeeck, Captain De Coninck, and Arent Van Jeveren had a private meeting in the stateroom. The purpose was to inform the boatswain of the situation and to find solutions to the problems the girl's presence posed.

All three men were troubled by the idea that she would have to face punishment, but it would not do for the captain to have two sets of rules. They decided that De Coninck would sentence her, Arent would execute the punishment, and Van Riebeeck would step in at the last minute and publicly prevent it from happening. De Coninck was willing to lose face in front of his men to spare the girl the ordeal of being whipped.

CHAPTER 8

"You want me to oppose you in front of all the passengers and crew?" Van Riebeeck had asked the captain.

"You have the authority," De Coninck shrugged, obviously not caring much for his reputation.

"I, for one, do not have the stomach to whip a girl, least of all this one. I knew her father. He was a good man," Arent added.

"Do you believe her story then?" De Coninck asked Arent.

"It doesn't matter if I believe her or not; it's not for me to decide," he replied, "but it's a nasty bit of business, that's for sure."

It was a sound solution to the problem. The only problem was that Van Riebeeck had no desire to challenge the captain openly. If he ever disagreed with the man, no matter his authority, he would address the matter in private. He would have to come up with a solution of his own – his wife.

* * *

Sebastiaan's mind was in turmoil as he paced his uncle's cabin like a caged animal. His stomach had made a neat flip when Barent told him what had transpired earlier in the dayroom. Striking an officer on deck was a serious offense, but striking the captain was unthinkable. She could receive the harshest punishment, and nobody would bat an eye. *'What had they done to her that drove her to such extremes?'* he wondered, remembering the quiet, vulnerable girl he had shared his dinner with the evening before.

Sebastiaan was gifted with a silver tongue, and he knew he could talk his way out of most troubles, but since his uncle was the one who had honed that skill, he doubted it would work this time. Could he do nothing right by this girl? Not for the first time was he left frustrated for his inability to save her.

"Are you trying to wear my carpet down?" the captain asked as he entered his cabin and moved to sit behind his desk. He looked at the young man as he paced the room. His nephew's movements held a catlike grace and the loose-limbed arrogance of a man who had pitted himself against man and nature and could peg more wins than losses. His broad shoulders and narrow hips were a far cry from the round tummy and knobby knees that had stood before him so many years ago.

Davit was there the night the boy was born. Abel De Vries and his sister Annabella De Coninck were childhood sweethearts. When they came of age, he proposed marriage; she accepted. He was ambitious; she was domestic. He left Holland to manage his business interests in Batavia, and she stayed in Amsterdam, eagerly awaiting his return. When she discovered she was with child, she had written him, knowing that he would return immediately upon receiving her letter, which he had done. He would have been in time, too, had the babe not decided to make his entrance into the world six weeks ahead of schedule.

Davit visited his sister as often as he could when she entered her confinement and even more so during the final stages of her pregnancy. She was alone, bored, and frustrated with her large body, swollen ankles, and inability to go anywhere.

They were having dinner when her pains started. She was convinced it was a false alarm, but he had sent for the family physician regardless. Ten hours later, he held his pink and wrinkly nephew in his arms. Little did he know that the tiny boy would later fill him with a paternal pride he had no right to expect.

After the birth, mother and babe were doing as well as could be expected. She had fought a mighty battle bringing him into the world, for her body was not entirely ready to deliver a child so early, and the babe was not breathing well. Davit canceled his commitments and stayed at his sister's side until her husband arrived. Guarding over the tiny boy, day and night, he slept next to his crib, ensuring the child kept breathing, gently blowing air into his little lungs when he struggled. Abel came two weeks after the birth, and Davit left to resume his life.

He did not see the child again until twelve years later when father and son boarded his ship destined for Batavia.

Sebastiaan abruptly stopped his pacing. Coming to a halt in front of the desk, he asked, "Uncle, what are you planning to do with Danielle?"

De Coninck didn't answer straight away.

"Are the two of you on a first-name basis now?" he asked, a warning flashing

CHAPTER 8

through his eyes.

Sebastiaan shook his head.

Heaving a deep sigh, De Coninck scratched his forehead. Fighting a wave of exhaustion, he replied more harshly than intended. "She will be punished."

Sebastiaan considered the meaning of his uncle's words, "What does that mean?" He paused, looking from side to side as if a revelation would come to him from either side of the cabin. "Surely, you don't mean to flog her."

De Coninck kept all emotion from his face as he leaned back in his chair. "She deserves no less."

Sebastiaan's body went cold and numb. He felt the blood abandon his face before rushing back, threatening to boil to the surface of his skin.

The captain saw the blush rush up his nephew's neck.

"Uncle, she is not a member of your crew. She – "

De Coninck interrupted, "Of course, she is not a member of the crew. She is a stowaway," he said, enunciating his words as if speaking to a particularly slow child. "Which, you will recall, is a crime. Understand this," he gave the young man a hard stare, moving his hand in a circular motion, "this is not a democracy. You don't get a vote. Here you live and die by my word."

There was nothing avuncular about his tone. His voice was cold as steel and just as strong as he punctuated his words with his finger stabbing the table's surface. As far as he was concerned, the conversation was over; he was tired and not in the mood to defend nor discuss his decisions with the whelp.

His stance on stowaways was not a secret, nor was it unclear or open for interpretation: they were not tolerated. Any fool stupid enough to hide on his ship would be quickly rewarded with ten lashes for his efforts. Sailors talk, and soon every urchin in the harbor towns where De Coninck's ship docked knew to look elsewhere for a free ride. Every stowaway had a story, but he did not let himself be influenced or swayed by any of it. For him, the matter started with the discovery of the unwanted guest on board his ship. Then there was the matter of her striking him, which, had it happened in private, he would brush aside, but she had done it before witnesses. He was not about to bring the matter up now. Best to let the boy draw his own conclusions.

De Coninck watched Sebastiaan battle with the circumstance. "I have to punish her. You know that," he said in a softer tone.

"No, I don't know that. Exceptions can be made." Sebastiaan's voice caught on the words. He was stubborn and pushing it. "She did not mean to board the ship and would have left as soon as it was safe. She was hiding from men who most likely were going to kill her. Uncle, please, you must understand this."

He was embarrassed at the pleading tone of his voice. Running a frustrated hand through his hair, he dropped his arm forcefully down the side of his body, exhaling sharply through his nose. Sebastiaan thought it best not to discuss her other offense at this point.

His uncle's face remained aloof, his attitude calm and resolute. Sebastiaan got the distinct impression that he was talking to a stone wall. He scanned the desk, searching for something to destroy, craving the satisfaction of seeing it shattered into pieces with the force of his vexation. He suppressed the urge, knowing that such behavior would land him swiftly on the other side of the cabin door.

"*If* I allow this," the captain said. Seeing the hope spark to life in Sebastiaan's face, he shook his head. He continued, "*If* I look the other way and let this incident go unpunished because she is a woman, how long do you think it will be before the sailors think they can hide their sweethearts among the barrels? I am not prepared to run a brothel out of the hull." De Coninck's voice was getting a hard edge.

"Uncle, she is an innocent woman – "

"Sebastiaan, my boy," his voice dropped to a low rumble, "Eve was also an innocent woman," the captain replied deadpan, waving his hand, impatiently dismissing his nephew.

Sebastiaan knew the argument was lost. Red-faced and huffing, he turned on his heel and left the stateroom. De Coninck stared at the door long after the young man had closed it.

Sebastiaan prowled the deck looking for the one man the captain would task to mete out this punishment. He couldn't be hard to find. It was a relatively small ship, and Arent was a fairly big man. Sebastiaan found him on his back, arms crossed behind his head, lying on his thin, grey, straw-filled mattress in

CHAPTER 8

the forecastle.

Fair weather allowed the ship to run on a skeleton crew tonight, affording most sailors much-needed time to rest. Men were scattered throughout the room. Light splashed from a few lanterns swaying lazily against the walls. One of the sailors played an improvised tune on a violin, four played cards, and some were grouped around Mattheys as he read from a book borrowed from the captain's small library.

Sebastiaan stood next to Arent's bed. "I need to talk to you."

Arent gave him a lazy look and, in a relaxed growl, said, "Speak, brother."

"In private," Sebastiaan said, tilting his head toward the open upper deck.

"Then it will have to wait till morning, 'cause I ain't getting up. Besides, there are no secrets here. How long do you think a secret can last on a ship this size?"

Sebastiaan heaved a frustrated sigh and went down on his haunches. "Did the captain speak to you about the girl's punishment tomorrow?"

Arent closed his eyes and replied, "Yes," dragging the word out as if Sebastiaan was confirming a suspicion.

"You are going to flog her?" he asked incredulously. "You are going to raise your hand against a defenseless woman?"

A drowsy "Hmm" was all the reply Sebastiaan got.

Seething, he grabbed a handful of Arent's shirt, twisting it in a ball and forcing his fist up under the boatswain's chin. "I won't let you. Do you hear me? I won't let you," he hissed.

Arent showed no reaction to Sebastiaan's words nor the manhandling of his shirt. Instead, he kept his eyes closed and his voice lazy. "You are spoiling for a fight, brother. I would urge you to go look for it elsewhere, but since we both know that I am the only one who can knock some sense into your thick head, I strongly suggest you find your bed and stop bugging me." Arent could hear Sebastiaan's ragged breath as his body shook with barely contained violence.

Frustrated beyond measure, Sebastiaan shoved down hard on Arent's chest as he pushed to gain his feet.

Arent watched his friend through slitted eyes. Only when Sebastiaan left the forecastle did he allow his body to relax.

Sebastiaan's legs made quick work of the distance between the forecastle and the hatch in the galley. Danielle was scared and alone tonight. He could keep her company, even if he couldn't bring her peace. One truth remained clear in his mind – it would be a frigid day in hell when he allowed anybody to harm her. He strode into the galley and was brought up short by the hulking form of Gabriel, a gentle giant at rest but fiercely narrow-minded when it came to executing his orders.

"Move, Gabe," Sebastiaan barked as he neared the hatch.

"Prisoner is not to receive any visitors, Cap's orders." There was a soft smile on the man's broad face, and his eyes were pleading with Sebastiaan not to push him.

Sebastiaan threw his head back, breathed loudly through his nose, and prayed for patience. There would be no rest for him this night.

***

Van Riebeeck had stayed late in the dayroom the previous evening, studying notes written by sailors from the *Haerlem* who were shipwrecked two years prior, at the tip of Africa. The information was invaluable, for the men had time to grow crops and interact with the local tribes. The sailors had established a good relationship with the Hottentots, a native tribe living near the coast. However, studying the journals was not the main reason he stayed up late; he was avoiding his wife. He was troubled by Miss Van Aard's circumstances and needed to find clarity before being subjected to his wife's questions. He knew if he went to bed early and she was still awake, she would drag the details of the meeting from him like a judge on a murder trial. Mercifully, by the time he reached their cabin, both she and Antoonie were fast asleep.

Maria woke slowly. It was morning but still dark outside. Instinctively, her hand went to the baby's forehead, relieved to find that his fever from the previous day was down.

Looking over at her husband, she said, "You came in late last night."

CHAPTER 8

"I had some reading to do."

She listened patiently while dressing herself as he described, in a sleep-heavy voice, the various vegetables that seemed to grow well at the foot of Table Mountain and how they compared to the vegetables grown in Japan. He talked about the wonderful varieties of fruit trees that could be planted and how all this fresh produce would benefit the health of the sailors on passing ships.

When she could no longer bear the direction of the conversation, she asked, "What was decided about the girl?" Standing by the side of the bed, she turned her back, waiting for him to fasten the laces of her corset.

"You poor thing. All the other women have each other's help to get dressed in the mornings, and here you have to settle for me." She could hear the smile in his voice as he deftly tucked the garment in place. Her husband did not view his position as one of power but merely another administrative cog that made the bigger ones turn. Most traveling governors and their wives were housed in gilded cabins with manservants and lady's maids at the ready, but these two preferred to keep a low profile without the pompous extravagance.

"Please tell me what I want to know. I didn't see her all day yesterday and planned to go to her this morning." Van Riebeeck applied all his attention to his wife's undergarments.

"Perhaps it is better to leave her be a while."

Instantly suspicious, Maria asked, "She is all alone. Why can't I see her?"

"Captain De Coninck will enter her in the log as part of his crew. She will not be alone for much longer," Van Riebeeck replied in a conversational tone.

"Part of the crew? But she is a girl." Maria turned around and gave him a narrowed look. She saw the slight twitch in his jaw, the flat pull of his eyebrows as he fought to keep all expression from his face, and the ring finger of his left hand lightly tapping against his thigh. "What are you not telling me?" she asked in the softest of voices, one the governor knew from experience was not to be ignored.

"Why do you assume I am hiding something from you?" He needed to buy a little more time.

"Husband, not only are you hiding something from me, you are also stalling," she said, pinching her lips firmly together, turning them into a hyphen rather than the full softness he was used to. "Out with it," she demanded, braiding her hair and expertly rolling it into a tight knot at the back of her neck.

Van Riebeeck knew it was best to lay the situation out as it was, unvarnished. His wife, despite her youth, was reasonable and level-headed. When presented with all the facts, she could be counted on not to overreact or indulge in hysterics, and she never lost her temper. He knew that for a fact, for he had driven her to the edge of her patience countless times. When angered, she got a faint blush. She would fold her hands in her lap and hold her tongue until her emotions were settled. Only then would she respond – never react. Secured in his wife's predictable good nature, he relayed the outcome of the meeting.

"She was held prisoner overnight in the hold and will receive only five lashes this morning for her punishment," he concluded.

"*Only* five lashes!?" With a shocked face, she protested, "That is barbaric. What has she done that deserves five lashes?" she asked, perplexed.

"It's not exactly legal to be a stowaway. She also attacked the captain." He rushed over the last statement before sweetly smiling up at her.

"Attacked the captain? How?"

"She slapped him."

"Where?"

"In the dayroom."

"Husband!"

"In the face."

Maria gasped, "Oh dear." Putting her hand over her heart, she rallied her troubled thoughts.

Once his wife decided to champion a cause, not much could divert her from her chosen path, and Van Riebeeck hoped that his wife's new path was Miss Van Aard's welfare.

"She did not plan to be a stowaway," Maria argued the girl's case. Turning to her husband, she searched his face with troubled eyes. "Furthermore, she went through a horrible ordeal on land, and on this ship, all by herself. No wonder she lashed out at the captain." Shaking her head in disbelief, she asked,

CHAPTER 8

"When is she to receive this punishment?"

"It is probably already done; it was set to occur after the morning service." Van Riebeeck employed his most soothing tone.

"Johan." She rarely used his given name. "You must do something. You cannot allow this to happen. As governor of the new colony, you are the highest authority on this ship. You can put a stop to this madness, *please*." Her brows drew together, forming a deep groove between her eyes.

"Wife, listen to me." His voice was soft but firm. "To start with, she is a stowaway, regardless of how she became one. Secondly, she kept herself hidden when she could have made her presence known. Thirdly she slapped the captain," he said, counting the arguments on his fingers and holding them up to her face, "Also, I am not going to publicly challenge the captain's authority. Lastly, I am not governor of a new colony; it's merely a halfway station."

"So, you will do nothing then?" she asked incredulously, ignoring his sound reasons.

"Have you not heard a word I said?" The frustrations of the moment gave his voice a regrettable edge.

She flinched as if he had slapped her. She was livid. The color was high on her cheeks as she looked him squarely in the face. He watched as she curled her small fists at her sides, no doubt fighting the desire to throttle him. He had never before seen her lose her temper so thoroughly. *She was magnificent.* Shaking her head in disbelief, she backed away, turned, and left the cabin, closing the door behind her with enough force to bounce Antoonie from his cot.

Van Riebeeck looked down into his son's bewildered eyes, smiled, and said, "Sometimes, my boy, a woman is the only cure. We just need to manage the dosage." Van Riebeeck was deeply relieved by his incorrect assumption of his wife's good nature.

* * *

The cat nipped at her hand in irritation as Danielle stroked the same spot for too long. Barent had brought her pants and shirt along with breakfast, but her stomach had tightened at the sight of the pale grey oat porridge. She had spent the night staring into the darkness. Her anger from the day before had burned away, leaving a deep emptiness in its wake. She had waited for the arrival of the morning like a pregnant mother waiting for the birth of her child, knowing it would bring fear and pain but unable to stop it from creeping closer. Fate had twisted her life into a bizarre series of events. She used to have a routine, days filled with purpose and certainty, but if the last ten days were any indication of what the future held, she was not sure she would live to see another Christmas.

By the time the bell announced the start of the morning shift, her apprehension had turned into annoyance, at herself. It was not as if she would be executed, she chastised herself. Besides, her father raised no weakling. She was a strong, intelligent woman who had done nothing wrong. The thought of the pain of the lashes terrified her, but she would push through it since there was no way around it. She prayed for strength and for time to pass quickly. If the good Lord could make time stand still for Joshua, He could hurry it along for her. Granted, Joshua was an important leader, and she was merely a girl, but they were both God's children, and she believed in His fairness and that He would not stoop to indulge in the pettiness of favoritism.

The hatch opened, and an unfamiliar face showed in the opening. "Let's go, sweetheart," the sailor called down and motioned her towards him. The cat jumped from her lap as her body tensed. Gaining her feet, the weight of the moment hit her. There was no kind face in sight nor a gentle hand to hold. She was utterly alone and at the mercy of others. A single tear rolled down her cheek, and her legs and feet felt heavy as she ascended the ladder. All the determination and brave conclusions she had reached during the night were swiftly deserting her.

She followed the sailor down the passageway, his hard bare feet slapping on the wooden floor. At the door, he took her by the arm and unceremoniously hauled her onto the upper deck. For the first time in more than a week, she breathed fresh air.

It was well before sunrise, the morning still grey and cool. Captain De

CHAPTER 8

Coninck was standing on the quarterdeck with a weathered red leather Bible in his hands. The deck was crowded, and her guard shouldered his way to an empty circle in the middle. Nearly everybody aboard had gathered, desperately vying for the best spot to witness the spectacle of her flogging. Some were hanging from the rigging to get a better view. Her presence caused a buzz among the spectators. A few were shouting ribald and lewd comments while the rest just stared in open interest. It was not every day that they were entertained by a beautiful young woman, wearing men's garb, being publicly flogged.

De Coninck opened his Bible, and as one, the crowd settled into a respectful silence.

The captain's voice rang across the deck, *"Deuteronomy 16:19, Thou shalt not wrest judgment; thou shalt not respect persons, neither take a gift: for a gift doth blind the eyes of the wise, and pervert the words of the righteous ...."*

Danielle stopped listening. Instead, she focused her attention on stopping her knees from shaking. Feeling her movement, the hand around her upper arm tightened. She squared her shoulders and lifted her chin in a slight private movement. With sheer force of will, she slowed her breathing and forced it in through her nose and out the same way. Taking a large lung full of fresh air, she stilled her face. She would face this moment with dignity.

With the morning service concluded, the humming and buzzing of the crowd increased, faces alight once more at the prospect of seeing blood. The circle around the mast tightened.

A mountain of a man stood next to the mainmast. He motioned her to a barrel that had been turned on its side. The man exuded violence and menace, with long, dark hair falling over impossibly wide shoulders. His face was savagely angular. His nose was wide but straight, and his black eyes dislodged a primal fear deep within her. She could see black, primitive-looking patterns edged into the bronze skin of his bare chest and arms. A limp whip hung at his side, the braided handle disappearing into his large paw. With a casual flick of his wrist, he sent the loose end of the weapon over his shoulder in two easy loops, leaving the handle to dangle over his chest.

Her whole body was shaking, and she swallowed several times to fight back the nausea that threatened to overcome her. Her heart was beating a tattoo that echoed from her chest into her head. She latched onto the beats in a desperate bid for composure and started counting. *One, two, three, four ...* The sight of the large man had shattered her control. She was on the brink of being swallowed by the noise around her. Fear was rising like a thundercloud in her belly. Her mouth filled with a metallic taste as her teeth sank into the sides of her cheeks. *Five, six, seven, eight ...* It was becoming too much to bear, and she folded in on herself. Sinking into the darkness of her body – nothing to see, nothing to hear, nothing to feel, just breathe. *Nine, ten ...*

A heavy hand took hold of the back of her neck and pushed her down until her stomach molded over the barrel. Her knees voluntarily folded in a kneeling position when she felt the wooden curve. The man took her wrists in one large hand and tied a coarse rope around them. The rope was then looped once around the mainmast and secured.

His touch pulled her back to the reality she so hopelessly wanted to avoid. She was kneeling over the barrel, facing the mast, exposed and vulnerable. Opening her eyes, she stared at the space between the deck planks. The weight of her head became too much, and she dropped it between her outstretched shoulders. *One, two, three, four.*

Arent took his time tying her down. When he took hold of her hands, he felt her shaking. She was frightened and alarmingly pale, but she did not utter a single word in protest – stoically accepting her fate.

Through the fabric of her linen shirt, he could see her spine protruding in a faint ridge along her back. She was slender and fine-boned. A full-force lash from his arm would flay her to the bone. Depending on the need, he could deliver twenty lashes neatly spaced across a man's back without breaking the skin. Or he could rip him to shreds with only three.

Arent took the whip from his shoulder and swung it a few times in a mock effort to loosen his muscles. The crowd frenzied, and one sailor screamed, "Show us her pretty skin, Arent."

He scanned the rowdy crowd. *Where the bloody hell was the governor?* They mistook the meaning of his look and cheered louder.

Sebastiaan had remained in the forecastle, for he knew his uncle would

CHAPTER 8

have him restrained were he to interfere with the girl's punishment, but the renewed uproar on deck cut through his resolve, and he started to move. His determined strides fell on the deck like drumbeats on a battlefield, causing the spectators to part before him; the few that were slow to move found themselves tossed aside in a ruthless instant. The edges of his vision blurred with his rage. Reaching the center of the deck, he saw Danielle bent over a barrel with her arms stretched out and her dark curls sweeping the floor. Keeping his eyes on her as he approached, he willed her to look at him, but she seemed unaware of her surroundings.

With clenched fists and a thunderous expression, he came to a halt in front of Arent, shielding the girl. Looking into Arent's black eyes, he saw nothing but an adversary. A bored expression was smeared over Arent's face as he coolly looked at the obstacle in his way.

"Put it down, Arent," Sebastiaan growled, gesturing at the whip. Arent shook his head and let the moment drag out.

"I told you. I won't let this happen." The promise of violence was dripping from every whispered word.

Sebastiaan was composed, but beneath that calm façade, Arent knew a lethal rage was boiling. If the governor did not make an appearance soon, things would turn ugly. The lad was by no means a green young pup anymore. His strength and skill matched Arent's in every way, and for the first time, Arent was unsure of the outcome were they to lock horns.

"I'll whip the bloody both of you. Now move, brother," he drawled.

Sebastiaan felt his last straw snap. His right fist snapped up and drove into Arent's left cheekbone with blistering speed. The heat of the moment slowed everything down, and Sebastiaan watched patiently as the boatswain's head fell back from the force of the impact, hovered a while, and then started to move upright again. The punch would have laid a lesser man out cold, but Arent's neck was thick with muscle. Sebastiaan's hands were already poised for the next strike, but he was robbed of the satisfaction when many strong arms pulled him backward.

Arent did not even see the lad throw the punch. The right hook slammed into his face with a potency that made his head whiplash and sent brilliant white light splintering across his eyes. A hushed shockwave rippled through the crowd.

"What is she to you?" Arent barked. His fists were itching for retribution, but he had to play his part in this farce. Sebastiaan was straining against the arms holding him back, and Arent knew it was only a matter of time before he broke free.

Sebastiaan realized that a brawl with Arent would not solve the matter. He needed to find a different way. "I will take her punishment. You can add a few more licks for that sweet kiss I just gave you," he called back, shrugging free from the hands restraining him. His voice, usually filled with good humor, was coarse as gravel.

Moving back to resume his position between Arent and Danielle, Sebastiaan let his arms hang harmlessly by his sides, his hands open and docile. Much of his anger had dispelled with the blow he had dealt Arent, but the same could not be said for his determination.

Arent glanced him over, fighting the urge to twitch his face. He could feel the makings of a fine bruise coming on. Sebastiaan had his temper on an admirably tight leash, but there was a stubborn set to his jaw and shoulders. Arent looked up to the captain standing on the quarterdeck. Captain De Coninck gave the deck a quick sweep, searching for the governor, and when he came up empty, he gave Arent a crisp nod, widened his stance, and crossed his arms over his chest.

"Very well. Untie her," Arent ordered. The crowd howled their disappointment.

Sebastiaan kneeled in front of Danielle. She lifted her head awkwardly towards him, and he felt a stab through his gut at the terror in her vibrant green eyes. Giving her a reassuring smile, he deftly untied the knots in the rope. Once free, he pulled her to her feet. She was shaking violently. He moved to draw her close when he saw Maria Van Riebeeck push her way through the layers of spectators, embodying calm and composure as she came to stand next to Danielle. Reaching out, she touched Danielle's elbow and spoke a few quiet words in her ear.

"I will take it from here," Maria said to Arent and Sebastiaan. She pulled

CHAPTER 8

Danielle from Sebastiaan's hands. The crowd parted like the Red Sea as the governor's wife led the girl to safety.

Sebastiaan waited until the two women disappeared from the deck before he stripped the shirt from his body and tossed it heedlessly to the side. He placed his hands on the mast in front of him and offered Arent his back. His muscles twitched as the morning sun's virgin rays played across his honey-colored skin. The blood lust of the crowd had dissipated. Sebastiaan was a favorite, and his chivalry had put them to shame.

Arent took a deep breath, raised his arm, and lowered the whip across his friend's back. An angry red welt rose instantly from Sebastiaan's right shoulder to his left side, where the skin split and wept a thick teardrop of blood that crept into the waistband of his pants.

With his face hard and expressionless as if carved from granite, Sebastiaan offered no reaction to the assault.

Five neatly spaced bloody slashes laid across Sebastiaan's back. A few drops of blood dripped onto the wooden planks at his feet, but Sebastiaan did not move from his position, defiantly waiting for more.

"It's done," Arent said in a harsh voice, shaking his head slightly.

Sebastiaan dropped his hands from the mast, bent down to retrieve his shirt, and left the deck without a word.

With a few sharp barks, Arent dispersed the crowd. The sailors resumed their duties, and the passengers found their cabins. Captain De Coninck turned towards his private quarters.

***

Knocking sharply, Arent entered the stateroom and was surprised to find the governor and the captain waiting for him.

"Well, that did not go according to plan," the governor said, breaking the tension. At least the man had the grace to look embarrassed; however, Arent ignored the observation and spoke to De Coninck, "Captain, I find myself in need of your fancy French brandy and two glasses."

Without delay, De Coninck handed the requested items over. His voice muffled as he was bending down, no doubt in search of some fortification for himself and his guest, when he asked, "Where's Sebastiaan?"

"In the hull," Arent answered over his shoulder as he turned to leave.

Chapter 9

He did not like crowds, didn't like it when others touched or rubbed against him; it made his skin crawl. But something was happening beyond just the regular morning service at dawn. The air on deck was thick with excitement. Sailors and passengers formed loose groups, sharing whispered opinions on what was about to occur. Keeping his back pressed against the bulwark, he inched closer to the group standing not too far from him. It was hard to hear what they were talking about, but the words 'flogging' and 'stowaway' drifted to him. There was a stowaway aboard. Could it be her?

The possibility made his palms break out in a layer of moisture, and he rubbed them absentmindedly against his sides. A commotion drew his attention. One of the men dragged a young woman to the center of the deck.

Her back was turned to him, and he focused on the long dark curls nestled between her shoulders. His eyes dipped lower to her waist, and he frowned when he saw how her bottom was devilishly on display by the gentleman's pants. Everything was making sense. She had been hiding in the hull all this time, dressed as a boy. He knew with absolute certainty that he had found her, but the thrill of his discovery was short-lived when a stab of jealousy angled through him at the man holding her captive. She was young and strong and would survive the flogging. The real problem was not the flogging but the infection from the wounds left by the whip that could prove lethal. He could not allow a paltry infection to rob him of the opportunity to continue their little game of cat and mouse.

A few curious eyes turned his way, and he became aware of the sound of his breathing and the sweat running down the sides of his face. With the excitement of seeing her for the first time, his breathing now resembled a pair of bellows. He had to leave. Embarrassed by his body's physical reaction to the woman, he rushed from the deck. Now that he knew what she looked like, there would be no more hiding from him. It was just a matter of time.

* * *

What's next? Danielle wondered. She had gone from nearly being publicly flogged to the warmth and privacy of a cozy cabin in a matter of seconds.

The woman gestured to a single chair adorned with a square patchwork cushion in the corner. Danielle sank onto it, not of her own volition. Her knees simply buckled, and her body followed. A sudden chill made her teeth rattle, and gooseflesh raced up her arms and onto her cheeks.

"You are in shock," the woman said while taking a blanket from the bed and wrapping it around Danielle's shoulders.

She clutched the ends close to her throat. The physical signs of her near-hysterical state were clear. Her heart was racing, her muscles trapped in never-ending shivers, and it felt like the blanket was sitting on top of the cold rather than expelling it.

"Danielle?" Kneeling in front of her, the woman searched her face with concerned eyes. She placed a hand on Danielle's knee, and the touch made her flinch, but the woman did not remove her hand. "You are safe. Do you understand?" Danielle nodded. The woman's voice sounded like it was coming from somewhere else.

"Good. Stay here. I'll be back soon."

Where was she going to go, in any event? She could run as far and fast as she liked and still be on the ship. Heaving a deep sigh, she scanned the room and came to rest on a small boy sleeping in a crib at the foot of the main sleeping bunk. His breathing was deep and even. The peacefulness and tranquility of the sight eased some of her agitation.

Perhaps one day, she would be a mother, give birth, and afterward smile

CHAPTER 9

and lovingly hold the tiny bundle in her arms. Having witnessed and assisted in many births, she could never fathom how mothers managed to smile so happily after enduring the agonizing pain and struggle amidst the ever-looming fear of death. The instant she held the baby in her arms, everything was forgiven and forgotten, and a love, fierce and tender, engulfed the new life. Could she do it? Could she ever love someone so unconditionally? Right now, sitting on a small chair in a stranger's cabin, on her way to some destination she would never have chosen, she realized that she didn't care. She didn't care if she ever became a mother or a wife or even so much as loved somebody. The realization left her feeling wonderfully empty.

The woman returned with the cook on her heels, carrying a tray of refreshments. Busying herself with pouring tea, she handed Danielle a cup with a dry oat biscuit on the side.

The cup rattled on the saucer, and the slight noise made Danielle's lips thin with annoyance. She needed to be alone, away from prying eyes.

Separating the offending pieces of crockery, she looked up to find the woman sitting on the sleeping bunk opposite her. There was no amusement or judgment in her face. The silence between them was strangely comforting, but Danielle knew that her state of mind was not to be trusted at this time. Her history with women was not a pleasant one. She perceived women generally as conniving and mean, and the more power they had, the worse they were. Finding herself at their mercy more than once in Texel, Danielle was the object of their gossip and snickering, cleverly hidden behind cupped hands or spread fans. They paid her the time of day only when they needed her herbs to rid them of an ache, an itch, or an unwanted babe in their bellies.

Her face involuntarily scrunched as she took a sip of the overly sweet tea. The soothing warm liquid slid down her throat, and she began to return to herself. Joining the cup to its saucer, this time without the accompanying rattle, she waited for the woman to say her piece.

The woman kept her steady eyes on Danielle, understanding that she needed privacy and wisely not allowing it.

"I'm Maria Van Riebeeck, the governor's wife." Her voice had a smooth velvet edge, "and that is our son, Antoonie," she said, pointing to the sleeping child.

Danielle introduced herself with the barest of words. If the governor's wife had noted her clipped response, she did not show it. Danielle had every intention of keeping her interactions with Mrs. Van Riebeeck to an absolute minimum. This repast was over. The tea had a restoring effect, and she felt much more in control of her limbs and emotions. She tried to gain her feet. It was time to leave.

With the half-full teacup still in her hand, she abruptly stood and belatedly registered that her legs were unsteady. It felt as if they were fashioned from aspic. She must have pitched, for the governor's wife instinctively reached a staying hand to her. The motion made Danielle pull back sharply, and she lost her balance, landing back on the chair that she had so gracelessly vacated a few seconds before. Tea spilled from the cup and stained her breeches.

"No, my dear, please keep still for a while." Concern and confusion washed over Mrs. Van Riebeeck's pale features. "Try to finish the biscuit. It will settle your stomach."

Danielle's instincts warned her that the caring woman before her was not to be trusted. The biscuit tasted like parchment, and she forced it down with a sip of tea. She remained in the chair only because her body was temporarily unable to do much else.

As the shock ran its course and her limbs quit shaking, her mind seemed to clear. Slowly she took stock of herself, starting at her feet. She was wearing her own clothes again, boots, workman's pants, bindings under a loose white shirt. It had all been returned to her early this morning, crisp and clean. Someone had seen to its laundering. She knew there were other women aboard. Perhaps one of them had done her the kindness. But she knew, better than most, that kindness was short-lived.

As a little girl, she was awkward. Growing up in a harsh world, without a mother, with only her father's guidance, had made her different from the other girls in the village. At first, she was pushed away the way small children do to unwanted little ones. As the children grew older, the pushing was replaced by underhanded cruelty. Early on, she had learned to avoid social interaction. She focused on being useful rather than popular. People in need

CHAPTER 9

seemed far less judgmental.

She never went on picnics or gathered in salons to embroider together, partly because she was never invited. Still, even if some brave soul had ventured to do so, she would most certainly have refused. Therefore having tea together in the afternoon and giggling over boys also fell by the wayside.

Her father had taken notice of her social isolation and awkwardness and thoroughly blamed himself for the situation. He had arranged get-togethers at their small house with a select few girls, but when no one showed up after the third attempt, he started to beg some of his patients to invite his daughter to spend time with theirs. She had agreed to go on a picnic to appease her father and stop his constant urging her to make friends. It turned out to be a glorious failure, for whilst the others were content to sit on a blanket, eating lemon tarts, shielded from the sun by their frilly parasols, she had wandered off in search of herbs. Their snickering behind her back bothered her more than she cared to admit, so she stayed away longer than she ought to. She had returned with armloads of flowers, leaves, and roots, but her defection, although fruitful, came at a price. The beautiful summer dress her father had insisted she wear was badly torn after it got tangled in a bramble bush, and her silk slippers were ruined beyond the point of restoration, and on top of all that was the reaction of the other girls. They had openly laughed at her, quickly gathered the blanket and food baskets, turned their backs on her, and left her behind as they headed back to the village. That was the last time she had ventured near a social gathering.

Pulling herself from the memories of the long-time-ago silly incident, she thought of all that had happened over the last nine days: her father's death, her time in the hull, and her near flogging this morning. For once, there were no tears, and she was grateful for the small mercy, for she was loath to embarrass herself before the governor's wife.

As she returned the cup to the saucer, her mind cleared. It was as if a dense fog she was previously unaware of was lifting. It was very much like when she had too much mustard and her nose cleared, followed by a rush of cold air so abrupt in its assault that she feared her heart might stop. That same sensation filled her now with the knowledge that she was no longer the same.

The knowledge sent a surge of power through her body akin to a lightning strike. She was no longer the scared girl who found refuge in her father's surgery or the rejected and insecure young woman she had been of late. She stood on the precipice of a new life. She could reinvent herself and live by her own rules.

"Mistress, I am grateful for your assistance but need only a few moments to collect myself before returning to the hull," Danielle said.

Maria nodded understandingly. The girl wanted to escape. She had been trapped in the hull for more than a week with nothing but darkness surrounding her. Waking in a stranger's cabin injured, under suspicion of murder and espionage, then rescued by a man whose intentions were as vague as the rest of the circumstances. It was enough to drive anybody to the edge of reason. She would explain all in due course, but first, another matter required her attention.

Danielle's face was very animated. It displayed every thought and emotion coursing through her mind. Her pale skin and dark hair emphasized the unusual color of her eyes. Maria could not decide if they were blue or green, but she was fascinated by the flash of defiance that shone through them. The girl was physically on the verge of collapse, but her spirit remained strong, and Maria felt an unexpected surge of protectiveness toward her. Reaching over, she took the teacup from Danielle's hands and returned it to the tray on the desk. The girl needed protection, and she needed a plan.

Her husband's words about having no female assistance drifted back to her. She needed Danielle tied to her in some official capacity. The girl's future would be much improved if Maria could prevent her from being conscripted into De Coninck's crew.

Enlisting Danielle as a crewmember was a solid solution from a man's point of view, but it was not practical, considering that Danielle was a female. Was she to scrub the deck all day? She would be alone and at the mercy of many sailors and soldiers. It was an impossible solution.

"Perhaps you could indulge me and have another cup of tea?" Maria turned to the task without waiting for an answer.

Danielle accepted the tea, and the ritual started again, this time mercifully

CHAPTER 9

without a biscuit.

She watched as Maria rearranged items on the desk. The cabin was not messy, but not tidy either – trapped in the gentle chaos of a family living in a small space. The bed was roughly made, as if done by a man. The baby's bedclothes were crisp and clean. On the desk, hairpins, ribbons, a few carved wooden animals, and journals competed for space – it was the desk of a family man. Maria's back was turned to her, affording Danielle the privacy she needed.

"It is pleasant and quiet in here, isn't it?" Maria spoke in a wistful voice. And she was right; it was peaceful in the cabin. Danielle observed the woman discreetly. They were the same build, not short nor tall but comfortably in the middle. Danielle's body was light and subtle, whereas motherhood had softened Maria's. Remembering how Maria had rescued her from the deck, she suspected a granite core lurked beneath the soft and gentle exterior.

Maria resumed her tidying, pushing books onto piles with journals at the bottom and letters at the top. Nothing was put away. Instead, similar objects were loosely grouped together, leaving the desk no less cluttered. Hairpins fell into a tin dish and pinged like small hailstones against a windowpane.

Danielle had to leave. Maria felt too much like a safe haven.

Her legs felt much steadier, and she pushed to her feet again. "Mistress, I –" but Maria swiftly interrupted her.

"No more of that," she said with a quick sweep of her fingers. "You can call me by my name. I'll call you by yours. Please sit down, for there is another matter that we need to discuss. I have an idea that involves you." Although her words were high-handed, they was delivered in a soft tone.

"You cannot return to the hull. It is not suitable accommodation, and well you know it." Maria gave Danielle a calculating look, her mind clearly at work. A pregnant silence hung between them. Danielle knew that the hull was most likely out of the question, and she would not be sad to never set foot in it again. It housed a pile of memories, and none were positive. She had lost track of time, for her thoughts had threatened to spiral down a dark hole once more, but Maria's plan finally seemed to reach a culmination point. When she spoke, her voice rang sure and true.

"First, I must ask: Do you like children?"

"Yes, I do," Danielle said, frowning at the odd twist in the conversation.

"You will do just fine, then."

Before Danielle could inquire as to the meaning of the statement, two brisk knocks fell on the door as if the person on the other side was in a terrible hurry with no time to waste. Danielle jumped from her chair just as little Antoonie's eyes flew open a short second before his first disgruntled cry filled the cabin.

Maria heaved a deep sigh and turned to the crib to pick up the little boy.

"Please enter, Mrs. Boom," she called over the howling child.

A stout, apple-cheeked, middle-aged woman entered the cabin, giving Danielle a passing glance before her eyes settled on the toddler in his mother's arms.

"Oh, what is the matter, sweetpea?" she cooed and reached her arms out to him. The little boy bucked his back and buried his face in his mother's neck, clearly not in the mood to be entertained by the newcomer.

"I just came by to –" she looked to Danielle. "Well, sit down, dear. You look close to fainting." The motherly frown stayed on her face as she pointed to the vacant chair. Danielle breathed deeply from the pit of her patience and sat back down again. It was beginning to feel like a Sunday morning church service – sitting, standing, sitting, standing – ridiculous.

"As I was saying, I came by to ask if Miss Van Aard would mind sharing a cabin with my girls. You see, four bunks are available, and they are preparing one for her as we speak." She looked expectantly at Danielle. Her mouth was lightly closed, eyebrows elevated, and it was clear that she expected a quick reply. When the response did not come fast enough to her liking, she snapped her eyes to the governor's wife, much like a lizard following the antics of a fly.

"Mistress?"

Antoonie's head was resting on his mother's shoulder, and he was loudly sucking his thumb while his large brown eyes shifted from one person to the next. Maria's body swayed rhythmically from side to side, rocking the child. She looked at Danielle and visibly tried to hide her amusement.

"Danielle, meet Mrs. Boom, the gardener's wife. She is the proud mother

CHAPTER 9

of two delightful sixteen-year-old daughters."

Mrs. Boom struck her hand out and gave Danielle's a firm, almost manly shake that rippled to her shoulder.

"Not much of a delight they are, but I am very pleased to meet you, my dear. So?"

"That is kind of you and your daughters, Mrs. Boom." Maria accepted on Danielle's behalf. "We appreciate your willingness to accommodate her."

It felt like somebody had emptied a bucket of cold water down Danielle's back. Dread and anger rose in equal measure within her. She was to share a cabin with two girls, and albeit they were three years her junior, venom did not require a vintage to be deadly. Words flooded her mouth, but before any could escape, Mrs. Boom exclaimed, "Very good," and clapped her hands together loudly, startling poor Antoonie, who immediately searched the refuge of his mother's neck again. "Come with me, and I will show you around. And perhaps we'll find you a dress."

Danielle was unsure what to do. Events were happening too fast, and she was about to topple over, like when she spun in a circle with arms stretched out to the sides. She looked to Maria, who smiled reassuringly and shook her head discreetly.

"Mrs. Boom, you are very kind, but if you could afford me and Miss Van Aard a few moments longer, I would bring her to you as soon as we are done here." Maria thanked her while rubbing the little boy's back with her free hand.

Danielle waited until Mrs. Boom closed the cabin door firmly behind her before releasing the breath she was unaware of holding.

"She's more bark than bite, don't worry," Maria smiled. "However, her little interruption did give me a moment to think. I tried to say earlier that I was hoping to convince you to take the position of my companion." She looked to Danielle before seating the child on the bed with a few toys to occupy him.

"What does that mean?" Danielle asked.

"It's a job. It means that you will be employed by the VOC and therefore receive payment for keeping me company, so to speak."

Danielle nodded, unable to fathom what such a position would entail. "What would you require from a companion? I've never been one before."

Maria looked out the window while rubbing her bottom lip with her index finger. "I am not entirely sure either. But it is more important that you agree to this arrangement."

She must have died and descended straight to hell. All her worst fears were coming true and in rapid succession: a job working for a powerful woman, spending time with her, and sharing living quarters with two girls. Her mind was swimming, trying to find alternatives. She would have to survive one day at a time until she could make her way back to Texel. But there was a matter that needed addressing first.

"Your husband believes me to be a spy," Danielle stated while looking Maria straight in the eye, searching for the slightest reaction.

Seeing the challenge in the remarkable green eyes of the younger woman, Maria smiled softly. "Are you sure about that?" she asked while raising her eyebrows in a challenge of her own.

Danielle was unsure what to make of the question. The governor believed in her innocence? Is that why his wife came to her rescue? Why she was offering her a position that would secure her safety? A companion to the governor's wife was nothing more than a fancy title for a glorified chambermaid. She was no stranger to carrying tea trays and cleaning chamber pots, and besides, anything was better than having to hide in the darkness of the hull.

"I agree to your proposal."

***

France and Holland were at peace, but that did not stop French pirates from molesting treasure-rich Dutch merchant vessels. The problem was worse around the Mediterranean and Portuguese coastlines. Since the *Drommedaris* had reached the coast of Africa, the threat of a pirate attack had diminished. Captain De Coninck could now consider lowering some cannons from the upper deck into the hull.

From the start of the voyage, the *Drommedaris* had been top-heavy, making it a nightmare to handle in heavy seas and leaving her to bob like a cork in a

CHAPTER 9

bathtub on good days.

Shortly after the dramatic scenes of the morning, De Coninck ordered nine cannons on the upper deck lowered into the hull, giving the vessel much-needed ballast.

Sebastiaan applied himself wholeheartedly to rearranging the cargo, making room for the cannons. His frustrations, and the irritation of his stinging back, propelled him to do the work of three men. Tools were hurled aside, landing in an untidy heap a few yards away. He needed to get his anger firmly under control before joining the rest of the crew – or most importantly, before facing his uncle again. There were not many ways available for a man to clear his head. He could beat the snot out of somebody or reorganize the cargo. The latter was closer at hand.

He lined barrels filled with seed against the wall, stacking them three high. His arms worked in a mindless rhythm as he tied the barrels down, wincing as tiny droplets of sweat ran down the crooked path between his back muscles and into the fresh cuts.

"What the hell are you doing?" Arent's rough voice came from near the opening.

"Making... room... for the cannons," Sebastiaan replied as his voice strained under the weight of the crate he was pushing.

"So, you will rearrange this shithole all by yourself?" Arent asked, scanning the space with a disapproving scowl. The bilges were not stinking for once, for all the foul water had been pumped away after the storm.

Sebastiaan straightened and looked to Arent, "What do you want?"

"Stop for a bit and come have a drink with me." Arent lifted the bottle of brandy.

"Shove it up your arse, Arent. I'm not in the mood," Sebastiaan growled as he turned his back on him and hurled an empty barrel to the side. The man needed to leave before he fed him his teeth.

An unwelcome memory bubbled through his violent thoughts and fought its way to the foreground.

As boys, Sebastiaan and Arent had become fast friends. Then, years later, en route to India, the *Drommedaris* was making her way south on the Atlantic, parallel to the African west coast, when she encountered a storm that kept all hands busy for three days. She had suffered mast and rigging damage and was challenging to handle.

With the crew exhausted, and the ship crippled, the captain had set a course for the Ivory Coast. That night the men slept as they were, on deck in the cold night air, and a blessing it was too. For during the middle watch, a ship with black sails had silently crept up on their stern. By the time the lookout had sounded the alarm, the monster galleon had already swung its grappling lines, and pirates were swarming onto the *Drommedaris'* deck.

Captain De Coninck had chosen his crew carefully. They were all fine sailors and fierce fighting men who never slept empty-handed. Within moments, the deck was crowded with men locked in mortal battle.

The galleon's sheer size and demonic façade had made cold sweat run down the seventeen-year-old Sebastiaan's back, but the moment the pirates released their bloodcurdling war cry, his fear vanished. He had been trained at the hands of his uncle, Arent, and big Gabriel for years. His uncle had taught him how to wield a sword with acute precision, Gabriel had taught him how to use his strength and every secret the cutlass held, and Arent had taught him how to cheat.

That night, his mind and body had fused, and he had met one faceless enemy after another with the same ferocity. Dead bodies and body parts had made movement difficult. The deck had soon become slippery with blood and gore. Eventually, when the moonlight had stopped glinting off the swinging cutlasses and the scrapes of metal against metal had died down, Sebastiaan found himself out of blades to cross. With his chest heaving and shoulders aching, he looked for the rest of the crew.

The fight had not gone the pirates' way, and they were trying to get back to their ship. But Arent was mad with battle fever, and instead of letting them go, he tried to prevent as many as possible from leaving the *Drommedaris*. He had made an error, for he was isolated from the rest of the crew and quickly found himself surrounded by four desperate pirates hell-bent on surviving. They attacked as a pack. While three were engaging the big man from his front and sides, the fourth crept around to attack Arent's unprotected back.

CHAPTER 9

Sebastiaan saw the moment before it could play out and leaped to the deck below. He rushed forward and buried his cutlass to the hilt in the first pirate's back. The long, curved point protruded from the front. One of the other pirates had seen Sebastiaan's approach and was quick to repeat the same battle strategy, but this time aimed for the young sailor's back. With only two pirates confronting Arent, Sebastiaan realized the ploy in time to twist his body sideways, but he was not fast enough to evade the approaching blade. Instead of piercing him, it cut into his side.

Not wanting to leave the *Drommedaris* without anything to show for their efforts, the captain of the black ship had rushed forward, knocked the cutlass from Sebastiaan's numb hands, and whipped a rope around his neck. Sebastiaan was hauled with them as they scrambled back to their ship.

As the pirates dragged Sebastiaan over the bulwark, he saw Arent drop his cutlass and raise his hands. The pirates would not waste a gift horse, for both men were young and strong and would fetch a decent price.

The pirates hacked the last of the grappling lines free, and the black ship leaned into the wind and bore away from the *Drommedaris*. Her cannons were in clear range, but Sebastiaan knew his uncle would not give the order to open fire for fear of killing him and Arent. The *Drommedaris* was too crippled to follow.

The black ship's captain ordered them below decks after Sebastiaan and Arent were searched for weapons. A knotted rope cracked across their backs, herding them down the companionway and into the slave deck. The wound at Sebastiaan's side was bleeding steadily. All the while, he was aware of Arent's solid presence.

The slaver must have sold its cargo only recently, for the deck was empty, but the stench was fresh. The headspace was less than half that of an average deck height, and they were forced to crawl until the guards pushed them down and secured their wrists and ankles with chains. Lying side-by-side on their backs, they could only sit up but not turn over. Men, women, and children would spend months chained to the deck like this. Their bowels would empty where they lay, and if anyone were to die – and many did – the corpse would stay where it was until the end of the voyage.

All the pushing and pulling had torn at Sebastiaan's wound. His life's blood was steadily draining from him, and he was drifting in and out of consciousness. In one of his lucid moments, he felt something tucking at his wrist. When he opened his eyes, he found Arent kneeling beside him.

"How the hell did you come loose?" he asked through the fog in his mind.

"Their search wasn't as thorough as it could have been." Arent was very creative when hiding weapons on and in his body. "I still have my arse blade."

Sebastiaan was about to ask another question when Arent hissed at him to be quiet.

Somebody was opening the hatch. They could hear the banging at the wooden pegs. Arent abandoned his task of freeing Sebastiaan and moved towards the sound, making sure to stay in the shadows.

The hatch opened, and a man came down the companionway. When he was on the second to last rung and could still stand upright, he loosened his breeches, let them drop to his ankles, and emptied his bladder. The fresh stench of urine filled the air, followed by laughter and a steady stream of insults in a foreign language. As the man bent to pull his slops up, Arent emerged like a djinn from the dark. He clamped his hand over the man's mouth and nose and hauled him away from the stairs. Sebastiaan heard scuffling and the snap of a neck, and then Arent was at his side again, working his blade on the remaining locks.

"Stay awake, goddamn you," he growled close to Sebastiaan's ear. "We'll have to make a run for it before those arseholes discover the open hatch."

As soon as the chains fell from Sebastiaan's limbs, they crawled to the opening, and Arent pushed him up the ladder. Once outside and breathing fresh air, they paused to scan the deck ahead. Sebastiaan struggled to keep his eyes focused and his feet steady. He was cold and nauseous from blood loss, and the blackness threatened to claim him.

Seeing Sebastiaan sway on his feet, Arent hoisted him over his shoulder and ran for the bulwark. Musket fire erupted behind them. Sebastiaan felt a bullet strike him sideways in the upper arm where it dangled over Arent's back. Arent's sure strides carried them swiftly across the deck, and as they reached the bulwark, he tossed Sebastiaan overboard in a fluid motion.

CHAPTER 9

Sebastiaan's mind had snapped to attention the instant his body hit the cold water. He had dropped deep and immediately began to push his way back to the surface. Not wanting to call out for fear of drawing the pirates' attention to their position, he scanned the water for Arent, praying that he'd made it safely overboard. Then Arent's head cleared the surface a few yards to his port side. The sailors aboard the black ship couldn't spot them in the dark water, and after a while, they quit searching for their lost prey and disappeared into the night. With no direction to swim in, they trod water. By dawn, Sebastiaan's body had reached the end of its endurance. Although the cold water had slowed the bleeding of his wounds, it had not stopped it, and there was too little left to sustain him.

"Arent," he croaked, "my uncle will come for you." Arent's lips were purple and cracked from the assault of the seawater. "Tell him ..." he broke off, and when he looked again, Arent was not where he last saw him.

Not having the energy to search for him, Sebastiaan closed his eyes and let his body sink. His descent was interrupted when a pair of strong arms clamped around his chest and pulled him back to the surface. Arent lifted the back of Sebastiaan's head against his shoulder and, with one hand under his chin, kept his head above the water and effectively stopped him from speaking.

"Shut up," Arent's voice was coarse with fatigue, "save your energy."

Sebastiaan shook his head.

"Shut the fuck up and keep breathing."

Those were the last words Sebastiaan remembered.

He woke in his bed, bandaged and warm, with his uncle sitting in a chair beside his mattress. Arent had kept them afloat for more than five hours until De Coninck's sloop had found them. The captain himself had hauled them from the water.

Sebastiaan felt the heat of his anger fade in the face of the memory.

"It wasn't supposed to happen the way it did," Arent said as he saw the rage leaving his friend. "We had a plan. The governor was supposed to stop the whole damn thing, but he didn't show. And so ..." He let the moment speak for itself.

Squinting to see what Arent was holding up, Sebastiaan conceded, "You have good taste."

Arent's shoulders dropped. "I have good taste, but I lack patience."

"Don't you think it's a bit early for that?" Sebastiaan censured in a last effort to remain stubborn, although his heart wasn't in it.

"When is it ever?" Arent's reply left absolutely no room for debate.

Sebastiaan dragged over the same crate he and Danielle had used a few nights ago and sat down on the floor with his arms resting on his bent knees. Arent divided the brandy between the two glasses, nearly filling each to the top.

"I don't think that's how it's done," Sebastiaan said with a smile.

"Who cares? We're going to finish it, may as well save time. How's the back?" Arent asked as he gingerly peeked over Sebastiaan's shoulder.

"You tell me."

"I had to draw blood. Anything less would've been an insult."

"I don't know if I should be pissed or pleased."

"Well, now you definitely need some tending."

"Not the surgeon, though," Sebastiaan replied lazily, swirling the brandy in his mouth before he swallowed.

"No, not the surgeon." Arent concurred with a shiver. "You'll need some sort of ointment, I think. Perhaps I'll ask Miss Van Aard if she would mind taking a look?"

Sebastiaan stared at the goat pen, nodding slowly in agreement, a slow smile curving his lips.

"Thank you, brother."

"You are most welcome," Arent raised his glass to Sebastiaan and drained the last of the brandy.

***

By mid-morning, two days later, Sebastiaan and four sailors emerged from the hull onto the upper deck drenched in sweat. The hull was finally ready to receive the cannons. Tilting his head back, he filled his lungs with fresh air.

CHAPTER 9

The *Drommedaris* was peacefully lying at rest on a calm, oily ocean. There was not even enough wind to stir the ensign. Under any other circumstances, the quiet would be a thing of beauty, but not today. The ship's upper deck was awash with activity. The hatches were lifted, opening most of the deck to the hull below. Bazaar-like noises came in layers: the frantic screams of the goats, men shouting, girls giggling, wheels grunting, and ropes straining. All that was missing were the calls from sellers peddling their wares.

Sebastiaan walked over to the barrel of fresh water near the mainmast. Removing the mug from the hook, he dipped it and downed it with a few greedy gulps. Wiping his mouth with the back of his hand, he watched as a goat was lifted from the hull, the harness leaving the animal's round belly to bulge between the front and back fastenings. Its bulbous eyes were wild, and the purple tongue concave as the frantic animal let loose an ear-splitting scream. Barent presided over the entire affair and herded his goats, once freed from the harness, with gentle endearments onto the bow where the chickens were already clucking away in their box pen.

"It's all right, my darling Duchess," came Barent's soothing voice. His arms were wide as if he wanted to embrace the dangling caprine.

Sebastiaan raised his eyebrows, "Duchess?" he murmured to himself with a slight shake of his head.

"He's given them all titles," his uncle replied, standing next to him. Then continued without looking to Sebastiaan, "Lad, I don't want you to do any heavy lifting today." Sebastiaan's head snapped around to meet the captain's gaze.

"We will have two teams lowering the cannons. I want you and Arent to oversee each team. Should one of those cannons slip, it will fall right to the bottom of the ocean, leaving a neat gap in the hull."

"In that case, I'll wager we'll touch the bottom before the cannon does." Sebastiaan smiled at his own wit.

"Precisely. I need cool heads and sharp eyes," and with that, his uncle looked up at the man in the lookout basket. He nodded an acknowledgment and left the upper deck.

It seemed that everybody wanted to share in the activity and sunshine. The

Boom twins' excited voices and giggles could be heard above the din of the deck. They were allowed to watch the goings-on with strict instructions to stay on the poop deck, well clear of all the activity. Niklas was, as usual, staring out over the ocean with a casual hand caressing the whip staff. His primary purpose for the day was to keep Orion in the stateroom and the twins out of the way – a task he efficiently managed with a scowl and a grunt depending on who stepped closer to wherever he deemed close enough.

Sebastiaan made a quick round of the deck, ensuring Lukas had everything he needed to keep the ropes tarred and ready. Barent was on the bows tending his animals. Most of the passengers were observing the proceedings from the aft deck. He scanned the small group but quickly lost interest when he didn't see Danielle among them. Neither was Maria Van Riebeeck, leaving him to believe that the two women were spending their afternoon together.

"Where are Mattheys and Orion?" Arent asked Sebastiaan as they passed each other.

"Barent sent Mattheys to mind the soup, and Orion is cleaning the stateroom. Lord Niklas will keep an eye on him."

"You are not serious?"

"Why?" Sebastiaan was confused. "You ordered them out of the way for the day."

"Yes, I did, but do you not remember the last time Mattheys tended the soup? We were sick for three days." Arent yelled while holding up three fingers to drive his point home.

"I'll fix it!" Sebastiaan called over his shoulder as he hurried toward the galley.

"And I don't want you in front of that damn soup kettle either!"

His uncle ran a tight ship, and his strict rules were worth every pain in the arse they caused in moments such as these. There was no confusion as to who assumed which task.

Ropes as thick as a man's wrist looped around the cannons. The heavy cargo was attached to two separate lines, threaded through pulleys, and connected to the main and the aft mast platforms, from there down to the hands of two seven-man teams.

CHAPTER 9

"Three, two, one, BOWSE!" Arent's voice thundered across the deck, and the two teams tightened the ropes as one, lifting the cannon and its base off the deck.

Sebastiaan's team took a few steps back as Arent's team moved closer to the deck's opening. Inch by inch, the cannon moved to the center of the open space, and the painstaking process of lowering the three-ton object began. As the gun reached the hull floor, more hands guided the iron wheels onto supporting spars and pushed the heavy weapons into designated areas, lending precious balance to the ship.

It was late afternoon, and only two cannons remained. Sebastiaan scanned the deck, pointing to the next seven men to take their places when the call from the watchmen brought all activity to a sudden halt. "Man overboard, starboard side!"

Sebastiaan and Arent shared a mutual exasperated look. Arent's chin dropped to his chest, and with pinched eyes, he blindly made his way to the ship's side. Sebastiaan was already moving to strip his shirt, not paying any attention to the hush of murmurs at the sight of his bloody back.

"Avast." Arent grabbed Sebastiaan's forearm as he reached to haul himself over the side. "Let the bastard steep for a bit. How many times have we told him not to dangle off the side by himself?" The veins on Arent's neck were protruding with his annoyance.

"I don't think he can swim," Sebastiaan observed, leaning over to get a better look, wholeheartedly agreeing with the boatswain.

"Sure don't look like it," Arent heaved a deep sigh. "I'll get him," he said as he reached for the rope handed to him by a sailor. "The line will cut into your back." He tied the rope around his waist and then passed it to Sebastiaan.

"Time to go fishing." Arent shrugged his shirt and neatly dove over the side, entering the water mere meters from where Mattheys was churning it with wild swings and loud splutterings.

Danielle was on her way to the galley when she heard the watchman's distress call. She hadn't been on the open deck since the morning of her near whipping, but she changed her course and headed towards the rush of fresh air.

The deck was as busy as she remembered it the last time, only now, instead of gawking at her, everybody was hanging over the side, searching the waters below. The situation couldn't have been too grievous, for the mood was light; a few sailors were even betting on the outcome of the unknown calamity.

"Bet you my ration of beer he doesn't make it."

"Nah, he'll make it," the other said in a low, lazy voice.

Next to the bulwark, Sebastiaan was hauling something onto the deck. Her breath caught as she saw the damage done to his back. Her eyes scanned the expanse of his flesh. His golden skin was marred with deep, angry, bloody cuts resulting from him taking her punishment. He had the body of a seasoned sailor shaped and battered by physical adversity. A wave of guilt swept over her as she watched his hard, lean muscles bulge and coil defiantly under the wounds.

He leaned back and pulled the heavy load onto the deck with long overhand movements. Another sailor joined him in his efforts, and moments later, they hoisted a dripping old man with a ramshackle appearance over the side, followed by a very annoyed and savage-looking boatswain. Danielle wondered if the boatswain knew any emotions other than annoyance and anger. Sizing up his naked upper body, she was deeply grateful that the damage to Sebastiaan's back was not worse.

She watched in quiet fascination as Sebastiaan let go of the rope and knelt beside the old man, his face alight with amusement.

"Do you need to cough up some water, Mattheys?" he asked as he playfully pounded him on the back, the force of which made the old man bow over like a praying monk.

"No, he doesn't," growled the boatswain, "he already spewed everything he had all over my forearm."

Barent came to stand next to Danielle. "I'll get some broth for him. You see him to the forecastle and make sure he's warm."

She liked Barent. He had become an anchor for her new life for the past two days. She now shared a cabin with two sixteen-year-old girls. The situation grated her nerves for its lack of privacy. On the other hand, they seemed to take her presence in their stride. They were used to sharing everything from

CHAPTER 9

a hairbrush to a chamber pot and accepted her without batting an eye.

Being Maria Van Riebeeck's companion was still a vague concept, for she seemed to expect nothing from Danielle. Idly lying about listening to the chatter of two sisters was not an option, so Danielle had foisted herself on Barent and demanded a job in the galley. She was well accustomed to Barent's routine from her time in the hull. Every morning long before the grey of dawn, he started the cooking fire, and yesterday she was waiting for him, ready for whatever task he could throw her way.

She forced her attention back to the scene on the deck. The boatswain was not done with the old man yet. With his hands planted in his sides, he stood in front of him, legs akimbo, giving him a loud piece of his mind.

"How many times, Mattheys?" he roared. "How many times must we tell you not to dangle on the outside by yourself? And *today*, of all days."

Her heart broke when she saw how dejected the old man looked. He was sitting on his bottom, with his legs pushed out in front of him, not quite able to flatten them all the way, his bony knees protruding severely. He kept his head low, not making eye contact or offering any rebuttal.

Instinctively, she moved towards him just as Sebastiaan wrapped a heavy arm around his frail shoulders and lifted him to his feet. The burly boatswain shook his head as he watched the pair make their way to the forecastle, one strong and virile and the other nothing more than a skeleton wrapped in thin leathery skin.

Danielle made to follow the men, but the captain's voice halted her. Her stomach dropped, and she slowly turned toward him, pinning her eyes to his throat. He waited until she could bear the weight of the silence no longer and slowly looked into his still face.

Reaching out, he pushed the familiar medicine box into her hands.

"Time to earn your keep."

Chapter 10

"You don't smell like an old person," Danielle said as she pressed the mug to his lips again. There were so many things wrong with that statement that Mattheys decided to address the offending issues in order of importance.

"Why the hell would you be sniffing me?" he grumbled, his Adam's apple bobbing up and down with indignation. It had been a while since he'd felt this scandalized, and Sebastiaan's chuckle was only heightening the effect.

Danielle ignored the question. He had been surly and uncooperative ever since Sebastiaan had helped him to his mattress, and she adamantly tried to divert his attention from his helpless state.

Walking into the forecastle took all the courage she had. These were the same men who had cheered for her punishment. She could still hear the filth they had flung her way. Clutching the medicine box to her chest, she'd squared her shoulders and decided then and there that wallowing in her hurt and hiding in the galley was a fool's errand. Barent had seemed to understand that her hands needed to be busy while her mind was reeling. She felt a slight burn of embarrassment for hiding behind Barent and hanging on to his proverbial apron strings. Instead, she fixed her eyes on her destination and blocked everything else from her mind. This was her life now, and if she wished to stay sane, she needed to embrace the opportunity afforded her.

Her trepidations were unnecessary, for the men in the forecastle paid her no attention. Not for the first time did she appreciate the difference between men and women. Men seemed to live in the moment, take what it offered, and move on.

CHAPTER 10

"One more sip, come on," she urged.

"You haven't answered my question," he growled from behind the cup. Danielle looked at Matthey's's gnarly hands as they closed around the mug. Remembering how he had suffered the boatswain's wrath, her heart warmed for him, for underneath all the grumbling and snarling lurked a good man. It was written in the lines on his face, and the light in his eyes.

"Finish this broth, and I'll answer every question."

"This broth tastes funny," he said, smacking his lips.

"I've added some herbs to help you settle down." She had added a little valerian to the broth. He would be sleeping soundly in no time.

He rolled his eyes as he grabbed the cup from her hands and downed the contents in three loud gulps. The cup protested with a dull thunk as it was slammed down on the wooden floor. He looked at her with his wiry eyebrows raised. "Go on then," he challenged.

Danielle smiled and felt her cheeks redden.

"I wasn't *sniffing* you, for goodness' sake, I merely noticed that you smelled …" she searched for the appropriate description, "clean and a little bit salty."

"That is because those arseholes," he said, pointing to Sebastiaan, "let me stew in the brine for too long." Danielle looked over to Sebastiaan, assessing his reaction to the accusation, finding him utterly amused. "And I don't need settling down," Mattheys grumbled more to himself than to her.

"It doesn't matter. It's all in now." She started to get up, but his next question made her sit back down again.

"What were you calling me old for?" This time Sebastiaan's laughter roared through the cavernous space of the forecastle.

"She misspoke, you surly turd. She meant ancient."

Mattheys only shook his head and looked at her with his watery eyes. The stubborn gleam had gone and was replaced by a tinge of sadness – or was she seeing her own emotions in the old man?

"Last question, and then you can patch the lad up."

She knew he was not done teasing her yet.

"Tell me, young lady, what does an old person smell like?"

"Dusty," she said without turning a hair and hastily gathered her medicine box. This time, her response elicited a full bark of laughter from Mattheys. "Well, that's what you'll get from sticking your nose where it doesn't belong."

"Mattheys!" The warning in Sebastiaan's voice was unmistakable, but the old man ignored the rebuke, turned on his side, and closed his eyes.

The peace she felt tending to Mattheys dissipated the instant she turned to the other bed. Sebastiaan had visited her in the hull, brought her food, rescued her from being whipped, and taken her punishment. How was she supposed to face him? The best course of action would be to tend his wounds as best she could and repay her debt to him. He seemed completely unaffected by their brief history, whereas all her intentions of being aloof fled her like a swarm of gnats on a stiff breeze. Her heart was speeding up, and her hands were turning clammy, but as her discomfort rose, so did her irritation with herself. She was nothing if not sure of her skill, and that was all that was needed at this moment.

Danielle knelt next to Sebastiaan's pallet with the medicine box open at her side. Her gaze traveled across the room for no reason other than that she could not face the half-naked man idly sprawled on the thin mattress.

The forecastle was not a private affair. Neatly spaced sleeping pallets lined the walls, and a few lanterns lent a cheerful warmth to the wooden room. A long table and twin benches split the space in half. Three men were playing a game of cards a few beds away, their laughter and banter reaching her at the far end of the cabin. Another man collected empty dinner bowls from the table, balanced them in a high pile, and headed for the door.

Slowly she turned back to Sebastiaan. He was relaxed, with no unease or tension and no mention of the injury she had caused him. Their gazes locked and held. There was so much she needed to say, to ask, to apologize for. But somehow, it all clogged in her throat, and no matter how desperately she tried to force her voice past the obstacle, her words seemed stuck. Frustrated, she whipped her head down to the medicine box, her hands finding the familiar objects she needed. Plucking the herb bottles from their moorings, she yanked the stoppers away and tipped the contents into the wooden bowl; dried green leaves landed in the bottom.

How anybody could think this girl was a spy was beyond Sebastiaan's

CHAPTER 10

comprehension. Every thought and emotion she had played across her face. She was wearing a skirt instead of her signature breeches, and her fingers were rubbing the fabric together absentmindedly. Her back was ramrod straight and her legs neatly tucked beneath the fall of her skirt. Her narrow shoulders were pulled almost to her ears. She was scanning the room, most likely looking for an escape, but he was not about to let her go so easily. He hadn't seen her in two days and if he had to fake a few aches and pains to keep her at his side for a bit longer, then so be it. Her large green eyes were almost black in the room's darkness, and with pinched lips and a deep frown, she stubbornly refused to look at him. Still, he waited, simply enjoying looking at her. The lanterns on the wall gave her skin a smooth, honeyed tone. Finally, when there was nothing left for her to study, she looked at him, but the moment was over too soon, and she attacked her medicine box.

"What are you doing?" he asked, slightly concerned at the intensity with which she was mixing a concoction that he hoped was meant for his back and not to be swallowed.

She shook her head, clearly hearing the smile in his voice, but refused to look up from her work.

"Don't do that. It looks painful."

Her insides felt like they were turning to stew when her eyes snapped up, only to find him still smiling at her. The intensity of his stare stripped her of her defenses and left her feeling shaken, in desperate need of hiding. The unconfirmed but genuine knowledge that he could see past her sadness and hesitation was unsettling. Her father was the only other person who ever looked at her with that much certainty. Over the last few weeks, she had vowed never to let anyone that close to her again. Those close to her tended to disappear, leaving gaping holes in her heart, too large to fill.

Sebastiaan watched as one emotion after the other flitted through her eyes – none of them good.

"Don't hide away. Talk to me," he pushed.

"I'm not hiding away." Her words were defiant, but they lacked conviction.

"Yes, you are. When you are upset or uncomfortable, you seem to crawl into yourself. So, instead of telling me what is bothering you, why don't you tell me what you're doing."

She wondered when she had become so easy to read.

"I am mixing herbs with honey to make a paste for your wounds." Her words were clipped and more abrupt than she meant, but she was deeply grateful for the ability to speak without choking.

"Does it require violence?"

A small, hesitant smile spread across her face, her shoulders dropped, and her hands stilled. Sebastiaan turned onto his stomach without further needling her, folding his hands beneath his chin. The movement pulled on his back, and he could feel a slight trickle as some of the cuts oozed fresh blood.

Nature had bestowed a reckless amount of beauty on the man's body. Deep shadows were carved into his shoulders by the lantern's light. Following the groove of his spine, nestled between ridges of muscle to where it disappeared beneath the waistline of his pants, she swallowed thickly and forced her attention back to the task at hand. It was just another body in need of care, nothing more. It was late and an eventful day, and she hadn't had much sleep since moving into the cabin with the twins, for there could be no other explanation for this discombobulated state of mind.

The first three wounds were not as deep as the last two. She'd seen it before. Blood would coat the whip and cut deeper into the skin as it became heavier. The bottom two lashes would leave a mark that would, hopefully, fade over time. Her fingers spread the ointment over the broken skin, his muscles rippling from her touch.

"I'm sorry." She had to apologize for his injuries. Guilt over his condition mightily oppressed her conscience.

"Stop sounding like the world rests on your shoulders. It is not half as bad as it looks." His chin pressing on his hands muffled his voice.

"Still, I owe you a debt." The silence between them lingered as she finished the treatment of his wounds.

"There is a way you can make it up to me, now that I think on it," he drawled. Her hands stilled as she waited. "You could come back and tend to me every evening until my wounds no longer torment me so."

CHAPTER 10

Her face froze in a blank expression he couldn't articulate, but a slow frown began to crease between her brows, and her lips started to thin. She was flustered, and he knew he was making her nervous.

"It was a jest. You are allowed to breathe, Danielle," he said.

Oh, but the man's arrogance could rival the ocean beneath them for its vastness. She wished she had a sharp reply to lay claim to, but her traitorous mind was uncharacteristically blank, so instead, she pinched her lips, at least pretending to bite back a scathing remark.

He was dangerous and safe all at once, and she found the combination most frightening. The need to flee was paramount, and she hastily gathered her supplies and stuffed them back in the wooden box. Slamming the lid shut, she came to her feet in a near stumble.

"Blasted skirt." She was so used to wearing her breaches that she gained her feet without sparing a thought to the ample amount of fabric stuck beneath her foot.

Sebastiaan's laughter followed her through the door and onto the open deck.

* * *

Her skirt snapped around her ankles as she made her way to the quarterdeck. It was sheer luck that he was on deck when she emerged from the forecastle. He was standing in the shadows talking to one of the sailors when a movement drew his attention.

He was running out of time. He needed to kill the chit sooner rather than later. There was another of Du Bois's men on the expedition, but the other man's location was unknown to him. He rather disliked the feeling of somebody watching him. The consequences would be severe if reports were to reach Du Bois that he was dragging his feet. Also, they were bound to encounter a returning VOC ship. It would be best if he were in a position to send a report of his own, stating that the deed had been done. No, for all that was practical, his cat-and-mouse game with the girl was wasting time. He needed to end it.

The deck was unusually quiet tonight, with only a handful of men tending to the sails. He looked up. The lad in the lookout basket was vigilant but relaxed, keeping his gaze fixed on the water, not the deck below. He excused himself from his conversation and quietly followed the girl as she made her way to the companionway leading to the quarterdeck. A quick hand over her mouth and nose would ensure stealth, and a twist of the neck would end it. When her body became heavy in his arms, he would toss her over the railing, watch it disappear into the black water, and be done with it.

She ascended the stairs without a backward glance. He kept his distance. With luck, the navigator would acknowledge her presence and return his attention to his instruments, ignoring the shadow following her a few seconds later. But the air crackled with the boatswain's voice. "Stay for a while," he said.

The girl startled, her instincts sharpened instantly, judged by the tension in her shoulders, and he knew that his hopes of following her undetected onto the upper decks were dashed. He suppressed a frustrated grunt and turned away into the dimly lit passageway.

This assignment was turning into a farce, pushing him to the outer limits of his ample patience. Soon, Du Bois would realize that he couldn't run his illegal smuggling operation without him. He was the one who would always be Du Bois's shadow, sweeping his tracks clean. Making sure he could move with grace and freedom among all the other aristocrats, knowing he had Samual Henders to thank for it.

* * *

The ship at night looked like an enchanted village from a childhood fairy tale. Lanterns swayed with the waves, creating large yellow circles like giant fireflies. A single brazier glowed near the mainmast, and dark wooden structures and deep mysterious shadows were all around. A few sailors patrolled the deck, setting about the tasks to keep the small wooden world gliding smoothly across the Atlantic. Muffled voices drifted on the warm night air. Water splashed against the hull, and the canvases snapped as

CHAPTER 10

a light breeze licked through them. How quickly life could change from chaotic to tranquil. One moment she was dazed and stunned from losing her father, violently at the mercy of others, and now she was bathed in moonlight, enjoying the smell and sounds of the ocean. Mindlessly she made her way onto the empty space of the quarterdeck. A streak of light shone from underneath the stateroom's door.

An unexpected voice brought her to a halt. Her head snapped to her right, searching for the source. A large man stood next to a structure in the middle of the deck. His face was illuminated from below by a candle in the glass-covered box housing the navigational instruments. The effect was most startling. Her breath left her body in a shudder. The boatswain exuded a menace that frightened her to the marrow. She whipped around, ready to flee.

"Stay for a while," he said. There was a rough edge to his deep, baritone voice as it rumbled across the deck.

She shook her head and retreated before any sound passed over her lips.

"I need to go," she croaked and forced a swallow down her instantly dry throat.

"I said: Stay," he spoke in the same tone as before, but she sensed that his patience had drastically plummeted between his first and second command. Clearly, the man was used to barking orders and having them obeyed. She stood deathly still, barely allowing her chest to move as her breath moved through her mouth, her arms defensively clutching the wooden medicine box to her chest. A small boy appeared at her side, with a bowl of stew in one hand and a bread roll in the other. She could not see much of his features in the dark, but he smiled up at her, and when he spoke, his voice was in stark contrast to Arents.

"Barent sent you dinner. He kept it for you," the child said, holding the items in his hands out to her.

"Take Miss Danielle up to the weather deck. She can have her dinner there," the boatswain growled, but the child seemed unaffected by his gruffness.

The small body headed for the companionway. "Come on then," he called over his shoulder, and again she followed orders.

"Orion?" the boatswain called after them.

"Yeah?"

"Make sure she doesn't fall over." The child giggled as he danced up the stairs in the dark without spilling a drop of her dinner.

They reached the deck that formed the roof of the captain's cabin below. The boy stood in the center, waiting for her. She set the medicine box on the white wooden deck boards, and he placed her dinner on top.

"I can get a lantern if you want," he smiled again, teeth shining white in the moonlight.

She found herself oddly relaxed in the child's company. His beautiful, delicate, dark features and innocent confidence washed her anxiety – brought on by so many changed circumstances – away. It was a heady feeling, as if a fog lifted from her insides or, more accurately, from her soul. In a moment of light-heartedness, she remembered her favorite childhood game.

"No, thank you, I think I will dine by the *luminosity* of the moon," she said with dramatic flair, noting how he scrunched his face in confusion.

"The what?"

"The moonlight," she said quickly. "It's a game my father used to play with me when I was little. He would use big words, other times made-up silly words, and I had to guess the meaning." He just stared at her, judging the soundness of her mind. Fearing he would leave, she said, "Now it's your turn to teach me something."

Chewing his bottom lip, he thought for a bit and said, "I was named after the stars. Do you want me to show them to you?" She nodded with a mouth full of stew. Danielle sat cross-legged by her makeshift dining table, and Orion lay flat on his back next to her, his finger pointing to the constellations above. He showed her Orion's Belt and told her how ancient Egyptian gods were born from the very same stars he was named for. He recited the names of three of the brightest stars, Alnilam, Alnitak, and Mintaka, before he went on in search of Venus.

"How is it you know so much about the stars?" she asked, thoroughly enjoying his company.

"I have lessons. Cap teaches me every day," he told her proudly. "He also

CHAPTER 10

teaches me my numbers and my letters." For some reason, she found the image of the stern and staunch captain teaching a small boy endearing.

Orion turned his head sideways and looked at her before he propped himself up on one elbow. "It is also how sailors and pirates navigate their ships," he said in a low voice. He quickly scanned the deck to make sure they were alone, crooked his finger at her, and as she moved closer to him, he whispered conspiratorially. "When I grow up, I'm going to be a pirate. But it is a secret, and you're not supposed to tell."

"I won't tell," she whispered back.

"Captain said he would peel my arse if I turned pirate one day." Danielle stifled a snort of amusement at the crude statement. She studied his upturned face. His features were fine, almost feminine, beneath his mop of dark curls.

"Do you have a family?" she asked, for he could be no more than six years old and, therefore, too young to be a cabin boy. Perhaps he belonged to one of the passengers.

"Nah," came a carefree reply. "Arent bought me," he said with a tilt of his chin in the direction of the boatswain below.

"Bought you!" How appalling.

"Yeah, at a slave market, but I don't remember much. I was plenty little."

Danielle was horrified at the thought of this sweet child being sold as a slave. What happened to his mother? She had seen the state of the slaves as they were dragged from slavers docking in the Texel harbor. Many had died right there on the docks, others later in her father's surgery. The ones who survived the hellish journey were nothing more than empty husks.

"My friend is sick," he said unexpectedly. "He has scurvy." Nodding in an adult fashion. "Probably going to die."

Before she could respond, he jumped to his feet. "Gotta go. It's my bedtime," he announced and disappeared into the darkness.

"The mistress came looking for you," Elsje, the blonde twin, informed her as soon as she stepped over the doorsill. "Said that you should meet her in her cabin when you're ready."

It was still early, and the sun was merely an hour over the horizon, but Danielle had already helped Barent serve the morning oat porridge and dry biscuits and prepare the stew for lunch. She had returned to the cabin to collect empty bowls and mugs, for the twins preferred to break their fast separate from the rest of the passengers. It was a practical consideration more than a moral one, for they were slow to rise and easily distracted. By the time they were dressed and brushed, it was almost high noon. Not that they were spoiled with trunks of clothing; they simply couldn't manage to keep the first dress they put on staying on. Garments would be tossed back and forth between them, hair ribbons were swapped and squabbled over, and finally, they would settle into brushing and braiding each other's hair until their scalps were red and tender.

Danielle only possessed two sets of clothing; therefore, her choices were much more straightforward. From the first moment she had entered the cabin, they had eyed her like a pair of starving street rats, measuring her with their eyes and whipping fabrics in her direction. As of yesterday, they were openly planning a new wardrobe for her against her sternest protestations. She was convinced she would wake one morning with her hair brushed and braided.

They were a pair of natural problem solvers, and a conundrum of some sort could always be invoked in the absence of a problem.

"Do you want me to braid your hair before you go?" And there it was.

"Why? Is my hair not acceptable?" Danielle asked Leesa. Danielle felt a pang of guilt when she saw how her face fell at the harsh question. Leesa was the quieter of the two and hardly ever spoke out of turn. It would be a mistake to take Leesa's silence as innocence, for she was the brains behind their mischief.

These girls were different from what she imagined, and she often found herself delivering rather grinding remarks. Although she could see that they hurt Leesa and grated on Elsje, the girls always absorbed her words quietly.

"I must go to the governor's wife, but perhaps tomorrow?" Leesa nodded without looking her way, but Elsje gave her a smile of approval.

The following week passed in a blur of social activity. Danielle found herself exhausted from mental confusion and readjustment by the end of each day. She was not used to having lengthy conversations and no privacy. The twins

CHAPTER 10

took to her presence like ducks to water, hardly even noticing her in their already crowded lives, but sharing a cabin was a challenge for Danielle. Her only solace was when she lay on her bed, closed her eyes, and imagined herself in her old bedroom, trying to remember the sounds from the street below.

She'd quickly realized that her life in Texel was a world away from her life on the *Drommedaris*. Every morning she worked with Barent in the kitchen. He didn't talk much, but they worked in companionable silence, preparing meals for the day ahead. They were well attuned to each other. He would pass a knife before she knew she needed it. She would clean around him as he worked without once being underfoot. They cooked together, and she fed off his grunts of approval and growls of dismay. Meals became a team effort where she would taste, he would season, and all commented on the improved flavor of the ordinary meals flowing from the small galley.

When everything was cleaned and stowed away, she would go straight from the galley to the governor's cabin. Maria Van Riebeeck's only demand was that she bring a tea tray with her. The rest of the morning was absorbed by her duties as a companion to the governor's wife. Nothing, and everything, drifted through their conversation, and slowly Danielle learned what it was to engage in female tête-a-tête. When their conversation found its natural quiet moments, little Antoonie would demand her attention, and slowly something would spark their banter again.

Danielle had grown to appreciate the quiet yet strong presence of Maria. She was a mere three years older than Danielle, and despite the power of her position, she was unassuming and compassionate. As the daughter of a parish pastor, she had learned from an early age to look at life through the eyes of somebody born to serve rather than receive. Antoonie was like a fat little woodworm, slowly but persistently burrowing his way into Danielle's heart. Lately, he had crawled into her lap at nap time, falling asleep with his tiny arms around her neck and his fingers tangled in her hair while Maria spent the time writing her journal.

When he was not sleeping on her lap, he was content to play around her on the floor, amusing himself with his wooden toys. "He's quite a shy child, but he has taken to you for some reason," Maria had commented while creating one of her many charcoal drawings. Danielle reached over, tickled his foot, and was promptly rewarded with a squeal of delight.

"Oh, he's full of sunshine. Aren't you, darling?" He gave her a sparkling smile so bright she felt it glow in her stomach. It never failed to amaze her how he somehow knew when Mrs. Boom was coming down the passageway, for that brilliant smile would fade, his eyes would snap to the door, and he would scurry to his mother seconds before two firm knocks would herald her arrival.

At first, she took her luncheon with Maria and Antoonie, for the governor spent most of his day with the broad committee in the dayroom, but they were interrupted when a sailor came knocking and begged Danielle's assistance with a cut to his hand. His hand was wrapped in a rag, but the cut was deep and required several stitches.

"Take your food!" Maria had called after her as she hurriedly ushered him from the cabin, horrified by the large blood droplets on the floor.

Since then, she'd thought it prudent to have her midday meal in the forecastle, on one of the long benches next to Sebastiaan, medicine box at the ready.

The crew had claimed the afternoon as their time to be tended to. Danielle addressed everything from blisters to constipation, no ailment or complaint too minor or too old to receive attention. She was met with heavy resistance and loud discouragement when she offered to call the ship's surgeon. It was unanimously agreed that the man should only be called for the most severe cases since he was most likely occupied with his sick child. They would all prefer to brave her herbal concoctions and ointments than risk the attention of the sawbones, as he was called behind his back.

Then there was the day that a tooth had to be extracted. It was a terrible ordeal, for the tooth was so rotten that she could not get a proper hold on it with her small forceps. It kept crumbling. She had to make a small incision in the sailor's gum to push the forceps beneath the gum line and get a better hold. The poor man was screaming with pain, and his face was swollen with the poison of the rotten molar. Some people were more sensitive in their mouths than others, and clearly, he could withstand all the rigors of a sailor's

CHAPTER 10

life but not the pain of an abscessed tooth.

At her wit's end, she suggested they send for the physician when Sebastiaan came to her rescue. He had put the sailor to sleep with a deft fist to the jaw. She had quickly made the incision and forced the forceps as deep as possible to get a firm hold of the tooth, making good use of his unconscious state. But the roots were deep and the angle awkward, and she found that it required more strength than she possessed. Sebastiaan had replaced her hands with his on the forceps and pulled the tooth free. When green pus followed the extracted tooth, he had turned abruptly and left the room. Apparently, there was a limit to his robust constitution, and pus oozing from the mouth was it. The crowd that formed to witness the procedure had dissipated, but she'd gained a new level of respect among the crew.

* * *

"How are you getting on with the twins?" Maria asked. It was a beautiful morning, and the sunlight washing through the cabin's large windows made Antoonie's hair glimmer like spun gold.

Danielle was rolling fresh bandages for her medicine box. She doubted she would ever require wound dressing again with all the off-cut pieces of cloth from the twin's industry.

A soft smile curved her mouth before she answered. She looked at Maria with a defeated expression. "I think they've adopted me. They told me they don't have siblings, and I would do nicely. I don't think they see each other as a separate person."

"They are two sides of the same coin. Your wardrobe, on the other hand, shows a vast improvement." Maria looked Danielle over. She was wearing her men's shirt tucked into a skirt with an unfashionably wide waistband. "You can start a new trend once we reach the continent."

"I don't even recognize my life anymore and am forever grateful that we don't have a looking glass in our cabin, for I fear I would not recognize myself either." There was no sting in Danielle's voice. Over the last three weeks, her busy schedule and the constant company of others had melted the bitterness in her heart. She was no longer consumed by sorrow and anger.

Life aboard the *Drommedaris* was not at all dreadful. The situation aboard the other ships was quite different. Most of the soldiers were on the other ships, and according to the twins, no woman would dare go near them, let alone share a journey for months on end in their company – barbarians, the lot of them. Of the one hundred and eighty-seven souls on the *Drommedaris*, only fifteen were soldiers, and their most persistent medical emergency seemed to be foot rot. She didn't mind tending their ailments, but they often looked at her with a wicked glint in their eyes that sent chills down her spine. She was not the only one who took notice. Sebastiaan had walked into the forecastle one afternoon while she was tending two of the soldiers. He had passed a single glance over them, promptly dismissed them from the room, and ordered that if any future discomforts arose, all soldiers should seek the attention of the ship's surgeon. Danielle was stunned by his transformation as he addressed the soldiers. Gone was the ever-present good nature from his face, replaced by eyes cold and hard and lips curled in a menacing snarl. From then, she only tended the sailors, most of whom were young and knavish but never disrespectful.

"My husband informed me that a ship with friendly flags was spotted this morning. We will know more by tomorrow." Maria spoke, her focus remaining on the charcoal sketch in front of her.

"A ship returning to Holland?" Danielle asked as her stomach tensed into a tight ball. This was her chance to resume, or rather return to, her old life.

"I would assume so." There was something in Maria's eyes when she looked at Danielle, but she looked away before Danielle could discern the emotion.

Danielle excused herself from Maria's company and returned early to her cabin, only to find it in an increased state of dishevelment. The twins were chattering like monkeys, punctuating their excitement with shrill shrieks and small bounces.

Danielle navigated her way around them and made it to her bed without incident. She sat down, lifted her feet from the floor, and crossed her legs. She was going back. Home. The apothecary was gone, but their home was

CHAPTER 10

still there, waiting for her. Everything would be as they'd left it that morning. The house would need cleaning, and she'd need to fill the pantry, but it was still there. She would start again, rebuilding her apothecary supplies. It would be easy enough to run her industry from her kitchen until she could afford to rent a small space somewhere. She'd talk to Mrs. Lint and see if that extra room at the candle shop was still available. Living alone would take some getting used to, especially now that she'd grown accustomed to always having voices and noise around her.

Two sets of slim fingers were flicking in front of her face.

"Danielle, are you listening?" Elsje's annoyance was clear from how she deemed it necessary to enunciate every syllable of Danielle's name.

"I'm sorry, dearest. What were you saying?" She'd realized Elsje's high drama diffused instantly when an endearment was directed her way.

A most unladylike grunt left Elsje's throat, and Leesa sighed heavily.

"We are meeting up with a ship returning from the East," Leesa informed her.

"We've been on a ship for over a month, by my calculation. Surely another one can't be the source of this much excitement." Danielle failed to see the significance. On the other hand, many ships returning from warmer climates brought back sailors with afflictions she'd never witnessed before. There could very well be an interesting new illness aboard. She was starting to share in the excitement reigning over the twins.

"We are each allowed five bolts of fabric! Isn't it wonderful?" Elsje squealed.

"The governor said we could choose anything we like, and he would pay for it – personally," Leesa added.

"Why?" Danielle was instantly suspicious. She could only imagine that the twins were so full of mischief that the governor took to bribing them into good behavior.

"For your wardrobe, of course, and whatever else we might need. We were thinking of creating some bright-colored shirts for little Antoonie. He is such a sweet darling..." Elsje's voice trailed off as Danielle absorbed the revelation.

"No bright colors," Danielle warned. But they both looked at her with narrowed eyes, and she knew her warning was falling on deaf ears.

GOOD HOPE

"You will be the best-dressed woman in the Cape."

Chapter 11

"You are free to return to Holland tomorrow, with the *Lieffde*, if you so wish," De Coninck's eyes barely left the charts in front of him. He glanced at her as if to ascertain that she was standing in front of his desk and continued his perusal. The lanterns on the walls bathed the cabin in warm orange light.

"If I so wish?" she asked incredulously. "Do I have a choice in the matter?" She could not keep the bitterness from her voice. Her life had been in the hands of others for over a month now, and she had given up hope of ever controlling it again. She was pushed and pulled in random, nonsensical directions – like a rudderless ship on a stormy ocean. And now, to discover that she had a choice in a significant event concerning her was laughable.

"Yes." De Coninck looked up from his studies, elbows resting on the desk, his lips pursed, and his expression blank, bordering on boredom. She expected him to look down again and continue with whatever he was doing, but he held her eye, and his gaze sharpened. He had heard the edge in her voice and was not impressed.

In the pit of her stomach, she knew this was one of those defining moments in life one often looked back on and wondered: What if I had chosen the other option, or said the opposite, or nothing at all? What if I had walked away instead of staying, or vice versa? What was even more alarming was the finality of her decision and the speed with which it came. She could leave, or she could stay. Returning to Texel was her goal ever since she'd found herself stuck in the *Drommedaris'* hold.

"What if I want to stay?" she asked, her voice clear and definite. For the first time since their acquaintance, she recognized the emotion passing through his eyes. The man was surprised, and he made no effort to hide it. "That is if you would allow it," she added belatedly, experiencing the strange urge to please him.

He regarded her for a moment longer. "I don't have a say in the matter. The Van Riebeecks, not me, employ you, and this is their expedition."

Could this be why Maria was so adamant about hiring her as a companion?

"If it were up to me, you would be sent back, but now, it seems, you have a choice. I suggest you take the night to think it over. The *Lieffde* heads north in the morning."

The *Lieffde* had appeared on the horizon three days earlier, and the sweet smell of spices had reached them long before she came to rest at their port side.

"Thank you, Captain." She had slowly turned to leave when he spoke again.

"I meant what I said. Don't make a rash decision. Take the night to think it over." He paused, but she knew there was more to come. "You did not ask for my opinion, but I will give it nonetheless." She turned back to face him; he was still looking at her. De Coninck had an arresting presence. His eyes shone with intelligence, and the rigid lines of his face commanded respect. "Now is the time to be selfish. It would be decidedly wise to put your needs above anybody else's in this matter. You are young and a talented apothecary. Your future is stretching before you. Do what is in *your* best interest, disregarding all else." He spoke to her as if he cared, giving her a pang in her chest. She missed her father.

* * *

Used to rising early, Danielle lay in her bunk bed listening to the sounds of her roommates sleeping. It was Sunday morning, and Barent had declared she could behave like a girl and idle the morning away without being needed in the galley. The Boom twins had accepted her into their lives without hesitation. The three of them shared a small cabin, a space constantly cluttered with clothing, hair ribbons, and pieces of fabric in varying stages of becoming a

CHAPTER 11

garment. Since she had only a pair of male pants and a shirt to her name, she became the perfect outlet for their combined creativity. They spent their days altering some of their dresses to fit her and fashioning undergarments for her from what, she suspected, were bedsheets. The results were fetching, if not a little unorthodox. Regardless, their talents were undeniable, and she was now the proud owner of two skirts, a petticoat, one and a half shirt – and nowhere to store it. There was precious little room in the cabin, but ten bolts of fabric now occupied the remaining space as of yesterday. The twins announced they were a much-needed addition to the room since they were more beautiful than any masterpiece done by Michelangelo himself.

A sneeze erupted from the bunk above her. With a wistful smile, Danielle accepted that the quiet – and private – part of her day was now over.

* * *

"Antoonie, darling, slow down," Danielle called to the toddler as his small arms snapped out to break his near fall. He was running across the weather deck with alarming speed. The sunlight danced off his wheat-colored hair, and his cheeks were full and flushed. Maria was nervous about letting him play outside, with his skin being so fair and his health so unpredictable. It was also the first time she had been separated from him since boarding the ship, an idea that appealed bittersweetly to the young mother. Danielle had fallen in love with the toddler from the moment he had reached for her from his mother's hip, and their bond had only grown stronger with each passing day.

Leesa was trying to hem a skirt when Antoonie sat next to her. "How am I supposed to do this chore when you are sitting on the fabric, sir?" she asked in mock annoyance while staring the toddler down. He responded by throwing a large section of the garment over his head, effectively winning the argument. Leaving them to their negotiations, Danielle made her way to the railing overlooking the goings-on on the upper deck below.

The *Lieffde* was making her way back to Holland from Batavia, heavy with spices and silk. She must be carrying more than just spices, judging by the number of culverins on deck. She lay so low in the water that her lower gunports were almost awash.

Today, the two ships would part ways, the *Drommedaris* continuing south, and the *Lieffde* heading home. Yesterday in the captain's cabin, her instincts had overruled her reasoning, but she had taken his advice and spent the night in contemplation.

Home meant more than just a cozy little townhouse with herbs growing in the garden. Home was also where she was deemed unsuitable company by most of her peers. Over the years, she had led a peaceful existence, but it would be foolish to think it would continue now that her father was no longer there to protect her. She was a talented apothecary, but how long before she made a mistake, misdiagnosed somebody, or prescribed the wrong treatment? All it would take was a whisper from one of the women in town, and she would be labeled a witch. Gossip spread like wildfire in a small village like Oudeschild, and the truth mattered little if the story was sensational enough. There were rumors already, and only by the grace of her father and his influence had it not escalated. Without protection, she would be at the mercy of an unsympathetic community already predisposed to believe the worst of her.

At first, she'd thought that if her life continued down the last month's track, she would not survive to see another Christmas. If she were to return to Texel, she would be lucky to make it to the end of summer.

"Thinking of joining them?" Leesa asked, reading her thoughts. Danielle released a deep breath and pressed her back against the railing. Shaking her head slightly from side to side, she had thought about returning with the *Lieffde*. But to what end? For some inexplicable reason, she felt safe here, with these people. It had been a month since her near flogging, and it was as if it had never happened. She was unsure how much of that she could accredit to Sebastiaan's intervention. Their friendship had grown, and her acceptance among the crew with it. If she were to leave now, she would be alone again. Despite having no earthly possessions or family, a feeling of belonging had settled over her. She effectively dismissed the notion of returning to Texel without further thought.

CHAPTER 11

Leesa seemed to understand in her quiet way, and a soft smile warmed her face as she tilted it up to Danielle. "Good."

Danielle looked out over the decks below. Her eyes settled on the two captains as they clasped hands. Captain De Coninck was a complex man. He had frightened her at first, but he was fair and strong, and the resemblance to his nephew made a little knot turn in her stomach – the same broad shoulders and golden hair. Sebastiaan had been avoiding her since the *Lieffde* had appeared on the horizon, or perhaps he was unusually busy. Still, he was not there when she visited Mattheys, nor did he come looking for her at the end of his shift.

He was never far, for how could he be in a world as small as theirs? Danielle often saw him high up on the rigging, helping the sailmaker tend the ropes or bent over hammering at the deck, undoubtedly filling in for Mattheys. However, for the most part, he did not take note of her comings and goings, and it nettled her far more than she was willing to admit.

Instantly annoyed with the direction of her thoughts, she tore her eyes away from the captains. Near the upper deck railing, Mister Coopman was throwing a parcel to another man on the *Lieffde*, who deftly caught it mid-air. The man nodded and touched the brim of his hat with his free hand before turning away – letters, among them her affidavit, detailing the murder of her father – justice. Her mouth set in a hard line at the thought, and she scanned the deck until a familiar figure captured her gaze. Sebastiaan was leaning against the mainmast, hands in his pockets, feet crossed at the ankles, staring up at her with an unfamiliar expression on his face. She could not look away for all the will she possessed, but the trance broke when he smiled, turned, and disappeared into the forecastle.

A moment later, he returned and bounded up the companionway towards her, taking the steps three at a time. Antoonie was still playing with the multitude of fabric covering Leesa's legs, and Danielle turned her back to them and met Sebastiaan at the top of the stairs.

"What? Did you suddenly remember that you hadn't spoken a word to me in two days?" she asked, and there was a notable edge to her voice.

He looked down at her annoyed face, fighting the desire to touch her;

instead, he held out his hand.

"I meant to give it back the first evening you tended Mattheys, but then you sprinted from the room so fast, robbing me of the opportunity." Always teasing her.

She looked at his outstretched hand; in it lay her small knife. Behind her, the *Lieffde* was creaking as she pushed away from the *Drommedaris*, and below, the two crews were trading insults and laughter one last time.

"You could have given it back many times since." She reached out and closed her hand around the familiar bone handle. Her father had carved it to fit her hand perfectly. She flicked the blade with the pad of her thumb. Sebastiaan must have sharpened it.

"I forgot, and then, when I thought you might return with the *Lieffde*, I decided to keep it." His eyes were dancing with laughter as he watched her.

"Why?" Her question came on a breath.

"Something to remember you by," he said with a shy smile, one she'd not seen before, and in that unguarded moment, he looked self-conscious, almost unsure of himself. She found the revelation unexpectedly pleasing, but her triumph was fleeting, for he gave her a wink and jumped down to the deck below with indiscreet sure-footedness.

"Infuriating creature," she muttered while tucking the knife into her waistband. Then she turned to pull Antoonie from the tent he made with Leesa's sewing.

"Not a word," Danielle spoke with the authority of an older sister.

"You could do a lot worse," Leesa said, impudently ignoring the silent threat.

"I'm not going to do anything."

"Of course not, dear." Leesa gave her a sweet smile while tying off a piece of thread.

Danielle contemplated all manner of violent acts towards the younger girl while gently rubbing Antoonie's back as he lay his head on her shoulder. Squinting her eyes against the brilliance of the sun-sparkled water, she watched the *Lieffde* grow smaller. This was what it felt like to have friends, or perhaps even sisters. It was exhilarating and frustrating all at the same time.

"Too far to swim," Leesa said in her soothing low voice, eerily reading

CHAPTER 11

Danielle's thoughts.

"Without a doubt," Danielle agreed but kept her eyes on the water. Antoonie had gone heavy in her arms, and his small warm breath feathered across her neck.

"Any regrets?" Leesa asked.

"No." Danielle took a deep breath of ocean air and waited for Leesa as she gathered her supplies, and then, they slowly descended the stairs and strolled into the dark passageway.

Chapter 12

One could easily mistake the weather deck of the *Drommedaris* for a Turkish bazaar had it not been that almost every piece of cloth or clothing was white or as close to white as possible. Several lines ran from every conceivable structure, and over it slapped and danced under- and outer garments, bedclothes, and baby clouts. Every female hand on deck, except for the surgeon's wife, had been doing laundry since the crack of dawn. The days were hot and humid this close to the equator, with afternoon showers on most days. The women depended on today's rain, for they needed the fresh water to soften the laundry on the lines.

The women were grouped around three large tubs, all filled with seawater. The first had a curb board for washing, and the next two were for rinsing. It was an exercise in futility, for the soap did not take well to the saltwater. Instead of lathering, it floated on top like clabber.

"This will never dry," Elsje complained. Anything rinsed in saltwater took forever to dry, and once it did, the salt in the fabrics would soak up any hint of moisture in the air and turn the garment damp again.

"Let's pray the afternoon shower will rid it of most of the salt," Mrs. Boom's reply came from where she stood bent over the tub of insincere soapy water.

"Do you not have an herb or a droplet of oil we can add to the soap next time to improve the smell a bit?" She had tied her hair back with a handkerchief and another wrapped over her mouth and nose, one arm resting on her knee for support and the other rubbing a shirt vigorously up and down the scrub board. "Ever since I got pregnant with the girls, I can't stand the smell. It sticks to the back of my throat."

CHAPTER 12

"I have no idea how to make soap. We used to buy ours from a lady down at the docks," Danielle replied. She and Elsje were wringing the garments from the second rinsing tub and hanging them over the lines. "Why don't you let me do the washing then? We can swap tasks."

"No, my sweet, if you do this, your hands will be as rough as one of them sailors. You'll scrape the skins clean off poor Antoonie's bottom when you change his clout."

"Or Sebastiaan's face," Elsje chimed in a voice meant to be secretive, but hardly was.

"What?" Danielle protested before thinking better of it, her cheeks instantly flaming.

Elsje was a perennial pest, and nobody was safe from her sharp eyes and wicked humor.

"Oh, don't tell me the two of you have not laid a finger on each other. What with all the time you've spent together over the last few weeks?"

"Leave off, Elsje," her mother chastised. Danielle reflected on the truth of Elsje's observation with a small, rueful smile. She gave Elsje a leer through her slitted eyes and caught the end of a bed sheet as it flicked towards her, and the dance continued; she twisted to the left and Elsje to the right.

"Do you think they are murdering that beautiful cat down there?" Elsje asked when another ear-splitting squeal came from the cabin below. "Sounds bloody painful."

"Elsje – language," her mother's warning came instinctive and with a tone of defeat that made Danielle smile.

"*Bloody* is not a curse word, Mother. I might add that it is merely an accurate description of the state of affairs. Who knows what foul fate has befallen that poor feline?"

"To answer your question: soap is mainly just water, fat, and lye." Mrs. Boom wisely switched to the previous topic, knowing full well that to continue with Elsje was only to fuel her mischief. "It's the lye that stinks so." Her nose wrinkled as she spoke.

Danielle remembered that her father had bought her rose-scented soap once, but it was just ordinary soap with dried rose petals. It looked beautiful, but the lye scent was still strong. "I could try to infuse the fat with some herbs or flowers before you add it to the soap mixture next time." She took the other end of a bedsheet and twisted again, sending small rivulets of water running across the deck.

"Do you intend to make soap here on the ship?" Maria asked as she took a shirt from Mrs. Boom and submerged it in the murky rinsing water.

"Oh no, Mistress," Mrs. Boom sounded alarmed at the thought. "It is a task requiring one to be on stable and solid ground. The lye would eat a hole in the floor if we were to spill it accidentally. No, we'll do it once we set foot on land again." Mrs. Boom looked up just in time to spot little Antoonie dipping his arms over the rim of an out-of-the-way pile filled with bloody bedsheets and clothes.

"No, my angel, don't touch that. Leesa, put that book down and rescue Master Van Riebeeck." The woman was used to organizing others while holding a completely unrelated topic of conversation, all in the same tone of voice.

"I'm taking Antoonie inside. His cheeks are turning red from the sun." Leesa scooped the baby up and headed for the stairs.

Mrs. Boom discreetly pushed the lone cloth-covered pile to the side. The water was dark with pus and blood. She had collected the week-old garments from the surgeon's cabin the evening before. The child's mother had lost all sense of time. Her every waking moment was spent next to her son, holding his hand and laying cool rags on his forehead.

Danielle often saw the surgeon's wife standing at the stern railing at night, the wind folding her nightdress around her skeleton-thin body. Her boy was in the last stages of the illness. His feet and legs were completely black, and his gums never stopped bleeding. The scurvy was so far gone that there was nothing to be done for the child, except wait. The surgeon had forbidden anybody to come close to him or his wife, in fear of spreading the disease, even though it was a well-known fact that scurvy was not contagious. The man's gruff manner did not leave much room for debate or common sense.

Sebastiaan had also warned her to keep her distance when she mentioned that she would like to visit the child.

CHAPTER 12

"I know you mean well, but it will end badly," he had said with no small amount of sympathy. "The surgeon is a father and a husband, and the hopelessness of his circumstance makes him unreasonable."

"A circumstance of his own doing," she had argued. "Scurvy can easily be prevented with a proper diet. Look at the sailors, all healthy."

"Yes, and that is because my uncle threatens them with the whip if they don't eat their sauerkraut every day, a notion put in his head by your father." He gave her a pointed look. "Not all ships operate in this manner, and not all physicians and surgeons are as wise as your father." He had spoken as if her father was still alive.

Maria got up and walked over to the bucket with the sick child's clothes and bedding. She removed the cloth, closed her eyes, and turned her head away, forcefully swallowing the bile in her throat as the fetid smell of putrefaction rose above the tang of the lye.

"No, Mistress, don't," Mrs. Boom protested as she rose to her feet to pull the governor's wife away from the foul-smelling water.

Maria refused to be distracted. "Please let me. It is the only thing I can do for her," she said as she tied a handkerchief around her mouth and nose. Then she knelt next to the bucket and attacked the grim task with fierce determination, scrubbing as if to wash the sickness away, splashing brown water onto the deck and the bottom half of her white apron.

"Does anyone know the surgeon's wife's name?" Danielle asked.

"It's Gertrude," Maria answered, "her family is from West Prussia."

Maria had the gift of stillness and infallible memory. People trusted her instinctively and were often moved to share intimate details of their lives with her. Details such as where they came from, their deepest fears and insecurities, their grandmother's ailments – all of it, and she treasured every bit of information, tucking it away in her mind, never forgetting, judging, or repeating. Danielle herself had fallen under Maria's spell, and they spent many hours talking about their families and their backgrounds, sharing their joys and their pains. Much of the peace she experienced now, after her father's death, was due to Maria's solid presence in her life.

"Miss Van Aard," the captain's deep voice reached them from the deck below.

From his tone, she detected the undeniable evidence of a storm brewing. Danielle dumped the heavy dripping blanket she had just lifted from the water, unceremoniously and without warning, in Elsje's arms and ran for the stairs.

Reaching him in a few swift strides, she noticed his nostrils flared slightly, and his blue eyes flashed with something that made her wish she had come to a stop a little earlier. He had the look of a man very shy of patience this morning.

"Captain?"

"Your father played the violin?" He made it sound like an accusation. She frowned up at him, nonplussed.

"Yes?"

"And am I correct in assuming that he passed that skill to you?" The man was mad. That is the only explanation she could muster. They had been on water rations for a week now. Could it have affected him this badly? She resisted the urge to raise her hand to his forehead to test the temperature. Surely there must be some brandy somewhere to soothe whatever ailed him.

"Yes?"

"Good. Get in there." He said with a jerk of his head towards the stateroom. She saw him clenching his fists by his sides and wondered if he was fighting the need to manhandle her into his cabin.

Danielle stepped over the sill and entered the captain's living quarters. It was immaculate as usual, with a soft lingering scent of sandalwood. Sunlight danced across the desk and on the floor where Orion was sitting, cross-legged. The boy clutched a violin to his breastbone with one hand and strangled a bow with the other. He was chewing his bottom lip while sporting a fierce frown between the two black slashes of his eyebrows. It looked like somebody had violently stabbed the child with the round end of the instrument and left him to pull it free himself.

"Master Orion," Danielle greeted him formally, "what are you doing?"

"Playing the violin. Cap says it's a bit scratchy, but he can definitely hear something coming along."

She slowly turned to give the captain a wide-eyed look. But she found

CHAPTER 12

nothing save the inside of the cabin door and the man's receding footsteps on the other side, as he undoubtedly sauntered across the deck and as far away from the cabin as his physical environment would allow.

"Ah," she said as understanding dawned. "Where's the cat?"

"Dunno, haven't seen him today," the boy replied without looking up from his chest. Staring at his tense little body, she had a fleeting vision of a dashing, violin-playing pirate, and the image made her giggle. Orion's head snapped up, and she saw a shadow of hurt and defiance in his eyes.

She softly smiled at him and shook her head, apologizing wordlessly for her small but inappropriate outburst.

"May I have a look at that?" she said, pointing to the instrument. The smell and feel of the instrument instantly transported her to their small house, with its warm cozy kitchen and her father's violin a permanent feature on the dining table. It felt like years since she had last touched the smooth curves of a violin, though it was little more than a month ago.

In the evenings, she would cook, and he would play some bawdy song he had heard in the tavern over lunch, and then after dinner, he would teach it to her. She had him roaring with laughter as she added more notes than were necessary or tried to turn the song into her version of an Italian masterpiece, complete with facial expressions and body twists.

"Can you play?" Orion asked hopefully.

She looked at him sideways and smiled wickedly. "On occasion."

"Can you teach me?" he asked with a face too severe for his age.

"I can try. I've never taught anybody anything before, so lower your expectations. This is going to take some time." She was trying to lighten the mood, but his eyes were fixed on the instrument.

"You need to teach me a sad tune."

She gave him a concerned look. "What is the matter? Why do you want to learn a sad tune?"

"For when they tip him in the drink." She frowned and tried to make sense of the odd statement.

"I don't underst-"

"When Raphael dies," he interrupted her. "They're going to wrap him in his blanket and tip him overboard." He speared her with his almost black eyes, making sure she understood. "And then I want to play him a song, so he knows I am sad." A lump formed instantly in her throat, and her eyes burned. She raised her eyebrows as high as she could, to stretch the tears away, and swallowed until the lump subsided. She understood.

"I know a song that is..." she cleared her throat and continued, "appropriate. But there might not be enough time for you to learn it."

"Then you'll play it," he said with absolute finality, leaving no room for arguments.

***

"I have a leak in my ceiling."

"You know, I've been suspecting that for years." Setting the tar and oakum aside, Sebastiaan gave his uncle a deadpan stare, face patently bland.

The captain smacked his lips in annoyance. "I walked into that one." He scanned the deck out of habit and released a sigh as deep as the south-easterly itself. The tension left his body in a wave.

"I *am* going to miss you." The statement was heavy with emotion, and Sebastiaan felt it in his gut.

"This is the only life I know," he said, a little embarrassed for sounding like a twelve-year-old boy begging to stay.

"It's time for a new one."

Sebastiaan knew the truth of it, but he loved this life. The crew was as good as his family. He had a place here. He loved sailing and the solitude of the ocean, but there was more to consider now. His uncle sank down on his haunches and stared at the gap in the deck, half-filled with tar-soaked oakum.

"I'm not sure it is one I want," Sebastiaan said as he stared at the same gap and wondered if the tar was enough to fix the stateroom ceiling or if he would have to get more. The faint plucks of a violin tuning reached them, and they both turned their heads toward the sound. Yes, definitely more to consider.

"You don't have a choice, lad." His uncle placed his hand on his bent knee and pushed himself to his feet with a grunt, suddenly sounding much older

CHAPTER 12

than his forty-three years.

***

She did not go looking for him on purpose. It had been a wonderful day filled with laughter, and with the sun dipping behind the wrung-out clouds of the afternoon, she'd hoped it would end on a happy note as well.

She ascended the stairs to the weather deck, as she had done most evenings, when she heard the rhythmic tapping of the carpenter, set on his repairing task. Mattheys was different after his dip in the ocean. He was quieter and took to his duties with more vigor than before. The old man was desperate to prove his worth, though she doubted anyone else was questioning it. She reached the top rung to find Sebastiaan's broad back instead of Matthey's weathered coat-hanger frame.

He was laying tar-soaked oakum into the grooves between the floorboards, gently hammering it deeper with the caulking hammer and a chisel. Danielle smiled as she remembered the fuss Mattheys made when she'd first referred to the tool as a strange skinny thing. It was a beautiful tool made from hard dark wood with metal fastenings.

He stopped and half-turned, giving her a crooked smile. She returned his smile and went to stand by the railing, leaving him to his work.

The ocean looked like a painting done by an artist deep in his cups; the colors were confusing and mesmerizing. Ever since she could remember, her father had taken her for a swim in the ocean every year on the first of March, rain, shine, or snow. It was his way of celebrating the end of winter and the beginning of spring. She thought it was rather him, stubbornly thumbing his nose at the cold.

The ritual had strict rules. One had to go in one's underwear and could only leave the water once completely submerged. At first, Danielle had just lain down in the ankle-deep water and waited for small waves to cover her. With age came wisdom and the realization that speed was the key. She changed tactics; instead of waiting for the water to cover her, she charged at it in a dead run, knees high and ridiculous, until the water reached her chest. Then she dropped to the bottom and felt her heart stop as the icy water closed over her head. After that, it was a shambles of numb limbs and squeals until her feet could remember how to run again, and she would bolt for the folded blankets they left on the dry sand.

She closed her eyes and felt the warmth of the gunwale beneath her hands. Inhaling deeply and smelling the sweet scent of the wild grasses in the air, she released her breath and dropped her shoulders.

"My nose is playing tricks on me. I thought I smelled sweet grass, but it must be the scent of the oakum," she said as she turned to face Sebastiaan.

"It's not a trick, and it's not the oakum," he said without looking up from his task. "The African coast is not far, and the wind is blowing from that direction this evening."

"I'm going to miss this." She waved her hand, indicating everything and nothing in particular. "Perhaps not the water rations, but the ocean. She is so beautiful when she's not angry."

He put his tools aside, the floor effectively watertight again, and came to stand beside her. Close enough for her to feel his warmth radiating through his shirt, but not touching.

"No more leaks?"

"No more soap scum on the captain's precious maps," he said with raised eyebrows.

"No!" She'd thought that Orion's violin practice was to blame for the captain's black mood. She'd never considered the laundering.

He chuckled and turned to face the water. They stood side by side, facing in opposite directions.

"I'm going to miss this too," he said, a strange heaviness weighing on the statement. "This is to be my last voyage." She heard the regret in his voice, and something uncomfortable lodged in her heart. She was getting used to the rhythm aboard the ship and was comfortable in the day-to-day order of things, never allowing herself to think ahead or back, just the here and now. There was safety in that. No matter what happened elsewhere, here, the same people would be doing the same things. Lukas will mend the sails, Mattheys will paint something, Barent will cook, Sebastiaan will always be everywhere, smelling like the ocean, and one day when she must leave this small world, it will continue to exist. She would think back, and it would still be there, somewhere.

Sebastiaan saw the uncertainty and confusion followed closely by sadness playing across her face. She was getting upset and was letting her mind run ahead of her.

"What do you mean?" she asked. "You're not leaving, are you?"

"Well, yes, I am." He turned to sit down against the bulwark and pulled her with him. "It is a bit of a long story. If you are interested?" Rolling his head in her direction.

"When does your shift start?"

"Six o'clock tomorrow morning," he replied.

"Then we have time."

He started at the beginning: on the night his mother died, leaving her husband with their young boy, lost and shattered. She contracted scarlet fever, and a week later, she was dead.

His father dealt with the shock of her death as he did with most things. He removed all feelings, wrote the necessary letters, and arranged a simple but elegant funeral. However, after the practical matters were taken care of, he could not face his emotions and instead tried to drown them. A neighbor came twice a week with food. Another had sent a servant girl to clean and tend the laundry, but no one sent a mother to care for, or manage, a miserable twelve-year-old boy. Abel had pushed his son away, for he could not look at the child without seeing his wife staring back at him.

Days turned to weeks, and his father drifted further into his own darkness. One evening, he had called Sebastiaan down from his room. The boy was thin and unkempt, his hair knotted and his clothes stale. There was a resolute set to his father's mouth as he ordered the child to get his shoes; they were going to the docks to meet his uncle.

Sebastiaan had heard many tales about his mysterious uncle, who sailed the seas and was never in one place long enough to settle or visit. It was well after dark when they boarded the large merchant vessel. *Eendragt*, Unity, was proudly written in gold letters on the side. A young boy met them on deck and ushered them into the captain's cabin, where a man came around a heavy desk to meet them. He looked like an angel, tall and broad-shouldered with hair that glimmered like gold in the lantern light. Sebastiaan took a step behind his father, but the man reached around and offered him his hand. His uncle's grip was firm but gentle as the fingers wrapped around his small, bony hand, and he smelled of clean ocean air and something else.

"Sandalwood," Danielle said softly, and Sebastiaan almost jumped at the sound of her voice.

"Yes, sandalwood," he smiled with a puff of air through his nose. He would never forget that smell; it smelled of adventure, unlike his father, who had a constant tang of stale alcohol about him. Abel De Vries was drowning in his sorrow but was clear-headed enough to realize that he could not drag his child down with him. He had decided to hand him over to his wife's brother.

The captain had pointed to two chairs in front of his desk, but his father had declined. Abel had spoken only a few gruff words conveying his wishes and then left without warning or a fare-thee-well. Sebastiaan had watched him go, understanding that any life was better than the one his father was living, and so he had accepted his fate.

That first night he felt safe and scared at the same time. He was at the mercy of a familiar stranger whom he did not know but who looked so much like his mother – same eyes, same hair color, same shape of the face, different mouth. After his father left, he was given a plate of food and told to eat everything, followed by a bath in cold water. His uncle then set about to comb his hair, and since his father had forgotten his things, he was dressed in an oversized linen shirt with the sleeves rolled up in thick bundles that kept dipping over his hands. He was given a sleeping pallet in front of the desk, and he fell asleep to the sound of his uncle's deep voice as he read the ship's manifest and contents of the cargo hold.

"What became of your father?" Danielle asked, hypnotized by the rasp of his voice. She wondered if he had ever spoken these words before. He stared across the deck, reliving it, not seeing anything but the past.

"He eventually left Holland and settled in Batavia."

Abel could not face life in a place filled with the memories of his wife, and

CHAPTER 12

as soon as he could, he moved to Batavia. Within months, he had settled and started the beginnings of a vast and successful merchant network with tentacles reaching as far as Japan.

"Do you see him often?" He would visit Batavia at least once a year by her calculation, if not more. But he only shook his head slowly.

"No." The word was no more than a whisper but heavy with guilt.

His father had written many times. Every few months, there would be a letter from him, telling of all the new things he was doing, about the new house, the staff, the exotic places, talking to his son like he was still twelve years old. There was always a letter on his birthday, and one for Christmas a month later.

Sebastiaan read them all and slowly became less and less interested in the news. He enjoyed his new life; he had friends, a purpose, and freedom from uncomfortable emotions. However, his uncle was a constant thorn in his side, making sure he never forgot his mother and not allowing him to harden his heart against his father. But not once did he force him to enter a life for which he was not ready.

"No," he repeated in a more substantial tone. "I went to see him for the first time when I was about fifteen."

The three years at sea had changed him from a small and bony boy into a young lad whose face and body held the promise of the man he would become.

It was the *Drommedaris'* maiden voyage, and she had encountered a fierce storm that left them limping into the Batavian harbor crippled and desperate for repairs. With time on his hands, Sebastiaan decided on an impulse to visit his father. Everything in Batavia was either square or straight, with trees standing in painfully straight lines and precision gardens surrounding large houses.

His father's mansion was nestled deep within its tropical garden, away from the street and close to the canal. Sebastiaan followed the path through the garden and imagined that this was what the garden of Eden looked like, minus the water features, of course. Birds with long colorful tails swooped low between the trees, and monkeys curiously eyed him from high branches as he made his way to the heavy double front door. The air was thick enough to chew, and he could hear the heat buzzing. His palms were sweaty, and the brass knocker slipped from his hand and landed with a dull thud against the door.

A butler, more Indian-looking than Malay, dressed in a white tunic that reached beneath his knees, followed by wide, white pants and a pair of purple silk slippers with upturned noses, answered the door. Sebastiaan was given a quick once over and informed that servants used the back door.

"My name is Sebastiaan De Vries. I came to see my father." He had spoken with the same tone of authority his uncle frequently used on deck, all the while thanking his stars that his voice had not suffered one of those random cracks. If the toplofty butler was surprised by the announcement, he did not show it, but stepped aside and motioned Sebastiaan in.

"Wait here," he said and pointed to an exact spot on the foyer's black and white tile floor, then turned and marched down a wide hall with Sebastiaan on his heels. The now thoroughly peeved butler stopped midway, turned in the same manner somebody with a neck injury would, and gave him a questioning look, to which Sebastiaan replied with a one-shoulder shrug. Wisely the butler held his tongue and continued down the hall, the prodigal son in tow.

They reached a solid-looking door to what Sebastiaan imagined was the study. The butler gave a single knock and leaned his shoulder to push it open. Sebastiaan brushed past him before his presence could be announced. The door closed behind him, and he noted that the study was the size of a VOC ship's upper deck. What he saw next brought him to a dead stop. It was his father; that much was clear. He still had the look of a man sure of his worth. His almost black hair was completely white now, and he was thinner, with deep lines marking his face. The man looked up from his correspondence, regarding the prominent sailor's dress of the young man standing in the middle of his study, and then pure joy washed over the blank stare on his face. He leaped from his chair, toppling it over, and they met in the middle of the room.

Sebastiaan stuck out his hand for a shake, but his father closed the distance

CHAPTER 12

between them and wrapped his arms around his son. The embrace was awkward and stiff, and it lasted too long. His father smelled of leather, tobacco, and something foreign, like one of the flowers in the garden whose scent lingered, but you can't pinpoint the source.

"Are my eyes deceiving me?" He shook his head as if to clear it, unshed tears glimmering on the edges of his eyelids. He held the boy at arm's length.

"You look so much like your –"

"Uncle. Yes, I get that a lot." Sebastiaan was being an arse, but he could not bear to talk about his mother. Instead, he scanned the room, searching for something; he was not sure what, perhaps signs of another woman. Instead, everything was hard and purposeful: dark wood, leather coverings, deep-colored rugs, lamps to aid a task rather than enhance a mood, stacks of papers, maps, and books.

His father gestured to two couches and called for tea and something to eat. Eating was perhaps a good idea, for suddenly, Sebastiaan had nothing to say, and neither did his father. He opened his mouth several times, sharply inhaled as if to say something, then thought better of it and let the breath out again. They sat facing each other with tea, custard tarts, and the ghost of his mother between them.

Abel De Vries was looking at the young man sitting across from him. It was a joy and a shock to see his son. He drank the image of him in, not missing a single detail. The child he had left on the ship that dark night had changed into a fine young man. His roughly trimmed, boyish blond curls starkly contrasted with the premature muscles that corded his arms. There were calluses on his hands, and a few faint white scars proudly marked the sun-browned skin. His eyes were bright and intelligent as he scanned the room, and there was an almost arrogant set to his shoulders, or perhaps it was the uncomfortable silence that affected his posture. His mother would have been so proud. He felt the need to apologize or explain, but that would mean talking about his wife, clearly a taboo topic for now.

The shock of seeing each other had sucked the conversation right out of them both, and Sebastiaan could feel his tongue sticking to the roof of his mouth. He reached for the cup of tea, but his finger was too big to fit through the ear, so he grabbed it over the top and tipped the contents down his throat. It was a smite too hot, but at least his tongue was free to move again. He tested the mechanics with a few clicking sounds. To say that he was uncomfortable under his father's penetrating stare was an enormous understatement. The man was inspecting him like a botanist who had recently discovered a new species of insect.

He had expected to feel some level of anger upon seeing his father. It was not clear why he would feel anger, but it was an emotion that he could understand. What he felt instead was a mixture of relief and concern. The last memory of his father was not pleasant, and he was relieved at the state he now found him in, but there was a fragility to him that Sebastiaan did not think was there before. Sebastiaan was planning on spending three weeks with his father but decided, then and there, those thirty minutes were all he could muster; the silence was killing him. His father recovered first and latched on to the only thought that popped into his mind – the weather.

"It is quite a bit warmer here than in Holland," he remarked with a small clearing of his throat, simultaneously pointing to the large window at the opposite end of the room.

"That it is," Sebastiaan agreed, and with that, the conversation fell into a stop-start pattern. Soon, they had depleted the tea, tarts, and most topics suitable for making small talk. They had discussed the weather, their health, and the lack of clearly distinguishable seasons in this part of the world, which inadvertently led them back to the weather again.

One would repeat a question, and the other would politely pretend not to notice. Sebastiaan decided that it was time to end the tense visit. It wasn't anybody's fault. They were just too different and too disconnected. He got his feet under him, rose, and was ready to take his leave when he heard the familiar booming voice of his uncle harassing the butler.

"I don't take orders from a man wearing a dress, Poppet. Stand aside." And with that, the door to the study burst open, and Davit De Coninck entered. The tension in the room shattered, and his father and uncle embraced like brothers.

They stayed for three weeks.

CHAPTER 12

"Things got better between my father and me. Eventually, we started to talk again, but staying was not an option, and after three weeks, I left with my uncle. I saw him as often as possible, but we mostly communicated through letters. We're better that way."

There was a long silence between them. The air was still heavy with things that needed to be said, but Danielle did not want to push him. He startled her when he gained his feet in a sudden movement.

"Wait here," he said as he stood and left, returning promptly with a lantern and a letter, handing Danielle the latter. The paper was heavy, and the words were visible through the stain made by the dark red wax seal.

"Read it."

Sebastiaan sat beside her again as she slid her finger underneath the seal and unfolded the parchment. The handwriting was beautiful and confident, with an artistic flair.

August 13, A.D. 1651

To Mr Sebastiaan De Vries, VOC Merchant Fluyt Drommedaris

From Mr Abel De Vries

My Darling Son, Sebastiaan,

I hope with all my Heart that this Letter finds you well and reaches you before, or on your Birthday, and so wishing you once again a Blessed Birthday. As you well know, it is always hot here, so not much has changed on the front of our favorite topic – the Weather.

However, I am afraid to report that my Health has taken a turn for the worse. The pain has spread to most of my Insides, and the Physicians are at a loss. I am prescribed laudanum, but it dulls my senses, and I found that in the twilight of my life, I prefer my Wits to be sharp.

My deepest Wish, and I refuse to believe it would be my last, is to see your Face and hold your Hand again. I've built an Empire, and would like for the effort to mean something, and therefore I wish to pass it to you with all its Intricacies and Secrets explained and revealed. My Son, what you do with it afterward is up to you. You surely have no obligation to me, for I have failed you as a Father for most of your life.

I must admit, dying has its advantages. I will be with your mother soon, something I almost wish for, but for the need to see you once more before I go.

I am Proud of the man you've become and fear not at all for your future. So, I will wait.

Until we see each other again.

Your loving father,

Abel De Vries

She folded the letter back on its creases and held it between her fingers.

"He'd been ill for some years. I did not think it was that serious." Sebastiaan looked at her then, and Danielle saw guilt, chased by regret, flash across his face. He swallowed hard a couple of times.

"Did you reply?" she asked, worried for a moment that he didn't.

"Yes, I promised him that I would come. I owe him that much."

"That's good. Will you take over his businesses?" She tried to picture him in anything other than sailor's slops and open-neck shirts with the sun on his face and the wind in his hair.

"Yes."

Such a simple answer. Sebastiaan reached out and took her hand. The gesture made her breath catch in her throat. His hand was dry, and the skin was rough. She thought she detected a slight tremor running from him to her as his fingers tightened.

"I want..." He stopped midway, swallowed, and stared at her. The light from the lantern played on his face and chest. She could feel the groove between her eyebrows deepen as she waited, leaving her hand where it was.

"I want you to come to Batavia with me," he said, measuring each word as if he was weighing it on a scale. He needed to be careful. If he were to succeed in the next few moments, what he was about to do would have to be a practical consideration rather than an emotional one, and he would not allow her time to pull it to pieces. If he revealed the true depth of his emotions for her too soon, her mind would balk against the notion.

She searched his face, but he wasn't giving anything away. The impact of what he was saying was hitting her from top to bottom in single file. Her eyes

CHAPTER 12

went wide, her mouth dry, her throat thick, and her stomach jumped. She was relieved to note that her legs remained unaffected.

"How would that work?" she asked because the inevitable was happening, and she was somewhat unprepared. Her future was taking shape, her life was gaining direction, and she was not ready. It was too soon, and too unexpected.

The woman was nothing if not practical; he smiled at the thought.

"We both need to start new lives, and it would be easier if we do it together. Don't you agree?" Sebastiaan did not wait for her response, and she was grateful for it.

"I also want you to meet my father, and I want him to meet you," he reached out and took hold of Danielle's other hand as well. The letter dropped in her lap. His face was as serious as she'd ever seen it, with no trace of humor or teasing.

"I want us to marry. You will never need for anything, and you'll be safe. You can even have an apothecary again if that is your wish." He was speaking in measured tones; the words were coming with an air of anxiety. He had clearly thought about this matter before. However, she felt that the moment and the delivery came as a surprise to both.

"You want to marry *me*?" She heard him clearly enough but needed confirmation and to buy herself a little time.

"Yes." He punctuated the acknowledgment with a nod. It made her smile. She tried to pull her hands back, but he refused to release them.

"And you want me to give you an answer now?" He considered her question, then looked from side to side, ensuring there was nothing else for her to do.

"Yes."

A marriage to Sebastiaan was not a bad idea, one she had not considered before, but not a bad idea at all. She felt the beginnings of a smile pull at the corners of her mouth. Then she nodded slowly, slit her eyes, and looked at him like an artist considering a canvas before making the first brush stroke.

"Fine," she said in a business-like tone that suggested the parties can now hawk, spit and shake on the new deal. Sebastiaan pulled her close and kissed her. The kiss lasted longer than he had hoped for, but shorter than he wished. At the feel of her trembling, he released her slowly.

He noted that she was slightly out of breath and a little flushed. She looked at him, her face completely still, and for a nerve-wracking moment, he could not see what she was thinking. She would be his, and a wave of smug victory welled in his chest. She had kissed him back but was by no means swept away or off her feet, and he suppressed his smugness with a violent effort.

"Regretting your decision already?" he spoke somewhat hoarsely, not sure he wanted the answer.

"No, but I always thought I would marry for love," she said and smiled wistfully. "You know – every little girl's fantasy," she added with a noncommittal wave of her hand.

"We can have that. We're not there yet, but we'll get there." A soft, quick breath escaped her nose, and one corner of her mouth lifted as if pulled by an invisible line, then relaxed and fell back into place. Sebastiaan stood and reached a hand to her. He pulled her to her feet, and they both turned to look out over the ocean. She hooked her arm through his and rested her head against his shoulder. He closed his eyes and said a silent prayer of thanks.

He had made her a simple promise, and the confidence and absolute certainty with which he said it made something take hold in the pit of her stomach, something new, something precious. Absentmindedly, she placed her free hand on her belly. He had given her hope.

Chapter 13

She woke to a firm hand on her shoulder, shaking her urgently. Turning over, she found the governor's face above hers. Startled, she shot up from her pillow, almost bumping her forehead into his chin. He retreated and placed his pointer finger against his lips in a sign of silence; she nodded in understanding.

"Come quick, it's Antoonie," he whispered and turned to exit the cramped cabin. Danielle grabbed the blanket from her bed, wrapped it around her shoulders, reached for her medicine box, and followed the governor into the passageway. There was no light to navigate by, but she could see his form hurrying ahead of her. He reached his cabin door and held it for her to enter. Soft, warm light from several lit candles washed into the dark space, and the faint ring of the bell on the upper deck announced that it was four o'clock.

The baby's body was hot and draped limply over his mother's shoulder, his arms loosely circling her neck. Maria was staring at their reflection in the black window, rocking him gently from side to side, patting her own arm instead of his back where the skin was too sensitive with the heat of the fever. Danielle saw the chapped lips and the raw tear marks on his cheeks. He was sleeping.

Maria turned to Danielle. "You're here, thank God." Her voice was hushed but heavy with worry.

"What is the matter?" Danielle asked.

"Antoonie has a terrible fever. He woke before midnight and only just stopped crying. Danielle, this is different than before."

Danielle laid the back of her hand against the baby's firm, round cheek and then his brow; he was burning up. He was half-naked, wearing only a fresh clout.

When he opened his eyes at the sound of their voices, they were unfocused and slicked over. Danielle spoke a few endearments to him, but she could see he was not hearing her.

"Do you know what to do?" Maria asked urgently, her arms tightening underneath his buttocks as she felt him waking up.

"I can make a tea to help relieve the fever and ease the pain."

Danielle had often made this tea, but for adults, not babies. She worried briefly over the strength but dismissed the concern and rushed towards the galley. Maria asked something, but Danielle did not stay to listen; she needed to stoke the fire, boil the water, and steep the tea. It all would take time they did not have.

Once in the galley, she found the candles in the box next to the flint. It took her twice as long to light it – damn her trembling hands. Barent had prepared the galley stove the evening before; the stones were scrubbed clean, and the sand evenly spread. A triangle of wood was sitting patiently in the middle, waiting to start the morning cooking. She thanked him silently for his foresight and lit the fire. Hanging a small pot on the hook above the fire, she added two cups of fresh water, willow bark, and a few more dried herbs. While the water took its time boiling, she filled a bowl with fresh water, grabbed a few clean rags from the shelf, and headed back to the governor's cabin.

Maria had laid Antoonie on the bed and was sitting next to him. Her knees and feet held close together. One hand rested on his chest; the other was clenched in a tight fist in her lap. Danielle could see Antoonie's eyes move beneath the lids, and his head thrashed from side to side as he battled whatever demon his innocent, fever-soaked mind was conjuring up.

"Keep touching him," Danielle said. "My father told me you need an anchor when trapped in a fever nightmare." Placing a cool, wet cloth on his forehead, she handed Maria another to sponge his body. His skin was so red she feared it would come off if they touched him too often, but he seemed to settle somewhat as the coolness spread over him.

CHAPTER 13

Danielle rushed back to the galley for the tea and returned to find Antoonie awake and very agitated. His bloodshot eyes were turning slowly in their sockets, and she knew his head must be pounding. When she forced his mouth open, his tongue was dry and swollen, and his throat was raw and inflamed; it would hurt to swallow. His breath was hot against her face. She dipped the tip of the cloth in the tea and dribbled a few drops into his mouth. The warm, bitter water ran down his throat, and he swallowed instinctively; more followed. He gave a hoarse pleading cry, and a few precious drops of the tea escaped his mouth.

"We need to get more tea into him," Danielle said anxiously, "this way is too slow."

Maria lifted the child onto her lap and pressed his back to her chest. He was fighting her. The pressure of her fingers on his sensitive skin made him thrash wildly to fend off the touch. She wrapped her arm across his front, effectively restraining him. His cries had lost most of their sound, resulting in open-mouth heaves. The sight and sound of his little body suffering shattered Danielle's heart, but she lifted the cup to his cracked lips and tilted it slowly.

At the increased amount of liquid in his mouth, his legs started to pump in earnest. He shook his head, and the cup dislodged from her hand, spilling most of the tea onto his mother's lap. Danielle took hold of his chin and tilted his head slightly back, pouring a small sip into his mouth again, cooing soft endearments. Another small sip followed, and she waited for him to swallow, then repeated the procedure. What she was doing to him felt like torture. He was so small and helpless, but, in the end, he had drunk half a cup of the medicine. Danielle sighed deeply to dislodge some of the tension coiled in her belly and sat back on her heels.

Antoonie's thrashing ceased for a moment before his skin gained a pale green tinge and his breath caught in his throat. Danielle raised onto her knees, reaching her hand towards him, when a foul, sour-smelling burst of light green liquid erupted from his mouth. He screamed as the stomach acids burned his throat and cracked lips, making gurgling noises as he choked on the remaining vomit in his mouth.

"Tilt him forward," she called to Maria and frantically tried to wipe his mouth out with the tea-soaked cloth. His coughing fit ceased, and his mother held him upright again, giving him another sip of tea. He was done taking medicine. His head furiously jerked from side to side, and she knew if she tried to control him, she would bruise his face.

The vomit had hit Danielle high on her chest, just above her nightgown's neckline, and was dripping down between her breasts; she rubbed the fabric over the spot to stop the tickling.

Maria eased the baby back onto the bed and, at Danielle's suggestion, turned him on his side to prevent him from choking should he succumb to another attack. He seemed to have calmed a little after the violent episode. Positioning him again, Danielle dripped the liquid into his mouth once more. This time, he managed a few swallows without incident and promptly fell asleep.

There was a sour tang in the air. Antoonie was making mewling sounds in his sleep, but the cool cloth on his head and his mother's hand on his chest kept him calm.

"He seems better," Maria said, looking up at her husband, who sat behind his desk. In all the commotion, they had entirely forgotten about Jan. The governor was disheveled and pale. Gripping the sides of his face, he watched the bed with a horrified, helpless expression. His eyes glowed like coals with the force of his emotions. Closing them for a moment, he struggled to gain his composure.

Danielle touched Antoonie's clammy skin. He was not better, but not worse either, which gave her hope.

"What are you thinking?" Maria asked as she looked into Danielle's troubled eyes.

"You should get some rest. You're exhausted," she replied, sidestepping the question. Maria had dark circles under her eyes, and between her and her husband, Danielle could not decide who looked the worst.

Antoonie's short reprieve was over. His body started to shiver as another wave of fever washed through him.

"Shall we cover him with a blanket?" Maria asked. Fresh beads of sweat formed on his forehead, and the glands in his armpits were swollen; his skin was once more heating up.

CHAPTER 13

"No, he's too hot."

Maria had removed his sodden clout and placed a dry one under his hips but did not fasten it, for his skin was too raw from the chafing. Danielle sponged his chest, round belly, and down the little legs with a fresh, cool cloth. Water was running in small streams down his sides, soaking the bedding. The shivering did not subside, and he woke with a cry for his mother. Maria scooped his naked body up and clutched him to her. The short nap had revived him enough to scream with all his might.

Unable to sit still any longer, Maria started to pace the cabin, gently bouncing him in her arms while softly speaking to him. The fever doggedly refused to release its hold on the tiny body. Antoonie's skin was scolding hot, and his eyes were losing focus. His father jumped from his chair and reached his arms out to his son, but Maria only shook her head and continued her soft endearments. She stood with her back to her husband so that he could look into his son's eyes. He placed his hand on the sweat-soaked hair and stepped forward to kiss his baby's cheek.

The two events had nothing to do with each other, but Antoonie's body went rigid in his mother's arms as his father's lips touched his face. His eyes fluttered and rolled back in his head. His arms and legs jerked violently, and a stream of feces squirted from his bottom, over his mother's arms, and onto the floor. Instinctively she tightened her hold on him. Jan retreated in shock, and Danielle jumped to her feet and reached for Antoonie. His body was slippery, and his mother was losing her grip on him.

"Let go," she urged as she pried Maria's arms away from him, "we need to lay him down."

She placed the child on the bed. The seizure was ravaging the little body. Drool and blood ran down the sides of his mouth as he clenched his jaw. His small, sharp teeth were biting into his tongue and the sides of his mouth; the burning inside his body was getting worse, and his skin was turning a deathly pale color.

The seizure lasted too long; something was terribly wrong. Danielle heard an unusual commotion outside the door, fast-moving feet, muffled voices, but then she focused again on the shaking child, unable to do anything other than watch.

Maria had turned to her husband, and he clutched her to him. They were both staring hopelessly at their child, praying soundlessly for deliverance, moving only their lips with silent, helpless tears streaming down their faces.

They had lost track of time, but Danielle guessed it must be midmorning. Nothing bad ever happens in the morning; she firmly believed in that. Babies were usually born at night; her mother and father had both died at night, and most criminals set about their deeds at night. She couldn't think of anybody she knew who had died in the morning. Besides, children often get seizures from fever, but they also seem to recover from it; she had seen it before.

The seizure slowly released its grip on Antoonie. His exhausted body relaxed against the bedding. Color started to creep back into his face, and his breathing was less ragged. Maria gasped, and she and her husband moved closer to the bed. Danielle reached for the artery in his neck; the pulse was uneven but strong under her fingertips. She turned and smiled at the worried parents and stepped aside to make room for them.

Jan lifted his son in his arms and held him close to his chest, relief radiating from his face. The baby's body was relaxed and peaceful. Maria's shoulders slumped as a sob left her. She took his angelic face in her hands and kissed his forehead, nose, cheeks, and wet hair. Antoonie opened his beautiful blue eyes, gave his mother a brilliant smile, and released a deep breath before going limp in his father's arms, his head slumping onto Jan's shoulder.

There was a moment of confused silence. Jan looked to his wife. She called the boy's name, but there was no reaction. Reaching over, she shook him by his narrow shoulders, but still nothing. Danielle felt her throat close, and she swallowed fiercely.

"God, help me," she prayed, unsure if she said the words aloud, while reaching over to search for a pulse.

"Did he lose consciousness?" Maria's head snapped in Danielle's direction.

Danielle searched for the throbbing but could not find it. She licked her finger and held it under his nose – nothing. Kneeling, she pressed her head to his chest but couldn't hear any sound or feel any vibration from his beating heart. His head was limp against his father's chest, his eyes half open and sightless, and his small jaw hung slack. Danielle felt herself sink to the floor, shaking her head, unable to look at her friend.

A primitive scream tore from Maria's throat, a gut-wrenching roar a mother hoped only to give once – when the child was born. She flung herself onto her baby's body, and her husband closed his arms around them both. His shoulders were shaking as the sobs tore through him. A numbness washed over Danielle as she watched the scene; they needed privacy. She pushed to her feet and quietly left the cabin.

* * *

It was the woman's gait that caught his attention. Arent was standing at the whip staff, talking to Niklas, when he saw Danielle stumble up the stairs and onto the weather deck. He excused himself and followed her.

He found her hanging over the back of the ship. She was filthy and struggled to breathe.

"What happened?" his voice was rough with concern.

Turning to face him, she licked her lips and tried to speak twice before she could manage to attach sound to the words.

"Antoonie is dead." It was the first time she had spoken the words out loud, and the force of it took the last strength from her legs.

Arent saw her knees buckle and quickly stepped forward, taking hold of her elbows; he kept her upright.

"Who?" The surgeon's child had passed away a few hours ago. Could she be mistaken?

"The governor's baby," she explained.

"Yes, I know who he is. When?" he asked, trying to clear his confusion.

She lifted her face to his but stared right through him with a haunted look. Her breathing was coming in short, shallow fits. She struggled to produce an answer, but Arent drew his conclusions from the fresh stains on her nightgown.

When? It felt like hours ago, yet she could still feel his soft little hand if she closed her fingers. Shaking her head, she tried to clear it, but something was wrong. She was hot on the inside and cold on the outside; drawing breath into her tight chest was a struggle, and her racing heart made her dizzy.

"Breathe," Arent said while holding her stare. He could see how she was trying to force her breath and failing.

"Relax your shoulders. Now, take a long, slow breath through your nose." She did, and he could feel the strength return to her body.

This was not a woman given to hysterics. He had seen her sew a gaping wound on the cook's hand that had made his stomach roil while holding a perfectly normal conversation on how to bake a souffle. However, she was close to losing control now. Arent had no idea how to console a woman in distress, but he knew how to keep men on their feet amidst despair.

"Danielle," he said firmly, having never used her name before, and this, coupled with the slight shake of his hands, made her eyes focus on him. "You can fall apart later. Right now, she needs you." He did not have to clarify who *she* was.

"Come," he said as he started in the direction of the stairs, not letting go of her elbow but adjusting his pace to accommodate her stumbling feet, "you need to wash and eat."

"What time is it?"

"It's almost noon," he answered.

He led her to the cabin she shared with the twins. Only Leesa was inside. The girl was pale, and her eyes were red-rimmed. He paused at the door and turned Danielle to face him.

"I have to go," he said, his concerned eyes scanning her face.

Danielle wanted to thank him but couldn't manage it. Instead, she quietly turned away from him.

* * *

Time had stopped for Maria. Still sitting on the bed, she held Antoonie in her arms. His body was limp and heavy, and his head rested on her shoulder. She rubbed his back in circles, murmuring and singing while rocking him gently. Her other hand cupped his round, soft bottom. Slowly she lowered him into a sitting position on her lap. His head dropped to the side, and she nestled it back against her shoulder. The scorching heat had left his body a while ago. He felt so cold now; finding a blanket, she spread it one-handed over them.

Mrs. Boom had come to take him, but somebody had stepped in and taken her away; it was a man – not her husband. Her husband … Somebody had come and taken him away as well. Someone else had come to clean the floor and removed all evidence of the battle fought and lost. The cabin was clean and tidy and too quiet. A person was in there with her, but she did not care to take her eyes off her child. Her baby looked so peaceful. His beautiful tiny mouth was slightly blue, but it would be better soon; the blanket would help. His eyelashes rested gently on his pale round cheeks. The color of his skin was so much better than the purple-red of the fever. The light played with his hair, and the curls seemed to dance.

"Maria." A voice spoke from somewhere underwater; she ignored it. Only when soft, warm hands touched her arms did she look up.

"Let me take him," Danielle said softly.

"No."

"It is time."

"No."

"He won't remain this beautiful. Let me wrap him. I promise I will give him back to you."

Danielle walked to the door, opened it at a tight angle, and murmured to somebody on the other side. Moments later, Sebastiaan entered with warm water for washing, followed by Barent carrying a tea tray.

When the men left, Danielle turned to Maria. She pushed her arms gently under Antoonie's flaccid body and slowly lifted him from his mother's lap.

"You need to wash," she told Maria as she lay him on the bed. Maria rummaged through a chest against the wall. Danielle washed the small body, and then she dressed him in the warm clothes his mother had placed next to him. Bending over, she kissed him on the forehead before wrapping him in a bedsheet from head to toe, covering his face. Finally, she took the blanket from his bed and gave him a final layer against the cold.

Maria was clean and dressed when Danielle pushed her down into her husband's chair and then lay the body of her child in her arms.

"Where is your comb?" she asked while scanning the desk.

"I don't know," Maria replied, her hair hanging in damp clumps down the sides of her face. Danielle found the engraved ivory comb underneath pieces of parchment and set about arranging Maria's hair in a low chignon.

Sebastiaan had found Danielle earlier on her way to the governor's cabin after Arent had left her to Leesa's tender mercies. Sebastiaan was pale but composed as he relayed the day's events. Raphael had passed away around ten o'clock that morning. The surgeon and his wife had barricaded themselves in their cabin, but Mrs. Boom had made her way inside and was tending to the distraught parents. The captain had taken the governor to his cabin, and Arent was with Orion, preparing the boards and ropes for the funerals.

"Mrs. Boom had tried to prepare the baby earlier," he said, tilting his head toward the door, "but it seemed to upset Mistress Van Riebeeck more, so I took her away." She only nodded as she listened to his report. "I've asked one of the twins to help clean the cabin." He was worried – she could see it on his face as he held the door to the governor's cabin for her. Touching his arm briefly, she felt his strength, and it fortified her.

"I'll be right outside if you need me."

"Thank you," she said, and he closed the door softly behind her.

Looking down at Maria's neat blond hair, she knew there was nothing left to do, save wait. She did not know what exactly they were waiting for; her world seemed to contract to this tiny space, and it was difficult to imagine that life was continuing elsewhere.

The bell chimed six times, and the door to the cabin opened. Governor Van Riebeeck took a few tentative steps towards his desk and then stopped, his eyes riveted on the wrapped bundle in his wife's arms. Danielle came around the desk and placed her hand lightly on his shoulder. He smelled like soap and brandy, and his hair was a little damp.

Psalm 23

The Lord is my shepherd, I shall not want.
He makes me lie down in green pastures,

CHAPTER 13

He leadeth me beside the still waters.

He restores my soul. He leadeth me in the paths of righteousness for His name's sake.

Yea, though I walk through the valley of the shadow of death, I will fear no evil, for Thou art with me, Thy rod and thy staff thy comfort me.

Thou preparest a table before me in the presence of mine enemies, Thou anointest my head with oil, my cup runneth over.

Surely goodness and mercy shall follow me all the days of my life, and I will dwell in the house of the LORD for ever.

Orion knew the Psalm by heart; it was his favorite. Perhaps that's why the captain was reading it. It had to be for him because Raphael couldn't hear anymore, and Antoonie was too little anyways.

The captain's voice was a steady baritone as he read the passage from the Bible. He finished, looked up, and scanned the deck. Finding Orion next to Arent, he slowly closed the large, weathered book and bent his head.

"I want to stand by Raphael," Orion whispered to Arent.

"Shh," the big man softly hissed while shaking his head.

Orion fidgeted restlessly with the hem of his shirt. Arent bent down and took the small hand into his.

A somber quiet descended on the deck, and there was a ruffling of bodies. Davit De Coninck stood for a moment in silence, and when he spoke, his breath caught on the simple prayer.

"O Lord, we submit these children to your care and eternal love. Bless us and keep us. Amen."

"Amen," the congregation whispered.

"I didn't get to say goodbye. I want to see him," Orion spoke without pause, and his voice gained volume as he realized that the proceedings were moving ahead and nobody was hearing him. *Why was everybody just standing there?* He looked to the surgeon and his wife for help, but they looked like ghosts floating above the deck, so distant, and he was suddenly afraid of them. The governor and his wife stood near the captain; they were very still and silent. They didn't seem to hear or see anything.

"Orion," there was a warning tone to Arent's whisper.

Danielle noticed the exchange and picked up the violin, ignoring the slight shake of her hands.

"Orion, come stand by me, and we'll play for him," she said as she nudged the violin under her chin.

She sank down beside him on one knee and whispered in his ear, "Do you want to play for him?"

He looked at her, and his eyes were two big black pools, "I don't know any songs." He sounded defeated.

Everybody was witnessing the display. Danielle could feel their eyes on her back, but she did not care.

"You know two notes, remember? We practiced them yesterday."

Arent was shifting his feet, signaling his discomfort. Danielle looked up and shook her head discreetly. She had lost her fear of him somewhere between noon and sunset.

"No, you play it," the boy said as he pulled his hand from the boatswain's and reached for something in his pocket. It was a pebble. With a determined look on his face, daring anybody to stop him, he walked to his friend's body. Kneeling on both knees he placed the small offering on Raphael's chest.

The slow notes of the violin lamented through the assemblage as the two children were lowered into the water. Orion pushed between the sailors, but he could not see over the deck's railing; his head only reached the top, even if he stretched onto his toes. Then, strong hands lifted him onto a barrel, the captain came to stand next to him, and they watched as the black water closed over the children.

Sebastiaan was standing to Danielle's right, solid and quiet. The feeling that she was sinking was gaining momentum from deep within her body. As the last notes died away on the breeze, she felt his hand tighten around her elbow, and he pulled her away.

Maria's eyes were riveted to the spot where her child had disappeared. The scent of him was still warm in her nose. An unwelcome but inevitable image penetrated her mind: his tiny body alone on the ocean floor, swaying from side to side with the force of the water. Her husband quietly slid a blanket

CHAPTER 13

around her shoulders, too stunned to comfort his wife beyond that. It was well past dark, and the *Drommedaris* had silently sailed on.

Two children had died today. Two children without graves.

* * *

At midnight, a lone figure walked down the passageway. Her bare feet glided soundlessly on the wooden floorboards as she ascended the stairs to the weather deck. The low-lying mist silenced and darkened the night. Small droplets clung to her hair and the skin on her face. Reaching the stern railing, she hoisted herself up and, with a swish of her nightgown, dropped into the invisible water below.

Chapter 14

It had been hours since the funeral, and a mist had settled over the ocean, effectively muffling the sounds of the sailors and fracturing the light of the lanterns. Maria returned to her cabin to find her husband behind his desk, staring at a closed ledger, his hands folded in his lap, his shoulders slumped under the weight of the cross he bore. She stared at him, waiting for any tangible emotion to register, but nothing came. Chewing the inside of her lip, she wondered what to do now. She looked around the cabin with an apathetic expression. A single candle flickered on the nightstand, for her benefit, not his. Everything was familiar, but nothing looked the same. Her eyes scanned the room and its contents without a hint of interest until they reached the foot of the bed. Her gaze narrowed, and she felt the first stirrings of emotion creeping up from the base of her spine.

"Where is it?" There was sand in her voice; she cleared her throat and tried again.

Her husband turned his head, and they stared at the same void.

"It's better this way," he whispered.

"Better?" She spat the word as if it were rotten in her mouth. "How can anything ever be better again? I want it back. I want his bed back where it belongs."

Jan only shook his head. This was his doing; she knew it. She would pound him until he restored her child's crib to its place. The force of her fury moved her feet before her mind had time to intervene.

He saw the precise moment his wife's grief broke her and gained his feet in time to receive the first blows to his chest. He welcomed her anger and let

CHAPTER 14

it wash over him, hoping the impact of her small fists would make him feel something. Finally, he lifted his arms and crushed her to him.

Smothered in the folds of his shirt, Maria felt her husband's arms close around her, and every single wall she had ever constructed throughout her entire life shattered, and she wept.

* * *

Danielle felt the pressure on her throat, slowly cutting the air to her lungs. Her body was heavy as it floated on the water. Antoonie's small plump hand slid from hers. Her eyes snapped open, and her mind sharpened as sleep receded. Danielle lifted her hand to her neck. There was nothing, only the heavy blanket resting against her skin. She swallowed a few times. Her body felt cold, and her skin cried out against the spreading gooseflesh. Somehow, the air still struggled to find its way to her lungs. Pushing the blankets aside, she freed herself from the bed. Once on her feet, it felt like the walls were closing in, and the darkness of the cabin became a suffocating mass. Dressed only in her chemise, she fled the room. Her feet seemed to have a destination in mind, for she headed for the galley without giving it much thought.

Her breathing came in short, belabored bursts, sounding ragged and feral. She opened the hatch to the hull and stumbled down the ladder. Scanning the familiar interior, she saw the chickens in their wire cage, the goats in the pen, dark shapes bulging in the dark, and then she found the stack of sails. Only when she was deeply tucked into her old lodgings, her back firmly wedged into a corner, did her breathing quiet down.

Antoonie, that beautiful baby, was gone. Had it only been twenty-four hours? It felt like many days, with so much happening. She remembered the funeral, how she worried over her lack of tears. After Sebastiaan had left her at her cabin, she'd gone straight to bed and had fallen into a deep sleep, plagued by strange dreams. Even now, the tears refused to come, but it made sense, for she'd cried so much after her father's death that she doubted she had any left to shed.

Earlier, she'd noticed an odd sensation swirling in her stomach, but she'd ignored it. That same emotion was still slithering inside her, forcing heat and sweat to the surface of her skin. Scalding, brutal, vicious rage flooded her body with the force of a freak wave. Her heart was racing, and the noise of the blood boiling in her veins hissed in her ears. A roar, raw and primal, escaped her mouth while her fist connected with the wooden side of the hull. Only after the initial froth of her anger was dispelled, like the warning blows of a volcano, did she let her head rest against the sails and close her eyes, surrendering to oblivion.

She woke to two worried, cry-swollen faces. Leesa and Elsje were staring at her from the foot of her small cave.

"Danielle?" Leesa asked, sitting down and reaching a hand to her.

Danielle ignored the hand and closed her eyes, hoping the girls would be gone when she opened them again.

"Danielle, dearest, come back to the cabin. It's so cold down here." Elsje had a pleading tone to her voice, and fresh tears brimmed her lower eyelids, making her look like a daisy in the morning dew.

"Leave." Danielle's voice sounded like an old crone's, scratchy and tired. Her anger was visceral and not at all under control, and she feared that she might do someone violence in her current state. She did not want their company.

"We'll sit with you until you're ready to come with us," Elsje tried again.

"Leave! Or as God is my witness, I will strangle you both," Danielle screamed, and her reaction was so bestial that the twins recoiled in shock. The harsh words broke the dam inside Elsje, and tears streamed down her face. Leesa wrapped a protective arm around her sister and led her to the ladder.

Danielle felt tired to her bones. All she wanted was to be left alone so that she could live inside her memories.

Once more, she closed her eyes, and once more, he was there, wrapping his soft, warm little arms around her neck and laying his head on her shoulder. She inhaled deeply and tasted the honey scent of his soft golden hair.

"Oh baby," she sobbed quietly and clutched her knees to her chest. He was not even her child, but she loved him deeply. She'd only known him for a month, but he would forever be a part of her heart. With his wet smile,

CHAPTER 14

sparkling eyes, and garbled words, he filled the space in her soul left by her father's death. He had saved her life, and she had failed him. She could not save him when he had needed her most; she was not strong enough to keep death from wrapping its cold, hard claws around him and dragging him away.

"I'm so sorry, my love," she whispered to the little boy. He ran towards her, the sun bouncing off his golden curls and his smile sparkling with mischief. She caught him to her, and together they spun around, bubbles of laughter floating in the air.

Danielle drifted amongst memories. At times she was with Antoonie, and other times she was back in Oudeschild, in the surgery, talking to her father. Sometimes she heard the sound of her own voice. She did not want to lose the few precious memories; it was all she had left. Her mind was slowly losing its grip on reality. It was so much safer and better to stay with Antoonie and watch him play on the cabin floor, listening to his giggles and feeling his soft fingers playing with hers. She was vaguely aware of movement around her, but she paid no attention to it, for it threatened to intrude on the images playing in her head.

She did not recognize Sebastiaan's worried voice when he called her name and spoke soothing words to her. Nor did she feel his arms when he wrapped her in warm blankets. The food Barent placed at the edge of her hideout remained untouched.

"Danielle." A harsh, unwelcome voice penetrated the fog of her dreams, reaching out to her from another world. She pushed it away and kept her eyes shut, blocking whoever was trying to talk to her, clinging to the images floating through her brain like autumn leaves on a breeze.

"Danielle, wake up now." The voice was more urgent and very annoying. It also scared Antoonie, for he drifted further away the louder the voice became. The voice kept talking, and he was almost completely gone, his image fading.

"No, come back," Danielle called to him, but he was gone, and all that was left was darkness. She opened her eyes and had to blink several times before they could adjust to the harsh light of the lantern that was rudely swaying in front of her face.

"Go away," she spoke to the faceless voice behind the light.

GOOD HOPE

"I will most certainly not," Mrs. Boom's stern and unyielding voice reached her, "and if you don't crawl from that hole you've wedged yourself in, I will drag you out by your feet."

The lantern was moved to the side and replaced by Mrs. Boom's round face. She looked rather cross. *Well, good for you*, Danielle thought unkindly as she rolled her eyes at the older woman and remained with her back firmly pressed to the hull.

"Danielle, it's been two days. You've not eaten a crumb or drunk a droplet of water. It is only by the grace of God that you have not frozen to death. But perhaps you should thank that kind boy for that." Mrs. Boom spoke without taking a breath while hefting her skirts and trying to mount the stack of sails, firmly set to make good on her threat.

Danielle looked down at her body. A thick blanket was wrapped around her, and another lay at her feet.

"Come now," Mrs. Boom spoke again.

Danielle was startled when she felt a firm hand close around her ankle. The hand was strong and warm. It felt like it was pulling her from the depths of the ocean. She wanted to follow the hand but did not want to leave Antoonie.

"No," she protested, trying to resist, pulling back. "No, I can't leave him." But Mrs. Boom had both hands on her ankle and pulled with all her might. The woman was admirably persistent, and the situation was becoming ridiculous. Danielle pushed away from the wall and stumbled forward, and the next moment she found herself pressed against a large soft bosom and plump motherly arms wrapped around her shoulders.

Mrs. Boom was making the strangest sounds. Raw sobs tore from her, and her body was shaking. Danielle felt a hand rubbing up and down her back and somebody speaking soft words in her ear. Slowly her mind found its rhythm again. It was not Mrs. Boom crying; it was her, and it was the force of her sobs that was shaking the older woman's body.

"That's the way of it. Let it all out," Mrs. Boom murmured.

Danielle had never known what it felt like to be loved and cared for by a mother until that moment. Mrs. Boom was always in a hurry, arranging and rearranging the world around them, but now she was still and patient,

CHAPTER 14

absorbing Danielle's torment and weathering the storm with her.

Long after her tears had stopped flowing, Mrs. Boom's arms were still around her, stroking her hair and back, forcing life into Danielle's body. Gently, Danielle dislodged herself from the comforting circle. The need to crawl back into the darkness was powerful. Mrs. Boom must have sensed the direction of her thoughts, for she spoke once more with the authority of an army commander.

"No, none of that. Come along." And with that, she started to wiggle backward the way she came, for the space was too narrow for her to turn around and make a graceful exit. Under any other circumstances, the scene would have been amusing, but there was no room for levity in her life, not now, not ever.

Mrs. Boom landed with a dull thud on the hull floor and barked at the open hatch, "You can bring it down."

Danielle had shuffled towards the lantern's glow and was sitting with her bare legs dangling over the edge of the stack of sails, her chemise bunched around her thighs.

Sebastiaan appeared with a bucket of steaming water. He placed it near the lantern, his face contorted with concern as he did a quick scan of her body. She tried to smile at him, but it felt more like a grimace. He gave Mrs. Boom a beseeching look, to which she only nodded, and then he left again. Danielle did not understand the silent conversation that passed between them.

Mrs. Boom stepped closer, took hold of the chemise, and gently lifted it over Danielle's head. She obeyed like a small child, raising her arms and letting the light cotton garment slide from her body. Then Mrs. Boom took hold of her wrist and tugged her towards the pail of steaming water.

"Not exactly as comfortable as a bath, but if it were good enough for the governor's wife, it should be good enough for you. Now, step in," she ordered.

Maria. The thought hit Danielle like a blow to the face. She'd been so diligent in nursing her own agony that she'd not spared a thought for Maria. Guilt gnawed at the fringes of her tired mind, but she pushed it away and stepped into the warm water, naked as the day she was born and not caring.

Mrs. Boom rubbed the soap industriously across the cotton rag in her hand.

Danielle looked down at the dark water with the dried-up soap bubbles; it reminded her of the surgeon's child's stinking blood- and pus-soaked garments. The memory caught her by surprise, and she turned, bent over, and retched. The only consequence was a burning throat and a bitter taste in her mouth. Danielle's body shook uncontrollably, wracked by nausea and lack of food.

"Hold onto me," Mrs. Boom instructed and took Danielle's hand, placed it on her shoulder, bent down again, and washed and dried her body as if she was a small child.

"I'm not leaving," Danielle said. Now that she was clean and warm, her anger was returning.

"None of us are leaving, dear."

"I'm not leaving the hull." Danielle knew Mrs. Boom misunderstood her on purpose. Her statement gained no response. She should thank her and be grateful for the tenderness she showed her, but her lips remained shut. Again, her heart was slowly filling with guilt, but her mind refused to embrace it just yet. If Danielle thought Mrs. Boom would give her the fight she so desperately needed, she was dead wrong.

"I understand the loss of a child, my dear. Even though Antoonie was not yours, the two of you shared a deep connection." She looked at Danielle, and there was no scorn in her eyes, no judgment, only tired understanding. "Your grief is understandable, but you are not a child anymore; you must do as you see fit." Mrs. Boom scooped the discarded clothes up, gathered the soap and rags, and headed for the ladder.

Danielle was speechless. She had counted on Mrs. Boom to be a staunch opponent, never accepting opposition, and fierce in her opinions and demands. Danielle could lash out at her full bore without leaving a mark, draining her body of the aggression presently governing it.

Strong hands reached down and helped Mrs. Boom back into the galley. "She is ready." Danielle heard her speak to somebody, and all was quiet again.

Chapter 15

She was deathly pale and shaking like a reed in a light breeze. Thrice, she tried to raise the spoon to her lips, and thrice she failed, leaving the soup to run down her chin and drip onto her clean dress.

Sebastiaan reached over and took the utensil from her hand, dipped the spoon in the soup, and held it steadily against her lips. They had not spoken a word since he'd brought her the food. His concern for her grew with every passing minute. He had slept on the floor, at the foot of the stack of sails, for two nights, keeping her safe and waiting for her to return to this world. As she listlessly allowed him to feed her, a frown was deeply knitted between her eyes, informing him that he was intruding and thoroughly unwelcome.

This would not do. He was losing her. The longer she was allowed to wallow in the dark, the closer she was edging to giving up altogether. This was not just grief over Antoonie's death; it was the sum of all the losses over her short life. Sebastiaan knew the only way forward was to stir her anger. She did not need sympathy; she needed a purpose, and coddling her would not push her out of the murky waters of her dispiritedness.

"Are you done?" he asked when she swallowed the last of the soup. She did not answer but only nodded, and he knew she misunderstood the question.

"Good, you've moped around in the dark long enough." He watched her closely as he handed her a piece of dried biscuit. It would help to settle her stomach. If she did not retch it back up, she was likely to spit it at him. Either way, he had little hope of the morsel reaching her stomach.

It turned out that he was overly optimistic. Danielle slapped the food away from her face, and fire ignited in her eyes, turning them a phosphorous green.

He had sensed her anger before and knew it was burning just beneath the surface. All he had to do was to drop a little spark in that cauldron of oil.

"How dare you?" she spat at him. "Leave." Her arm snapped towards the open hatch. Sebastiaan ignored her. Instead, he looked toward the goat pen; sunlight was falling in small squares as it filtered through the lattice floor of the upper deck. It must be high noon.

"Leave," she hissed again and got to her feet unsteadily, swaying before she reached a steadying hand to the wall of folded sails. "I did not ask for your company." She sounded tired, and his heart gave a pang, but he could not afford to give in to her now. Instead, he turned slowly from the goats to face her and allowed a world-weary expression to creep onto his face before he topped it off with a cold smile. The combination proved successful, for she took a step forward and raised her arm, but the slap never made it to his face. She was too weak. Instead of making good on her threat, she stumbled. Sebastiaan grabbed her wrist more to support her than to restrain her. He could feel the tremors of her rage running in her arm.

"That's the problem, isn't it, Danielle?" he said while giving her a slight shake. "You don't ask for anything. Instead of facing your troubles, you crawl into a black hole and hide from the world. Don't you?" he spoke in a near shout, and his voice thundered through the hull.

Her eyes were large, and he could read the shock in them. She opened her mouth to speak, but he spoke before she could, still holding her wrist in a firm grip.

"No, you listen. My guess is that you've done that all your life." Her shock was fading and replaced by confusion.

"Whenever something did not go your way, or the world turned its arse side to you, you ran for a safe, dark spot to hide away, didn't you?" He did not wait for an answer. Even though he knew he was right, he was also overly harsh, but his fear of losing her was greater than his need to be gentle.

"Your whole life, you hid behind your father, needing him to protect you and make the world right for you." He paused for a mere second to see the impact of his words but giving her time to respond or defend herself would be a mistake.

CHAPTER 15

"You have no idea how to deal with a setback; no idea how to face a storm. You are one of the smartest people I know, and yet you can't seem to see past your own nose." She was too stunned to cry. Her only reaction was a sharp gasp of air. He let go of her wrist, and she sank onto the upturned crate she'd vacated before. Sebastiaan stood before her, legs apart and arms folded.

A cold silence stretched between them, and when she finally spoke, her voice was so soft, he almost missed it.

"Antoonie's death is not a mere setback. I loved him deeply." She sounded lost while trying to defend her actions.

"Antoonie is not yours to mourn." He was cruel, but she was sinking faster than he could save her.

"How can you say such a thing? Mourning does not require ownership." His face remained still. "This is pointless. I am not discussing this any further. Mrs. Boom understood. Why can't you?"

"Mrs. Boom is tired, Danielle. She's been running back and forth between Mrs. Van Riebeeck, the surgeon, and now you. She sure could use a little help. You are right, though; grief does not require ownership. But there is grief, and then there is self-pity, and you are nose-deep in the latter. All the while, the child's parents are grieving upstairs; your friend has lost her only child. The surgeon's wife lost her only child too, and the burden of that loss took her life." He did not have to elaborate, for her face was shadowed with guilt. Guilt he could work with; despair frightened him. He had seen it in his father, and he would be damned if he lost another person he loved because of it.

She took a moment, digesting his words. His point was clear, and it embarrassed her, but there was nowhere to hide. Danielle was stunned by the impact of his words and the force behind them. His anger was palpable, but it felt like an anchor in a churning maelstrom.

Everything he said was true. She had never faced the world alone, always hiding behind her father or her work. She had never needed to put her feelings aside for somebody else before, or perhaps the need was there, but she never saw it. She was always too wrapped up in her own world and all its wrongs and unfairness. What a child she was, what a foolish child. She raised a hand to her mouth as she closed her eyes. This is where he would turn his back on her and leave, and she would not blame him. Holding her breath, she waited, but he was not leaving; he was still standing right in front of her, and she could feel the heat radiating from his body.

Silent tears rolled down her cheeks and dripped onto her arms. The air between them felt brittle. Sebastiaan watched the shiny lines they left on her face, witnessing her torment, but resisted the need to reach out and touch her. She closed her eyes for a breath longer than a blink, opened them, and looked at him. His posture had not changed. His face was still expressionless. He would not give her anything to rage against or hide behind.

From the look on her face, Sebastiaan knew she was finally ready to talk, to let him see past the veil she so carefully kept wrapped around herself.

When she finally started to speak, her voice was raw with emotion. "My father's death was a shock, and I was sad, but the sadness was for myself, not for him." She felt a wave of guilt over her selfishness. Growing up without a mother, she never yearned for one. Her father had filled both roles seemingly effortlessly. He had protected her, nurtured her, and loved her. A teenage girl's concerns and worries had been met and solved with cuddles, kisses, and scientific explanations. And she took it all for granted. Never once paused to thank him. Oh, she told him she loved him, hugged him fiercely, and kissed his beard-roughened cheek, but she never sat down and told him how much he meant to her, how his love had filled her world and made it perfect and beautiful. So, when he died, she was scared and alone and mainly cried for herself – not for him.

"He made me fearless, and I miss that feeling. All I feel when I think of him is guilt." She searched Sebastiaan's face and saw the determined set of his jaw. He lowered himself onto his haunches, forearms resting on his thighs, head tilted, eyes sharp, mind working – his signature pose. Instantly self-conscious under his scrutiny, she fell silent.

"He was your rock, and when he fell away, you were adrift. As for guilt?" He scratched the back of his neck and wrinkled one side of his face. "I don't think anybody can reason that away; it needs to come from inside."

"Is that why you made your father the promise?" she asked. "Out of guilt?"

CHAPTER 15

"Perhaps," he paused for a moment, looking for a way to turn the conversation away from him. Everything he thought she needed to know about him, she already knew.

She turned her harrowed eyes to him, and he knew there was more.

"I can't go to Maria," she said.

"Why not?"

"I think I'm cursed." His eyes stilled on her face. "Everyone I love dies." She had that haunted look again, the same one she had the day she'd been tied to the mainmast.

"So, what will happen when I love you?" She swallowed thickly, staring at the dancing sun squares on the floor.

A rough breath left his nose. "You're not cursed." There was a warning in his whispered response.

Danielle was trying to find answers, but she was looking in the wrong direction. She needed to turn around and find them inside herself. She *was* fearless. If she saw herself the way he did, she would be unstoppable.

This conversation needed to end, and he needed to get her out of this godforsaken hull. The greyness in the air was oppressive. She looked stronger as the color returned to her face. He stood, reached out his hand, and pulled her up – time for the final push.

"Is this who you are then?" he challenged her in an even tone.

"What is your meaning?" Her voice dropped a few degrees.

"Defeated," his eyes raked down her body in slow measures. "Scared," following the same slow path upwards again until they met hers, his gaze hardened. "Broken."

Danielle felt her lip curl and her eyes slit. Her anger firmly pushed her guilt out of the way. The arrogant bastard was spoiling for her to lose her temper again, only to prove a point. She would not give him the satisfaction. But her rising ire would not let her take the high ground. On second thought, she would gladly give him both. To Hades with his opinion of her. He had deliberately lured her into a trap, made her talk about her father just so that he could use her vulnerabilities against her.

She took a step closer to him, tilting her face until it was mere inches from his, and hissed, "Go to hell, Sebastiaan." Then she turned, marched as well as her shaky legs would allow, to the ladder, bunched her woolen dress in one hand, and ascended gingerly without a backward glance.

Sebastiaan's mouth curved in a slow smile. He kept his eyes on her, ready to wipe the grin off his face should she turn around, but she didn't.

"Didn't think so," he said quietly.

* * *

Danielle brushed two gentle knocks on the door. There was no response, but after a while, it slowly opened. Mrs. Boom made to exit and belatedly saw Danielle.

"I'm sorry, dear. I didn't know you were there," she said, and Danielle could see the dark half-moons beneath her eyes. Her once-round apple cheeks were now pale and sunken. Danielle reached out and touched her hand, giving it a squeeze.

"Can I go in?" she asked, unsure what to expect from either woman.

Mrs. Boom turned to look at the dark cabin and then at Danielle. "She's not speaking, but I think she would love your company." There was not a trace of reproof in her words.

The cabin was uncharacteristically dark and equally tidy. Maria was sitting on the neatly made bed, feet together, hands loosely folded in her lap. Her hair was savagely tied in a chignon, her face ghostly white against the black of her dress. She was staring at the wall, and no expression indicated her thoughts, except her eyebrows were twisted slightly upward near the bridge of her nose. Her eyes blinked unevenly, and she struggled to hold her head upright.

The last time Danielle was in the cabin, sunlight was streaming through the windows, bathing the stunned mother and her dead child in golden light. The sight of Maria broke her heart. How long had she been like this? But Danielle knew the answer to her question. Guilt was cutting her insides to shreds.

She must have made a sound or a movement, for Maria slowly turned her

CHAPTER 15

head in her direction. When she saw Danielle, the cold glass that seemed to cover her face shattered, and a raw sob escaped her. Danielle moved without thought and gathered Maria in her arms. Neither of them cried. They clung to each other like two lost souls caught in a torrent. Danielle was stroking Maria's back in slow circles, rocking her gently like a mother would a distressed child.

"Maria, I am so sorry," she whispered. They were cheek to cheek, and she knew Maria heard her, but she made no sound. Her arms tightened slightly around Danielle's shoulders. The apology was the key, and for the first time, Danielle felt the knot in her stomach start to unravel. "I am sorry I was not here for you." She rocked Maria while she spoke.

"Where were you?" The unexpected words from Maria caused Danielle to still, but she kept her arms around her friend.

"I was in the hull," she said, and she felt worse than the coward she was.

"How was it?" Maria's voice was hoarse.

"Dark." Danielle pushed gently away and looked into Maria's eyes, searching for anything that could signify hope or life.

"The same as here then," Maria said, blinking slowly.

"Yes, but not as neat." Danielle looked about the cabin. It was so tidy as to be clinical. It almost looked as if nobody was living there.

"Mrs. Boom," Maria said by way of explanation.

"Can I open the shutters?" Danielle asked, needing some warmth to return to the dreary space.

"No, I hate the light." Maria searched the bed for something, couldn't find it, and gave up. "I'm so tired," she said but remained seated.

Danielle sank to the floor and unlaced Maria's boots, giving them a slight tug, and slid them from her feet. "Why don't you rest for a spell? I will be right here." Maria dropped to the pillow as if being shot. One moment she was sitting, and the next, she was lying on her side, legs still dangling from the bed. Danielle scooped her legs up and covered her in a woolen blanket, tucking the sides in and sweeping a few strands of hair from her forehead. Then she knelt on the floor next to the bed, took Maria's hand, and lay her head on the mattress.

***

She woke to a hand on her shoulder. Governor Van Riebeeck stood beside the bed with a candle in his hand.

Danielle's legs were stiff from hours on the floor, but she rose with his hand supporting her elbow. She looked at his grief-stricken face. There were no words. They shared an unspoken moment, and then she left. It must have been well after dark, for the sconces in the passageway were lit, casting the narrow corridor in lazy orange light.

Before retiring to her cabin, she needed to clear her head and fill her body with fresh air. She needed to mend fences with the twins. They had never treated her with anything but kindness and acceptance, and she was horridly mean to them. She was tired to her core. The previous couple of nights and days were molded into one haze of memory and mirage.

Her favorite part of the ship was the weather deck. She loved wrapping her arms around the lone flagpole fixed to the center of the aft railing, listening to the ensign swishing in the wind, and looking out over the vast expanse of water where they'd just been. It was a quiet and uncluttered spot. She could always count on a bit of solitude there, the water far below, gently swirling in the wake of the ship, closing and erasing its traces as if they had never been, wiping them from the ocean's memory. But not tonight. That place held too many memories, for she used to take Antoonie there to play in the sun, twirling and dancing with the wind. No, tonight, she headed in the opposite direction. She weaved her way across the upper deck and up the steep ladder to the ship's bow.

Chapter 16

The bow served his purposes even better. It had to be tonight. He was confident Du Bois's other man was not aboard the *Drommedaris*, and so he'd bought himself a little more time by sending a false report to Du Bois, with the *Lieffde,* stating that he'd done the deed. Then she'd disappeared for two days. At first, he thought she was with the governor's wife, but then he heard from the old fat woman that she was tucked away in the hull and guarded by that whelp that roamed the decks like he owned the ship.

The success of this mission would almost certainly bring him into Du Bois's innermost circle. After this, he would probably be asked to oversee the Asian operations, set up smuggling routes, and source new suppliers.

She cleared the top of the ladder, and he stepped into the shadows as there was no point in alerting her to his presence just yet.

He had removed his shoes earlier, and the deck was cold and slippery under his bare feet. With the rushing of the wind and rain, the ever-creaking of the lines, and the snapping of the sails, she would never hear his approach. He was prepared to follow her onto the weather deck, where she always went, but the bow was perfect for his plan. The weather deck was quiet and open, whereas the bow was cluttered, with shrouds and ropes running from the foremast to the deck.

Emerging from the shadows, he ascended the ladder, realizing his hand was coated in sweat when he placed it on the thin wooden handrail. Releasing a relaxing sigh, he continued his climb. At the top, he paused before stepping onto the bow. Above, the service platform of the foremast was unoccupied.

There was nobody there but her. Two lanterns spluttered dimly in each corner of the deck, and a few barrels were tied to the base of the mast to collect rainwater.

She made no effort to hide and stood in the front port side corner next to the lantern. Her shoulders were relaxed, her head slightly tilted back, and her arms spread wide on the railing. He could have made good use of that delicious body were he afforded the time and a bit more privacy, but he doubted she would bend over and accept his attentions quietly. His body reacted so violently to his thoughts that he was forced to swallow a cough, and warm sweat now coated most of his skin.

This moment had many times played itself out in his head. Over and over, he had imagined how he would take her life. The options were endless, given time and imagination, and he prided himself on his inventiveness. In his fantasies, however, he always had time on his side. Tonight would have to be quick and quiet. He planned to walk up behind her silently, let the wind carry her scent to him, and enjoy that little boon for a second. Then he would reach out and cover her mouth while lifting her over the railing and dropping her into the waters below, preferably close enough to the ship that it sucked her under. If anybody saw him, he could always claim that she threatened to jump and that he was too late to save her.

Danielle's eyes did a quick scan of the deck. There was nobody. The lookout above was empty as well. Rain was coming down steadily, strong enough that she could already feel fat drops running down her neck. Soon, she would be soaked through. This part of the ship was always windy, she thought with a wry smile, windy and noisy. With arms spread wide on the gunwale, she looked down to where the ship was cleaving through the water with white foam curling against the front.

Tonight, she welcomed the wind and the rain, and especially the noise, for the hull was quiet, and she was tired of the sound of her thoughts. The crowded forecastle below her feet gave her a feeling of safety. Most view sailors as rowdy and dangerous, but she'd come to trust them with her life. They were brave, honorable, and hardworking. The soldiers were a different matter, but luckily, only a handful were aboard.

CHAPTER 16

Something deep inside her was starting to fall into place. She tilted her head back to let the rain wash over her upturned face when she heard something sounding like a cough coming from behind.

Danielle whipped around, startled by the unexpected sound. Squinting into the darkness, she tried to identify the source of the disturbance. A man of medium build was standing in the shadows, having just cleared the steep ladder onto the bow's deck. He was not dressed in the loose shirt and wide-leg slops the sailors wore. For a moment, she panicked, thinking that one of the soldiers had followed her, but then she saw the outlines of the long black coat. The shape took form, and her body relaxed as she recognized the surgeon. The poor man had lost his child and wife in one day; his whole family was gone. She wished there was something she could do or say to ease his pain, but she did not know him well enough. He was not very social and only appeared a few times on deck. His mien was always so intense, just like now. A tremulous smile curved her mouth as she made to leave, for he must have sought out the bow for the same reasons she did – solitude, but not silence.

"Good evening, sir," she greeted him and gave a couple of steps toward the ladder. He opened his mouth to speak, but no words came forth. However, his hand rose slowly, staying her. His breathing sounded harsh as they stared at each other. "I'm so sorry for your loss," she almost whispered, her heart breaking for him.

He did not respond to her condolences but kept his eyes on her face as he stepped closer. The men did not like him overly much and would not go out of their way to engage him in conversation. Therefore, he must be lonely without his family and starved for company. Talking to somebody and sharing a burden is often healing on its own, but he was not speaking. Perhaps he needed time.

The air between them grew thick, and an uneasy feeling enveloped Danielle. The surgeon had walked toward her until they were no more than a foot apart. Their eyes locked, and she fought the urge to take a step to the side and away from him, but to do so, she would have to push past him, for he had her neatly trapped in the corner. Leaning slightly backward, she felt the railing pressed into her from behind, reminding her of the knife she wore tucked into the

209

waist of her skirt.

Not wanting to offend him by trying to avoid his presence when he was obviously in distress, she stayed where she was, but he was crowding her, and her unease was starting to ripen into trepidation. Her arms crossed defensively over her stomach as he closed the already too-small distance between them. He reached forward and, with one hand, trapped her arms to her body. The fingers of the other smeared along the length of her cheek. With the pale-yellow light of the lantern washing over his face, she saw the predatory gleam in his eyes, and a scream died in her throat, choked off by the tightening of her muscles.

Danielle forced her shallow breaths deeper into her lungs. His fingers were damp and cold, and the rancid, sharp smell of his sweat left a brackish taste in her mouth. Her knife might as well have been under her pillow, for there was no way she could free her hands to reach for it with his body leaning heavily into hers. She needed to scream for help, but her throat was so tight with shock that only air seemed to escape in ragged bursts.

He was not an attractive man, and even if he were, the odors secreted by his body would have cast a deep shadow over it like storm clouds bearing hail on an otherwise sunny day. His hair was a premature salt and pepper grey. There was nothing of interest in his features. His face was not wide or narrow, and his nose was straight but nondescript. The slight tilt at the outer corners of his eyes did not enhance his overall appearance. However, the true oversight in his creation was his mouth, for it was nothing more than a slit, a mere thumb's width above his chin. She briefly wondered if God was in a hurry when He had made him and merely forgot to add the lips. But the message she saw in his eyes chilled her blood. He was hungry for violence and the need to inflict pain.

"Hurting me will not lessen your pain." Her voice was guttural, but she thought to appeal to the anguish he must be carrying after losing his family. His bark of laughter hit her like a slap, and she turned her head away.

"Do you think I mourn a wife I didn't want and a child who wasn't mine?"

She snapped her head back to face him, her fears momentarily replaced by anger at his callous words.

CHAPTER 16

"Danielle." It sounded like he was testing her name to see if he liked it. He pressed harder against her and forced her to bend backward at a painful angle. Unable to free her hands, she felt the railing cut into her spine. "I'm not being paid to hurt you." A confused frown formed between her eyes. "Du Bois is paying me to get rid of you." She did not miss the triumph in his voice.

Du Bois had found her.

Then he bent his head and placed the flat of his tongue against her skin. He licked from her collarbone to the hollow beneath her ear. Her stomach made a neat flip at the unexpected sensation, and she gagged at the fecal smell of his saliva.

"Just a little taste before it's over," he growled close to her face.

She felt his body harden as he pressed against her. Since her hands were trapped between them, her only weapon was her knee, and she tried to raise it, but he felt her intent and slammed a thigh between her legs, lifting her higher against the railing. The skin on her spine burned as it was scraped away by the unyielding wooden barrier.

Looking down at the churning black water, the scream she had searched for before finally found its way into the night air and was as quickly swallowed by the rushing water and the snapping of the sails. Time stood still as the knowledge that her life was rapidly nearing its end dawned. How often had she heard others speak of how their lives flashed before their eyes or how they felt eternal peace when they described moments they miraculously survived? All she felt was the wish to see Sebastiaan one more time. He was angry at her the last they had spoken, and she knew that if she died tonight, he would carry the guilt of it with him, even though he was right and his words, harsh though they might have been, were true.

"What are you doing?" A sharp, clear voice spoke from behind them.

Surprise and instinct spun the surgeon toward the sound, and Danielle fell forward at the sudden release of the pressure on her body. Her wits returned with a vengeance now that her life was no longer quite literally teetering on the edge of the railing. Both her hands snapped behind her back. Her left hand yanked the shirt from the skirt's wide waistband, lifting it away as the fingers of her right hand found and curled around the handle of her knife, pulling it free in a single smooth motion.

Danielle was still crouching when she saw Orion standing a few strides from the surgeon, a deep scowl splitting his angelic face.

"Leave her be, you filthy piss prophet!" he spewed in his most determined voice. He had saved her life, and she knew, without a doubt, that the surgeon would not hesitate for a moment to extinguish his if he were to bear witness to her murder.

"Orion, run!" she shouted above the din of the wind and rain.

Her command failed and succeeded simultaneously. Orion defiantly stood his ground. Danielle did not have time to come up with anything more persuasive, for the sound of her voice had drawn the surgeon's attention away from the child and back to her. She pushed to her feet. The deck was slippery and felt as if covered in a layer of snot. Now she understood why sailors were always barefoot. Boots, freshly painted deck boards, and heavy rain were a poor combination when she could least afford it, but she managed to inch her way out of the corner where he had her trapped moments before.

The situation had become more complicated for the surgeon than he had anticipated. There was now a witness, and he was out of time. She was opening her mouth again, but whatever she planned to shout was silenced as he swung towards her. The momentum carried the back of his hand neatly across her face. It was not so much a slap as an open-handed punch. His knuckles instantly split the skin on her cheekbone, and she was again driven back into the railing. With large round eyes, she stared at him, daring him. The look on her face fueled his rage, for she was not cowering as he'd hoped, nor was there any sign of fear. Before his hand could snap out to throttle whatever unruly emotion was governing her, he saw a blur of movement and felt a sting across his face from his ear to the corner of his mouth.

The shock of the slap pushed Danielle toward the reality of the situation. If she did not fight for her life, she would forfeit it. She wanted to drive her knife into his stomach. He was close enough, but the blade was short, and his coat, waistcoat, and shirt would hinder its effectiveness. Instead, she swung her arm wide, aiming for his neck but missed and felt the blade slide off his face. Blood was streaming freely from the extended cut across his cheek, but he

CHAPTER 16

seemed unaffected. It was not a mortal wound. She'd hoped it would at least have the force to stop, or topple him over, allowing her to escape. However, his eyes turned wild, and a roar tore from him. He launched forward, pinning her to the railing with his weight, one hand closing tightly around her throat while the other grabbed hold of her knife-wielding hand and slammed it mercilessly onto the gunwale. His fingers bit into her wrist, and she could feel the ligaments part. White-hot pain shot up her arm. She tried to scream, but with his hand tightly around her neck, all she could manage was a broken croak.

He had learned his lesson earlier, for he had neatly trapped her legs between his. Blood was rushing through her veins in her desperate search for air, creating an awful swishing sound in her ears. She tried to ignore the sensation of her heart trying to escape her chest. The sooner she could calm its frantic beating, the better off the rest of her would be. The inability to breathe was starting to affect her vision. Her eyes were swimming in something that felt like a thick salve, causing shapes to blur and the edges to blacken. He must have pulled the knife from her limp fingers, but her focus was solely on gasping for air and finding none. Slowly, her brain was starting to release its hold on her senses. Her hearing failed her first, then her vision, and now her skin was uncomfortably numb. Still, the pressure on her throat persisted. There was no strength left in her limbs, and she would have crumpled to the floor had his body not pressed against hers and his hand not formed a vice around her neck.

At last, the blackness that threatened her vision's edges drew over her eyes, and the darkness sucked her into its peaceful depths.

The shrill of Orion's scream floated across the decks to where they stood. Captain De Coninck, Arent, and Sebastiaan all looked in its direction. Sebastiaan saw the small boy charge full bore into a solid black figure now hidden by lines and shadows. The three men moved as one towards the child's distress, with Arent first, Sebastiaan second, and De Coninck last, rushing up the steep ladder and onto the bow.

Orion had crept from his bed, begging the captain to allow him to search for the cat, which he was convinced was trapped in the rain. No amount of reasoning could dissuade him from his firm belief that his pet was in great peril, even though the cat was older than the boy and had navigated more storms and pirate attacks than some sailors aboard. Now, Orion lay on the deck in a pool of blood, a knife sticking at an odd angle from his side, his face deathly pale and his eyes closed.

De Coninck uttered a curse, foul even by sailor's standards, and rushed toward the fallen child, already stripping his overcoat to cover the small body and protect him from the rain.

A grunting noise sounded from near the port side railing. Sebastiaan saw a dark figure bent over a woman. He instinctively knew it was Danielle. He and Arent reached the man together. The combined force of their pull on his body lifted him clean off his feet and granted him a few moments of flight before he landed heavily on his back, sliding some distance before coming to a complete stop against the foremast.

De Coninck measured Orion's pulse and then searched the rest of his body for injuries. He was surprised to see the surgeon fly across the deck, but his surprise was quickly replaced by fury as his brain attached meaning to the events. It was a mistake to have allowed the piece of garbage aboard, but they were in a bind not having a surgeon when they had left Texel, and it was foolish to undertake a long voyage without a ship's surgeon. The blame for this most unfortunate event was solely his, for he should have questioned the man more vigorously. Sebastiaan was turning towards Danielle, and Arent was heading in the surgeon's direction. Confident that the situation was well in hand, he returned his attention to Orion.

Arent was in a savage rage as he stalked towards the surgeon with deathly calm strides. Sebastiaan lost all interest in the erstwhile attacker when he saw Danielle's lifeless body dropped to the floor. He nearly lost his composure when he noted the cut across her cheekbone, her small hand bloodied and bruised, and the red swelling around her throat that would be purple come morning. Feeding the hope that she was still alive, although her skin color argued otherwise, he knelt beside her, searching for her heartbeat. There was none, and then he cursed himself as he discovered he was searching in the wrong place on her neck.

CHAPTER 16

Thank God, he prayed silently upon finding her pulse flutter under his fingers. It was faint and uneven at first but was fast gaining strength.

"Arent," Sebastiaan barked a warning over his shoulder. He would kill the man as soon as he was sure she was all right. The thought filled him with vicious joy, and his attention was drawn back when he saw the faintest flicker of her eyelids.

Danielle gulped a large breath when the pressure was no longer around her throat. A blinding headache came with the blessed rush of air, and her eyes started protesting the darkness. Blinking vigorously, she forced her vision. There was no doubt in her mind that she was dead, but would she be so relieved to breathe if that were the case?

Sebastiaan was on his knees in front of her. He was talking, she could see his lips move, but her ears were still not working properly. His face was trapped in some urgency, and she thought he looked wildly panicked. She tried to give him a reassuring smile but feared he couldn't see it, for his eyes were misty and unfocused. Where was the surgeon? And Orion?

Fresh air fueled her senses to resume their duties. "Orion?" she asked, but Sebastiaan ignored the question, only lifting her off the wet floor when she started to shake uncontrollably. "Where's Orion?" Pressed against his warm body, with his arms locking tightly around her, she could not hear his reply.

Her throat burned with every sob-like breath she took, and she was still shaking, but the soothing tones of his voice were becoming clearer. She could still not attach meaning to what he was saying. Resting her chin on his shoulder opened her airways more, and her hearing returned in full. The sound of flesh slamming into flesh floated across the deck. Turning her head, she saw a large hulking figure slamming his fist repeatedly into the surgeon. The man's head limply fell from side to side with each impact. Arent was killing the surgeon. She knew it should matter, and yet – it didn't.

"Can you stand?" Sebastiaan asked, and at her nod, he climbed to his feet, bringing her with him. He pulled her to where the captain was kneeling near the middle of the deck. She let him guide her with one hand on her back and the other holding her arm. Her limbs felt heavy with each step, and she wished he could just let her sit for a moment. But the captain moved slightly sideways and yelled, "Arent, we need him alive."

Orion was lying on his back in the middle of the deck, his face deathly white, her knife protruding from his side. Danielle screamed at the sight, and her knees buckled.

She crawled to the fallen boy. Blood was staining his shirt, and a small pool had formed on the deck near his body. The diluted blood ran in faint pink lines between the grooves of the floor planks.

Captain De Coninck sat back on his heels at her approach. She looked up at his face. He was calm, and that gave her hope even before he spoke. "He's alive," he attested with perhaps more force than was needed, and the message in his eyes was not unclear – *and he will remain as such.*

Danielle laid her palm against Orion's cold forehead, and then her fingers moved toward the knife. She gently touched the entry wound, trying to determine the angle of the blade. The blade was not long, but what it lacked in length, it gained in sharpness. The cut was neat but not deep, and it was the only mercy for this night, for it might have missed his organs.

"We need to get him out of the rain," the captain ordered and moved to pick Orion up.

"Wait," Danielle croaked, her voice not fully recovered yet. It still felt like her throat would close up at any given moment. She tried to clear it a few times, but the abrasion proved too painful. Pointing to the captain's neck, she asked, "May I have your neckcloth?" De Coninck deftly tucked it from his neck and handed it over without question. Danielle wrapped the soft linen, still warm from his body, carefully but tightly around the blade. Then the captain lifted the child and made for the ladder.

"Try to keep it steady," she begged from behind him.

"Go with him," Sebastiaan spoke close to her ear after he had helped her safely down the ladder.

"We will be there shortly." His tone was brusque, and looking into his face made her take an involuntary step backward. There was nothing familiar about him. He was stark and cold; his face was edged in rigid, hard lines; his beautiful hazel eyes, always ready with a smile, were dead and unyielding. Though his touch was gentle and his tone soft, the transformation frightened

CHAPTER 16

her.

"Go on," he urged.

* * *

Orion regained consciousness when captain De Coninck placed him on the dayroom table. Tiny whimpers escaped him, but he bravely clamped them down when he saw the captain standing by his side. De Coninck stroked the boy's sodden black curls and told him how brave and strong he was while Danielle mixed a sedative. She thought no truer words had ever been spoken.

"I don't want the surgeon," he begged in a small voice. "He hurt us."

"Hush now," the captain spoke. "Danielle will tend to you. Will that please you?"

"Yes." His eyes closed, and his breathing turned from shallow and painfilled to deep and even as the laudanum started to work.

She waited until there was no longer movement behind the closed lids and his long black eyelashes made perfect semicircles on his cheeks, and then she unwound the stabilizing bandage around the knife. Touching the area around the entry wound, she determined the exact angle of the blade. Confident that it was safe to remove, she pulled it slowly from his body. Blood instantly started to pool around the clean lines of the cut. Four stitches at the most, she guessed. The knife was indeed too short to inflict life-threatening damage.

De Coninck had lit every lantern in the dayroom, and it was as bright as high noon. She worked fast, her mind a comfortable three paces ahead of her hands, cleaning and stitching the wound. The laudanum would wear off soon, and it was better if he was not given a second dose.

They still had no idea how Orion came to be stabbed, for Danielle's last memory was of the surgeon dispossessing her of the knife. After that, her memory was foggy. They would question him once he was feeling better.

She looked at her hands, covered in the child's blood. This boy would live, and it was not through any part she played. The wound would heal, regardless of whether she tended it or not. She could make it easier, to be sure. But she had no control over life or death, no control over the paths of others. The knowledge settled over her like a warm blanket. So simple a truth, but with such a life-changing impact. It was like she had found something she'd lost a long time ago. She was not cursed. Her life was no different from those around her. The only difference lay in the choices she made.

Some clarity deep inside her was trying to surface, figuring itself out. She needed time to think and analyze the past events that had led her to the false course she had been on for so long. But there was no time. Arent and Sebastiaan had just walked through the door. Danielle tied off the last suture and glanced over Sebastiaan as she reached for the honey and yarrow mixture. It was hard to reconcile the man standing opposite her with the warm and easy-going one she was betrothed to and thought she knew so well. Arent looked more or less under control, though his hair was wild, and he was covered in blood.

"How much of that is yours?" she asked, hinting at the wet stains on his shirt.

"None of it," he replied and moved to stand at Danielle's side, taking Orion's small hand into his, covering most of the thin forearm.

"Report," Captain De Coninck ordered the two men, his tone soft but a long way south of gentle.

Arent spoke first. "He was not exactly a well of information. He worked for Alain Du Bois. Apparently, saw himself as Du Bois's henchman, having gotten his hands wet in the man's name before. From what we could piece together, he weaseled his way onto the ship and into our hearts with orders to kill Miss Van Aard and rid Du Bois of the only witness to her father's murder."

Danielle kept her eyes on her patient, not wanting them to see her reaction to Arent's words.

"Did you at least try to reach the bottom of that well?" De Coninck asked, knowing that the chances of the surgeon surviving the interrogation were slim at best.

"Yeah. It was only when he started repeating himself that we thought it was time for the funeral," Arent finished without fanfare as if the matter was merely a side note.

Danielle briefly wondered if the surgeon died during his funeral or before.

CHAPTER 16

Either way, the distinction was by now moot.

De Coninck absorbed the information and raised a questioning eyebrow at his nephew, who had not spoken since entering the brightly lit dayroom.

Sebastiaan did not think there was anything more to add. Arent had pretty much summed it up.

"Couldn't have happened to a nicer joe," Sebastiaan said with a nonchalant shrug. The out-of-character response drew her attention. His face still wore the unreadable stone mask that had fallen into place earlier. His eyes were still cold and savage, and he looked like a person most would give a wide berth. Even though he was standing less than six feet from her, it felt like he was somewhere else, and she missed him.

* * *

It had been two weeks since the death of the children. Life aboard the *Drommedaris* had resumed its normal rhythm, but a mist of melancholy clung to the sailors and passengers.

The latter floated like wraiths across the deck, did what needed to be done, went where they needed to be, and then withdrew. Everybody seemed to adhere to the same rule of keeping to themselves, for they knew where any conversation was bound to lead, and nobody was yet strong enough to endure it. The death of three people on the same day in close quarters was a wound best left to heal by itself. The surgeon's demise was not one to be mourned and therefore had not contributed to any emotional hardship.

The camaraderie between the sailors and passengers, formed after the New Year's Day storm, remained strong, despite recent events. The sailors resumed their duties without a shift or an outward change in their spirit. With a different understanding of life and death, they left the passengers to deal with their sorrow as they saw fit, unsure how to bring peace and comfort to gentlefolk. For them, emotions and problems alike could be drowned with hard work and a ration of brandy. The only time a ripple of discomfort crept through was when the governor was among them. Van Riebeeck possessed a quiet dignity and a natural air of authority that wrapped around him like a rich man's cloak. His presence was met with downcast eyes, scratchy throats, and shuffling feet. What to say to a man like this after a thing like that?

The governor's wife mostly stayed out of sight and only emerged at night, to stand on the spot from where her child had been lowered. The deck was quiet then, and the sailors on shift gave her the necessary consideration. She was visiting his grave. Each time, before heading back to her cabin, she touched her fingers to her lips three times and then the railing. Once for Antoonie, once for Raphael, and once for the surgeon's wife.

On one such night, she became aware of a presence and saw a scrawny figure approach.

"Mistress," he greeted with a slight nod and a graveled voice.

"Mattheys," she sighed, wishing she knew his last name. It was a moonless and cloudless night. A light breeze made the ocean swell gently, moving the ship up and down much like the chest of a deep sleeper.

"A perfect night," Mattheys said, coming to stand next to her, resting his forearms on the gunwale, and filling his lungs to the brim with salty air.

"Yes, it is." She did not feel like talking, but his unassuming presence was neither unpleasant nor unwelcome. They stood in each other's company for a while, staring out over the black ocean.

He clicked his knuckles, and she looked at his hands. She was surprised by their elegance. His fingers were long, gnarly, and work-worn, but the nails were clean and neatly shaped. He seemed unaware of the annoying habit.

"Do you have a family, Mattheys?" Although the dark partly obscured his features, Maria thought she saw him squint.

"Not anymore."

"What happened?" Maria knew she was prying, which was probably rude.

"Life." A single, solid explanation. As he shifted his body, his head dropped to his chest, making his shoulder blades stick out under the thin gauze of his shirt. After a moment, he lifted his head with a sigh and spoke with a clear voice.

"Nothing ever stays the same, Mistress. We are sailors; we live by the stars and the wind." His eyes glimmered in the dark of his face. "Sometimes the weather is bad, and we suffer, but then it changes again." She listened without responding, and he continued. "If we don't change with the weather, if we behave as if the storm was still raging, we will sink the ship. We would hoist the wrong sails and make the wrong maneuvers. Do you see? To survive, we must accept what's coming our way and change accordingly."

He straightened, rapped his knuckles three times on the wooden railing, and made to take his leave.

"But what do I know? I see life through simple eyes. That said, I've lived, loved, and lost." A wry smile tucked at his lips. "You'll need something warm for your shoulders if you stay out here. When the stars are wet like that, it will turn cold soon. Good night, Mistress." He gave a slight bow and left.

She stared after him for a long while, the air felt thin and dry, and her breath made a small white puff as she released it.

* * *

"I don't know how they do it, spending months on end at sea. I've had enough. I need to feel something solid beneath my feet. Dirt, that's what I need. I want to feel, smell, and cover myself with dirt." Danielle sat flat on the floor with her back against the wall, mending a shirt.

Maria looked up from the charcoal sketch she was working on, trying to respond, but coming up empty.

Danielle met Maria's blank stare with a challenge, "What?"

"Did I kill him?"

In the weeks that followed Antoonie's death, Maria had refused to talk about him, and the abrupt question caught Danielle off guard.

"How?" she asked incredulously.

"I was washing Raphael's clothes that day. Did I carry a sickness to him – afterward?"

Danielle could not imagine that there was a link between the sick child's filthy clothes and Antoonie's fever.

"No," she breathed. Danielle understood better than most the unhinged thoughts of someone trying to grab hold of any shred of an explanation. Was there anything she could say to bring a grieving mother peace? Perhaps not.

Perhaps time was the only cure.

"What are you sketching?" Danielle could not bear talking about Antoonie, for her own wounds were still devastatingly raw. She loved the child deeply. Even though he was not hers, Danielle had often daydreamed about having a child of her own one day, just like him.

"Just a house," Maria replied and lifted the piece of parchment for Danielle to see. It was a beautiful sketch of a typical Dutch dwelling with a gabled façade, small windows, and a solid-looking front door. She was a talented artist but modestly kept her drawings tucked away. There were beautiful sketches of Antoonie. One depicted him as a newborn, sleeping peacefully. Another of him giving a wet smile with his first tooth proudly on display, and Danielle's favorite, Antoonie, standing on baby legs with round fat feet, holding onto a chair for support. There were many drawings of Maria's husband in various poses, reading at his desk, his face deep in thought, staring out the window, the light rendering one half of his face almost entirely in shadows. There was another where he looked straight at the artist with a mischievous smile; it was so lifelike that Danielle could see the velvet brown of his eyes shining through the grey portrait. Lately, Maria drew only buildings, ships, and empty furniture.

"It needs a tree." Danielle saw the subtle makings of a smile on Maria's face when she picked up the charcoal again.

A soft knock sounded, and the door opened at an angle upon Maria's permission. Sebastiaan's head popped around, his eyes scanning the room.

"Mister De Vries, please come in," Maria called. He stepped over the sill and then stopped.

"Good afternoon, Mistress. I wondered if the two of you would like to join me for a stroll on the deck?" He blushed brightly, and Danielle snorted softly, knowing that he had just made up the words on the spot. Maria gave her a scowled look, taking pity on his obvious discomfort.

"That is a lovely thought, thank you. But why don't you take my rather bothersome friend? I have a tree to draw and want to use the light while it is still good." She gave him a reassuring smile.

"Are you sure?" Danielle asked, but Maria only fluttered a charcoal-stained

CHAPTER 16

hand in her direction.

Still grinning at his expense, Danielle followed Sebastiaan and closed the door softly behind her, feeling guilty for leaving Maria alone, especially at this time of day. The no-man's-land between late afternoon and early evening was so depressing. The sun was about to set, and dust motes danced in the last streaks of sunlight as they fell on the wooden floorboards.

They left the confined space of the passageway. With his hand in the small of her back, Sebastiaan guided her across the upper deck and up to the ship's bow.

"No, why don't we stand on the weather deck? It is so much more peaceful there," Danielle protested. Since the attack, she'd not been to the bow. Just looking in its direction, let alone spending a few leisurely minutes up there, left her smelling the surgeon's foul breath on her face.

"Time for you to face your fear," he said while pushing her towards the ladder.

"I don't have a fear."

"Then what's the problem?"

There was no point arguing with him when he was in this mood, hiding his stubborn determination behind that mask of good-natured sweetness. The only people immune to that particular weapon were his uncle and perhaps Arent, but most certainly not her.

Leaning their bodies against the railing, they let the wind slap their faces.

"I can't remember ever coming out here and not feeling the wind on my face."

"Niklas has a special talent for finding a breeze." Sebastiaan looked over his shoulder across the ship at the navigator on the quarterdeck.

"That's one of my favorite places on the ship," he said, pointing to the prow. "I always go there if I need a moment of peace."

Danielle leaned forward to glance at the carcass-shaped structure above the waterline; it looked frighteningly uncomfortable and dangerous.

"It doesn't look very peaceful." She watched the water splashing beneath the wooden beams, unable to imagine how anywhere down there could be safe enough to produce a single coherent thought.

Sebastiaan turned to her, searching her face, "So?"

She could hedge, but it was only postponing the inevitable. In the end, he would force her to talk, and perhaps it was what she needed.

"I feel old," she said, and he laughed.

"Are you angling for compliments?" he asked, still smiling.

"Not old like that." She dropped her shoulders, only then noting how tense they were. "The night of the attack, I came up here to think on what you said before, in the hull."

He looked down at his feet, regret etched on his face. "I am so sorry for what I've said. I –"

"Stop," she interrupted, "it was all true."

"But also cruel." He shook his head as if he could not make peace with the thought.

"I didn't see it so. It was the lifeline I needed. It gave me perspective." She paused to give him a moment, but he remained silent. "I grew up that night." She stared out over the ocean. "When he had his hands on my throat, I knew I was going to die, and I was scared, not for myself, but for leaving you."

A dark shadow flittered across his eyes, and there was no trace of amusement on his face. "I was also scared for Orion." She looked toward the spot on the deck where he had lain, bleeding. It was crisp white, with all traces of violence cleaned away. "And I've discovered that it is liberating to not fear for oneself. To live from the inside out."

"What do you mean?"

"I don't think I'm cursed. Life is full of disappointments and disasters, oftentimes unavoidable. Sometimes you are the victim at the storm's center, and other times you are the spectator. I think things just happened to me, same as everybody else, and my suffering, if you will, is less when I turn my focus away from my circumstance. Looking to others and their needs, seeing them right, rather than focusing on my own needs and the desire to isolate myself from future pain."

Sebastiaan seemed to contemplate that statement for a while. "You are very black and white, aren't you? Something is either this or that, no in-between." He sounded annoyed.

CHAPTER 16

"What? How can you say that? You were the one who pushed me toward …" she could not find a word for where exactly he had led her, "toward this."

His reaction confused her. It was not so outlandish to want to help others. She'd spent a lifetime caring only for herself. It was time to shed her old skin and morphed into somebody she could be proud of.

"No, I didn't," he protested like a little boy, and for a moment, he looked it too, but the illusion did not last long. "I understand what you are saying. But, Danielle, if you take this view too far, it could destroy you." She was ready to interject, but he held his hand up. "No, you need to maintain a balance. Otherwise, you might run the risk of losing yourself."

"And that is why I have you," she said smiling, for she was sure he would pull her back whenever she leaned too far off course. He was her anchor.

"God, help me," he sighed.

Chapter 17

March 29, 1652

The *Drommedaris* messaged her two sister ships, the *Reijger*, under the boisterous command of Captain Hooghsaet, and the *Goede Hoop*, under the young Captain Turver. They were entering the last leg of their voyage and would need to stay close to each other until they reached their destination.

The three ships lay side by side at midday, and the captains gathered in the *Drommedaris'* dayroom, accompanied by Governor Van Riebeeck. Van Riebeeck pondered his position as he watched the three captains – quietly taking the measure of each. Theoretically, as leader of the expedition, all three captains bent a knee to him, but he could not see how such a feat would ever be accomplished – not that he cared for it either.

Perhaps Captain Turver could be considered pliable, but the other two were beyond anybody's control.

De Coninck was a man's man. His crew would follow him to the ends of the earth. And over the edge, simply because that's the direction he pointed them in.

Hooghsaet was a large, red-haired descendant of a Viking, for it was the only explanation Van Riebeeck could marshal to explain the man. The VOC had poached him from the navy decades ago. Initially, he had found adapting to civilian life a trifle difficult, but as a natural problem solver, he had fixed that minor nuisance by browbeating it into adapting to him. He commanded the *Reijger* with navy-like standards and discipline. De Coninck would be the first to admit that he owed his career to the older man. He was made

CHAPTER 17

First Officer under Hooghsaet's command, and the two of them shared a long history and colorful friendship, with stories that could burn the ears off the most hardened sailor.

And then there was the young captain, Turver. Partaking in the expedition to the Cape was his first long voyage as captain. Although the young man was competent, he did suffer from the occasional bout of rule-following. Captain Turver was impeccably dressed for the meeting. The fabrics of his garments were crisp, and his dark hair was neatly tied at his neck, effectively lending a rather piratical look to the other two.

"We are terribly short on water," Turver continued the discussion, sounding mildly panicked by the admission. He remained straight-backed and square-shouldered as he spoke, keeping his chin just that nudge too high and his lips barely touching.

"How short?" Hooghsaet asked, one arm draped over the back of his chair, his long legs stretched out in front of him.

"No more than a month's supply," Turver replied, "and that includes the beer."

Hooghsaet looked across the table and then around the room, slightly twisting in his seat as if he had dropped something and yearned to retrieve it. "Do you not have any brandy?" he admonished De Coninck for the oversight.

"Barent," De Coninck hollered. The sound of rattling glasses came down the companionway from the captain's cabin, and all four men turned in its direction.

"Ah, nectar from the angels themselves," Hooghsaet smiled. "The only good thing to ever come out of France."

After glasses were generously filled and clinked, the conversation continued.

"Our crew and passengers are healthy," De Coninck looked to Van Riebeeck for confirmation, to which the governor gave a single nod, "and we've been on strict water rations for more than a month now. I suggest you do the same. God willing, we might be able to reach the Cape before the end of April."

"We could tack a little closer to the African coast. The winds are stronger, and the seas are rougher, but," Hooghsaet looked to each captain, "with luck, we can cut down on our travel time." He turned his sharp eyes, hidden beneath red bushy eyebrows, to De Coninck, "Do you think the *Drommedaris* would hold up if we set a bit more east?" Although moving some cannons to the hull did help with the stability of the vessel, it did not solve the problem completely; the *Drommedaris* was still unstable and hard to handle.

"We're about to find out," De Coninck said with a shrug. He took a sip of brandy, swirling it around his mouth, and with closed eyes, swallowed slowly. When the burn died down, he spoke again, "I like this plan; however, we all need to agree on it. And from this point forward, we need to stay close together. Who knows what awaits us this far south?" Looking to Van Riebeeck, he asked, "Governor?"

Van Riebeeck spoke in a voice smooth and strong. "Gentlemen, you've brought us safely thus far." He halted briefly, and all knew he was thinking of his son. The moment passed silently.

"I, too, greatly favor setting foot on land as soon as possible. However, the ever-present threat posed by so many enemies must not escape our consideration. We have the French," he pointed to the brandy, "the Danes, the English, and the bloody Portuguese. It seemed the only country we might consider friendly is Liechtenstein, and that is simply because they are landlocked."

"Are we not at peace with England? Surely that is one force we do not have to worry about at this time." Captain Turver was correct in theory, but this far south, rules and treaties quickly got very blurry.

"I don't trust them," De Coninck remarked.

The VOC merchant ships were well armed to defend against enemy or pirate threats, but together, the three posed a formidable front.

"Yes, our arrival at the Cape can get a bit noisy with so many hypocritical friends and open enemies. The waters are teeming with privateers and corsairs. I say we shoot first and then see if it's worth asking questions after. How many guns do you still have on deck?" Hooghsaet asked De Coninck.

"Not enough," De Coninck sighed. "I could bring one or two back up, but what we gain in firepower, we lose in stability."

Hooghsaet pressed his lips together and shook his head.

CHAPTER 17

"No," his voice rang sure and deep, "keep them below decks and try not to sink. We'll watch your back." He sent Turver a look that made the young man nod earnestly in agreement, straightening more in his chair, the backrest now wholly abandoned. Van Riebeeck suppressed a smile and felt a pang of sympathy for the poor boy.

Saturday, April 5, 1652

Niklas found himself glued to the stern rail, his nautical telescope firmly pressed to his right eye.

"How long has he been standing there?" Sebastiaan asked. The captain was at the whip staff, and Sebastiaan and Arent stood close by. Sailing so close to the African coast had required all hands on deck to keep the *Drommedaris* afloat. The task pushed each man to the brink of his endurance. It was times like these that the crew's experience shined through. Rules tightened, and discipline sharpened, for tired men were prone to mistakes when there was no room for it.

"Since lunch," Arent replied.

"Damn, are we really *that* close? It's a touch ahead of schedule," Sebastiaan mused. The last week had been rough on everyone. The crew was exhausted, and the passengers had given up three days ago on being seasick. The *Drommedaris* was dancing on the ocean like an unbroken colt. On the bright side, they were still *on* the water and not beneath it.

"I don't know, but we know better than most not to doubt Lord Niklas, and he's been itching since yesterday." Arent gave his beard a raspy scratch and continued to scan the water.

"I'll give that boy all the Spanish reals in my purse if he is right," De Coninck grumbled.

"And how many do you have, Uncle?"

"Four."

Sebastiaan laughed, thanking Niklas for not being a greedy man.

"Table Mountain!" Niklas roared from the topmost deck. The call came at five bells past noon. The announcement was met with a stunned and grateful silence, quickly shattered by exuberant cheering that pumped renewed energy into all.

Captain De Coninck turned to Sebastiaan and Arent. "Hoist the flag and fire the shot," he barked his orders with a face-splitting grin.

Niklas came down from the weather deck with the same urgency one would display upon returning from a visit to one's elderly grandmother. Not a feather was ruffled as he resumed his duties at the whip.

"Well done, lad! Sharp as ever," the captain said, laughing as he slapped Niklas repeatedly on the shoulder. The navigator looked down; his lips moved as if to say something, but he only nodded quietly, ill at ease with all the praise and attention.

Moments later, Sebastiaan hoisted a yellow and blue ensign, followed shortly by a crash of gunfire as a single shot rang from the main deck, sharing the good news with the *Reijger* and *Goede Hoop*.

On deck, the exhaustion and lethargy of the last few days evaporated like steam. Men scrambled up and down from the hull to the main deck, carrying tools and barrels; others were preparing the sloop to take the scouting party ashore. Passengers flooded the deck, shaking hands and backslapping the sailors, offering help of all and any kind. De Coninck decided to let the chaos reign for a bit longer and turned to find the governor; they had much to discuss.

* * *

"I find myself momentarily at a loss for what to do." Governor Van Riebeeck was lounging in a chair in front of De Coninck's desk.

The captain nodded awkwardly, with his head tilted back against his chair.

"Well, we won't be able to do much for the rest of the day. Tomorrow we'll send two men in the sloop to scout the bay and see if any nasty surprises await us. Much will depend on their report."

Van Riebeeck and De Coninck sat in companionable silence, enjoying the noise from the decks outside. A knock fell on the cabin door, and Barent entered.

"Just coming to inform you of the menu for dinner, Cap." De Coninck gave

CHAPTER 17

the cook a heavy-lidded stare.

"It will be salted meat and stale bread. Again. Knowing that it is mostly everybody's favorite." The cook gave a hearty chuckle that made his belly shake. The good-natured comment elicited a bark of laughter from Van Riebeeck.

"And an extra ration of brandy for all. Thank you, Barent." That brought a scowl to the cook's face.

"Cap, I would have to open the last barrel then," he protested.

"The only crime worse than mutiny, Barent," De Coninck reasoned, "is to ration brandy with our destination in sight."

* * *

It was past dark when the governor and his wife stood side by side at her spot on the deck, knowing that the last connection to their son would be lost when they set foot on land. He looked to his wife, and his heart swelled with tenderness. She was still so young and had had to bear so much.

All three ships had dropped anchor close to land, having sailed past the bay during the afternoon, making sure to stay out of sight of any enemy eyes scanning the horizon. Now they were lying close together, tucked behind The Lion's Rump, so named for that part of the mountain looked somewhat like a lion resting on its haunches.

She sighed and rested her head against his arm, listening to the waves crashing on the beach beyond.

"Welcome to our new home, my darling," Van Riebeeck said and turned to kiss the top of her head.

"Home," she exhaled, "would such a thing be possible?"

She knew what a halfway station would mean to sailors' health and well-being on long voyages. Having a place to stop and replenish their fresh food and water supplies would be a godsend, and with His good grace, they would be able to make it so. She also knew that her husband was an ambitious man. His drive was one of the things she loved most about him. He could see the advantages of establishing a fort and gardens at the Cape, for he had campaigned vigorously in favor of it. Still, she doubted he intended to remain on the African continent for the rest of his days.

Since the debacle in Japan, where his superior's overzealous opium trading also tarnished *his* reputation, he felt he needed a project to prove himself to the mighty Seventeen, and the establishment at the Cape was just that.

"Husband, I know you have your heart set on India."

He looked at her sharply, surprised by the direction of her thoughts.

"But I am compelled to inform you that unless I can walk there, we're not going."

"Then the Cape of Good Hope will have to do."

Chapter 18

"Do not scratch my paint," Mattheys yelled at the men lowering the sloop over the side of the *Drommedaris* and into Table Bay, as they had come to call the turbulent bay in honor of the flat-topped mountain guarding over it.

"Mattheys," Arent's warning came shortly on the heels of the carpenter's grumbling as he turned towards the forecastle.

A crowd had gathered on deck. In fact, everybody was on deck this morning to wave off the three men who would scout the bay for enemy ships.

There was a disturbance among the onlookers as one man pushed his way to the front. It had taken the combined efforts of the expedition's three captains to explain to the governor why he could not join the scouting party. It was strictly a scouting mission. They needed to know if there were any enemy ships in the bay and, if so, whether they should prepare for attack or defense. The governor had conceded the point the previous evening, but obviously had a change of heart overnight, for there he was, angling towards Arent, no doubt to renew his pleas to be allowed aboard the sloop.

Arent had already chosen the two men who would accompany him. Sebastiaan because there was no chance he would venture into any uncertain circumstance without knowing his back was covered. Adam Hulster, the bookkeeper, because the man had eyes like a hawk.

"Mister Van Jeveren," the governor chose the path of deep respect. "I would like to be part of the scouting mission. I think it would be extremely beneficial to …" The governor stopped speaking when he noted how tightly Arent was pinching his eyes whilst vigorously shaking his head. When the governor's voice trailed off, Arent lifted one finger, and the universal signal for silence was observed and understood. Arent answered to one authority on this planet, and it was not to God, or to the Seventeen Lords in Amsterdam, or to Governor Van Riebeeck. It was to Davit De Coninck, and to him alone. Anyone beyond that held no significance, but he was nothing if not polite.

"Governor, it is not a good idea." It was a good explanation by his standards. Furthermore, he had used a gentle tone and even added a smile for good measure. The governor mistook the response as offering room for discussion. Arent narrowed his eyes and looked at the sun. It was past nine already, and they were wasting time. The swells were only growing higher, and he suspected that by noon, white caps would be forming, impeding, and dramatically taxing their rowing and ability to see. They needed to get a move on. He turned to the governor, fists planted in his sides, his legs the required shoulder-width apart and bending slightly at the waist to bring his eyes level with the shorter man's. Somebody in the crowd giggled nervously, and De Coninck bit back a smile and looked down to study his fingernails.

Arent took a deep breath. It was time to dig up and dust off his long-suffering diplomacy skills.

"Governor, with all due respect. Entertaining as it might be to watch you run around a crispy white beach with a Hottentot arrow in your arse, I don't think the event would benefit the longevity of this fledgling colony *or* your dignity, for that matter. We'll scout, and when I give the all-clear, you follow, after and not before. Until then, you sit tight and wait." With the matter settled, Arent turned and barked at his two companions.

Governor Van Riebeeck was undeterred by the boatswain's high-handed manner. He stepped closer and waited for the man to return his attention to him. Arent heaved a frustrated sigh. Ideally, he would have preferred to count to five, but time was of the essence, so when he reached two, he wordlessly looked at the governor and raised his eyebrows.

"Would I be able to wave goodbye from the railing?" Van Riebeeck asked without missing a beat, mischief dancing in his deep brown eyes.

Slapping the governor on the shoulder, Arent disappeared over the railing, the sound of his laughter following him into the waiting sloop.

CHAPTER 18

***

The sloop had returned two hours before dark. Arent, Sebastiaan, and the bookkeeper had surveyed the bay and all its coves, finding it devoid of any ships. Thus, they determined that the bay was safe enough to move closer to land.

Their only view of the new land was the large cone-shaped mountain they were hiding behind. Yesterday they had a brief view of Table Mountain, edged by a hazy white line, but from that distance, it looked like the mountain was floating in the ocean and not the southern tip of the mighty African continent. Now, long past sundown, it was no more than just a black mass, but the air was crisp and filled with the scent of plants, rich earth, the sound of birdsong, and the waves crashing against the rocky edge of the Lion's Rump. The *Drommedaris* was at rest, her sails clewed, and her anchor dropped. She had reached her destination and had brought her passengers safely to their new shores. The three-and-a-half-month journey was arduous, but she was intact and would serve as home to most passengers until temporary dwellings could be constructed.

The aim was to start the construction of a fort and gardens as soon as possible. It would provide shelter from the elements and protection from attacks, both from sea and land.

Danielle was standing on the weather deck, breathing in the sweet-smelling air and staring at the outline of Table Mountain. Like all aboard, she was eager to go ashore, but the captain and six soldiers were going on the morrow to scout the area and search for any correspondence from passing ships. Hopefully, they would return with vegetables or fruit, fresh fish, and by the grace of all that is holy, fresh water.

A deep sense of peace had settled over her. It was autumn, something she would have to get used to. It would be mid-spring in Europe, and the days were growing longer. Here it was the opposite. The remaining heat from the day radiated from the land, and she closed her eyes at the sensation. It would be wonderful to start fresh, to create a home here in this unknown wilderness, but not for her. She was only here for a short while before leaving with

Sebastiaan to start her life elsewhere. It would be hard to leave her friends. The twins had become like her sisters, annoying, loud, messy, and loyal, and she loved them. Maria was her friend, and the thought of what they'd been through together made Danielle's throat swell thickly with emotion.

"What are you thinking about?" Maria asked gently, and Danielle nearly jumped out of her skin at the unexpected intrusion. Maria laughed, a sound so beautiful it rolled like pearls across the deck.

"I'm sorry, I did not mean to startle you. I thought you heard my approach."

"Don't apologize. I can't remember the last time I heard your laugh."

Maria came to stand next to her, and together they stared at the horizon.

"I need to go ashore. My medicine supplies are dangerously low." Danielle needed to stock up for the journey ahead as well.

"Believe me, everybody has a pressing need to go ashore, but you have to bide your time. We must wait for the captain to return tomorrow. Perhaps we could go the day after."

"We?"

"Well, yes, I would love to go with you, and you can teach me all about the plants you use to make medicine."

The message was clear. Somebody would have to do it when Danielle left, and Maria was thinking ahead. The thought filled Danielle with a strange emotion she was unwilling to examine at present, so she pushed it aside.

"That would be wonderful. Oh, to feel the dirt under my feet and earth that does not move."

"The men will want to be sure it's safe before they allow us to go. As Arent explained so eloquently this morning, it would not do for us to be running on the beach chased by Hottentots," Maria said and laughed at the memory of Arent's words to her husband. "Besides, I am a terrible runner. They would easily catch me, and then who knows what would become of me."

"Are they hostile?" Danielle asked.

"I honestly don't know. There are so many mixed reports. I guess we'll find out soon enough." She paused for a moment. "My husband is optimistic, but then again, he's always had the heart of an adventurer."

CHAPTER 18

***

Captain De Coninck left with ten armed soldiers and two oarsmen directly upon completion of the morning service, significantly shorter than his regular Sunday service due to the governor's impatience.

The captain's departure was not met with any drama, for the governor had come to learn that no matter the firmness of his orders or the severity of his threats, nothing would sway De Coninck. He would stay aboard until the captain was confident it was safe to go ashore.

Shortly after sunrise, the *Reijger* dropped anchor next to the *Drommedaris*. The two crews celebrated the event by flinging censurable insults back and forth.

Captain Hooghsaet boarded the *Drommedaris* and joined the governor on the weather deck.

"Good morning, Governor." Hooghsaet bowed respectfully the instant he cleared the companionway. He liked the governor; there was a fire burning in his belly that showed in his eyes. What he admired most was that the young governor did not waste time with subterfuge. He was as straight and true as an arrow. This morning the governor's shoulders were pulled tight, his back ramrod straight, and his fingers were drumming a steady rhythm on the railing. Impatience crackled around him like a lightning storm.

"Good morning, Captain Hooghsaet," Van Riebeeck greeted with a bow of his own before he turned back to stare at the little sloop being tossed about by waves bent on crashing it to pieces.

"That looks uncomfortable," Hooghsaet chuckled.

"I've prayed in earnest for their safe landing, but I've now taken to repeating only the highlights. May the good Lord forgive my lack of rhetoric." Van Riebeeck sounded so earnest in his concerns that Hooghsaet let out a bark of laughter.

"Aye, it's a bit rough. You can be glad not to be aboard."

"I'm not relieved in the least," Van Riebeeck said, and his voice took on an edge that drew Hooghsaet's attention. "It's a sore topic, and I have no wish to discuss it," the governor stated, not taking his eyes from the struggling sloop.

Hooghsaet understood instantly. The governor was itching to go ashore. "He's making you wait, isn't he?" he asked, just to see what reaction he might get. He was not disappointed.

Sensing an ally, Van Riebeeck turned to Hooghsaet. "That beach is as bare as a baby's bottom," he pointed vigorously at the hazy, white strip of land hugged tightly by a dense, lush forest, "and yet, here I am, reduced to a mere spectator. We seem to be forever scouting for trouble. Yesterday it was an empty bay, and today, an empty beach." The governor elegantly cleared his throat as he aired his discontentment.

"Most inconvenient," Hooghsaet agreed. His hulking frame dwarfed the governor, so he bent forward and rested his forearms on the gunwale. With squinting eyes, he watched as the men wrestled the sloop onto the beach. It would be better to deposit the governor onto land from the mouth of the river, where the waters were calm. That surf was not conducive for a man to remain in possession of his dignity.

"Most," the governor lamented, and both men turned when Barent appeared with a tray of refreshments.

Shortly after lunch, De Coninck returned with the two oarsmen, various vegetables, and a net heavy with fish. He swung over the railing and handed the governor a packet of letters wrapped in thick oiled leather.

Clasping hands with Hooghsaet, the two captains exchanged news as the governor wasted no time and unceremoniously unwrapped the bundle, scanned the contents, and selected a letter.

De Coninck had left the ten soldiers on land with orders to keep watch. He was tired and looked forward to a hearty meal, a glass of French brandy, and good company. Tomorrow the governor would want to go ashore. After that, their daily routine would change. This afternoon would be one of the rare moments of peace where all was as it should be. His musings were cut short when the governor drew his attention.

Van Riebeeck explained that a returning fleet had passed the Cape in January and had left two horses and tools with a local tribesman. He handed De Coninck the letter and turned to Hooghsaet as he discussed the content. When De Coninck finished the lengthy report, he carefully folded the parchment

CHAPTER 18

on its creases.

"It is all settled then. Captain, when you are ready." Van Riebeeck looked to De Coninck, his hands planted in his sides and his feet rolling onto their balls and back.

"When I am ready for what?" De Coninck did not understand the expectation in the governor's mien.

"To depart," Van Riebeeck's explanation sounded more like a command as he turned towards the ladder leading down to the sloop.

Too late, De Coninck grasped the governor's meaning while Hooghsaet roared with laughter.

"Wait. No. Governor Van Riebeeck, just wait a moment, please." It must have been De Coninck's pleading tone that halted the governor. "Don't you need to dress for the occasion? Or have a flag? This is an auspicious moment. We'll go tomorrow." De Coninck could not fathom why the man was in such a hurry, but more so he did not look forward to making that trip twice in one day.

"Captain," the governor was visibly holding on to his patience. "You will notice that I am dressed. Also, we do not need a flag, for we are the only ones in the bay, and I can assure you, the natives would not care for the meaning, one way or another. However, I agree with you; it will truly be an auspicious moment if we make it to the beach in one piece, indeed." He looked from one captain to the other, waiting for more objections. When none were forthcoming, he continued, "Now then, where are your ten soldiers?" he asked as his eyes focused on De Coninck.

"I left them on the beach."

"Perfect, let's make haste."

When Governor Van Riebeeck had watched the sloop make its way to shore earlier in the day, it looked like a mighty struggle. Sitting in the middle of the small vessel, clinging onto a length of rope, he found the trip a hellish ordeal. The swells rolling to the beach lifted them so high as to have a clear view of their destination and, in the next instant, dropped them so low that they were surrounded by nothing but walls of water.

When they reached the breakwater, Van Riebeeck knew that hell was several levels deeper than he anticipated. White foamy water slammed between their shoulder blades, pushing them forward, only to be assaulted by a similar wall of water slamming into their faces as the front of the sloop fought the wave ahead.

The two oarsmen in the front, and captains De Coninck and Hooghsaet behind him, kept them from capsizing. Van Riebeeck watched as four oars lifted and pushed down at precisely the same time, keeping the small vessel perfectly balanced. The sloop lifted high on the crest of a wave, all oars lifted, and in the next heartbeat, its belly slammed down on the white froth. The oars dipped, pushed back, lifted, swung forward, dipped, and pushed again. The steady rhythm transfixed him. The last wave drove them at breakneck speed towards the fast-approaching land, and the governor tightened his hold on the thick rope.

As the wave lost its power and the sloop slowed down, the four men leaped as one over the side. They were waist-deep in the water as they clutched the sloop's sides, steering it toward the white sand. Van Riebeeck made to get up as well, but Captain De Coninck shook his head at him; water was streaming down his face. It still amazed him how these men seemed to communicate without words and act in perfect unison.

Van Riebeeck glanced from De Coninck on the port side to Hooghsaet on the starboard side and was taken aback by the boyish looks on both faces. With hair plastered to their heads, drenched to the bone, and waves crashing into their backs, they both grinned from ear to ear.

"Stay put, Governor," De Coninck ordered, "we need you to keep the sloop on the water." Van Riebeeck gave his captain a perplexed frown.

"Aye, if you get up, it'll tip right over." Hooghsaet laughed as he shook his mahogany hair from his face. Convinced that he was the butt end of their joke, Van Riebeeck sat back down.

When the four men pulled the sloop from the water's edge, De Coninck nodded to Van Riebeeck. The governor rose, straightened his sodden coat, and stepped from the small vessel onto the golden African sand. It felt strange to be standing without movement under his feet. His brain was so used to adjusting his balance to the moving floor that it took him a few moments

CHAPTER 18

to grow accustomed to the solid earth. The men paid him little attention as they pulled the sloop further away from the water. Once the sloop was safely embedded in the dry sand, the two sailors took a fishing net and headed for the river.

Five armed soldiers with bare feet and flapping shirt tails came running towards the new arrivals. They stopped a few yards away from the governor and the captains, each in his own time. Hands raised to foreheads in what must've been an attempt at a salute. Hooghsaet growled, and De Coninck turned to Governor Van Riebeeck, "They're your probl-," he paused, then rethought his statement, "they're yours to command now, governor."

The governor regarded the line of undisciplined soldiers, then bit back the scathing remark they so thoroughly deserved and asked, "Where is the rest of your company?" His displeasure must have shown, for the men tried to straighten themselves when the oldest of the group answered.

"Three Hottentot men arrived about an hour ago, wanting an audience. We told them to wait till morning." Realizing that he'd not answered the governor's question, he added, "The other men are guarding them."

"Guarding them?" Governor Van Riebeeck's anger was at a steady simmer, but he held it tightly under control. "Where are they now?" he demanded.

"Sitting on the dune over there," the soldier replied, tilting his head in the direction from whence he came. Van Riebeeck narrowed his eyes at the man, who then ended his statement with a belated, "Sir."

"Take us to them," Van Riebeeck barked, and the soldiers turned, one accidentally bumping into another, to lead the way.

Five men were loosely lounging around a fire, and the smell of roasting fish clung to the afternoon breeze. Five muskets rested on their butts against a large rock, muzzles pointing upward, accompanied by ten rapiers, tips in the sand. They waited until the approaching party was about ten feet away before they concocted a counterfeit look of surprise and jumped to their feet. Thumbs scratched foreheads in what could only be yet another feeble attempt at a salute.

Three native men, each a generation apart, were squatting on the crest of a dune a small distance away. They did not bother to rise when the governor approached. Instead, they narrowed their eyes and assessed the newcomers with deep interest.

Van Riebeeck scanned the girdle of half-eaten fish and then looked each soldier in the eye when he spoke.

"Do we not extend our hospitality to our guests?" His tone was deceptively low and mild.

"Governor?" one of the men asked, his dull eyes too lazy to stay focused at one point for long.

"Did you share your food with the three men on the dune?" This time Van Riebeeck's voice held a sharp edge, and it seemed to straighten the man a few degrees.

"They are savages, Governor." The man had the gall to look perplexed. He even twisted his head like a dog begging for a treat. The anger Van Riebeeck was suppressing since laying eyes on the first soldier reached its boiling point. He resisted the urge to kick the girdle from the coals; showing such undisciplined behavior would make him no better than the nitwits standing before him.

"Fall in," the governor barked. The authority in his voice, accompanied by the cold stares from the two formidable-looking captains, left no room for misinterpretation. The ten soldiers scrambled to form a saw-toothed line.

Van Riebeeck counted his blessings, for he did not think they would understand the command. He was no military commander but had already made his mind up to spend considerable time and ingenuity in the endeavor to improve these men's military prowess. He doubted they would ever be disciplined or effective soldiers, but by God, they would be less irritating when he was done with them.

The governor started towards the three Hottentots. Captain De Coninck followed the governor, and Captain Hooghsaet turned towards the crooked line of men; a soft smile lifted the tips of his copper-brown mustache.

One of the Hottentots rose and patiently waited as the two white men made their way up the dune. His companions on either side of him remained in their squatted positions.

Governor Van Riebeeck reached the top, slightly out of breath. Regaining

CHAPTER 18

his composure, he assessed the man staring at him. He looked deep in his middle years, with greyish-brown skin, wrinkled as if it was used to housing a much larger man. The bones in his face and chest stood out in stark relief. He was naked except for a small loincloth covering the essential parts and the skin of what must have been a small antelope over his shoulders. His lips formed a firm line under his wide nose, but it was the clear, sharp black eyes that held the governor's attention.

Van Riebeeck executed a perfect deep bow de rigueur with those at the royal court, lifted his hand, and placed it over his heart.

"Jan," he introduced himself in a clear voice, deciding his first name would be easier to pronounce than his lengthy last.

The Hottentot repeated the gesture and introduced himself as Harry.

Van Riebeeck was taken aback by the unmistakable accent and the unexpected name. He turned to share a brief look with De Coninck, who looked similarly bemused.

"English?" De Coninck asked Van Riebeeck in Dutch.

When Van Riebeeck looked back at Harry, he noted a proud smile splitting his face. He must've heard and understood De Coninck's question.

A broken conversation in English and Dutch accompanied by various hand gestures followed. Harry had learned many words from previous shipwrecked sailors, enough to convey the information Van Riebeeck needed.

Yes, he was in possession of tools and two horses, which he would hand over on the morrow in return for a length of copper wire as compensation for the safekeeping of these items over the last four months. When Van Riebeeck inquired as to what constitutes a length of copper wire, he learned it was equivalent to roughly two yards. It was an exorbitant fee, but the governor reckoned they could have eaten the horses, given their apparent malnourished state; they didn't.

Van Riebeeck explained their presence at the Cape of Good Hope and what they aimed to achieve over the coming months and years. It was a difficult concept to convey in basic broken language, and many questions followed. In the end, the governor took a stick and outlined the fort and something resembling fruit trees in the sand. All three Hottentots scurried closer to the drawing and studied it from various angles. A lengthy deliberation ensued in a language entirely put together by clicking sounds. Harry seemed to be doing most of the explaining, with the others nodding in contemplative agreement.

Returning his attention to the governor, Harry offered to show him the gardens created by the shipwrecked sailors of the *Haerlem*, two years earlier. Interestingly, he seemed in favor of the construction of the fort.

When the governor asked about the likelihood of other tribes in the area, Harry explained that three tribes visited the Cape during the course of a year. The Khoikhoi came from the west coast down to the mountain for fishing. They seemed to be peaceful and in possession of some cattle. From what Van Riebeeck could deduce, Harry's daughter was one of the wives of their chief.

The second group, the Saldanhars, came from the east. Harry's movements became more animated and his face more expressive as he described the evil, violent tribe that owned many head of cattle but refused to share their wealth. Upon hearing the name of their hated enemy, the older man spat to the side, and the younger nervously fidgeted with the edge of his loincloth.

Then there was the third group, the Beach Rangers, or Hottentots, to which Harry and his family belonged. They were a peace-loving tribe that mainly remained in the south and lived off the sea.

They all seemed nomadic in nature, and Governor Van Riebeeck was beginning to understand Harry's partiality towards constructing a fort. It would be a permanent source of food and protection for him and his tribe.

With most of the critical topics discussed, Van Riebeeck gestured toward the cooking fire below on the beach. He invited the three Beach Rangers to join them for an early dinner provided by the two oarsmen who had returned with a net heavy with coppery red *steenbras*, a local fish of the sea bream family.

The soldiers had undergone a transformation that the governor thought would take him months to accomplish. They stood at attention in a painfully straight line, shirts neatly tucked, shoulders back, chins high, and eyes staring into the forest beyond. Captain Hooghsaet was contentedly sitting on a nearby boulder, sucking on his pipe and blowing perfectly round smoke rings.

CHAPTER 18

Chapter 19

It was the second time she was summoned to the dayroom by the captain. This time, she was not facing the broad committee but the three captains and the governor. During the first meeting, she'd physically attacked Captain De Coninck, but now she had little desire to repeat the performance. The incident felt like it happened years ago, not merely a few short months. So much had happened between then and now.

"Thank you, Barent," Captain De Coninck said, and once more, the dayroom door closed quietly behind the cook, leaving her standing in the middle of the room.

"Miss Van Aard," he acknowledged her with a curt nod and then turned to a large middle-aged man with red hair. He was draped like a piece of laundry over the chair he occupied.

"This here is Captain Hooghsaet of the *Reijger*." The older man nodded to her with sparkling eyes and a warm smile. She liked him. He exuded a magnetic vitality that was hard to ignore; worse, she suspected he was well aware of the fact.

"And Captain Turver of the *Goeie Hoop*." Captain De Coninck pointed to a young man with dark hair, pale skin, and a tight upper lip. He was very proud of how he dressed. That much she could deduce, for his ensemble was well put together. But the strains of the long journey showed, especially in how the once-white shirt was valiantly clinging to its former elegant shape. The *Goeie Hoop* was clearly running low on starch. She paid him the due respect and then greeted the governor. Governor Van Riebeeck's warm eyes and soft smile made her feel at ease, and the tension left her posture.

CHAPTER 19

"Please take a seat," De Coninck said, pointing to a chair. Danielle was no fool. She can clearly remember how the conversation went the last time he invited her to sit down.

"I'll stand if it's all the same, but thank you."

De Coninck stared at her, his lips pinched and his eyes calculating. No doubt entertaining various creative ways in which he was going to wring her neck later. For some inexplicable reason, he let the matter go with an annoyed, "Fine."

Captain Hooghsaet released a loud "Ha," slapped the table with the flat of his hand that made the crockery rattle, and declared, "Aye, she'll do."

Danielle glanced nervously from one man to the next, unsure what to make of the outburst of enthusiasm.

Captain De Coninck continued to explain how disease had broken out on the *Goeie Hoop* and that little more than a handful of men were affected. However, the ship's surgeon was old and needed assistance; since the patients could not come to him, it meant he would have to climb up and down the companionways.

"Could he identify the disease?" she asked Captain Turver, who seemed taken aback by her direct question. Unsure if he would lower himself to answer a woman, he looked to De Coninck, who encouraged him with a nod.

"Yes, he believes it to be dysentery."

As far as Danielle was aware, there was no cure. The disease would run its course in about seven days at most, if the patient and his bedding were kept very clean. Otherwise, it would recur until the patient died.

"Of course, I will do whatever I can."

"Excellent," De Coninck concluded. "We'll row you over tomorrow morning, with an escort, naturally."

"No," she immediately protested. "I mean, yes. Tomorrow morning, but no escort."

Captain De Coninck was instantly annoyed, thinking she was just being contrary again.

"Why not?" he demanded.

"The disease is highly contagious. I don't want others to be exposed to it and spread it to the *Drommedaris*. I would probably have to stay on the *Goeie Hoop* until it is under control."

"Out of the question," De Coninck declared with so much vehemence she thought it would be supremely foolish to oppose him. "You will come home every night. Is that understood?"

Home. Danielle smiled softly. He would not know how much that misspoken word meant to her.

"Yes, sir. It should mitigate the problem if I scrub down entirely and dress in fresh clothes before leaving the *Goeie Hoop*." She fought the tears that threatened to gather in her eyes. She had a home. "I think," she added belatedly.

The matter was thus settled. Danielle would be rowed to the *Goeie Hoop* every morning at sunrise with a spare set of clothes and back every evening at sundown.

* * *

The *Goeie Hoop* was anchored near the mouth of the Fresh River. It was a humble little river carrying water from the mountain to the Atlantic. At five fathoms, the mouth was deep enough to accommodate the vessel comfortably and allow it to lie close to the shore in relatively calm waters.

The view was breathtaking. It was like the continent had rushed towards the sea and, at the last moment, changed its mind, coming to a stop against itself, creating the beautiful, flat-topped mountain with its two cone-shaped companions on either side, pushing at its foot a lush green forest that ended in a brilliant white beach.

Energetic waves violently pounded the shoreline. It would be easy to think this paradise, were it not for the corpses lying in a neat line on the glittering sand.

Three sloops had already made several trips since yesterday, carrying the dead to the beach for burial. The stench engulfing the vessel was thick enough to be described by its color. A heady south-easterly had been blowing for the last three days, and Danielle realized that the wind was blowing the smell

CHAPTER 19

inland. No wonder nobody aboard the *Drommedaris* had smelled anything.

She'd purposefully left her medicine box behind. There was no point in depleting her stores. It was best to use what was available on board.

The two men rowing the sloop to deliver her to the *Goeie Hoop* had waited until she was safely aboard before returning to the *Drommedaris*. Now she was standing on the upper deck, trying not to vomit. Captain Turver was striding purposefully toward her.

"Good morning, Miss Van Aard," he greeted, and she wondered what he found so good about the morning. From where she was standing, the smell would suggest otherwise. But true to form, he maintained a stiff smile, and she had the feeling he was having trouble keeping his eyes on her face and not letting them run over her form.

"Allow me to show you to the surgeon's room." He took her elbow, and she let herself be guided to a small cupboard-sized cabin. An old man was bent over a desk writing a few notes by the flickering light of a candle, for there was no window.

"Mister Rose, your assistant has arrived," Captain Turver spoke in a voice loud enough to startle her. When the man managed to turn himself around, there was a questioning scowl on his old face.

"Your assistant," Captain Turver nearly yelled.

"My what?" Mister Rose yelled back.

Captain Turver abandoned the attempt at civil introductions and turned to leave while mumbling something in her direction she thought sounded like "good luck."

The surgeon leaned closer to Danielle with narrowed eyes. At first, she thought he was about to sniff her, then she came to suspect that he was not only hard of hearing but nearly sightless as well.

"Who are you?" he barked at her.

She explained the situation with exaggerated hand gestures and a loud voice that came out slightly shriller than she'd anticipated.

"You're a woman." This time the bark had a strong accusatory slant to it.

Danielle suspected he could hear higher-pitched sounds better and responded while bending her voice to accommodate him.

"What am I supposed to do with a woman?" Beggars and all that crossed her mind, but she kept the thought to herself, thinking the question rhetorical. She decided not to abuse her voice by trying to answer. In response, she offered a shrug and decided to follow him around until he led her to the sick men.

They descended into the main deck. Danielle had left her satchel with clothes in the surgeon's little room, only extracting a broad, long bandage from the bag. She would have sagged to the floor if it were not for her hand pressing against the wall. The sight was not unfamiliar after having seen dysentery before in her father's surgery. One case of dysentery was a challenge to a person's constitution; more than a hundred in a confined space was diabolical.

Two lanterns valiantly tried to light the room but only managed a small circle around themselves, leaving the rest in a dusty greyness. Several windows lined the wall, and Danielle could see thin slices of sunlight trying to cut through the boards nailed in front of it. There were no beds or hammocks. The sick were lying on the open floorboards. She took a hesitant step while tying the bandage around her nose and mouth. Her fingers were numb, and she swallowed hard several times to force the content of her stomach back. Her feet made a sloshing sound every time she took a step, and it was not hard to imagine what caused it. Judging by the smell, she deduced that a thick layer of bloody feces and vomit covered the floor. The patients were lying on the floor, in their own misery, without so much as a blanket beneath them. All were naked and in various stages of dying. Those still lucid looked at her with hollow eyes. Never had she seen or imagined a scene so hopeless and devoid of humanity.

The large room led into the galley, with a fire burning in the grate and freshly flayed fish on the chopping board. But then it suddenly all made perfect sense. This room used to be the mess hall, and there should have been a long table in the middle with benches on either side. They had removed all the furniture and turned the room into a sickroom. It was sheltered from the elements and close to the upper deck to remove the dead. The forecastle was then most likely for those not already sick.

CHAPTER 19

The surgeon was walking among the men, mumbling and scribbling on a piece of parchment. Danielle followed at a sedate pace, wondering if he even noticed the suffering at his feet. He did an admirable job of ignoring her, but then she thought the odds were more likely that he had already forgotten that she was there.

Death was ruling with an iron fist in this antechamber of hell, and its old minion walked among the suffering, keeping tally. The surgeon was careful not to touch any of the sick. On occasion, he would stoop over a body, apparently gathering some information using his remaining senses, and Danielle thought herself overly optimistic thinking of such in the plural. Then he straightened, hawked, and spat, adding to the soup sludge on the floor before shuffling along.

Somewhere in the darkness, a man coughed, and the sound was accompanied by his bowels releasing with a wet sound. Instinctively Danielle scanned to see which of the patients it was when her foot hooked on something, and she lost her balance. She snapped her arms out to break her fall, but her hands slipped away, causing her to land flat on her belly. She managed to turn her face sideways and lift it away from the floor.

No matter how hard she swallowed, she could not keep her rising vomit at bay any longer. Gaining her feet, she rushed from the room and up the companionway, yanking the bandage from her face. Once on the upper deck, she ran to the bulwark and emptied her stomach repeatedly until she was heaving with nothing left to throw up. Hanging over the side, she gulped the fresh air with tears streaming down her face.

A firm hand on her back brought her upright. Captain Turver took a step backward, brushing the hand that had touched her forcefully on his breeches. Wiping her mouth on her sleeve, she turned to look at him.

"Good heavens, woman, what happened to you? Are you ill?"

"I am not ill. I am shocked." Danielle's throat burned, and her mouth tasted bitter. "Water, please," she managed, and to her surprise, the pompous little man turned to scoop water from a nearby barrel with a mug that looked like it should better serve as something to carry ashes from the stove. He handed it to her but kept his distance. Danielle rinsed her mouth and spat the water over the side.

A look of disgust leaped onto his face, where it froze in abject horror. Captain Turver looked her up and down, but there was nothing lecherous in the gesture. Danielle followed his gaze. It became instantly apparent why he was so horrified. The front of her once-white shirt was wet and hung limp under the weight of the brown moisture. Thankfully the stays she wore underneath made it not stick to her skin. The hem of her skirt was sodden with evidence of what was happening below decks.

Good men were dying like animals stripped of their dignity, with nobody caring for them. Men who had fought and survived the same storms as those on the *Drommedaris*. Men who joined this expedition not looking for adventure or to advance their careers but to feed their families, who loved them and were waiting for them to come home. Looking at the young captain, she squared her shoulders and found her voice.

"Yes, sir, this is the look and smell of human suffering." She would wear these stains as marks of honor. The surgeon was in dire need of help. And that was precisely what he would get.

"Mr. Rose asked that water be boiled and brought down to the sickroom," she lied, hoping the young captain would do as she asked. Holding her chin high, she stared him down until he nodded and walked toward the forecastle, calling for an aide.

As she reached the hellhole below decks, a plan was starting to take shape. First, they needed fresh air, so she began prying the wooden planks from the windows. Wedging her fingers between the rough planks, she pulled them from the opening. When she reached the third window, the surgeon became aware of the change in the room. He was clearly not in favor of it and ordered her to immediately cease the lunacy and replace the window coverings. Arguing with him was pointless, so she stubbornly shook her head and kept going. Even if this were all she accomplished today, it would be an improvement. She was fairly sure the planks would be back in place come morning, but she planned to beg a tool from Mattheys to make removing them easier. This was a battle she would win out of sheer determination and stubbornness if nothing else. These men would not die in the dark.

CHAPTER 19

Captain Turver was nothing if not good at following orders, and a steady supply of hot water was delivered to the top of the companionway for the remainder of the day. Each time Danielle returned to collect a fresh bucket, she would empty the used one over the ship's side with strict orders for it to be thoroughly cleaned before being filled again. Finding a pile of rags in the galley, she knelt next to the man she thought was closest to death and started to wash his sweat and feces-covered body before moving on to the next. Most of them were unconscious, and she doubted they would last the night.

It was late afternoon when Danielle emerged from the main deck. Begging a cabin and a pail of hot water from Captain Turver, she stripped and scrubbed her body and hair thoroughly with soap she brought with her before washing her filthy clothes in the same water.

As promised, the sloop returning her to the *Drommedaris* arrived just before sunset. She made her way down the rope ladder, cursing the inconvenience of her skirts as she went. But ascending the corresponding ladder of the *Drommedaris* was near impossible. She was tired and frustrated with the ample fabric constantly getting stuck under her boot. Bending down, she grabbed the hem and tucked it between her teeth, not caring much for the effect. This was the last time she was wearing a skirt. From tomorrow she would be back in her breeches.

Even as she made the silent vow, she knew it would come to naught, for it was precisely what she'd decided to do this morning. Sebastiaan nearly suffered chest pains when he saw her walking across the deck in her breeches and shirt. Nobody on the *Drommedaris* paid her any attention, but he pointed out that it would probably be the first sight of a woman in breeches the men on the *Goeie Hoop* had ever had, and he was not having any of it.

"Is that what you'll be wearing today?" he had asked with raised eyebrows and waving a finger in a manner that encompassed all of her.

"Yes, why?"

"Don't you think it will cause a bit of a stir, you prancing around in your breeches in front of men who've never seen a woman dressed such?"

"Almost all on the *Goeie Hoop* are sick. They would not be paying attention to what I wear."

"Danielle, a dead man will pay attention," he said, and the look he gave her did not match the gruffness of his voice. Danielle felt herself blush so deeply that even the tips of her ears glowed.

"Sebastiaan, all of me is decently covered," she defended.

"Not in that, it's not. Every line of your arse is clearly visible like it's been drawn by Mistress Van Riebeeck's charcoals." He was enjoying this, the impossible man, and she knew she might as well give in, for he would win this little battle of wills.

"I'll wear my coat."

"Hmm, and it's a lovely coat, to be sure. But …" Sebastiaan smacked his lips and looked towards the horizon as if an answer to this problem would come from that direction while moving his body in front of the ladder, blocking it. Danielle rolled her eyes.

"Those men are waiting for me. I don't have time for this." She pointed past him to the two men waiting in the sloop below.

"Better change quickly then," he suggested, in a tone dripping with glee.

Moments later, she returned to the upper deck dressed in a skirt that nearly kissed the floor, only to find Sebastiaan still standing in the same spot, with an arrogant little smile playing across his face.

"Better?"

"You are a vision," he had said, clearing the way to the ladder with dramatic flair.

* * *

Finally, clearing the bulwark, she emerged onto the deck of the *Drommedaris* and nearly fell into Sebastiaan's arms.

"Please, don't touch me," she said and stumbled back.

"Why not?" He frowned in confusion and took a step toward her but halted. "What's that smell?" He sniffed the air around her, trying to locate the source of the foul odor.

"It's me." She sounded pathetic, even to her own ears. She watched as

CHAPTER 19

various emotions flitted across Sebastiaan's face, his forehead deeply furrowed as he contemplated how best to deal with the problem.

"I'll get Mistress Boom."

It must have been close to midnight when Danielle finally found her bed and collapsed into a deep sleep. Mrs. Boom had given her one look and ordered Barent to boil water and bring food, then she had bullied her husband from their cabin, locked the door, and scrubbed Danielle from head to toe with lavender soap she had procured from the *Lieffde* weeks earlier.

"Where are your dirty clothes from today?" she asked. Danielle explained how she'd laundered and left them on the *Goeie Hoop*.

"Bring them back tomorrow, and we'll wash them properly," she'd ordered, but Danielle had refused, stating that she did not want anybody else to get sick. Her concerns were met with a firm "nonsense," effectively ending the discussion.

* * *

A new day did not make it a better one. Six men had died during the night. Their wrapped corpses lay on the upper deck of the *Goeie Hoop*, waiting to be transported for burial. Unlike the day before, Captain Turver was not there to meet her when she cleared the ladder.

Danielle made her way to the surgeon's little cabin, noting a few curious glances from the men. Instead of the old surgeon, she found the captain bent over the desk, attempting to read the notes in the yellow of a single candle.

"Good morning, Captain Turver," she greeted.

"No, Miss Van Aard, nothing is good about this morning. Our surgeon, Mister Rose, died last night."

Danielle was stunned into silence. Thinking back, she did not believe that he was sick. Sure, he was old and defective in too many ways to mention, but she would have noticed if he was that close to death.

"He suffered apoplexy, or at least, that is what the cook thought was the cause of death." His hand fluttered along with the rushed words. It dawned on her that this dire situation was now entirely resting on her shoulders.

"Do you have any idea what he fed the sick?" His question was laced with frustration. "Cook does not know, and I've been trying to read these notes but have been unsuccessful in my endeavor."

He looked so thoroughly lost that she felt a stab of sympathy for him but quelled it before it could grow into something substantial. This situation might now rest on her shoulders, and she might very well be held responsible for every death from this point forward. But this entire fiasco could have been avoided had the captain acted differently. There was no illness on the *Reijger* or the *Drommedaris,* for their captains enforced strict hygiene rules. She'd seen a man flogged for urinating against the bulwark. At the time, she'd thought it an overreaction, but now her view was greatly altered.

"I don't think they were fed." She studied his expression at the revelation. He looked genuinely shocked.

"I beg your pardon?"

He held up his hand when she opened her mouth to repeat herself.

"No, I heard you the first time. How can you make such an accusation?"

"It's not an accusation – merely an observation. Why do you think the cook does not know what to prepare?" she asked, hoping now, with the surgeon gone, the captain would begin to see the scope of the disaster.

"Dear God, have mercy."

If ever there was an opportune moment to campaign for her cause, this was it.

"Captain Turver, I need ten men to help me below decks. We need to wash the sick and clean the main deck. Also, I need a steady supply of hot water, same as yesterday." She kept her voice cool and to the point, and when he wanted to speak, she cut him off. "Ask the cook to prepare a thin fish broth." Having stated her needs, she waited.

"They wouldn't help you, and I don't think I can force them." He stared out over the upper deck at the men milling about.

"I need you to try," she pushed.

He shook his head absentmindedly, and then she understood; he wanted to be liked and was afraid to do anything that would make him unpopular,

CHAPTER 19

but he was going about it all wrong. That, however, was not her problem, or perhaps it was; time would tell. She needed to get below decks. There was more work to be done than hours to do it.

"Order them, threaten them, flog them if you have to, but get me the help I need."

"Miss Van Aard," his posture tightened, "you are forgetting yourself."

"Yes, much like you are trying to forget the hundred men dying beneath your feet," she said. Her plan for today was simple: feed and clean the sick, find blankets for them and then clean the room. As she walked away, she called over her shoulder, "Ten men, Captain."

An hour later, a burly man who looked like he was Arent's closest relative, *sans* the hair, came down the companionway carrying two pails of hot water. It was the first time anybody but the cook made it down the stairs. Danielle put the broth she was dripping into a patient's mouth aside and stood to meet the newcomer.

"Adam," he said as she tilted her head back to see his face. After hearing the name, she stared at the man on the floor. "No, not him. Me."

"Adam," she repeated. The longer she looked at him, the more he resembled an angel. "I'm –," she started, but he interrupted.

"I know who you are, miss. Everybody knows who you are." He looked around the room, and the sadness on his face was unmistakable.

"My brother was one of those who died last night. We were not allowed in this room, so I could not be with him."

"I'm so sorry," she said, and her heart must have shown in her eyes, for he looked at her and gave her a poignant smile.

"What do you need?" he asked.

"I need nine more men and blankets." He did not bother to answer but turned and left the room with determined strides.

The windows were still open when she arrived this morning, but what she gained in fresher air, she lost in temperature. The men were shivering. However, when she reached for the planks to cover the windows again, one of the sick, still strong enough to speak, protested with all the energy he had left.

Adam came back bearing a mountain of blankets. It appeared that the men would give their blankets, but not their help, and she could hardly blame them.

"I couldn't get you the nine men, miss," he growled.

"Adam, I would not trade you for a hundred. Start covering them, and if we have blankets to spare, put them aside for tomorrow. We might need to wash some tonight."

The ends of the bandage she'd tied over her nose and mouth hung down her back. It was long enough to cut in half. She handed one of the pieces to Adam.

"I don't mind the smell, miss," he responded without taking the bandage.

"It's not for the smell. It is to protect us so we don't breathe in some of the disease." He did not understand the logic but took the bandage nonetheless and tied it as she showed him.

Then he bent down and carefully covered the patient nearest to him with a coarse woolen blanket, much like a father would his child.

"Miss, a bad draft is coming through the floor planks," he said as he straightened.

She knew, but there was nothing for it.

By the end of the second day, Danielle knew she was fighting a battle she could not win. The main deck needed to be cleaned if anybody was to have a fighting chance of survival, and she needed more help. Adam was a gift from God. He had carried bucket after bucket of water up and down the companionway. It had taken them all day to feed and wash the sick, but the room was still in the same condition as she'd found it, and tomorrow she would be stuck in the same loop, and nothing would actually have been accomplished. They were merely treading water.

Danielle emerged from her borrowed cabin with a bundle of filthy clothes under her arm when she noticed Captain Turver strolling towards her, elegantly balancing a teacup containing his afternoon refreshment.

"Report, please," he ordered. He was still sour over their conversation this morning, for his lips were stiffer, and his chin just that smidgen higher. She did not know if it was his posture, the teacup, or his tone, but something

CHAPTER 19

inside her snapped.

After several deep breaths, she finally felt composed enough to answer.

"All the patients have been fed, but I don't know how many will survive the night. I am fighting a battle I cannot win. The disease grows in the unhygienic conditions in which the men find themselves. Today we've spent washing and feeding the sick, and tomorrow we will do so again. But none of that means anything if we cannot stop the disease from spreading. I need more help. Adam alone is not enough." She was planning on pleading with him but feared she might have failed in the attempt because she'd dropped the laundry and was wildly gesturing with her arms. Judging by the look on the captain's face, it was clear he did not detect her pleading tone either.

"Miss Van Aard, you seem like the sort for whom nothing is ever enough."

She wanted to protest, but he held a well-manicured finger in front of her face.

"I have complied with all your demands: I've provided hot water for two days without pause, I've provided the exact food you demanded, I've provided assistance, and still," he shook his head as if he could not fathom her ungratefulness, "you are not satisfied. What will it take?" His voice rose as he spoke, and he was close to shouting by the end of his tirade.

Heavens, who knew he had it in him, she wondered.

"I want the men moved off this ship. All of them, hale *and* sick."

"Have you taken leave of your senses?" He was horrified by the suggestion. "Where would you put them? On the beach, exposed to the elements and all the wildness that exists just beyond those trees?" He pointed towards the shoreline.

"Anywhere would be better than here. Everybody needs to leave the ship, including you, and not a soul should be permitted back aboard until the whole thing has been scrubbed top to bottom." It was sound advice, and anybody with half a brain would see it — except Captain Turver.

"Miss Van Aard."

If he *'Miss Van Aard'* her one more time, the crew would be burying their captain next to their surgeon.

"Our surgeon is not yet cold in his grave, and you act as if you own each patient on board."

"Captain, if I choose to own anything, I can assure you it would not be this. Besides, this is about saving the lives of *your* men. We need to break the cycle of the disease. They need to be moved off the ship."

"What makes you think that moving them would do them any good? Moving these men to shore would only infect more, and more would die."

"And I could probably treat them. Getting these men out of these *horrid* conditions is the logical first step. The disease breeds in the filth, but if we can put them somewhere clean, they can start to heal. I am not acting on a whim, sir. My father was a gifted physician, and this was his view on treating the disease."

"It is out of the question. They stay where they are." He made to leave, but her next words halted him dead in his tracks.

"Then, sir, you will be guilty of their murder, for that is what you are doing in refusing them proper care. You are *murdering* them!"

To his credit, he kept a level head.

"Miss Van Aard, this is not the time to make enemies." The quietly spoken words were as cold as his eyes as they bored into hers.

He probably had more to say, but Danielle was tired, and her patience was thin. She needed a different tactic.

"Captain Turver, imagine you contract this disease, and you might still." She could feel her temper simmering, but it was tightly under control. "I would be the only person standing between you and the most humiliating and undignified death imaginable. The question is, *Captain*: Do you want to make an enemy of *me*?"

That uncomfortable truth hit home with the force of a trebuchet.

The captain took an involuntary step backward. The way she'd spat his rank was one reason, but the green fire in her eyes swiftly outweighed it. The woman looked positively possessed when her ire was stirred.

Danielle had the advantage. To retreat or give him time to respond would be a mistake. She closed the gap between them.

"This ship is a cesspit of disease. Living conditions are atrocious. To reach the sick, I must wade through shit, blood, and vomit every day. *They need*

CHAPTER 19

to be moved off the ship." She made sure to emphasize every word of the last statement.

He was shocked to his core at her use of language. Who could have guessed that such vile words could flow so easily from something so delicate? Unfortunately, he did not have time to ponder the phenomenon, for she was speaking again, and this time each word was punctuated with a small, sharp finger stabbing his chest.

"If not," her words were seductively low and smooth, which only managed to heighten his trepidation, "I will bring the governor and the other captains here to witness these conditions. Not only will you drown in shame, but you will be demoted to a position so low that cleaning the head twice a day would be an honor."

Turver was not one to think on his feet. He needed time to consider the consequences of his words and choose them with care. This woman, on the other hand, suffered no such impediments. He could throw her off his ship this instant; he certainly could. But her threat was not empty, and she seemed motivated enough to see it through.

"Fine, Miss Van Aard, you win. We'll move the sick on the morrow. Where to, I have no idea."

She needed to talk to the governor about erecting a tent for her patients. He was eager to start construction of the fort, and as far as she knew, he had already marked the foundations. Her request would delay his plans, but she did not doubt that he would see the sense of her appeal.

* * *

Once more, she was led to the dayroom. She'd begged Barent to let her interrupt the meeting between the governor, Captain De Coninck, and Captain Hooghsaet.

"Miss Van Aard, please take a seat," Captain De Coninck greeted her. Too exhausted to stand, she sank down in the nearest chair.

She was unsure if she should simply start speaking or wait to be invited. All looked relaxed and friendly enough. Erring on the side of caution would perhaps be advisable.

"You asked to speak to us," Captain De Coninck prodded.

"Yes, thank you," she cleared her throat and started. "The situation on board the *Goeie Hoop* is quite dire, I'm afraid. More than a hundred men have taken ill." She scanned the three faces, and all shifted in their chairs, looking less relaxed and more concerned.

"We were not aware of the severity. We were led to believe that only a handful of men were affected." As Captain Hooghsaet spoke, all good humor left his face. Captain Turver had deliberately downplayed the situation to his peers.

"Perhaps that was the case at the time, but I can only report on what I've witnessed." Danielle continued to describe the past two days' events, highlighting only the crucial obstacles and concerns. She needed these men on her side. Plucking their heartstrings and painting Captain Turver as a villain would not accomplish that. They would prefer facts to emotions and solutions to problems.

"My solution is to build a tent large enough to house all the patients. It would be easy to clean, the patients would be warm, and I could start preparing medicine to ease their suffering and aid their healing," she concluded.

"Slow down for a moment," Captain De Coninck said with a raised hand. He was now leaning forward in his chair, resting his forearms on the table. "Thank you for bringing the matter to our attention. We will discuss it and make the necessary arrangements. Why don't you find your bed? You look tired."

This was not good. She couldn't leave the meeting without a clear idea of what would happen to her patients. Danielle made no effort to stand. On the contrary, she pushed her bottom firmer into the chair.

"Captain, please," she pleaded, "we do not have time to sit about and discuss the matter over tea. It is quite urgent. Those men's lives are in great peril," she said, pointing in the direction of the *Goeie Hoop*.

The short fuse of Captain De Coninck's temper instantly caught fire.

"Miss Van Aard," his voice whiplashed, "I said we would discuss the matter. Whether we do so over tea, *or not,* is none of your concern."

CHAPTER 19

"This is just like Homer said, '"Old men talk, while young men die."'

"Who are you calling old?" Hooghsaet barked from his side of the table.

Did she say that out loud? That was a mistake; she silently cursed her tired mind.

"Young lady, you are a long way out of line," De Coninck's warning was softly delivered but very real. She could afford to make an enemy of Turver, unfortunate as that was, for she'd genuinely liked him, but she needed the support of these men. The governor would never oppose the captain and *vice versa*. She must have both on her side.

"I apologize. I meant no offense. Please." If De Coninck was surprised by her apology, he did not show it. "The situation is dire. Men are dying as we speak."

She looked to the governor, silently begging his assistance.

"Danielle," it was the first time the governor had used her given name, "we understand the problem, and I give you my word we'll find the right solution." He spoke gently and quietly, but Danielle was unmoved.

"You don't understand the problem, and you don't have to look for the right solution. Those men need to be moved off that ship if they are to have any chance at survival, and I can't put them on the beach. I need a shelter." He was her only hope, and she did not like the direction he was steering the conversation.

"I don't understand the problem?" Governor Van Riebeeck's tone lost its warm notes, and a warning flashed through his eyes. He had a fort to build and would not allow anything to stand in his way. For the first time, Danielle understood why he held the position he did. He was fair, humble, and reasonable but also ruthlessly formidable.

"Perhaps it is time for a little perspective. Allow me." He looked at her, warning her not to speak, and when she remained quiet, he continued. "The rains will start soon, making the construction of the fort and gardens difficult, if not impossible. A delay will severely affect the lives of thousands of sailors who depend on us to provide them with fresh water and food." He looked at her, but she remained mute. "Everybody is currently living on the ships. These ships are not at our disposal indefinitely. We must unburden them of their cargo and passengers as soon as possible. I can't simply order people onto the beach with nowhere to house them while waving goodbye to the only shelter we currently have." Much like she was going to do tomorrow morning. "So you see, the need for a sick tent can simply not take precedence over everything else."

Captain Hooghsaet was quietly observing the exchange, and, to her surprise, so was Captain De Coninck. She'd fully expected the latter to throw her from the room. The governor's response was unexpected. She'd thought he would support her. Without him, she was alone, and come tomorrow, she would be moving a hundred sick men onto an empty beach. If the illness did not kill them, her decision most certainly would.

Danielle rose from her seat. She needed a new plan. Perhaps she and Adam could scavenge discarded sails from the ships and construct a makeshift shelter. Perhaps Sebastiaan could help her, but he and Arent were gone every day to fish or hunt for meat.

"Governor Van Riebeeck," Danielle had nothing left to lose. She recklessly looked him square in the eye, leaning forward on the table. "If you do not build the tent I want, the disease will spread to every man, woman, and child on this expedition, and there will be nobody left to build your precious fort and gardens. And this idea of a halfway station will perish even before it has a chance to live." She'd said enough. Gaining her feet, she turned to leave, sick and tired to her marrow of fighting and arguing.

"Darling," Captain Hooghsaet's deep voice reverberated around the room, "when do you want this tent of yours?" Danielle slowly turned around. She felt like hugging the man, but now was not the time to go soft.

"Tomorrow at daybreak," she said and left, not seeing the smile De Coninck hid as he, once more, found something fascinating about his fingernails.

"*Jesu*, that girl does not understand the art of subtlety," Hooghsaet grumbled once the door to the dayroom closed behind Danielle. "Did young Turver lie to us?" he asked his companions.

"It would seem so," De Coninck answered.

"She could have exposed him," Hooghsaet said.

"But she didn't," the governor said. "Is it possible to build a sick tent in such

CHAPTER 19

a short time?"

"I've seen dysentery before," De Coninck answered, "and she is not wrong. We need to get the situation under control sooner rather than later." He looked to the others. "We'll build the shelter tomorrow, but know this," he paused for effect. "You gave her what she wanted today. Tomorrow she will be back, asking for more. And that fire you see in her, the one you like so much right now, is going to singe your arse. Mark my words," he said, pointing a finger at Hooghsaet.

Chapter 20

The *Drommedaris* was lying close to the *Goeie Hoop*, in the mouth of the Fresh River. The beach was no more than an easy swim away. Sebastiaan was already waiting for her when she stepped onto the upper deck. The sight of him took her breath. He was dressed in a loose linen shirt that draped from his broad shoulders, and he had swapped his sailor slops for breeches and boots.

"You had a busy day yesterday," he greeted with a smile.

"I'm afraid I behaved rather like a shrew."

She looked endearingly embarrassed, and he laughed.

"How much did you hear?" she asked, afraid of the answer.

"Directly? None of it. Indirectly? All of it."

She groaned.

"I told you, you would be unstoppable, didn't I? We've been here four days, and what goes up first? Not the flag or the fort, but your hospital."

She could hear the pride in his voice, and it made her extremely self-conscious, so she bowed her head and kicked at something that was not there. Where was a pebble when you needed it?

"See over there?" She followed his outstretched hand and looked at the beach. Large poles were sticking up from the sand. "Those are the poles for your tent."

The sun was not an hour above the horizon, and so much had already been done. She watched as two sloops beached; Adam and three others carried two stretchers to the shade of a nearby tree. Adam paused to ensure the stricken men were comfortable and covered under their blankets before returning to

CHAPTER 20

the sloop to fetch the next stretcher.

"Who's that?" Sebastiaan asked as he followed her gaze.

"Adam. He was the only man willing to help me yesterday."

Sebastiaan's face darkened as he silently contemplated the man, nodded as if he'd reached some conclusion, and reached for his cutlass. After strapping the vicious blade to his waist, he took Danielle's hand and led her to the ladder.

Poor Adam, he was such a gentle giant. "Sebastiaan -" she was about to protest his reaction and whatever decision he seemed to have reached.

"Your patients await, my lady," he said casually, cutting her short, then helped her into the sloop below, where twelve men were already waiting for them.

Their voyage to the beach was quick and uneventful. Danielle was tightly wedged between Lukas, the sailmaker, and Sebastiaan. Arent was already ashore; she could hear him barking orders. When the sloop's front touched the sand, Sebastiaan scooped her up and carried her to where the sand was dry.

Adam and his team had just placed another pair of patients in the shade when Sebastiaan walked toward him and pulled him aside. Danielle held her breath as she watched. They were too far away for her to hear, but Sebastiaan was speaking, and Adam was nodding. Then Sebastiaan reached for his cutlass. The sun caught the blade as he flipped it in his hand and handed it to Adam. What was he doing? Her palms were damp, and she released a shaky breath.

Sebastiaan's blond curls stirred in the morning breeze as he strode back to her, his gait easy and shoulders relaxed.

"I have to go up the river with Arent and my uncle to fish and do a bit of hunting for dinner. We'll be gone most of the day, but Adam will stay close and watch over you." He tilted his head and studied her face. Danielle felt her cheeks redden with embarrassment at her thoughts.

"Thank you," she managed. Sebastiaan was trying not to laugh; she could see how he bit the inside of his bottom lip and how his eyes crinkled and sparkled. Then he bent down, kissed her forehead, and said, "I'll take you back this evening. Wait for me."

She only nodded and watched as he turned away and walked in Arent's direction.

By midmorning, she and Adam had dribbled enough broth into each man that she was confident they would reach midday without any more deaths. They had shaped the warm sand around the sick sailors' bodies, and all were as comfortable as could be expected. They lay waiting while the tent was still under construction. Many of the sick were lucid and each met her eye with unfiltered gratitude, introducing themselves as she moved from one makeshift bed to the next.

One dark-skinned man kissed her hand and whispered, "Thank you, Malaikat."

"Don't thank me, just get better. That would be thanks enough," Danielle said and squeezed his large, calloused hand.

"Adam, what does *Malaikat* mean?" she asked when they shared a quiet moment in the shade of a tree.

"It's Javanese for angel," he said and winked at her.

The moniker deeply touched her. However, she doubted the governor and the captains would share the view. They would most likely protest the name with a signed document of some sort. She chastised herself for having such uncharitable thoughts. Those men had put all their plans on hold to build her a hospital. She vowed never to disobey or contradict any of them ever again. From this point forward, she would toe the line.

Allowing herself time to relax, she leaned forward and folded her arms around her knees.

God must have made this part of the world on a Saturday, for He sure took his time. The ocean was a deep sapphire blue, and as it neared the shore, the waves were a clear blue-green that towered with crisp white tops and then thundered onto the sand, leaving white spray and foam to shoot high above the black boulders that studded the beach. Some of the boulders were twice as high as a man, and she wished she could climb them. Perhaps tomorrow.

She'd never seen sand like this. It was not coarse and yellow like that on Texel, but powdery fine and white. She mistook it for snow when she first saw it from the *Drommedaris'* deck. Wherever the water touched, it turned a pale gold that quickly faded as the waves pulled back. Danielle removed her boots and hose and stuck her tender feet into the warm sand, covering them to create small sand caves, which immediately collapsed when she pulled her feet free.

The part of the beach where the sick were temporarily placed was perfectly secluded, sheltered by boulders and vegetation, large trees providing ample shade from the midday sun. A plant with fleshy leaves, covered in what looked like little water blisters, was creeping over tree roots and sand, chasing dapples of sunlight, its purple flowers abundantly on display. If she were a painter asked to venture an interpretation of heaven, this vista would come to mind.

"I'm going for a short walk. I need to see what herbs I can find for easing their pain or bringing down the fever," she said and made to stand.

Adam was remarkably quick for a man of his size, for he reached his feet before she did and held a firm palm out to her, not to help her up but to keep her where she was.

"No, miss," he said in a stern voice. "You are to stay put until I can go with you, and I can't go with you now since we can't leave these men. One of us will have to stay with them." The last he added almost as an afterthought.

"I'm just going over there," she pointed to where the salty-looking plants were being infiltrated by varieties she thought looked familiar. "You would be able to see me at all times, I promise." Adam shook his head while his eyes seemed to look right through her. She'd seen that look many times on big Gabriel, the most kindhearted man she'd ever met but stubborn to his core when it came to obeying his orders.

"Miss, I promised Sebastiaan I would guard you. I can't do it if you're over there." He pointed with his eyes in the direction she was planning on going.

"Promised Sebastiaan? You did not even know him until a few hours ago. You and I go way back." She argued using all the weapons in her arsenal: raised eyebrows, curled upper lip, wagging finger, all of it – none of it worked.

"Yes, all the way to yesterday," he said, looking very pleased with his display of wit. "I was told to tie you to a tree if you don't want to listen. I would not like to do it, but I will if I must." Danielle knew it wasn't a threat but a statement of fact.

One of the sick men croaked his opinion, "We might not be able to do much, and more's the pity, but we agree with Adam on this. You need to stay put."

She was about to threaten him with no dinner, but that was too mean.

"Oh, fine," she huffed and kicked up a wad of sand, giving action to her annoyance. Her little tantrum earned her a few warm chuckles but nothing more.

It was shortly after lunch when Lukas announced that the tent was ready. He had sewn damaged sails together to create a roof, so high it was far beyond her reach, and sides firmly tied to pegs and weighted down with sand, effectively sealing off any drafts. To Danielle's eye, damaged sails had never been more beautiful.

She placed the sickest patients on the left and the others on the right. The groups met almost precisely in the middle of the back wall. Trunks with the men's belongings had been arriving from the *Goeie Hoop*, and she used them as markers for the evenly spaced beds dug in the sand, as the tent had no floor. Due to the nature of the disease, a floor would only be a hindrance. This way, soiled sand could simply be shoveled away.

Tomorrow, Danielle planned on cutting some of the tall grasses that seemed to grow everywhere to serve as mattresses.

Outside, Adam was tending a fire. Those not working on the fort carried firewood and water to the tent. She'd set strict rules of hygiene in place. Everybody entering the tent must wash their hands and arms, and the ritual was to be repeated upon exit. Those who argued or protested were met with Adam's ferocious scowl. A few buckets of water were placed along the center path for her and Adam to wash their hands after tending each patient. Those were regularly emptied, cleaned, and refilled.

Empty buckets were available to be used as latrines. The men were hesitant to use the buckets with Danielle in the tent.

"Miss, we can't do this with you watching us," they protested.

"Neither dignity nor shame has a place in a sickroom," she told them. "Was it not yesterday that I had washed every one of you, top to bottom?" Only after a few chuckles did she notice her poor choice of words. "You will use the

CHAPTER 20

bucket, and that's that. I cannot run from the room every time you develop the need. I will get nothing done."

"Yes, but do you have to inspect it afterward?" one of the older ones asked.

"I do. I need to see how much of the inflammation still lives in your body," Danielle explained.

"And how does staring at our shite tell you that? Is it like reading tea leaves? I had an aunt who did that."

Danielle bit down hard to keep from laughing. "No, it's not like that. I need to see if any pus is mixed with the excrement. If it's getting less, then it's a sign that the inflammation is starting to clear up, then your fever will lower, and your belly- and headaches will start to fade."

"What was that?" one of the men on the right side of the tent asked. Danielle heard it too, and so did Adam. They both froze. The shouts were laced with tension and sounded different from those floating around them all day.

"Oh, no, you don't," Adam said, holding both arms out to his sides like he was trying to herd cattle into a small enclosure.

Danielle had already scooped up her medicine box. "Adam, somebody could be injured. I must go."

"Aye, she has to," one of the sick chimed in.

"Shut up, Pieter. You just want to know what's going on," Adam snapped at the man.

"You can come with me," Danielle said to Adam.

"We can't leave them." He looked at the two lines of men. Today was a good day; it was past noon, and there were no deaths. More men seemed to have strengthened than to have declined. Those who had a foot firmly planted in the grave a day ago were now starting to pull it back.

"We'll hold," Pieter said. "I'll keep an eye on the others."

"You are too weak to stand, you dolt. I had to carry you to your bed," Adam ruthlessly reminded the chatty patient.

"Well, I'm the best of the bunch, so at least we wouldn't be going anywhere."

In the few short minutes since it had started, the shouting seemed to have escalated in its urgency, and Danielle was already out the door when she heard Adam's labored breath behind her.

Not bothering with her boots, she hurried away from the beach and inland to where the new fort's foundations were being dug. Salty ocean air mixed with the mossy scent of the forest created a heady combination.

Cresting the dune behind the hospital tent, Danielle paused to find her bearings. About a hundred yards ahead, only the heads and shoulders of the men digging a trench were visible. The trench would soon become part of the foundation for the new fort's outer wall. The site was well chosen. The fort was going to occupy a generous, elevated, relatively level patch of land that offered a clear view of Table Bay. It was far enough from the waterline to be out of the ocean's reach but close enough for the cannons to offer adequate protection to the south. The Fresh River formed the western border and, in time, would be diverted to create a moat encircling the structure. Next to the building site, in a large clearing, a crowd was beginning to form.

Lush, green, sea-hardy vegetation veined the white sand. Danielle made her way toward the melee; she regretted leaving her boots behind with every step she took.

The scene resembled something like a before-action battlefield with spectators. The crowd consisted of three distinct groups. At the far end and backed by the forest, ten dark-skinned men, weapons in hand, stood in a determined formation. They varied in age, but all were tall with lean muscles and skin, a deep shade of walnut brown, that shimmered in the sunlight. Their faces were stern but not violent. The weapons, medium-length spears and straight wooden clubs with round heads, were held more like a promise than a threat.

To the side, sailors and soldiers gathered. Some sailors were leaning on their shovels as they observed the warriors. Having faced many pirate attacks at sea, they were not concerned. They knew the look of an enemy with murder on his mind. The soldiers were decidedly more nervous, clutching their rapiers with white knuckles, hoping the governor would forget that they had joined the expedition.

Most of the noise came from a tight cluster of natives near the center of the clearing. It was a rag-tag bunch of three men, a handful of women, and roughly the same number of children. They looked distinctly different from

CHAPTER 20

the warriors. They were smaller in build, withered looking, with tawny, dull skin.

Danielle slowed her walk but kept her eyes on them. The older women wore small leather head coverings molded to the shape of their heads, decorated with tiny beads. The others had shells and leather throngs knotted into the tight curls of their hair. Around their necks hung strings of beads, bones, and seashells. They were dressed in large pieces of animal skin made into aprons that managed to shield them from waist to knee in the front but failed to reach their behinds and upper bodies.

A young mother held a suckling baby to her breast. A few small children were hanging on their mothers' skin covers. One had her finger stuck in her nose; another was sucking his thumb. The children were all as naked as the day God had made them. Three men stood in front of the women and children, dressed in nothing more than a loincloth. The men had no spears or clubs but were armed with a respectable-sized rock in each hand, as they held defensive stances and loudly communicated their distress and intent to launch their missiles. The panicked women added to the cacophony by loudly sobbing and wailing as if the world was coming to an end.

Adam took Danielle by the arm and dragged her toward the group of sailors. She recognized Lukas, the *Drommedaris'* sailmaker, and headed in his direction.

"Lukas, what's going on?" she asked, reaching his side.

"What are you doing here? Did I not just build you a tent?" he challenged, looking down at her in alarm.

"Yes, a tent, not a prison. Besides, I heard the noise." He sighed and shook his head at her.

"The Saldanhars," Lukas pointed to the ten men, "want an audience with the governor. The Beach Rangers are Harry's family," he said, pointing to the Hottentots in the middle. "They were here since yesterday. So here we are, waiting to see what's what."

"Who's Harry?" Danielle rose onto her toes to get a better look.

"The taller of the three men," Lukas replied with a more pointed gesture.

"Why are they so upset?" she asked, gesturing with her chin toward Harry's family.

"I think there might have been a dust-up between the two tribes earlier," he explained.

"How do you know all this?"

"Harry can speak a few words of Dutch and English, plus he is very creative with his hand gestures."

"Where's the governor?" Lukas pointed to the construction site where Governor Van Riebeeck and Captain Hooghsaet were making their way toward the disturbance.

The men cleared a path for the governor. After a few words, an unhappy-looking Captain Hooghsaet remained at the edge of the group of Dutchmen while Governor Van Riebeeck stepped forward alone. A warrior stepped from the group of Saldanhars with an air of authority, indisputably marking him as their leader.

He was taller than the others, with an open face and sharp features. A well-prepared ox hide mantle hung from his shoulders to his knees. He flicked one side of the cloak over his shoulder as he neared the governor, exposing his well-toned body. A small loincloth, held in place by a narrow leather string tied around the waist, hung in front of his private parts. For some of the men, it offered concealment, but for others, including their leader, it failed miserably, and Danielle wondered why they even bothered.

The sight might have been distressing a week ago. She'd seen men and women in various stages of undress before, but her father had always protected her innocence. All his male patients were invariably covered from the waist down by bandages, blankets, or undergarments.

Since her arrival on the *Goeie Hoop* a couple of days ago, there was no longer an inch of the male anatomy that held any mystery for her. Apart from the skin color and the proportions, the sight was not new. What drew and held her attention was the long cut that ran in a jagged line from the top of his right thigh nearly to the knee. The wound was gaping and ugly. It must be causing him an incredible amount of pain. He seemed unaffected by it, considering he moved with the grace of a predator towards the governor, with nary a hint of a limp. He reminded her of the dandies she saw strutting down the streets of Oudeschild, clad in brightly colored outfits cut in the latest fashion, purses fat with gold. The memory would have made her smile had the moment not been so charged.

"It's a pissing contest now," somebody commented from behind. Danielle did not care for the contest's outcome. So long as they all left here with a pulse, she would call it a win.

The governor and the Saldanhar chief stood a few feet apart. Neither spoke, and a tense silence stretched between them as they took each other's measure. From the look on the chief's face, Danielle got the impression he had never seen a white man before.

Van Riebeeck stood motionless, keeping his eyes locked on the man in front of him, his face carefully blank. The chief studied the governor with a furrowed brow. He tilted his head as he tried to see beneath the governor's hat, then abandoned the headdress and focused on the face. For a long minute, he stared into the governor's eyes, narrowing his own slightly, before his gaze dipped to the large white collar, scanning the shoulders, the arms, and the empty hands. He continued his perusal down the governor's body until he reached his booted feet. He exhaled a frustrated sigh, for the clothing concealed too much vital information. His eyes snapped back up and held the governor's gaze before giving a crisp nod.

Van Riebeeck took the gesture as a greeting and responded with a bow, making sure not to move his feet but instead only lowering his torso and head.

The chief began to speak in his language. His eyes never left Van Riebeeck's. He spoke at length, and as his speech progressed, he became more animated. The governor patiently waited for the chief to finish.

When it was his turn to talk, Van Riebeeck started in full Dutch, stating scrupulously his desire to establish an equitable trade relationship with the Saldanhars. The chief was not as polite as the governor, for halfway through the governor's speech, he started laughing and shaking his head. Their exchange was at an impasse, considering neither could understand a word the other was saying.

Governor Van Riebeeck turned to look at Harry and then waved him over.

That was a mistake, as Harry's family immediately took exception to the gesture and voiced their outrage by renewing their death lament. As for his part, Harry shook his head and waved his arms to emphasize the explicit "No!" he bellowed back. The chief seemed to understand the dilemma and took it upon himself to bark a few sentences in a dialect they seemingly shared. The attempt proved to be a disaster. Not only did Harry visibly pale under the chief's command, but his whole family took several steps back, increasing the distance between them.

Both men turned back to each other, ignoring the screaming Hottentots. Van Riebeeck was struck by inspiration. He raised a finger in the air and then searched the ground at his feet until he found what he was looking for. With a stick, he drew the shape of a cow and then another until ten stick-figure cows, complete with horns and udders, were neatly scratched into the loose sand. Underneath, he drew a squiggly line the length of the ten cows. Upon completion, he stepped back, planted his fists in his sides, and nodded at his artwork, looking decidedly pleased with himself.

The chief slowly walked down the line of cows giving each his full attention, and when he reached the end, he bent down abruptly and squinted at the line beneath them. Looking to Van Riebeeck, with a face contorted in confusion, he uttered a word that could only be interpreted as "What?"

The warrior watched as Van Riebeeck walked to the group of Hottentots, starting another wave of hysteria, and pointed to the copper wire wrapped around Harry's arm. The chief nodded, returned to the drawing, and doubled the line in length.

Van Riebeeck shook his head and erased half of the new addition with his booted foot. The chief responded by walking to the drawing's other side and erasing half the cows. Van Riebeeck extended the line a little and restored one cow. The chief shook his head and laughed. However, his laughter did not sound humorous. The sound held the sharp edges of a warning.

Danielle started to wonder if they were achieving anything or just trying to see how far one could push the other. Until the governor held up five fingers. The chief pointed to Harry and his family and nodded. The Hottentots immediately understood what was transpiring and renewed their initial protestations with gusto. Van Riebeeck shook his head.

Something in the air shifted. The noise from Harry's family became louder; the nine Saldanhar men shifted their feet and moved their hands on their weapons; the sailors straightened from their shovels, and the soldiers took a step back. Governor Van Riebeeck kept his eyes locked on those of the Saldanhar chief. Neither man was smiling. Both looked cold and unyielding.

Danielle saw how the governor's shoulders straightened, and his spine stiffened. The chief raised his hand, and a heavy silence fell over the clearing. Danielle held her breath, then the chief extended his arm and forcefully pointed toward the group of Hottentots. His face was stark and fierce, and the detachment in his eyes chilled her blood. It was a face of a warrior ready to do battle. Again, Van Riebeeck shook his head.

The chief had no weapons, but that did not diminish his menace. His unarmed state did not last long, for he turned to catch his spear, followed by his club thrown to him by one of his men. Turning back to the governor, he pointed the spear's tip at the underside of Van Riebeeck's chin. Governor Van Riebeeck stood his ground, keeping his gaze steady and his face empty. Danielle saw the rise and fall of his shoulders; he was taking deep, even breaths. A buzz like an angry beehive started among the sailors, but Captain Hooghsaet raised his hands in a silent call for calm.

When the warrior spoke again, his loud voice carried effortlessly; though the words were foreign, the meaning was clear. He would agree to the governor's request for five heads of cattle in exchange for Harry and his family. Governor Van Riebeeck's response was the same, only stated more carefully this time because the spear's tip was scraping his skin.

"He should let him have them," Lukas spoke quietly.

"Lukas," Danielle chided.

"What? They bring us nothing but empty bellies. They've been sitting under that tree all day, not lifting a finger, just waiting for us to feed them."

Danielle knew how stubborn the governor could be, and the chief did not seem keen on letting the matter rest. Instead, his face was shrouded by a dead man's mask, except for his eyes. He was not hiding his intentions; she knew he was moments away from running the spear into the governor's brain, killing him where he stood. The muscles in his other arm rippled to life as he adjusted his grip on the club.

Maria was going to lose her husband on this day, and for what? How was her friend to survive the loss of both her child and her husband in the span of a month?

Danielle moved, but Adam's hand around her upper arm halted her.

"Adam, stay," she ordered and pulled her arm free. The man was too protective by far, and with that glint in his eye and Sebastiaan's cutlass in his hand, he could very well be the spark that set this whole powder keg alight.

Lukas was speaking to her, but she ignored him, and with her medicine box tightly clutched under her arm, she walked towards the pair in the middle of the clearing.

She had no idea what to do but was confident that inspiration would strike by the time she reached them.

Her unexpected appearance drew the attention of both men, and they looked at her with identical expressions of disbelief and confusion. The distraction lessened the tension by a small degree, and Danielle swallowed dryly, looking from one man to the other, much like a child would glance between bickering parents.

The murderous burn receded from the chief's eyes, the muscle near his jaw stopped pulsing, his spear-wielding hand lowered, and his shoulders relaxed. The governor went the other way: his jaw tightened, his carefully blank eyes caught fire, and his fists clenched at his sides. He was furious.

"Let me tend his wound," Danielle spoke in a small voice, for her confidence was deserting her with alarming alacrity.

"What?" the governor asked, and he had to shake his head to clear his hearing.

Danielle released a light cough and repeated, "Let me tend his wound."

She pointed to the large wound on the chief's thigh, gesturing more for the governor's benefit than the chief's, as he seemed to struggle with the meaning of her request.

The governor was still staring at her with the same expression, but she could see his mind working behind his narrowed eyes. He turned his attention from

CHAPTER 20

Danielle to the wound, making a show of studying it with a furrowed brow, then he straightened and looked the chief in the eye, raising his eyebrows in question. The chief did not react or respond.

Van Riebeeck pointed to the wound and then to Danielle, gave a short nod, and took a step to the side. The warrior stood motionless.

Danielle looked down at the injured leg, but she could feel his black eyes boring into her. It took her a good few moments to gather enough courage to face him. She had stupidly placed herself in this precarious position; now was not the time to cower. Returning his stare, she tried not to let her fear show.

The violence that emanated from the warrior earlier was replaced by curiosity, and Danielle was not sure which alarmed her more. Judging by the look on the governor's face, he was close to offering her to the chief in exchange for a chicken.

The chief studied her features in much the same way he had the governor's. However, he seemed less guarded now. A look of surprise lighted his features, and he stepped closer, the tension of earlier entirely forgotten.

She knew the instant he noticed her unusual eye color when he leaned forward and frowned into her eyes. Dropping the club at his feet, he grabbed hold of her chin and tilted her head to the sun. The glare made her eyes water, but she kept still, feeling very much like Lot's wife, rooted to the spot like a pillar of salt.

Removing his hand from her chin, he closed his fingers around a lock of her hair. Rubbing it and letting it fall like sand through his fingers, he picked up a thicker tumble and raised it to his nose, and again, he let it fall from his hand, fascinated by how it drifted down to her shoulders.

Danielle's heart was beating in her head. The Saldanhar chief took a step backward, and with an expression of deep interest, he deliberately let his obsidian eyes take in every detail of her body, starting at her head and ending at her feet. She felt like a newly discovered insect but was drawn from the trance when he pointed to her bare feet and motioned for her to give him her foot. It was an odd request, and she decided to ignore it. Besides, her legs were still somewhat unstable with fear, and she did not want to risk lifting one and falling over. He made an impatient grunt and repeated the gesture. Danielle frowned and shook her head. Then he bent down, took hold of her ankle, and lifted her foot.

She swallowed the shriek that followed the unexpected behavior and snapped out her hand to stop herself from falling over, grabbing hold of his hide-covered shoulder. He seemed unaware of her touch, for he was prodding at the sole of her foot, running the rough pad of his thumb from the ball all the way to the heel. It tickled, and she tried to pull her foot back. Apparently, the soles of her feet did not meet with his approval, as he was making pitiful clicking sounds with his tongue and shaking his head.

Releasing her foot, he nodded to the governor and turned towards his men. Some unspoken agreement had just been reached.

"What just happened?" she whispered to the governor.

"I think you are allowed to tend his wound," he answered, sounding more befuddled than angry.

"What did my foot have to do with it?"

"I have no idea. Let's go," Van Riebeeck said, pointing to where the group of men now sat on their haunches in the shade of a large tree, weapons at their sides. Mercifully, Harry's family had quieted down and was watching the goings-on from a safe distance.

The day settled back into the harsh rhythm it had before the disturbance. Captain Hooghsaet's orders rumbled across the clearing. The soldiers were to remain on the perimeter, eyes on the governor, while the sailors were ordered back to the building site.

Governor Van Riebeeck was sitting with the Saldanhar men. They were engrossed in a conversation that took on the characteristics of a game of charades. All seemed enthusiastic enough, and Danielle walked to the chief, where he lounged a distance away against a tree trunk, one leg bent and the other straight. His hand was resting on the weapons lying by his side. The gesture seemed more a habit than a sign of impending trouble.

She kneeled next to his outstretched leg. The wound had clotted a while ago, but it didn't look older than a day. Prodding the flesh around it gently, she found it firm and slightly warmer than the rest. Bending over, she sniffed the gaping laceration. There were no signs of putrefaction. It needed stitching, and she wondered if she had enough catgut.

When she opened the medicine box, he craned his neck to see inside. She turned it so he could look at the contents. He did not touch any of the strange bottles and parchment sachets. She reached for the long, thin bone needle, lifting it for his perusal, unsure how he would react if she were to stick it into his skin unexpectedly. He was intrigued by the object at first, but when she made sewing motions in the air over the wound, understanding dawned. He jerked his leg to the side, and his hand snapped out to take the needle from her, but she was faster and pulled back, holding it out of his reach. He looked thoroughly disgusted, and she laughed.

The wound was deep, and she would need to layer the stitches, meaning she had to sew the deepest part on the inside first and then close it by pulling the skin together. It would be a painful procedure, and she would have preferred two or three men to hold him down. But asking four sailors to pin the Saldanhar chief to the ground while she tortured him with her bone needle would only result in a bloodbath, and then she would definitely be short on catgut.

There was no way to prepare him for what was to come. Best to just start and see where it all led. At the first sensation of the needle entering the inside wall of the wound, he grunted and involuntarily jerked his leg. She paused, and her eyes snapped to his. He gave her a hard stare. His mouth was pulled in a tight line, and beads of sweat dotted his upper lip, but he made no move to grab any vital part of her body.

The animated conversation between Governor Van Riebeeck and the Saldanhar men quieted at the chief's grunt. Van Riebeeck rose to his feet, but Danielle shook her head and pointed to the man sitting beside him. He was young and muscular, with many scars marring his skin. He did not look like the squeamish type.

The young warrior's reaction to her was almost identical to the chief's earlier, but when he reached out to touch her, the chief's harsh command stopped his hand mid-air. With a few pointed hand gestures, she mimed to the chief what she needed. He nodded his approval, and she showed the young warrior how she wanted the leg held. Once the familiar procedure of closing the wound started, her hands took on a life of their own. They were steady and sure as she finished three more stitches deep inside the wound, tying the walls neatly together. The young Saldanhar kept the leg steady, but after the first stitch, he turned his head away and stared sightlessly into the dense forest.

She stitched the skin in the middle of the wound together first, followed by ten more on either side. The chief had ordered the young man back to the shadows after the fourth stitch. He had relaxed his back against a tree and held perfectly still, quietly watching her work.

When the wound was tidily closed with twenty-one evenly spaced, firm stitches, she pulled gently on one of them. He frowned at the unpleasant sensation, then she wagged her finger and shook her head. He grinned.

Danielle reached for her honey and yarrow ointment, lifted it to her nose, inhaled deeply, and then held it under his nose. He inhaled and nodded again, and she covered the line of stitches with a thick layer, then wrapped it with a long bandage, split the end, and secured it in place with a tight knot.

She did not doubt he would discard the bandage at his earliest convenience, but the catgut would hold for at least ten days. Closing the lid of the medicine box, she gave the chief a smile and a shrug, signaling that she was done.

When she stretched her hand to help him up, he frowned at the offending gesture, gained his feet effortlessly, and walked to where his men were waiting.

There was a slight stiffness to his gait, but she thought it might be due to the unfamiliar sensation of the bandage, which positively glowed against his dark skin. The chief touched Governor Van Riebeeck's shoulder and held five fingers in the air. The governor waited for the demand to follow, but when none was made, he gave the chief a deep bow, then the warriors gathered their weapons and disappeared into the forest without a backward glance.

Chapter 21

"No!" the child screamed with all his might and swatted Arent's outstretched hand away from his body.

"Orion, stop your screeching. You must learn to swim." Arent spoke in his on-deck voice, sending a flock of birds fluttering from a nearby tree in search of a more peaceful perch.

"No, I don't," the child spat back, pushing the boatswain's already stunted supply of patience to its limit.

Captain De Coninck chuckled covertly at the scene from where he lounged against a tree on the riverbank, a fire crackling not far from his feet.

After searching the forest for nearly three hours and finding nothing more significant than a dog-sized antelope, they decided to quit the hunt and cast the fishing net instead.

Sebastiaan had discovered the rock pool further downstream. It was a large hole surrounded by boulders and heavy trees drooping over the dark water. The air was buzzing with insects and bird calls. A large flat-topped boulder, which must have dislodged itself eons ago from the mountain, had come to a rest near the middle, or perhaps the boulders had come first and then the river. Who knows? De Coninck pondered the beauty of their surroundings as he watched the three naked bodies in the water.

Sebastiaan glided through the water with breathless elegance, causing gentle ripples on the surface as he crossed the pool in easy strokes, enjoying the licks of the cool, sweet water over his skin. He and Arent had raced earlier while his uncle had shown Orion how to build a fire. Arent had quit the monotonous activity a while back and was now aggressively trying to intimidate Orion into a swimming lesson. The child was having none of it. Sebastiaan flipped onto his back and closed his eyes against the dancing sunlight. Hearing Arent's impatient tone, he dropped to his belly again and disappeared under the water.

Sebastiaan broke through the surface near the boy, laughed, and shook his sodden curls, sending water in a shower of light sparkles around his head. Orion's delightful squeals bounced off the boulders. Pinching his eyes shut, he fended off the cold drops with small, outstretched hands.

"Again," he shouted.

Sebastiaan turned his back to the boy and signaled for him to climb on.

"No," Orion protested.

"I won't dip you, I promise," he said smoothly and waited as Orion edged closer.

A soft, warm weight settled on his back as Orion climbed on and clasped his arms tightly around his neck. "Ease up a bit, will you?" Sebastiaan dislodged the death grip and moved the child's hands to his shoulders before taking slow steps away from the rock.

"Ready?" he asked and felt the little body move with what he assumed was a nod.

Carefully, he pushed forward in the water and swam with even strokes, keeping close to the surface so the child's head and upper body stayed above the water. He swam until he felt the rise of a sandbank under his feet, then turned and made the trip back to the rock in the middle of the pool. Depositing Orion back on the rock, Sebastiaan was rewarded with a brilliant smile, which instantly dropped when Arent stepped closer.

"Right, now you know what it feels like," Arent said as Orion scampered back to safety. "Come on, get in the water." Arent slapped the water by his side, resulting in the child taking two steps in retreat, gingerly stepping over the rapiers lying at the ready. He thought if Orion continued his retreat, he would end up in the water anyway; the possibility was starting to hold great appeal.

"Cap, order this whelp to get his scrawny backside in the water." Having run out of encouragements, he turned to help from a higher power.

CHAPTER 21

"No," De Coninck replied languorously. "He's yours – bought and paid for. You teach him. Besides, I've done my part. I've taught you and Sebastiaan how to swim when you were much older, and it was a lot harder." He watched as Arent glared at the child, fists on his hips. De Coninck laughed and said, "Try again."

"Orion, get in the *bloody* water right now, or I am going to ..." The threat died on his lips as ten native soldiers stepped through the dense forest and onto the riverbank. Sebastiaan and Arent reached for the rapiers as Captain De Coninck closed his hand around his musket and got to his feet in a fluid motion.

The musket was a poor weapon of choice as it was only good for one shot, and preferably not in close quarters, but De Coninck suspected that the noise would be enough of a deterrent. It would be a shame to spill blood on such a peaceful day.

"Orion, stay on the rock," Arent spoke softly.

"Yeah, *now* you want me to stay on the rock," Orion whispered back.

"Hush," Arent pinched his lips to stop his smile from spreading.

The Saldanhar chief surveyed the scene near the waterhole. An older man with the sky in his eyes was staring at him. A long thick stick draped over the man's forearm. His posture was relaxed, and there was strength in his shoulders and power in his hips, but the knowledge was more an instinct than fact, for again, he could not see what lurked beneath all the coverings on his body.

The chief's eyes shifted to the two men stepping from the water, one with the sunlight in his hair, the other with a witch's markings on his arms and chest. Warriors, no doubt, for their muscles were fine and their bodies scarred. They held their weapons by their sides, easy to see and ready to use. A little boy stood proudly on the rock behind them with a curious expression. The child showed no fear, which meant he had faith in the warriors.

Turning to his men, the chief gave an order, and they sank to their haunches. He stepped toward the older white man.

Sebastiaan watched as the dark warriors crouched as one. Their weapons were primitive but well made, and he wished for a set of his own. The spear looked light enough to travel a great distance, and the club would crack a pirate's skull with one swing. Instinctively, he licked his lips.

The white bandage around the young buck's thigh caught his eye. At first, he'd not paid it any attention, but now the significance was like a punch to his stomach that forced the air from his lungs. *Danielle.*

He pushed the panic from his mind. She was well protected as long as she stayed in the tent or near the sailors. Scanning the men, he noted that they did not look like they came fresh from a fight. He relaxed and returned his focus to the chief. He was young, tall, and slender, but when he flicked his cloak over his shoulder, Sebastiaan caught the way the muscles rolled and stretched under the scarred dark skin. The lad was tough and agile; he would be a mean, fast fighter.

The chief stepped closer to his uncle until they were only a few inches apart. His uncle held his ground, but Sebastiaan knew he was itching to step away or order the young chief to back off. He was exceedingly territorial about his personal space, and the chief was well within its boundaries.

The chief shifted both his weapons to one hand, and with his free hand, he reached out, snaked it around his uncle's neck, and drew him into an embrace. Sebastiaan could almost hear the knuckles of his spine crack as his uncle bent rigidly into the gesture, keeping his free hand by his side. A tight frown had knotted itself into Arent's brow. This was definitely a first for all.

Stepping back from the stiff embrace, the chief looked his uncle in the eye, smiled, and held five fingers in the air. De Coninck nodded his agreement and watched blankly as the warriors rose and quietly moved off into the forest again.

"What the hell?" Arent muttered.

Captain De Coninck was rooted to the spot, staring into the forest where the men had vanished. His impassive expression had given way to one of acute confusion.

Sebastiaan broke the stunned moment by stepping forward and pulling his uncle into a tight hug, his shoulders shaking with silent mirth.

"What?" his uncle exclaimed. "Get off me, you idiot," he grunted and shoved his nephew away.

CHAPTER 21

Sebastiaan laughed and ducked out of the way of the fist, aimed at his jaw.

* * *

It was long past the lunch hour when Governor Van Riebeeck walked Danielle back to the hospital tent, with Adam trailing a discreet distance behind.

"How I wish we could keep the events of today between the two of us," he spoke pensively, as he walked with his hands clasped behind his back.

"Are you wishing to keep it from your wife or Captain De Coninck?" she asked.

He breathed a deep sigh and lifted his face to allow the sun's rays to wash over his features.

"Preferably both and in that order."

"You were not at all pleased with me today," she ventured, not understanding why his approval was important to her.

He paused their slow walk and turned to her. "Danielle, you secured us five heads of cattle. It's four more than I hoped for. How can I be displeased with you?" They continued the rest of the way in silence.

"So, what was all the fuss?" Pieter asked as soon as she cleared the tent's entrance.

"We had an important visit from one of the tribal chiefs," Danielle said as she glanced at each patient. One of the older men on the left's condition had worsened.

"We've had ourselves an important visitor as well," Pieter spoke again, but did not offer more until he was sure he had Danielle's full attention.

"Well?" Danielle stared at him. "It will save time if you tell me, or do you want me to guess?"

Ignoring her snappish tone, he continued, "The governor's wife and her friends, that's who. Nice lady. She even touched old Dirck's brow." He said and gestured to her dying patient.

Maria was here. Danielle missed her friend. With all the tumult of the last few days, she hadn't spent any time with her. She longed to sit with the twins and listen to their endless chatter, or Mrs. Boom's to-the-point conversations that usually revolved around solving the problems of those around her.

With a wistful smile, Danielle turned to Adam.

"Would you mind begging a little broth for Dirck from the cooks? I've no more herbs to brew. I don't know what else to do for him." She gathered another blanket and covered the frail body of the old sailor. The sand underneath him was clean; his bowels had run empty, but he was losing the battle against the raging fever.

"The other lady, who came with the governor's wife, and the two younger ones were planning to go with the gardener to search for feverfew. It sounds like something you could use." Pieter looked to Danielle as she nodded her agreement. "She looks like the sort to get things done. If you get my meaning?" he finished his report.

Pieter was right. If Mrs. Boom went in search of feverfew, she would not return without it or something like it. It would be a godsend. Danielle would then be free to cut some long grasses, which grew at the beach's edge, for mattresses.

Adam returned with Captain Hooghsaet and an older man.

"Miss Van Aard," Captain Hooghsaet said, "this is the *Reijger's* surgeon, Mr. Hoek. He is eager to be of service." He shoved the surgeon towards the entrance with a hearty slap on his back.

"Mr. Hoek, I am so grateful for your assistance." Judged by the sour pinch of the man's face, it didn't look like he'd volunteered his services.

"He will take the night shift so that you can have a bit of rest," Captain Hooghsaet stated.

Danielle had not realized how tired she was until that moment, but she could not let him enter the tent without a few instructions.

"Ensure you wash your hands after tending each patient, also …" but the surgeon turned away from her and disappeared into the tent without regard for her apparently unwanted advice. Danielle frowned and made to follow the obstinate man when Captain Hooghsaet stayed her with a hand on her shoulder.

"Come sit with me for a spell," he said, dragging her away.

"No, I can't," she protested, but he put his arm around her shoulders and

CHAPTER 21

steered her toward a cluster of boulders and a new cooking fire.

"Child, you are dead on your feet from exhaustion. Look at you, pale as a topsail, with dark patches under your eyes. When was the last time you had something to eat?" He studied her with a concerned scowl.

"I can't leave them. Some might not make it through the night." She looked over her shoulder to her hospital.

"Neither will you if you don't take care of yourself. Hoek will tend them during the night. He's a good man, with nary a mean bone in his body."

The evening held a festive mood. Cooking fires dotted the beach, with the smell of roasted fish and cooked sorrel filling the air. An unfamiliar sound rumbled from afar.

"What was that?" Danielle asked, looking in the direction of the sound.

"A lion, but he's not near." Hooghsaet's voice was easy, without a trace of concern.

It was the most primal sound she'd ever heard, and it caused the fine hairs on her spine to rise.

"I've never seen a lion," she confessed.

"Aye, and let's pray you never do," Hooghsaet said as he reached to take a cooking girdle and pewter plates from Barent, dismissing the cook with a curt nod.

The hunting party had returned, and Arent saw to the fair distribution of the day's catch.

"Now, if only we had something to eat," Captain Hooghsaet rued from the opposite side of the fire.

"At your service, my lord," Captain De Coninck raucously announced as he planted a bucket with fresh fish next to Hooghsaet. Sebastiaan dropped next to Danielle with a content sigh and, in one smooth motion, hauled her up beside him.

"Excellent, I'll clean, you cook," Hooghsaet announced to De Coninck, and the two set about preparing the fish for dinner, leaving Sebastiaan and Danielle a moment to exchange the day's news.

De Coninck chuckled as he heard Sebastiaan's "Jaysus" and watched his nephew rub a hand over his face and rest the back of his head against the boulder. She must've told him about the incident with the chief. Van Riebeeck had intercepted him earlier and relayed the incident. Judged by the governor's carefully chosen words, De Coninck had the suspicion there was more to the event than what Van Riebeeck was revealing.

Slowly their group around the fire grew. First, Arent joined them, with Orion on his heels, chewing on a large piece of flatbread. With a grunt, Arent lowered himself onto the sand and stretched his legs in front of him. Orion darted to the fire to inspect the fish.

"Come settle your bones," Arent's tone was deep and lazy. "Plant your little arse here before you fall into the fire," he ordered Orion as he patted the sand next to him. "Remind me never to have children," he spoke to nobody in particular.

"You probably have one in every port from here to Tokyo," De Coninck laughed.

Arent growled and glared at the captain with all the dignity of an offended house cat.

Their amiable banter was interrupted when Governor Van Riebeeck and Maria strolled toward them with a hesitant Captain Turver in tow. Over the last week, the young man had lost weight, and his eyes were haunted and sunken. He was clearly uncertain of his welcome, but when Hooghsaet passed him a plate of fish, he accepted it gracefully and sank next to the fire, quietly picking at his food.

The deaths of so many sailors under his command weighed heavy on his conscience. Danielle felt a stab of sympathy for him as she closed her eyes and rested her head against Sebastiaan's shoulder.

* * *

The previous night Danielle had thought there was nothing more beautiful than an African sunset. The day had ended with a fiery celebration as the sun dipped behind Table Mountain, painting it in adamant relief against a sky feathered with purple and pink wisps of clouds, leaving the beach to glimmer in pools of molten gold.

CHAPTER 21

Now, twelve hours later, she was hard-pressed to revise her opinion. She'd found that every day started with its own sense of selfhood. This morning, powder blue skies whispered over a smooth silver ocean, timid in its fragility yet so powerful it stilled her breath.

"This is something, isn't it?" Sebastiaan's voice breathed over her ear as he came to stand behind her, close enough that she felt the heat from his body.

Nothing seemed to stay constant. Colors and sounds were always in a state of change, except for the waves. Their continuous pounding of the beach was like a trusty old mantle clock keeping time.

Some lives travel in a circle, starting at a point and returning after a journey to find themselves slightly altered for better or worse. Hers was a straight line, always moving forward, forever changing. She would probably never return to Oudeschild; there was nothing left for her. She found the thought did not hurt as much as it used to. Danielle felt grounded and confident for the first time in her life. Her future stretched sure and beautifully before her, anchored by Sebastiaan's steadfast presence.

"What are you thinking about?" he asked.

"Nothing," she laughed. "Everything."

"How is your hospital coming along?"

"It's clean," she smiled and leaned back against him.

"Do you have everything you need for it?" he asked, and she sensed he was leading somewhere.

"No, why?"

"We are leaving in nine days," he said.

The shock of the casual statement straightened her spine, and she turned in the circle of his arms.

Shaking her head, "Nine days? So soon?" She looked at him with a furrowed brow.

"Yes, we are leaving with the *Reijger*, Captain Hooghseat informed me last night. He would've stayed longer, but with the chief's promise yesterday, he will have a good supply of fresh meat and can set sail sooner."

"I thought we would leave with the *Drommedaris*."

"No, the *Drommedaris* will stay for a few months in service of the new settlement. I can't wait that long."

Instantly a sunny smile spread across her face, and her eyes sparkled with renewed vigor.

"I'll be ready. I'll need a lot of help, but I'll be ready," she promised, then grabbed his hand and pulled him across the deck to where the other women were waiting to be rowed to the beach.

Chapter 22

The following week flew by in a blur. Work on the fort was progressing slowly, much to Governor Van Riebeeck's dismay. Every day, more tents were erected at the edge of the clearing near the building site. Heavy rains over the last few days had washed much of the foundation away, forcing the workers to mix the soil with rock and underwood to prevent a similar disaster in the future.

Many of the men working on the site were unacquainted with their task, and with only a few skilled tradesmen among them, it was a trial-and-error endeavor, with much time spent fixing mistakes. With the constant rain and building woes, morale was at a low, and where morale steered, ingenuity and productivity followed.

Captain Hooghsaet and Governor Van Riebeeck oversaw the fort's building, and with the rain clearing, a brilliant idea had taken hold. They decided to hold a competition. All the men were divided into groups, each competing against the other to see which team could dig the most foundation trenches in a day.

At first, nobody was particularly keen on the new megrim. However, Hooghsaet's announcement that the winning team would be rewarded an extra ration of beer at the end of the day drummed up the required enthusiasm.

Now, once more, the air was filled with loud shouts as the men cheered each other on. Any attempts at sabotage were quickly quelled and harshly punished. The offending team would forfeit their ration of beer for three days, leaving the offenders with pitifully long faces, miserably clutching their mugs of fresh water, come dinner.

Captain De Coninck had declared early on that he had no interest whatsoever in anything related to building, whether it be a tent or a fort. He would, however, ensure no one went hungry. With Sebastiaan and Arent's vigorous assistance, there was always fresh meat for the dinner pot, whether it be fish or game. Cattle supplied by the Saldanhars were slaughtered, with half the meat set aside for immediate consumption and the other half salted and cured.

Most days, they would catch up to seven hundred steenbras. The fish was a great favorite for its delicate taste. "Better than any that can be found in the Fatherland," Governor Van Riebeeck declared.

One late afternoon, the hunting party came crashing through the edge of the forest, and into the clearing, with all the grace of a disgruntled elephant bull. They were battered and exhausted, hauling a makeshift stretcher lashed over their shoulders. Fashioned from roughly cut poles and hewn together with the rope from the fishing net, the stretcher bore the giant carcass of a hippopotamus. The belly was cut open, which had caused it to deflate around the four stubby legs protruding from the grey mass. The broad head with its tiny ears dangled close to the stretcher's bottom end, and thick, dried blood crusted the edge of the destroyed right eye socket.

As more men became aware of their presence, work ceased, and the sailors crowded around the fascinatingly grotesque animal. Hooghsaet pushed a few onlookers aside, clearing a path for him and Governor Van Riebeeck.

The three hunters had encountered the beast shortly after casting their fishing net that morning in a new section of the river when the hippopotamus calf emerged from the depths.

De Coninck had not wasted a moment in reaching for his musket and taking careful aim before shooting it neatly through the eye. After the exhilaration of the kill had worn off, they faced the dilemma of transporting the nearly two-thousand-pound prey.

The rest of the morning was spent gutting the hippopotamus, followed by felling and stripping young trees to construct the stretcher. Then they set about the herculean task of hauling it back to the settlement.

CHAPTER 22

"Well done, my boy," Hooghsaet bellowed and slapped De Coninck vigorously on the shoulder, eliciting a loud groan. He looked to see what had caused the sound and found that all three men's shoulders were bloody from where the ropes had cut through their shirts and into their skins.

"Stop gawking, you bunch of ninnies. Three men to a pole and three to the ropes," Hooghsaet hollered his orders at the gathering men. "Take it to the cooks. That's it. Move sprightly now." He turned to the governor, who stared at the scene with open-mouthed fascination. "Governor, why don't you follow along and make sure they don't lose it on the way?"

De Coninck accepted the brandy flask Hooghsaet pushed into his hands and took a few restoring sips before passing it to Arent. Arent tilted his head back and had tipped the flask high when Sebastiaan plucked it from his hand, securing the last few drops for himself.

"On to the beach, then, lads. I know a fetching lass who can patch up any scratch." Hooghsaet laughed as he led the way.

* * *

"Can I have the tooth?" Orion asked, fingering the large, sharp canine in the animal's bottom jaw.

"It's almost as long as your arm," De Coninck said, ruffling the child's shiny ebony curls as he stepped away from Danielle, his shoulders neatly cleaned and bandaged.

"It would be my first treasure. Please," Orion begged, dragging out the last syllable of his plea.

De Coninck laughed. "Yes, you can have it, but it needs to lay in the sun for a month before you can touch it. Do you understand?"

"Why?" the boy asked, wrinkling his nose and frowning at the inconvenience.

"The sun needs to clean it," De Coninck explained.

"But can't we wash it in the river?" Orion persisted.

"Orion," Arent's impatient voice rumbled from where he sat, hunched over under Danielle's careful ministrations, "do you want the tooth or not?"

"I want it," Orion said emphatically.

"Then you'll wait. Aye?" Knowing when a battle was lost, the little boy hung his head, hiding the shameful tears of his disappointment.

"Orion?" Mrs. Boom called from near the fire. "Do you remember the honey you and Sebastiaan collected yesterday?" She continued at the boy's demure nod, "I made honey cakes. Would you like one?" He leaped from De Coninck's side to receive the sweet treat from Mrs. Boom, her face an open book of delight as she watched him wolf it down, with honey dripping from his chin and over his small hands.

"I assume it can be eaten," Van Riebeeck said as he watched Barent and the other cooks preparing the carcass. "But I am most curious as to the taste. Has anyone *tasted* hippopotamus before?" Van Riebeeck asked, contemplating the extravagance of the question as he wrapped his arm around his wife's shoulders.

"The lions seemed to like it. Figured we might too." Arent's logic was too shocking to warrant an argument.

"Well, if we can't eat it, we might use it for bait," De Coninck mused.

"Good heavens," Van Riebeeck exclaimed, "what on earth are you hoping to catch?"

"Perhaps one of those whales you've been eyeing the last couple of days." De Coninck sounded half asleep, but a smile curved his mouth as he spoke. The governor knew De Coninck was pulling his leg, for he had been positively sulking since he'd seen the large mammals within easy reach of the shore. If only they had the equipment necessary to undertake such a hunt successfully. All in good time, he'd promised himself, but he made sure all knew of his misgivings and frustrations.

It was nearly dark when Barent approached the governor with the first of the hippopotamus steak. Van Riebeeck stood up to receive the dish, signaling the importance of the event. Barent nervously waited, hands clasped behind his back as the governor took the first bite.

Van Riebeeck chewed, closed his eyes, and swallowed. All around the fire watched in anticipation.

"Well?" Hooghsaet demanded.

CHAPTER 22

"Well done, Barent," Van Riebeeck praised, and the cook beamed under the governor's approval. "It is delicious: mild and gamey, doubtless more flavorful than beef and not as chewy as one might suspect."

"Pity we don't have the innards. I could have done something with the heart or the liver. Lots of good food there," Barent bemoaned the loss.

"I'd say you have enough to keep you busy as it is," De Coninck admonished his cook.

"Aye, we'll probably work through the night. Would be a shame for any of it to go to waste." Barent's words trailed behind him as he returned to his task of cutting the meat into manageable pieces.

"Well, Captain, no need for feeding it to the whales then," Governor Van Riebeeck spoke to De Coninck as he handed his wife a morsel of the meat.

"I don't think whales feast on hippopotami," Turver added with an austere look of concern. No one paid the observation any attention, apart from Arent, who rolled his eyes at the dainty fop.

For his part, Captain Turver proved to be an adept naturalist. He had spent many hours with Hendrik Boom and Leesa in search of fertile soil for growing fruit and vegetables. His records and illustrations of the sites and native plants were painstakingly detailed.

Leesa found the unpredictable nature of most young men quite unsettling and preferred to avoid their rambunctious behavior altogether. The young captain's quiet intelligence and passion for plants and animals, which he sketched with the softest and surest hand, had slowly drawn her from her shell. With him, she discovered a confidence she'd not known she possessed. She laughed at his wit, and he listened with deep interest as she voiced her opinions. On occasion but only when he persisted did she offer a gentle critique of some of his sketches.

Turver had made several trips to a nearby island and had returned with images of penguins and seals. Upon seeing the sweet, smiling face of a baby seal, Leesa had jested that the island should be called Robbin Island in honor of the sweet-faced *robbe* or seals. Turver had promptly picked up his quill, carefully dipped it into the ink well, and in an elegantly slanted hand, wrote the name across the island on his naval chart.

To Leesa's bitter disappointment, he would not allow her to accompany him to the island.

"The seas are too rough, and you are far too precious to be put to such perils," he had explained, and of course, she understood, touched by his concern. Still, she wished to see the beautiful seals and laughed at the waddling penguins he so adroitly described.

"Had he kissed you yet?" Elsje asked her one evening as she bent to scoop stew from a pot hanging over the cooking fire, her eyes sparkling with mischief. The inquiry was ill-timed, for the *'he'* in question was walking towards them in the company of Sebastiaan and Arent, fairly dwarfed by the two burly men.

Leesa couldn't think of an answer quickly enough because her heart was beating frantically. The palms of her hands were moist, and her cheeks flaming, as she looked at the approaching men, her eyes fixed on only one. The question startled her into nearly dropping her meal into her lap if not for Danielle's quick rescuing of the bowl.

Elsje wriggled her eyebrows and gave Danielle a wink. Danielle smiled secretly, thinking the young captain was not as slow on the uptake as she had judged him to be. Luckily the *Goeie Hoop* would remain at the Cape for a few more months.

"What about you?" Danielle teased Elsje.

"What do you mean?" she feigned innocence.

"Is there anyone you wished would kiss you?" Elsje was a favorite among all at the settlement. She cut a swath through the men with her bright hair, sparkling eyes, quick wit, and sharp tongue.

"Listen to me," Elsje said, looking Danielle straight in the face. "When I marry, it will be to a man with clean fingernails and a big yacht." Danielle had snorted her stew all over her skirt as Elsje demonstrated the size of the yacht, which bore no resemblance to a nautical vessel at all.

"I am going to marry a silk merchant," Elsje stated, "and he will bring me luxuriously fine silks of every imaginable color from the East."

"But he will never be home," Danielle countered.

"So?" Elsje looked at her in confusion. "I'll be busy sewing the most exquisite

CHAPTER 22

garments and will hardly notice."

The picture Elsje was painting was not hard to believe, and Danielle could see her blissfully happy among brightly colored bolts of fabric, lost in her creations.

***

Every morning the governor and the women were rowed to the beach. Danielle spent all day in the hospital tent, nursing the sick men back to health. Four more had passed away since leaving the *Goeie Hoop*. The last two days were without any casualties, and she was beginning to believe there would be no more.

Leesa often brought a basket of herbs, and Danielle had tied small bundles to the stitching of the hospital tent for drying, lending an earthy smell to the enclosed space.

Every evening she would hand over the care of her patients to Mr. Hoek, who had warmed to her and her strict rules in his own time. He was a man of few words, but his hands were gentle, and his soul devoid of cruelty. How such a gentle, soft-spoken man managed to endure under the command of someone like Captain Hooghsaet was a mystery.

"He is not soft-spoken," one of the patients said. "He is non-spoken. The man does not utter a word. It is as quiet as a crypt here at night." His complaints were bolstered by grunts from the others.

"You can quit your whining," Danielle scolded them. "Nighttime is for sleeping, so there is no need for conversation and noise. Besides, this is a place of rest and recuperation and should always be quiet."

"It is never quiet when you're here."

Danielle frowned at that unwelcome bit of truth.

As soon as Mr. Hoek entered the tent, Sebastiaan would drag her away. They walked hand in hand along the beach, enjoying the feeling of the sand under their bare feet, knowing that soon they would have to swap it for the constantly rolling wooden deck of a ship. Sitting in their secret hideaway, which was nothing more than a large boulder shrouded by the overhanging branches of a tree, they planned their future, drinking in the last rays of the day and watching as the ocean changed gradually from pink to purple to grey.

"My father's house is quite large, with beautiful gardens surrounding it," he said. "We can stay there, and after we get married, we can move to a place of our own."

She shook her head before speaking. "No, if your father approves of me, I think we should stay with him. It would be unfair to take you away from him."

"He will approve of you," Sebastiaan's voice was soft, but she detected a hint of steel underneath the velvety tone.

"How can you be so sure?" He did not bother to answer and only laughed at her ignorance.

They would stay under the tree until it was time for dinner, then make their way back leisurely, dragging their feet through the wet sand, leaving long twining patterns in their wake.

Since coming ashore, life had found a new cadence. It was not, however, without its struggles. Cuts and gashes were not out of the ordinary, and Danielle was becoming equally adept at stitching wounds as she was at treating dysentery. The men from the *Goeie Hoop* were steadily recovering, but every day one or two of those working on the building site would fill the recently vacated spaces, sharing the symptoms of their predecessors.

But it was Maria who haunted Danielle's thoughts. In the wild struggle of creating a habitable settlement, Maria seemed to float in and out of everyone's day. There was a time after Antoonie's death when she appeared to have found peace. But peace seemed to be a finite commodity. For Maria, it had run out.

Some mornings she spent with Danielle in the hospital, and other times she wandered through the forest with the gardener, returning empty-handed and seemingly unaware of the fact. Her eyes were dull and inward-looking, searching for a meaning she could not find.

Most afternoons she spent in the shade with Orion, having temporarily taken over his education from De Coninck. Other times she would stare sightlessly out over the ocean. At first, Orion was a balm to her aching heart, but his boisterous nature soon proved too much for her. To the boy's endless

CHAPTER 22

delight, his schooling was suspended, and he was free to spend his days running and playing on the beach under Mrs. Boom's ever-watchful eyes.

"My husband has the fort to build and a settlement to start. You have your patients," Maria had said as she and Danielle took a few moments to enjoy their luncheon in the shade. "Mrs. Boom has taken over the cooking. Even the twins seemed to have found a place for themselves." She exhaled a sigh so deep as if to empty her heart. "I was supposed to chase after my boy, watch him play in the sand, teach him about all the new things that would form his world." She shook her head sadly. Her eyes were dry and raw with sorrow, with no more tears to spill.

"You'll have another baby," Danielle said. "You can't give up."

"I'm not giving up, Danielle." Maria stared into Danielle's eyes, searching for something. "I'm standing still in the eye of a storm." Danielle understood that. Not so long ago, she was standing in the eye of her storm, and it was Maria who'd reached out to her. She had no idea how to reach out to her friend. Maria was like a small vessel quietly and inexorably drifting away in the night.

Chapter 23

Danielle noticed Maria's absence on deck four days into their last week as they readied themselves to row ashore. Maria's mood had become increasingly melancholy over the last few days, and Danielle thought that perhaps her friend had decided to stay aboard and lose herself in her drawings.

The morning was hazy, even though the sky was clear. A morning like this signaled wind in the afternoon and perhaps an oncoming storm. Danielle would have to fortify the tent's walls in case her suspicions proved true.

The beach was already a hive of activity, with sloops filled to the brim with provisions for the *Reijger*. They were to set sail in three days. Mr. Hoek would be leaving with them, and Danielle had decided to ask Mrs. Boom to take over the hospital until a surgeon arrived with the two large cargo ships already en route to the Cape and expected to arrive any day.

Entering the tent, she relieved Mr. Hoek of his duties and listened to his report of what transpired during the night. As per usual, nothing much happened, and thus the recall was quick and concise. They were now well and truly ahead of the disease. The key was to recognize the symptoms early and treat the victims quickly and effectively. By doing so, the infection rate had been slowed; she believed they might eradicate it within the next week.

Shouts and cheering drew Danielle's attention away from her careful notes on the native plants she recognized and their medicinal uses. Quickly checking on her four remaining patients, she left the tent.

People were dancing on the beach and waving their arms in the air. Danielle spotted Elsje amidst the chaos.

CHAPTER 23

"What's going on?" She asked.

"Two ships," she pointed out to sea. "Can you see them?"

Danielle followed her outstretched hand and squinted at the horizon, where a few specks of white appeared and disappeared.

"Are you sure?" To her mind, it could be anything from waves to clouds. It was too far to see.

"It's the *Walfis* and the *Olifant*." The *Whale* and the *Elephant,* the expedition's two cargo ships. The vessels had been delayed in Texel and had set on their journey almost an entire month late.

"How do you know?" she asked Elsje.

"Barent said so."

"Would recognize those sails anywhere," Barent chimed in. Danielle just shook her head at the cook and set to return to the tent.

"Can't even be sure it's a sail, let alone which," she murmured to herself as she walked away.

A fierce wind had whipped the bay into a madly churning cauldron; it took the ships two days to drop anchor some distance from the shore.

The mood amongst the onlookers on the beach was somber. Strong winds and sheets of rain that felt as if they could cut skin were violently bearing down on them. All silently waited for the storm to lay claim to the battered vessels and sink them to the bottom of Table Bay.

By late afternoon, on the second day after the two cargo ships had dropped anchor, the wind changed, and fear gripped Danielle's heart with cold fingers. The smell that reached the shore told of indescribable suffering, a suffering Danielle had witnessed firsthand aboard the *Goeie Hoop* – dysentery.

Frantically she ran to the hospital tent. With no notion of how many patients would soon flood the space, she had to make room and protect her almost hale patients.

"Adam!" she screamed to be heard above the roar of the wind. Her trusted assistant appeared at her side, and from the stricken look on his face, she knew the same fears were coursing through him.

"We need lots of water from the river, and we need a shelter ..." There was too much to do. "No, wait. Please find Sebastiaan," she said and headed for the tent.

No fires were lit along the beach, for the wind was too strong, and there was the general concern of it being whipped into the forest. Therefore, the only water for the sick was that which Adam had hauled from the river.

The new patients would need warm water as they would have to be washed from head to toe.

Sebastiaan came crashing through the tent's opening with a murderous look. He scanned the space before his eyes settled on Danielle, finding her safe and unharmed, and only then did his countenance soften.

"Adam said you needed me?" he asked, his voice heavy with worry.

"Yes, have you smelled the air?"

"I have. It smelled like the *Goeie Hoop*. Dysentery?"

"I have no doubt. But I need a fire to boil water for washing and cooking." He grasped her meaning before she had to ask.

"Aye, you need a shelter built first. I'll fetch a few lads. Do you need Mrs. Boom?" he asked. The men had built a shelter for Mrs. Boom and the cooks in the clearing so they could continue their work.

"Yes, I do," she said without hesitation. Danielle watched him leave with determined strides, and she sent a quick prayer of gratitude that she would never have to live without him.

The *Reijger* planned to set sail tomorrow for Batavia, but she was certain Captain Hooghsaet would wait for the storm to die down before attempting to leave the bay.

Danielle was dividing herbs into bundles when Mrs. Boom swished into the tent.

"What do you need done, my dear?" Her presence was a mercy, for where Anke Boom went, order followed.

"Sebastiaan is building us a wind shelter. I need –" but Mrs. Boom interrupted her.

"No, dear Sebastiaan sent a handful of lads with instructions on what must be done. He left with the other rowers to rescue the men on those ships, for the captains fear that the storm is sure to sink them." Seeing the shock on Danielle's face, Mrs. Boom wrapped her in a tight embrace.

CHAPTER 23

"The waves are too high," Danielle almost cried as she clutched the older woman's shoulders.

"You must have faith, my darling. You know he is a strong rower and an even stronger swimmer. Besides, that beast of a boatswain is with him. He'll be just fine." Mrs. Boom's words soothed some of her fears. Danielle stepped away from her and raced outside. She had to see him before he left, but she was too late. The departing sloops were nothing but black spots against the waves. She could not even distinguish his blond hair.

"Oh God, please keep him safe," she prayed as she wiped the tears from her face.

Turning into the wind, she let it blow her hair back before she gathered it into a tight bundle. After twisting it in a braid, she flung it onto her back. It would not do for her to fall apart, she reprimanded herself sternly. Time to earn her keep. The memory of De Coninck's command, all these months ago, invoked a wry smile.

The men were building a wind shelter at least six feet high from a type of bramble bush. It was a hardy, thorny shrub that clung relentlessly to anything and everything, making it the perfect barrier against the wind.

Adam and Pieter, her former patient, carried barrel after barrel of fresh, clean water from the river. Soon Mrs. Boom would start the fires to heat the water and cook the broth.

Danielle leaned into the wind as she fought her way up the dune behind the tent. She needed to cut long grass for the sleeping pallets. The sick would be feverish; there were enough blankets, but a few more would not hurt. She just hoped somebody had the presence of mind to rescue the blankets on those ships before they sank.

* * *

Many eager hands awaited the returning sloops. Wading into the rough surf as far as they could, the sailors onshore dragged the sloops away from the pounding water; some rowers were so exhausted that they collapsed into the arms of their waiting shipmates. Fresh arms quickly replaced them, and as soon as the small vessels were relieved of their burden, they immediately returned to rescue more from the stricken ships.

Adam and Pieter dragged the sick men to the hospital tent. A few could walk on unsteady legs, but most were too close to death to manage the distance unassisted.

Danielle and Mrs. Boom stripped the sodden and filth-encrusted clothes from their bodies. Laying them side by side in hollows dug in the sand, lined with a layer of long grass, they washed each man with patient diligence.

"We need more help," Mrs. Boom said as the stream of sick men trickling into the tent seemed like it would never end.

"No," Danielle shook her head from where she was kneeling next to a young sailor, "best not to expose too many to the sickness. We'll manage. Besides, there must be surgeons on the ships."

"They died weeks ago," one of the new patients said. "We had to stop at St. Vincent to leave the worst of the sick behind."

Mrs. Boom listened as the sailor reported the sorry tale. "I suppose we'll have to manage on our own then. You've done it before." There was a note of admiration in the older woman's voice as she spoke to Danielle.

"I had Adam." Thinking back, Danielle couldn't imagine how she would have managed without Adam by her side. He was a loyal friend.

"Miss, what do you want to do with the dead ones?" Adam's voice called from near the entrance.

The question, so casually asked, shook Danielle.

"How many?"

"So far, we have eight," he replied.

There was nothing she could do for the dead. All her attention and care were for those clinging so valiantly to the little life still left in them.

"Adam, line them up near the wind shelter and cover them with something." It occurred to Danielle that some might still be alive, and she rushed outside.

As she kneeled over the first corpse, it was plain as day that the man was no longer alive, but she searched for a pulse before straightening his body and moving on to the next one. Her breath caught when she brushed the hair from the pale blue face. It was one of the sailors from the *Drommedaris*.

CHAPTER 23

She recognized him, even though she couldn't remember his name, a flash memory of a young sailor hanging from the shrouds, laughing down at his friend on deck, filled her eyes with unexpected tears.

"How?" she asked Adam. He did not answer but turned his back on her as he stalked to the shoreline to collect more sick and dead bodies. Danielle ran after him, grabbing hold of his arm.

"Answer me." She did not understand his behavior. "Adam," she begged.

"Go back to the tent, Danielle," he said in a voice so stern and unyielding that she took a few steps in retreat.

"No," she shouted, "answer me."

"Two sloops have been lost with all hands," he said and watched as the meaning of his words hit her.

"Who –" there was more she needed to know, but he cut her off.

"We don't know. They are only just starting to wash up."

Danielle started up the beach, where sailors dragged a sloop from the water. She watched as the rowers were replaced and then ran towards them, calling Sebastiaan's name.

"He's not here, miss," an unfamiliar voice said.

"Have you seen him or Arent?" she asked.

"No, miss."

The storm was intensifying, and the rain sliced through her clothes, running in cold rivulets down her body. She called for Sebastiaan many more times, and each time, her calls were met with shaking heads. One man waved her away as one would a bothersome insect.

A raw cry shredded her insides as it left her body. Her legs could no longer support her, and she sank to her knees in the wet sand.

Please God, she prayed.

Strong arms wrapped around her and lifted her to her feet.

"Come, miss," Adam's voice cut through her misery, "we know nothing for sure. Come now," he coaxed. "The men need you, for as God is my witness, they will die if you don't see to them."

Danielle moved toward the hospital as if in a dream. Inside, the scene was eerily familiar. Sick and dying men lined the sides of the tent, so close to each other that there was just room for her to walk between their sleeping pallets.

Mrs. Boom looked up as Danielle entered and read the desolation on her face.

"Child, stop this nonsense immediately," she snapped in a voice Danielle had never heard from her before. "Until you cradle his dead body in your arms, he is still alive." Somehow the callous words cut through the fog that shrouded Danielle's mind.

"Get to work, missy." Mrs. Boom's voice fell with the tenderness of a whiplash across the tent.

Danielle resumed her task of stripping, washing, and covering the men as Adam and Pieter dragged them in, one after the other.

"Miss, I think this one is still alive," Adam announced as he walked into the tent backward, hauling a sailor under his arms. The man's bare heels drew deep tracks in the sand. "I put him with the dead at first, but when I returned, he made a sound. Now I'm not sure if my mind is playing tricks on me."

Adam deposited the man near the entrance. His skin was a pale grey, and his fingers were blue. Danielle searched for a pulse in his neck and wrist, finding none, but as she reached over to straighten his head, she saw his eyelids flutter. The movement was so faint as if not to have happened at all. Without waiting for further evidence, she grabbed two blankets and wrapped his filthy wet body.

"Should we not clean him first?" Mrs. Boom asked.

"As soon as he is stronger, we'll clean him," Danielle replied. She felt a surge of protectiveness for the unknown man. Death would not claim him, not tonight, not while she could stand between him and The Reaper.

Earlier, they had prepared an herb mixture that Adam suggested they steep in broth.

Danielle reached for a bowl of broth, lifted the sailor's head into her lap, and slowly dribbled a few drops into his mouth.

Time passed without meaning or reference. Adam and Pieter worked as men possessed, carrying slop buckets back and forth, ensuring a steady supply of warm water and broth.

"Adam, please don't empty the dirty water into the river," Danielle said.

"No, miss, we dug a hole earlier. It all goes in there. Figured it's best not to pass the pestilence to the fish." Smiling at his reasoning, she realized that she couldn't remember the last time a pleasant thought had invaded her troubled mind.

Sebastiaan should have returned many hours ago; he hadn't.

Dawn was approaching, turning the sky a somber grey. Danielle straightened and headed outside. Pushing her fists into the small of her back, she pulled her shoulders back and straightened, tilting her head before she let it roll to the corpses lining the wind shelter. Fifteen lives were lost. She stopped by each, drawing cold lids over eyes frozen in the horror of death, brushing hair from the faces with a maternal gentleness, and ensuring limbs were neatly straightened for easy burial. She wondered if she should bind the sagging jaws but decided against it.

How extraordinary that in death there was no status, no honor, nothing; we are all the same. She hoped that when it was her turn, there would be a gentle hand to close her eyes.

Sebastiaan was not among the dead. Was he lost and washed up somewhere along the beach with sand in his hair, eyes staring coldly into the morning air? Nobody had seen him since he first rowed out to the ships. The sun was starting to rise. If he were alive, he would have come to her by now. *Where are you?*

I'm right here.

She would forever hear his voice filling her head and echoing through the rooms of her heart. Tears streamed over her face, and her shoulders shook with the force of her anguish.

Heaving a deep sigh, she turned back to the tent, and there he stood, battered and tired, looking like an angel in all his golden beauty.

"You're alive," she breathed.

A cocky smile curved his tired mouth, and he opened his arms to her.

"Of course," he croaked above her head as she barreled into his chest with a force that drove them back a few steps.

"It's over," he said as he closed his arms around her. Opening her eyes, she saw what he meant. The storm had spent itself during the night, leaving the morning clear and fresh as if it had not been at all. Evidence of its violence was everywhere. The beach was littered with driftwood, and Danielle knew that all Governor Van Riebeeck and Captain Hooghsaet had accomplished over the last week was once again washed away. "The ships are safe, and we'll be leaving after midday," Sebastiaan's voice cut through her exhausted thoughts.

"You must get some rest," she told him.

"This time, I'm not part of the crew. We'll have all the luxury of passengers, with nothing but rest for the next three months." It sounded like heaven.

A sound behind them disturbed their embrace, and Danielle withdrew slowly from Sebastiaan, mourning the loss of his nearness.

The governor was standing with his wife in his arms. Her long, blond hair was knotted and stringy as it hung free from where her head rested against his shoulder. One arm dangled in front of his legs, the other crushed against his chest. Her feet were bare. Evidence of the sickness streaked the pale skin of her legs. Her nightdress shone sparkling white in the early morning sun.

Governor Van Riebeeck looked stricken, pale, and on the verge of collapsing. Sebastiaan was the first to move, reaching to take Maria from his arms, but Danielle's voice stopped him.

"No, don't touch her," she said in a hoarse whisper. She could not risk him getting sick as well. "Bring her inside," she motioned the governor forward with her hand on his back, watching him walk with the effort of an old man.

Now that she knew Sebastiaan was safe, her mind snapped into place. A hundred and forty souls occupied the tent, but the far-right corner was reserved as a storage space, and she led the couple there.

Shoving the clean blankets and crates with herbs aside, Danielle motioned for the governor to lay his wife on the bare sand.

"Adam," Danielle called. The large sailor rushed toward her, stopping dead in his tracks as he recognized their newest patient. She read in his eyes what she feared in her heart: Maria was too close to death to turn back.

"I need a partition for privacy," she said, "but first, a bowl of broth. Then send Pieter to cut long grasses for a pallet." Adam turned with the zeal of a soldier on the parade ground. Danielle wrapped Maria in a blanket, then

CHAPTER 23

lifted her head in her lap.

Looking up at the governor, she asked, "Why did you not bring her sooner?"

"She didn't want me to." His eyes were bewildered and fixed on the form of his wife. His shirt was stained with a mixture of sweat, feces, and vomit. It was only a matter of time before he would show symptoms.

"How long has she been sick?"

"Three days. It was only when she lost consciousness that I could bring her."

Danielle understood the hell he had been going through, knowing how stubborn her friend could be and how soft her husband's heart was where she was concerned. He would not act against her wishes.

"During the heights of her fever attacks, she kept calling for Antoonie." His voice broke as he spoke, and he let the tears stream down his face without consideration or shame. "Oftentimes, she smiled, as if she was looking straight at him. She kept calling for him, no matter how much I begged her to stay with me." His shoulders shook as his silent sobs trembled his body. "Danielle, she is leaving me. Make her stay. I *cannot* live without her. Please make her stay." He was breaking apart as he pleaded for his wife's life.

Danielle's own eyes were burning with tears. His words tore her heart to shreds. What could she say? She could make no promises and give no assurances. False hope was worse than no hope at all.

"I will do my best, I promise."

When Adam rushed with the news that Maria had fallen ill, Mrs. Boom dropped the blanket in the sand at her feet and ran to the tent. Mrs. Boom had done all she could for the men in the tent and had taken on the new task of washing the soiled blankets. With Pieter's help, they rinsed them in the ocean first and then in freshwater before they spread them over the bramble bushes to dry in the sun.

She came to a halt at the foot of Maria's pallet, her eyes large and wild as she took in the miserable state of her friend.

"Dear God, she's –" Her exclamation was cut short when Danielle shook her head, the warning clear in her eyes. *Don't you dare say the words.*

"Mrs. Boom, I need you to take the governor back to the *Drommedaris*."

Danielle knew his cabin would be in an unliveable state, but Mrs. Boom would see to it and care for the governor as if he were her own child.

"I don't want to leave her," Governor Van Riebeeck protested.

Danielle could understand his reluctance, but there was nothing he could do now, and the longer he stayed in the hospital, the more vulnerable he would become to the sickness. He needed a good, hot bath, a hearty meal, and a sleeping draft to help him settle. She handed Mrs. Boom a pouch of herbs.

"Steep this for him. It will aid his sleep." She watched as Mrs. Boom went to the bucket in the middle of the tent and scrubbed her arms and hands before leading the governor away.

Adam had cordoned off the entire back section of the hospital with a sail curtain, affording Maria precious privacy. By lunch, her condition had turned better and worse all at once. Danielle had managed to administer a few drops of the medicine broth, resulting in a violent reaction from Maria. She was pulled from her unconscious state when her bowels forcefully emptied as she brought up the contents of her stomach. After that, her body was ravished by violent shudders as the fever tightened its grip.

Danielle had no choice but to strip away the soiled nightgown and wrap her friend's naked body in a fresh blanket. There was a moment when she was sure Maria had breathed her last breath, but after many agonizing seconds, her chest had weakly started to rise and fall again. The effort had cost her dearly, for she had again sunk into a deep unconscious state.

"Danielle," a deep voice spoke from the other side of the curtain.

She rose to her feet and walked towards the sound, pausing to wash her arms and hands. Sebastiaan was waiting for her. Everything about him was in severe disagreement with where he stood, and she wanted to chase him from the hospital before any of its misery sullied him. His face was clean-shaven, framed by freshly washed golden curls, and he smelled clean, with a hint of spice from the soap he'd used.

"It's time to go," he said as she emerged from behind the curtain. It took a moment for her to register the words. She'd forgotten that they were set to leave today. His hand tightened around her elbow as he led her from the tent.

CHAPTER 23

The beach was once more alive with activity. The *Reijger* had moved from the mouth of the Fresh River and was now lying in the bay, ready to set sail. A sloop waited at the water's edge to transport the last passengers to the ship. Captain De Coninck and Arent were in deep conversation with Captain Hooghsaet. Shouts came from the *Reijger* as sailors waved and shouted farewells to those staying behind. A gentle breeze stirred the air, and the surface of the water was generously sprinkled with sunlight, making it sparkle with bright white brilliance, adding to the festive mood. Danielle felt like she was in a dream. She blinked a few times to clear her eyes.

"I can't go," she breathed.

"Danielle, we *have* to leave now. The ship is ready to sail. If we wait, the tide will turn, and exiting the bay will become very difficult." Sebastiaan's voice was tight, but he kept it even as he spoke.

"I can't leave her. Not like this." She looked at Sebastiaan, and her heart broke as she saw how his face contorted with an emotion she'd not seen before. She felt the slight tremble in his hand when he reached out to draw her aside, affording them a little more privacy.

"Danielle, don't do this," he begged. His eyes were glistening with moisture, and his voice was raspy.

Danielle could not leave Maria when she needed her most. The force of the moment was paralyzing. She was at a crossroads and faced a decision that would severely impact their lives, one way or the other. The moment was hauntingly similar to when she stood in De Coninck's cabin and chose to stay rather than leave with the *Lieffde*, a minor concern compared to what she faced now. This time, it was not just her life affected by her decision, but Sebastiaan's too.

Sebastiaan looked down at the woman before him. How different she was from that frightened, injured girl who'd stared at him with so much fear and apprehension as she lay in his uncle's cabin so many months ago. The fine, white line of the wound she'd suffered to her forehead was still there, and he traced his thumb over the small imperfection. He'd once told her that she could be unstoppable if she only saw herself as he did, and here was the evidence of his words. She stood before him, tired and filthy but strong, boldly sacrificing herself. He pulled her tight against his chest.

"I can't go," she repeated.

"Then I will stay with you."

It was a fool's errand. His father was dying, and he knew as well as she that he couldn't stay. He had to go.

"You can't. You *must* go to your father." Her voice was muffled, but she continued, "You can come back for me." She felt the movement of his body as he shook his head.

"I can't leave you," he breathed into her hair.

"You must. I'll wait for you. See to your father and then come back for me." It was the logical course but also the hardest.

"Is it because we are not married?" he asked, desperately clinging to anything that would make her change her mind. "Because if it is, we can march to my uncle right now and fix that." He let go of her and took a step back.

She wanted to reach for him again but refrained. "Even if we were married, I would still ask you to leave me here."

He closed his eyes and dragged both hands through his hair, leaving it in disarray.

"Danielle," his voice was pleading, and a sad curve twisted his mouth.

"Sebastiaan, come back for me." She took his hands in hers. "This is bigger than us. So many lives are at risk. Mr. Hoek is leaving with the *Reijger* today, leaving the settlement without a surgeon."

"I'll make him stay," Sebastiaan said, and hope sparked through his words as he gripped her shoulders.

Danielle shook her head. "How could I live with myself if Maria died, knowing I had left her? How would you be able to live with yourself knowing you had abandoned your father? Our love would be tainted." He just stared at her, not speaking, but she could see the heartbreak on his face and in the set of his shoulders. The situation was hopeless.

"Soon, more ships will come, and hopefully, they will bring physicians. Then we can have our life, free of guilt and what-ifs."

Sebastiaan heard his uncle call to them. Their time was up. Hooghsaet was

CHAPTER 23

already seated in the sloop. If he forced her now, he *would* lose her. If he let her have her way, they *could* have a future.

"Do you have your little knife with you?" he asked, and there was a tragic note in his voice.

She frowned at the strange question but nodded as she reached for it.

"Give it to me," he spoke as he reached for his dagger.

"What are you doing?" His odd actions confused her.

"I'm not leaving you without a decent knife," he said as he flipped his dagger over in his hand, offering it to her. "Now give me yours," and he stretched his other hand out.

She closed her fingers around the handle of the large, heavy dagger as she placed the small knife in his palm, severing the remaining bond with her past. It was the last thing she had grabbed the night her father was murdered, and she was forced to flee the surgery. She'd used it to cut salted meat and cheese while hiding in the *Drommedaris'* hull and defended herself against Samual Henders when he attacked her. It was a part of her, and now it was the part of her that would go with him, along with her heart, until he returned for her.

He tucked the small knife into his waistband before embracing her with fierce tenderness, his mouth covering hers.

"Wait for me," he spoke against her lips.

"I'll wait for you," she promised, pressing closer.

Then he released her, turned, and walked toward the waiting sloop.

THE END

Want more?

Join C.M. O'Neill's exclusive Reader's Group to receive sneak peeks of upcoming works.

If you have enjoyed this book, please take a moment to leave a few words in a review. To an author, a review is worth its weight in gold.
   Review at Amazon.com
   Review at Goodreads.com

For more relaxed and interactive hangouts, C.M. O'Neill can be found on Facebook @CMoNeillAuthor and Instagram @c.m.oneill.

Aknowledgements

Most importantly, I'd like to thank my readers for their support. We are all writers until someone buys our book, then we become authors. So, thank you for making me an author. I hope you enjoyed Danielle's journey.

Next, I wish to thank my daughter Esti, the most talented writer I've ever known – if only she would sit on her *derriere* and finish her book! That aside, without her, I would never have been able to finish this book. I've pestered her endlessly with, "Can you just read this and see if it works?" She is an absolute rock; her patience, support, and creative insights are second to none.

Thank you to my husband, who worked as tirelessly on this book as I did. He has read the manuscript countless times, fixing errors and providing honest and invaluable, constructive criticism. "Thank you for being my soundboard on all our coffee dates."

I wish to thank my son, Liam, for being Sebastiaan's eyes, Orion's laughter, and everything good and true that lives in the heart of all boys who grow to become breathtaking men. All the children in this book are boys, and each of them, in some way, was inspired by you.

Interview with the Author

Q: Why this book? What prompted the idea?

A: I came across Van Riebeeck's journal. Although widely published, it's not exactly something people read for fun. After that, I started reading South African history books with particular attention to the early days of the Dutch settlement. I was surprised that the journey from Texel to the Cape is nothing more than a one-liner. But after reading the journal, I discovered the intensity of that journey. Many of the significant events in my book are true, and they came from the journal. It provided most of the characters, and my plotline was as true to the actual events as possible.

More than anything, though, I thought that little Antoonie deserved a place in history.

Q: What part of the book did you have the most challenging time writing?

A: The beginning.

Q: Anything else? Can you elaborate? ...

A: It was horrible! I changed it three times, and it's yet to work. That first chapter is still out of step with the rest of the book. But ... it is what it is; there's nothing I can do about it now.

Q: What part of the book did you have the most fun writing?

A: I love writing, and when it flows, the whole process becomes very enjoyable. The scene I enjoyed the most, though it's not really a fun scene, was Danielle's whipping. Initially, I wanted to whip her for real, not flay her open, just enough to leave a few scars. However, my husband campaigned so vigorously for her to be spared that I altered the scene.

Danielle was perhaps the most complex character to write. It took me a long time to understand her, but once I did, it became a lot of fun.

Q: Is there going to be a sequel to this book?
A: Yes, this book is the first in the trilogy.

Q: What came first, the plot or the characters?
A: The plot. It was driven by Van Riebeeck's journal. I didn't have to think up the plot; it was already there for me. I just had to bring the people back to life and bring in a few fictional characters to help it flow.

Q: Which characters in the book were real historical figures and which were fictional?
A: Van Riebeeck and his family were real, and so were all three captains of the ships. Arent was real, as well as Harry and his family. Many of the support characters were real, such as the Booms and the surgeon – although I don't know his real name, he was referred to as 'the ship's surgeon,' so I gave him a fictional name, and he also didn't try to murder anybody. The surgeon's child was also on the ship and died of scurvy, though I also invented his name. Most other characters were fictitious: Danielle, Sebastiaan, Mattheys, Orion, Barent, and Du Bois.

Q: You stated that the book is based on true events. Which key events were real and which were fictional?
A: The storm and the freak wave were real, and their effect on the ship. Van Riebeeck took time to write a quick entry on the day of in his journal that simply read: "Ship at beam's end. Great danger."

Then – this is not a significant event – but the fact that the ship was unstable and hard to handle was real and caused great consternation and frustration during the journey, making it a miracle that they survived the storm.

Symon Jansz's death was real. He died the day after the storm of apoplexy.

Antoonie's death was real, but it was never mentioned. Van Riebeeck was very private and did not like mentioning his personal life. We know Antoonie boarded the ship, but there's no record of him getting off. He's never mentioned again, so we have to assume he died on the ship. There's no record of his death, so I had to invent how he died and when.

The first meeting between the three captains was real – the one where Turver announced his ship was short on water and where they decided to band together to protect the *Drommedaris,* as her guns were below deck and she was quite vulnerable to attack.

Van Riebeeck mentioned in his journal that a man fell overboard and was rescued. He didn't say who it was, so I figured I'll toss Mattheys.

Obviously, the arrival at the Cape was real. Arent scouting the bay and the first meeting with the Hottentots were real.

Dysentery broke out, although it wasn't on the *Goeie Hoop*. It was on one of the cargo ships that came two weeks later, but to make the timeline of the novel work, I had to change that. Also, Maria became very sick.

The hippopotamus scene was real, and the scene by the river where the Saldanhar chief embraced De Coninck.

Q: How do you feel about De Coninck as a person? He feels like the central pillar of the whole story, as the captain of the flagship.

A: The VOC chose him to be the governor of the settlement should anything happen to Van Riebeeck on the journey, so he was quite a significant person. It is a fact that there was never any illness on his ship; he was strict but fair. That's as far as historical fact goes. He was by far my favorite character to write. He's like the glue that keeps everything together – the eye of the storm; he's everybody's safe place.

Q: There are many female characters in the book. Is there a character that resembles you?

A: No. However, a little bit of me came out in all of them. Some things are more personal than others, for example, Mrs. Boom's glass face is most definitely mine.

Q: Of all the male characters, which was your favorite?

A: Arent. Sebastiaan is unhealthily dishy, Orion you can just eat up, and De Coninck is difficult not to have a little crush on. But Arent was my favorite. His personality is based on a friend of mine. He doesn't know it, and we shall keep it that way for my health and safety.

Q: What inspired Du Bois? He's the catalyst for the whole story and a striking character, but his presence in the book is short-lived.

A: Du Bois is entirely fictional, but he is my absolute dream villain, and maybe one day I'll write a spin-off where he is the lead character because parts of his backstory were real. For example, Cardinal Mazarin was a politician who served as the chief minister to King Louis XIV of France, and he, Mazarin, was murdered. To this day, we don't know who killed him, and I figured that sounds like the kind of thing Du Bois would do.

Q: What was the research for this book like? You had to learn about so many things and skills that are outdated today.

A: It was insane. If anybody were to look at my internet search history, they would come across things like 'how to operate a bilge pump on a 17th-century ship', 'what is the actual depth of a fathom of water,' 'how to cook a hippopotamus steak,' 'what does hippopotamus steak taste like,' all through to the term 'piss-prophet' and whether it was real (it was).

But in all seriousness, the danger with that much research is that it can lead to info-dumps in writing, which is awful – nobody should do that. So, the challenge was to weave all that information through the book and make it sound like everyday life.

Q: Last question: is C.M. O'Neill your real name?

A: Yes and no. C.M. are my real initials, and O'Neill was my maiden name's original form from the Irish Vikings many moons ago. My real name is very… un-English, and if I ever see a book with that name on the cover, I don't think I would buy it.

Other works

Also, by C.M. O'Neill

From Lambs to Lions
Book 2 in the The Cape of Good Hope Trilogy

1653 - In the untamed wilds of Southern Africa, a fledgling colony fights against the unforgiving grip of nature and the specter of starvation. Amidst this crucible of hardship, a spirited, young woman emerges, seeking her place in a world where survival demands more than resilience – it demands rebellion. Brave, compassionate, and unyieldingly stubborn, she navigates the treacherous landscape, only to find herself ensnared by her own daring. The perilous path woven by her actions intertwines with heartbreak and sacrifice, molding her destiny.

Inspired by true events, *From Lambs to Lions* is a tale of tenacity, impossible choices, and unbreakable spirits determined to defy the odds.

Printed in Great Britain
by Amazon